HOUSE OF EARTH

Now available ███████████████ck, the *House of* ██████████ brings together three engrossing, best-selling novels—*The Good Earth, Sons,* and *A House Divided*—in the epic saga of the House of Wang that follows three generations of farmers, warlords. merchants, and students through the sweeping events of half a century.

"The mightiest monument of American letters." —*Philadelphia Forum*

"An impressive achievement, revealing and rich in humanity." —*The New York Times*

A HOUSE DIVIDED

"Do not miss *A House Divided* even if you have not read the others of the trilogy. It is a book of tremendous strength, beauty, and grace." —*Providence Sunday Journal*

"Written from the inside with impressive detail and with rare beauty of workmanship." —*Boston Herald*

A HOUSE DIVIDED
was originally published by
The John Day Company, Inc.

Books by Pearl S. Buck

The Angry Wife
A Bridge for Passing
Come, My Beloved
Command the Morning
Death in the Castle
Dragon Seed
The Exile
Fighting Angel
The Goddess Abides
God's Men
The Good Earth
Hearts Come Home and Other Stories
The Hidden Flower
A House Divided
Imperial Woman
Kinfolk
Letter from Peking
The Living Reed
The Long Love
Mandala
The Mother
My Several Worlds
The New Year
Pavilion of Women
Peony
Portrait of a Marriage
Sons
The Three Daughters of Madame Liang
The Time Is Noon
The Townsman
Voices in the House

Published by POCKET BOOKS

PEARL S. BUCK

A
House
Divided

PUBLISHED BY POCKET BOOKS NEW YORK

A HOUSE DIVIDED

John Day edition published 1935

POCKET BOOK edition published March, 1975

L

Standard Book Number: 671-78797-7.
This POCKET BOOK edition is published by arrangement
with The John Day Company, Inc. Copyright, 1935, re-
newed, ©, 1963 by Pearl S. Buck. All rights reserved. This
book, or portions thereof, may not be reproduced by any
means without permission of the original publisher: The
John Day Company, Inc., 257 Park Avenue S., New York,
N.Y. 10010.
Front cover illustration by Jim Avati.
Printed in the U.S.A.

A
House
Divided

I

IN this way Wang Yuan, son of Wang the Tiger, entered for the first time in his life the earthen house of his grandfather, Wang Lung.

Wang Yuan was nineteen years old when he came home from the south to quarrel with his father. On a winter's night when snow drifted now and again out of the north wind against the lattices the Tiger sat alone in his great hall, brooding over the burning coals in the brazier, as he loved to do, and always he dreamed that his son would come home one day, a man, grown and ready to lead out his father's armies into such victories as the Tiger had planned but had not seized because age caught him first. On that night Wang Yuan, the Tiger's son, came home when none expected him.

He stood before his father, and the Tiger saw his son clothed in a uniform new to him. It was the uniform of the revolutionists who were the enemies of all lords of war such as the Tiger was. When its full meaning came to the old man he struggled to his feet out of his dreaming, and he stared at his son and he fumbled for the narrow keen sword he kept always beside him and he was about to kill his son as he might kill any enemy. But for the first time in his life the Tiger's son showed the anger he had in him but which he had never dared to show before his father. He tore open his blue coat and he bared his smooth young breast, brown and smooth, and he cried out in a loud young voice, "I knew you would want to kill me—it is your old and only remedy! Kill me, then!"

But even as he cried the young man knew his father could not kill him. He saw his father's upraised arm drop slowly down and the sword fell mildly through the air, and staring at his father steadily, the son saw his father's lip tremble as though he would weep, and he saw the

old man put his hand to his lips to fumble at his mouth
to steady it.

At this moment when the father and son stood thus
facing each other, the old trusty hare-lipped man, who
had served the Tiger since both were young, came in
with the usual hot wine to soothe his master before he
slept. He did not see the young man at all. He saw only
his old master, and when he saw that shaken face, and
that feeble changing look of anger suddenly dying, he
cried out and running forward, he poured wine quickly.
Then Wang the Tiger forgot his son and he dropped
his sword and with his two trembling hands he reached
for the bowl and he lifted it to his lips and he drank
again and again, while the trusty man poured out more
and yet more from the pewter jug he held. And again
and again the Tiger muttered, "More wine—more
wine—" and he forgot to weep.

The young man stood and watched them. He watched
the two old men, the one eager and childish in the comfort of the hot wine after his hurt and the other bending
to pour the wine, his hideous split face puckered with
his tenderness. They were only two old men, whose
minds at even such a moment were filled with the
thought of wine and its comfort.

The young man felt himself forgotten. His heart, which
had been beating so hard and hot, turned cold in his
bosom, and a tightness in his throat melted suddenly
into tears. But he would not let the tears fall. No, some
of the hardness he had learned in that school of war
served him now. He stooped and picked up the belt
he had thrown down, and without a word he went aside,
holding his body very straight as he went, into a room
where he had been wont to sit as a child to study with
his young tutor, who later was his captain in the school
of war. In the darkness of the room he felt to find the
chair beside the desk, and he sat down, and he let his
body be slack, since his heart was so dashed.

It came to him now that he need not have let himself be so passionate with fear for his father—no, nor so
passionate with love for him, either, that for this old

man's sake he had forsaken his comrades and his cause. Over and over again Wang Yuan thought of his father as he had just seen him, as he even now was in that hall where he sat drinking his wine. With new eyes he saw his father, and he could scarcely believe this was his father, the Tiger. For Yuan had always feared his father and yet loved him, though unwillingly and always with a secret inner rebellion. He feared the Tiger's sudden rages and his roarings and the swift way he thrust out the narrow bright sword he kept always near at hand. As a little lonely lad Yuan waked often in the night, sweating because he dreamed he had somehow made his father angry, although he need not have been so fearful, since the Tiger could not be truly angry with his son for long. But the lad saw him often angry or seeming angry with others, for the Tiger used his anger as a weapon with which to rule his men, and in the darkness of the night the lad shivered beneath his quilts when he remembered his father's rounded, glaring eyes and the way he jerked his coarse black whiskers when he raged. It had been a joke among the men, a half-fearful joke, to say, "It is better not to pull the Tiger's whiskers!"

Yet with all his angers the Tiger loved his son only, and Yuan knew it. He knew it and he feared it, for this love was like an anger, too, it was so hot and petulant and it lay so heavy on the child. For there were no women in the Tiger's courts to cool the ardor of his heart. Other lords of war when they rested from their battles and grew old took women to amuse them, but Wang the Tiger took not one. Even his own wives he did not visit, and one, the daughter of a physician who, being an only child, had inherited silver that her father gave her, was years gone to a great coastal city where she lived with her own daughter, the only child she ever bore the Tiger, to give her learning in a foreign sort of school. Therefore to Yuan his father had been everything of love and fear, and this mingled love and fear were hidden hands upon him. He was held imprisoned and his mind and spirit were fettered often by this fear of his father and the knowledge of his father's only, centered love.

Thus had his father held him fast, although the Tiger did not know he did, in that hardest hour Yuan had ever known, when in the southern school of war his comrades stood before their captain and swore themselves for this new great cause, that they would seize the very seat of government of their country and put down the weak man who sat there, and wage a war for the good common people who now were at the cruel mercy of the lords of war and of the foreign enemies from abroad, and so build the nation great again. In that hour when youth after youth so swore his life away, Wang Yuan drew apart, held by fear and love of his father, who was such a lord of war as these cried against. His heart was with his comrades. A score of harsh memories were in his mind of the suffering common people. He could remember their looks when they saw their good grain trampled down by the horses of his father's men. He could remember the helpless hate and fear upon an elder's face in some village when the Tiger demanded, however courteously, a tax of food or silver for his men. He could remember dead bodies lying on the ground and meaningless to his father and his men. He could remember floods and famines, and once how he had ridden with his father on a dike, and water was everywhere about, and that dike was dark with lean hunger-ridden men and women, so that the soldiers must be ruthless lest they fall on the Tiger and his precious son. Yes, Yuan remembered these and many other things and he remembered how he had winced to see these things and hated himself that he was a war lord's son. Even as he stood among his comrades he had so hated himself, even when for his own father's sake he withdrew secretly from the cause he would have liked to serve.

Alone in the darkness of his old childish room, Yuan remembered this sacrifice for his father, and to him at this hour it was all a waste. He wished he had not made it, since his father could not understand it and did not value it. For this old man had Yuan left his own generation and their comradeship, and what did the Tiger care? Yuan felt himself misused and misunderstood his whole life long, and suddenly he remembered every little hurt his father ever gave him, how he had forced his son out to see his men do their feints of war when the lad was reading a book that he loved and was loath to leave it, and how his father had shot down the men who had come to beg for food. Remembering many such hateful things, Yuan muttered behind his closed teeth, "He has never loved me all his life long! He thinks he loves me and that he holds me the only dear thing he has, and yet never once has he asked me what I really want to do, or if he did, it was to refuse me if what I said was not his wish, so that I always must take thought to say what he wanted and I have had no freedom!"

Then Yuan thought of his comrades and how they must despise him, and how he now would never have a share with them in making his country great, and he muttered rebelliously, "I never did want to go to that school of war at all but he must force me to go there or nowhere!"

This soreness and loneliness grew in Yuan so that he swallowed hard and blinked his eyes quickly in the darkness and he muttered furiously as a hurt child mutters to himself, "For all my father knows or cares or understands, I might as well have turned a revolutionist! I might as well have followed after my captain, for now I have no one—no one at all—"

So Yuan sat on alone, feeling himself the loneliest soul and very dreary, and none came near him. Throughout the hours left of the night not even one serving man came near to see how he did. There was not one who did not know that Wang the Tiger, their master, was angry with his son, for while the two quarrelled there were eyes and ears at the lattices, and now none dared to turn that anger on himself by comforting the son. It was the first time Yuan was paid no heed, and so he was the more lonely.

He sat on and would not search for any way to light a candle nor would he shout for any serving man. He folded his arms upon the desk and put down his head upon them and he let the waves of melancholy sweep over him as they would. But at last he slept because he was so weary and so young.

When he woke it was faint dawn. He lifted up his head quickly and looked about him; then he remembered he had quarrelled with his father, and he felt all the soreness of it in him still. He rose, and he went to the outer door upon the court and looked out. The court was still and empty and grey in the wan light. The wind was dead and the snow had melted as it fell in the night. By the gate a watchman slept, huddled in a corner of the wall for warmth, his hollow bamboo and his stick with which he beat upon it to frighten thieves away laid down upon the tiles. Looking at the man's sleeping face, Yuan thought with gloom how hideous was its slackness, the jaw loose and hanging and open to show the ragged teeth; although the man was at heart a very kindly fellow and one to whom in his childhood, and not many years ago, either, Yuan had often turned for sweets and toys at street fairs and such things. But to him now the man seemed only old and hideous and one who cared nothing for his young master's pain. Yes, Yuan now told himself, his whole life had been empty here and he was suddenly wild with rebellion against it. It was no new rebellion. It was the breaking of the secret war he now felt had always been between him and his father, a war grown he scarcely knew how.

In his childish early days Yuan's western tutor had taught him, trained him, plied him with the talk of revolution, of reshaping the nation, until his child's heart was all afire with the meaning of the great brave lovely words. Yet he always felt the fire die when his tutor dropped his voice low and said most earnestly, "And you must use the army that is one day to be yours; for country's sake you must use it, because we must have no more of these war lords."

So unknown to Wang the Tiger did this hireling subtly teach his son against him. And the child looked miserably into the shining eyes of his young tutor, and he listened to the ardent voice, moved to his core, yet checked by words he could not speak, although the words shaped too clearly in his heart, "Yet my father is a lord of war!" Thus was the child torn secretly throughout his childhood, and none knew it. It made him grave and silent and always heavy-hearted beyond his years, because though he loved his father, he could take no pride in him.

In this pale dawn, therefore, Yuan was wearied past his strength with all these years of war within himself. He was of a mind to run away from it, and from every war he knew, from cause of every kind. But where might he go? He had been so guarded, so kept within these walls by his father's love, that he had no friends and nowhere he could turn.

Then he remembered the most peaceful place he had ever seen in all the midst of war and talk of wars in which he had been from childhood. It was the small old earthen house in which his grandfather once lived, Wang Lung, called the Farmer until he grew rich and founded his house and moved it from the land so that he was called Wang the Rich Man. But the earthen house still stood on the edge of a hamlet and on three sides were quiet fields. Near it, Yuan remembered, were the graves of his ancestors set upon a rising bit of land, Wang Lung's grave, and other graves of his family. And Yuan knew, because once or twice or more, he had passed there as a child when his father visited his two elder brothers, Wang the Landlord and Wang the Merchant, who lived there in the nearest city to the earthen house.

Now, Yuan told himself, it would be peaceful in that small old house and he could be alone, for it was empty except for the aged tenants his father let live there since a certain still and grave-faced woman Yuan remembered had gone to be a nun. He had seen her once with two strange children, one a grey-haired fool who died, and one a hunchback, his elder uncle's third son, who became a priest. He remembered he thought the grave woman almost a nun even when he saw her, for she turned her face away and would not look at any man, and she wore grey robes crossed upon her breast; only her head was not yet shaven. But her face was very like a nun's face, pale as a waning moon is pale, the skin delicate and tightly stretched across her small bones, and looking young until one came near and saw the fine and hair-like wrinkles on it.

But she was gone now. The house was empty except for the two old tenants and he might go there.

Then Yuan turned into his room again, eager to be off now he knew where to go, and he longed to be away. But first he must take off his soldier's uniform he hated, and opening a pigskin box, he searched for some robes he used to wear and he found a sheepskin robe and cloth shoes and white inner garments, and he put them on in haste and gladly. Then silently he went to fetch his horse, stealing through the brightening court, past a guardsman sleeping with his head pillowed on his gun, and Yuan went out, leaving the gates ajar, and he sprang upon his horse.

After Yuan had ridden awhile he came out from the streets and into lanes and alleys and out from those into the fields, and he saw the sun come slipping up beneath a blaze of light behind the distant hills, and suddenly it rose, nobly red and clear in the cold air of that late winter's morning. It was so beautiful that before he knew it some of his dolefulness was gone and in a moment he felt himself hungry. He stopped then at a wayside inn, from whose door, cut low in earthen walls, the smoke streamed out warmly and enticingly, and he bought hot gruel of rice, a salty fish and wheaten bread sprinkled thick with sesame, and a brown pot of tea. When he had eaten everything and had drunk the tea and rinsed his mouth, and paid the yawning keeper of the inn, who combed himself the while and washed his face cleaner than it had been, Yuan mounted on his horse again. By now the high clear sun was glittering on the small frosty wheat and on the frosty thatch of village houses.

Then being after all young, on such a morning Yuan felt suddenly that no life, even his, could be wholly evil. His heart lifted and he remembered, as he went on, looking over the land, that he always said he would like to live where trees and fields were, and with the sight and sound of water somewhere near, and he thought to himself, "Perhaps this is now what I may do. I may do what I like, seeing that no one cares." And while he had this small new hope rising in him before he knew it words were twisting in his mind and shaping into verse and he forgot his troubles.

For Yuan in these years of his youth found in himself a turn for shaping verses, little delicate verses which he brushed upon the backs of fans and upon the white-washed walls of rooms he lived in anywhere. His tutor had laughed at these verses always, because Wang Yuan wrote of soft things such as leaves dropping down on autumn waters, or willows newly green above a pool or peach blossoms rosy through the white spring mists or the dark rich curls of land newly ploughed, and all like gentle things. He never wrote of war or glory, as the son of a war lord should, and when his comrades pressed him to a song of revolution until he wrote it, it was too mild for their desire, because it spoke of dying rather than of victory, and Yuan had been distressed at their displeasure. He murmured, "So the rhymes came," and he would not try again, for he had had a store of stubbornness in him and much secret willfulness for all his outward quietude and seeming docility, and after this he kept his verses to himself.

Now for the first time in his life Yuan was alone and at the behest of no one, and this was wonderful to him, and the more because here he was, riding alone through such land as he loved to see. Before he knew it the edge of his melancholy was tempered. His youth came up in him and he felt his body fresh and strong and the air was good in his nostrils, very cold and clean, and soon he forgot everything except the wonder of a little verse rising shaped out of his mind. He did not hasten it. He gazed about him at the bare hills, now mounting sandy clear and sharp against the blue unspotted sky and he waited for his verse to come as clear as they, as perfect as a hill bare against an unclouded heaven.

So this sweet lonely day passed, soothing him in passing, so that he could forget love and fear and comrades and all wars. When night came he lay at a country inn, where the keeper was an old solitary man and his quiet second wife was not too young and so did not find her life dull with the old husband. Yuan was the only guest that night, and the pair served him well, and the woman gave him little loaves of bread stuffed with fragrant seasoned pork ground small. When Yuan had eaten and had supped his tea, he went to the bed spread out for him and he lay weary with good weariness, and though before he slept the memory of his father and the quarrel came stabbing once or twice, yet he could forget this, too. For before the sun had set that day his verse came clear as he had dreamed it, shaped to his wish, four perfect lines, each word a crystal, and he slept comforted.

After three such free days, each better than its yesterday, and all full of winter sunshine, dry as powdery glass upon the hills and valleys, Yuan came riding, healed and somehow hopeful, to the hamlet of his ancestors. At high morning he rode into the little street and saw its thatched earthen houses, a score or so in all, and he looked about him eagerly. About the street were the farmers and their wives and children, standing at their doorways, or squatting at their thresholds upon their heels, eating bread and gruel for their meal. To Yuan they seemed all good folk, and all his friends and he felt warmly to them. Over and over had he heard his captain cry the cause of the common people, and here they were.

But they looked back at Yuan most doubtfully and in great fearful wonder, for the truth was that although Yuan hated wars and ways of war, yet although he did not know it, still he looked a soldier. Whatever was his heart, Yuan's father had shaped his body tall and strong and he sat his horse uprightly as a general does, and not slack and anyhow as a farmer may.

So these people now looked at Yuan doubtfully, not knowing what he was and fearful always of a stranger and his ways. The many children of the hamlet, their bits of bread clutched in their hands, ran after him to see where he was bound, and when he came to the earthen house he knew, they stood there in a circle, staring at him steadily, and gnawing at their ends of bread, and pushing each other here and there, and snuffling at their noses while they stared. When they were wearied of such staring, they ran back one by one to tell their elders that the tall black young man had come down from his high red horse before the house of Wang, and that he tied his horse to a willow tree and that he went into the house, but when he went in he stooped because he was so tall the door of that house was too low for him. And Yuan heard their shrill voices shouting these things in the street, but he cared nothing for such children's talk. But the elders doubted him the more after they heard their children and none went near that earthen house of Wang, lest there be some evil about to come upon them from the tall black young man, who was a stranger to them.

So did Yuan enter as a stranger this house of his forefathers who lived upon the land. He went into the middle room and he stood there and he looked about him. The two old tenants heard the noise of his entering and they came in from the kitchen and when they saw him they did not know who he was and they too were afraid. Then seeing them afraid, Yuan smiled a little and he said, "You need not be afraid of me. I am son of Wang the General, called the Tiger, who is third son of my grandfather Wang Lung, who lived here once."

This he said to reassure the old pair to show them his right to be there, but they were not reassured. They looked at each other in greater consternation and the bread they held ready in their mouths to swallow went dry and stuck in their throats like stones. Then the old woman put down upon the table the stick of bread she held and she wiped her mouth with the back of her hand and the old man held his jaws still and he came forward and ducked his tousled head in a bow and he said, trembling and trying to swallow down his dry bread, "Sir and Honored, what can we do to serve you, and what would you have of us?"

Then Yuan sat down on a bench and smiled a little again and shook his head and answered freely, for he remembered how he had heard these people praised and so need not fear them, "I want nothing at all except to shelter myself here awhile in this house of my fathers —perhaps I may even live here—I do not know, except I have always had the strangest longing after fields and trees and water somewhere, although I know nothing, either, of such life on the land. But it happens just now I must hide myself awhile, and I will hide here."

This he said still to reassure them and again they were not reassured. They looked back and forth to each other and now the old man laid down his stick of bread, too, and he said earnestly, his wrinkled face anxious and his few white hairs trembling on his chin, "Sir, this is a very ill place to hide. Your house, your name, are so well known hereabouts—and, sir, forgive me that I am only a rude coarse man who does not know how even to speak before such as you—but your honored father is not loved well because he is a lord of war, and your uncles are not loved, either." The old man paused and looked about him and then he whispered into Yuan's very ear, "Sir, the people on the land here so hated your elder uncle that he and his lady grew afraid and with their sons they went to a coastal city to live where foreign soldiers keep the peace, and when your second uncle comes to collect the rents, he comes with a band of soldiers he has hired from the town! The times are ill, and men on the land have suffered so full their shares of wars and taxes that they are desperate. Sir, we have paid taxes ten years ahead. This is no good place for hiding for you, little general."

And the old woman wrapped her cracked, gnarled

hands into her apron of patched blue cotton cloth, and she piped also, "Truly it is no good place to hide, sir!"

So the pair stood doubtful and eager and hoping he would not stay.

But Yuan would not believe them. He was so glad to be free, so pleased with all he saw, so cheered by the bright shining day, he would have stayed in spite of anything, and he smiled with his pleasure and he cried willfully, "Yet I will stay! Do not trouble yourselves. Only let me eat what you eat and I will live here awhile, at least."

And he sat in the simple room and looked about him at the plow and harrow set against the wall, at the strings of red peppers hanging there, and at the dried fowl or two and onions tied together, and he was pleased with everything, it was so new to him.

Suddenly he was hungry and the bread wrapped about garlic, which the old pair had been eating, seemed good to him, and he said, "I am hungry. Give me something to eat, good mother."

Then the old woman cried, "But, sir, what have I fit for a lord like you? I must first kill a fowl out of our four—I have only this poor bread, not even made of wheaten flour!"

"I like it—I like it!" answered Yuan most heartily. "I like everything here."

So at last, although doubtful still, she brought him a fresh sheet of bread rolled into a stick about a stem of garlic, but she could not be content until she found a bit of fish she had salted in the autumn and saved, and this she brought him for a dainty. He ate it all, and it was good meat to him, good above any he had ever eaten, because he ate in freedom.

When he had eaten he was suddenly weary, although until then he had not known he was, and he rose and asked, "Where is a bed? I would like to sleep awhile."

The old man replied, "There is a room here we do not use commonly, a room where your grandfather lived once, and after that the lady who was his third, a lady we all loved, so holy good she turned a nun at last. There is a bed in that room where you may rest."

And he pushed a wooden door at the side and Yuan saw a little dark old room that had for window only a small square hole over which white paper was pasted, a quiet, empty room. He went into it and shut the door and for the first time in his guarded life he felt himself truly alone for sleep, and loneliness was good to him.

Yet as he stood in the midst of this dim, earth-walled room, for a moment he had the strangest sudden sense of some stout old life going on there still. He looked about, wondering. It was the simplest room he had seen in his life, a hemp-curtained bed, an unpainted table and a bench, the floor the worn and beaten earth where many feet had worn hollows by the bed and door. There was no one there except himself, and yet he felt a spirit near, an earthy lusty spirit he did not understand. . . . Then it was gone. Suddenly he ceased to feel the other life and he was alone again. He smiled and was so sweetly weary he must sleep, for his eyes were closing of their own will. He went to the great wide country bed, and he parted the curtains and he threw himself down, and he wrapped about him an old blue-flowered quilt he found rolled there against the inner wall. In the same moment he was asleep and so he rested in the deep quiet of the ancient house.

When at last Yuan awoke it was night. He sat up in the darkness and parted the curtains of the bed quickly and looked into the room. Even the square of pale light in the wall had faded, and there was only soft, silent darkness everywhere. He lay back again, resting as he had never rested in his life because he woke alone. It was good to him to see even no servant standing near to wait for his awakening. For this hour he would not think of anything, only of this good silence everywhere. There was no single noise, no grunting of some rough guardsman who turned himself in sleep, no clatter of a horse's hoofs upon a tiled courtyard, no shriek of a sword drawn suddenly from its scabbard. There was nothing but the sweetest silence.

Yet suddenly there came a sound. Out of the silence Yuan heard a sound, the sound of people moving in the middle room, of whispering. He turned himself upon the bed, and looked through the curtains to the ill-hung unpainted door. It opened slowly, a little, and then more. He saw a beam of candlelight, and in the beam a head. Then this head was pulled back again and another peered in, and beneath it more heads. Yuan moved then upon the bed so that it creaked and at once the door shut, softly and quickly, a hand pulling it closed, and then the room was dark again.

But now he could not sleep. He lay wondering and awake, and he wondered if already his father had guessed his refuge and sent someone to fetch him. When he thought of this, he swore to himself he would not rise. Yet he could not lie still either, being so full of his impatient wonder. Then suddenly he thought of his horse and how he had left it tied to a willow tree upon the threshing floor, and how he had not bade the old man feed or tend it, and it might still be waiting there, and he rose, for he was soft-hearted about such things more than most men are. The room was chill now and he wrapped his sheepskin coat closely around him, and he found his shoes and thrust his feet into them, and he felt his way along the wall to the door and opened it and went in.

There in the lighted middle room he saw a score or so of farmers, both young and old, and when they saw him they rose, first this one and then that, all staring at him and when he looked at them astonished, he saw not one face he knew, except the old tenant's face. Then came forth a decent-looking, blue-clad farmer, the eldest of them all, his white hair still braided and hanging down his back in an old country fashion, and he bowed and said to Yuan, "We come to give you greeting, who are the elders of this hamlet."

Yuan bowed a little and he bade them all be seated, and he sat down, too, in the highest seat beside the bare table, which had been left empty for him. He waited, and at last the old man asked, "When does your honored father come?"

Yuan answered simply. "He is not coming. I am here for a while to live alone."

At this the men all looked at each other with pale looks, and the old man coughed again and said, and it could be seen he was spokesman for them all, "Sir, we are poor folk here in this hamlet, and we are much despoiled already. Sir, since your elder uncle lives in that far foreign city on the coast, he spends more money than he ever did, and rentals have been taken from us forcefully far more than we can pay. There is the tax we pay the lord of war, and the toll we pay the robber bands to keep them off us, and we have almost nothing left to live on. Yet tell us what your price is and we will pay you somehow so that you may go elsewhere and so spare us more sorrow here."

Then Yuan looked about him in amazement, and he said, with sharpness, too, "It is a strange thing I cannot come to my grandfather's house without such talk as this! I want no money from you." And after a moment, looking at their honest, doubtful faces, he said again, "It may be best to tell the truth and trust you. There is a revolution coming from the south, and it comes against the lords of war in the north, and I, my father's son, could not take arms against him, no, not even with my comrades. So I escaped by night and day and with my guardsmen I came home, and my father was angry when he saw my garb, and so we quarrelled. And I thought I would take refuge here for a while, lest my captain be so angry with me that he search me out to kill me secretly, so I came here."

And Yuan stopped himself and looked about the grave faces, and again he said very earnestly, for now he was eager to persuade them, and a little angry at their doubtfulness, "Yet I did not come for refuge only. I came also because I have the greatest love for the quietness of land. My father shaped me for a lord of war, but I hate blood and killing and the stink of guns and all the noise of armies. Once when I was a child I came by this house with my father and I saw a lady and two strange children here, and even then I envied them, so that while I lived among my comrades at a school of war, I thought about this place, and how some day I might come here. And I envy you, too, who have your homes here in this hamlet."

At this the men looked at each other again, none understanding or believing that anyone could envy the life they had, because to them it was so bitter. They were only more filled with doubt of this young man who sat there speaking in his eager willful open way because he said he loved an earthen house. Well they knew how he had lived, and in what luxury, for they knew how his cousins lived, and how his uncles, the one like a prince in a far city, and Wang the Merchant, now their landlord, who grew rich so monstrously and secretly upon his usury. These two they all hated, while they envied them their riches, too, and they looked with coming hatred and with fear upon this young man, saying in their hearts they knew he lied, because they could not believe there was in the whole world a man who would choose an earthen house when he might have a great one.

They rose, then, and Yuan rose, too, scarcely knowing if he need or not, since he was not used to rise except to his few superiors and he scarcely knew where to put these plain men, dressed in patched coats and in loose and faded cotton garments. But still he wished to please them somehow, so he rose, and they bowed to him and said a thing or two in courtesy, and they answered, their doubts clear enough upon their simple faces, and then they went away.

There were left only the old tenant and his wife, and they looked anxiously at Yuan and at last the old man began to plead, and he said, "Sir, tell us truly why you are here so that we may know ahead what evils are to come. Tell us what war your father plans, that he sends you out to spy. Help us poor folk, who are at the mercy of the gods and of the lords of war and of the rich men and governors and all such mighty evil ones!"

Then Yuan answered, understanding now their fearfulness, "I am no spy, I say! My father did not send me —I have told everything, and told it truly."

Still the old pair, too, could not believe him. The man sighed and turned away, and the woman stood in piteous silence and Yuan did not know what to do with them, and was about to be impatient with them, until remembering his horse he asked, "What of my horse?— I forgot—"

"I led him to the kitchen, sir," the old man answered. "I fed him with some straw and dried peas, and drew him water from the pond." And when Yuan thanked him, he said, "It is nothing—are you not my old master's grandson?" And at this suddenly he dropped to his knees before Yuan and groaned aloud, "Sir, once your grandfather was one of us upon the land—a common man like us. He lived here in this hamlet as we do. But his destiny was better than ours is, who have lived on poor and hardly always—yet for his sake who once was like us, tell us truly why you are come!"

Then Yuan lifted up the old man, and not too gently, either, because he began to be very weary of all this doubt, and he was used to being believed in what he said, being son of a great man, and he cried, "It is only as I say, and I will not say it over! Wait and see if any evil comes through me upon you!" And to the woman he said, "Bring me food, good wife, because I am hungry!"

They served him then in silence, and he ate the food. But it seemed not so good to him tonight as it had been earlier, and he soon had enough of it, and at last he rose with no more words and went again and lay down upon the bed for sleep. For a while he could not sleep, because he found an anger in him against these simple men. "Stupid fellows!" he cried to himself. "If they are honest, still they are stupid—knowing nothing in this little place—shut off—" And he doubted they were worth fighting for, after all, and he felt himself very wise beside them, and comforted by his greater wisdom he fell asleep again deeply in the darkness and the stillness.

Six days Yuan lived in the earthen house before his father found him, and they were the sweetest days of his whole life. No one came again to ask him of anything and the old pair served him silently and he forgot their doubts of him and he thought of neither past nor future, but only of each day. He did not enter any town nor go once to see his uncle in the great house, even. Each night at dark he lay down to sleep, and he rose early every morning in the sharp wintry sunlight, and even before he ate he looked out of the door across the fields now faintly green with winter wheat. The land stretched out before him, far and smooth and plain, and he could see, upon its smoothness, the flecks of blue which were men and women working to make the earth ready for the soon coming of spring, or some who came and went across the paths to town or village. And every morning he thought of verses, and he remembered every beauty of the distant hills, carved out of sandy stone and set against a blue cloudless sky, and for the first time he saw the beauty of his country.

All his childhood long Yuan had heard his captain use those two words "my country," or he said "our country," or sometimes to Yuan he said most earnestly "your country." But Yuan had felt no quickening when he heard them. The truth was Yuan had lived a very small, close life in those courts with his father. He had not often gone even into the camp where the soldiers brawled and ate and slept and even when the Tiger went abroad for war Wang Yuan lived on surrounded by his special guard of quiet men in middle years, who were bade to be silent near their young lord and tell no idle, lustful tales. So always there were soldiers standing near Yuan between him and what he might have seen.

Now every day he looked where he would, and there was nothing between him and all that he could see about him. He could see straight to where the sky met earth, and he could see the little wooded hamlets here and there upon the land, in the distance to the west the wall of the town, black and serrated against the porcelain sky. Thus looking every day as far and freely as he would, and walking on the earth or riding on his horse, it came into his mind that now he knew what "country" was. Those fields, this earth, this very sky, those pale, lovely, barren hills, these were his country.

And here came a strange thing, that Yuan ceased even to ride his horse because it seemed to lift him off the land. At first he rode because he had always ridden a horse, and to ride it was to him the same as using his own feet. But now everywhere he went the farming people stared at him, and they always said to one another, if they did not know him, "Well, that is a soldier's horse, surely, and it never carried any honest load," and within two or three days' time he heard the gossip of him spread and people said, "There is that son of Wang the Tiger, riding his great high horse everywhere and lording it as all his family do. Why is he here? It must be he looks upon the land and tallies crops for his father and plans some new tax on us for war." It came to be that whenever Yuan rode by they looked sourly at him and then turned away and spat into the dust.

At first this scornful spitting made Yuan angry and astonished for it was new to him to be so treated, who had never feared anyone except his father, and who had been used to servants hurrying to his bidding. But after a time he fell to thinking why it was, and how these people had been so oppressed, for so he had learned in the school of war, and then he turned good-humored again and let them spit to ease themselves.

At last he even left his horse tied to the willow tree and walked and although it came a little hardly to him at first to use his own legs, yet in a day or two he was used to it. He put aside his usual leathern shoes and wore the straw sandals that the farmers wore, and he liked to feel beneath his feet the solid earth of path and roads, dry with the months of winter sunshine. He liked to pass a man and meet his stare as though he were any stranger and not a war lord's son to be cursed and feared.

In those few days Yuan learned to love his country as he never had. And being so free and lonely, his verses rose shaped and shining and ready to be written down. He had scarcely even to search out a word but only to write down what was in him. There was no book or paper in the earthen house, and only an old pen that once his grandfather had bought, perhaps, to set his mark on some purchase deed for land. Yet still the pen could be used, and with it and a broken bit of dried ink block he found Yuan brushed his verses on the white-washed walls in the middle room, while the old tenant stared, admiring yet half fearful of the magic written unknown words. And now Yuan wrote new verses, not only of willows brushing silent pools, or of floating clouds and silver rains and falling flower petals. The new verses welled up from some deeper place within him, and they were not so smoothly written, for he told of his country and his new love of it. Where once his verses were pretty, empty shapes, like lovely bubbles on the surface of his mind, now they were not so pretty, but were filled more full of some meaning which he struggled with, not understanding wholly, coming with rougher rhythm and uneven music.

Thus the days passed, and Yuan lived alone with his great swelling thoughts. What his future might be he did not know. No clear form of anything came to his mind to make his future plain. He was content for this time to breathe in the hard bright beauty of this northern land, glittering in the cloudless sun, its very light seeming blue, it poured down from so blue a sky. He listened to the talk and laughter of the people in the little hamlet streets; he mingled with the men who sat at wayside inns, listening, seldom speaking, as one listens to a language scarcely understood, but very sweet-sounding to the ear and heart; he rested in the peace where there was no talk of war, but only of the village gossip, what son was born, what land was sold or bought and what its price, what man or maid was to be fed, what seed due to be sown, and such good common things.

His pleasure in all this grew greater every day, and when it grew too great, a verse came shaped into his mind, and he wrote it down also, and so was eased awhile, although here was a thing so strange it made him wonder at himself even, that while he found pleasure in these days, his verses came up out of him always not merry but tinged with deep melancholy, as though there were in him some hidden well of sadness, and he did not know why this was.

Yet how could he live on like this, the Tiger's only son? Everywhere the country folk were saying, "There is a strange tall black young man who wanders here and there like one witless. They say he is the son of Wang the Tiger, and nephew to Wang the Merchant. But how can a son of men as great as these wander like this alone? He lives in that old earthen house of Wang Lung, and it must be he is out of his mind."

This rumor reached even to the ears of Wang the Merchant in the town and he heard it from an old chief clerk in his counting house, and he said sharply, "Of course it is no brother's son of mine, for I have seen and heard nothing of him. And is it likely true that my brother would let free his precious only son in such a way? I will send out a serving man tomorrow and see who it is who lives in my father's tenant house. I gave no one such a leave to live there for my brother." And secretly he feared the sojourner might be some pretending, robber spy.

But the tomorrow never came, for those at the Tiger's camp had heard the rumor, too. That day Wang Yuan rose as his habit was now and even as he stood in the doorway eating bread and sipping tea, and looking out across the land and dreaming, he saw in the distance a chair borne upon men's shoulders and then another and about them walked a guard of soldiers, and he knew the soldiers for his father's by their garb. He went inside the door then, suddenly not able to eat or drink any more, and he put the food down on the table and stood waiting, and to himself he thought most bitterly, "It is my father, I suppose—and what shall we say to each other?" And he would have liked to run away across the fields like any child, except he knew this meeting must

come upon some day or other, and he could not run
away forever. So he waited very troubled, and forcing
back his old childish fear, and he could eat no more
while he waited.

But when the chairs drew near and were set down,
there came out from them not his father nor any man at
all, but two women; one was his mother, and the other
was her serving woman.

Now could Yuan be astonished indeed, for he seldom saw his mother, and he never knew her to have left
her house before, and so he went out slowly to make
his greeting, wondering what this meant. She came towards him, leaning on her servant's arm, a white-haired
woman in a decent garb of black, her teeth all gone so
that her cheeks were sunken. But still there was good
ruddiness upon her cheeks, and if the look upon her
face was simple and a little silly, even, yet it was kind,
too. When she saw her son she cried out in a plain,
country way, for she had been a village maiden in her
youth. "Son, your father sent me to say that he is ill
and near to death. He says you are to have what you
will if only you will come at once before he dies. He
says to say to you he is not angry, and therefore only
come."

This she said loudly and for all to hear, and in truth
even by now the villagers were clustering to see and
hear a new thing. But Yuan saw none of them, he was
so confused by what he heard. He had strengthened himself through all these days not to leave this house against
his will, but how could he refuse his father if he were
truly dying? Yet was it true? Then he remembered how
his father's hands had shaken when he stretched them
out in eagerness to take the comfort of the wine, and
he feared it might be true, and a son ought not to refuse
a father anything.

Now the serving woman, seeing his doubt, felt it her
duty to aid her mistress, and she cried loudly, too, looking here and there upon the villagers to mark her own
importance. "Ah, my little general, it is true! We are all
half-crazed and all the doctors, too! The old general lies

at the end of his life, and if you would see him living, you must go quickly to him. I swear he has not long to live—if he has, then may I die myself!" And all the villagers listened greedily to this and looked at each other meaningfully to hear the Tiger was so near his end.

But still Yuan doubted these two women, the more because he felt in them some hidden secret eagerness to force him home, and when the serving woman saw his continuing doubt, she threw herself upon the ground before him and cracked her head upon the hard-beaten threshing floor, and she bellowed in loud, feigned weeping, "See your mother, little general—see even me, a slave—how we beseech you—"

When she had done this a time or two, she rose and dusted off her grey cotton coat and cast a haughty stare about upon the crowded gaping villagers. Her duty now was done, and she stood to one side, proud servant of a high proud family, and so above these common folk.

But Yuan paid no heed to her. He turned to his mother and he knew he must do his duty, however he might hate it, and he asked her to come in and seat herself and this she did, while the crowd followed after and edged into the door to see and hear. But she did not heed them, being used to common folk who always gape to see their betters.

She looked about the middle room, wondering, and said, "It is the first time I was ever in this house. I used in childhood to hear great stories of it and how Wang Lung grew rich and bought a tea house girl and how she ruled him for a while. Yes, the greatest tales of how she looked and what she ate and wore were told from mouth to mouth in this whole countryside, although it was a thing of the past, even then, for he was old when I was but a child. I mind now it was said Wang Lung even sold a piece of land to buy a ruby ring for her. But afterward he bought it back again. I saw her only once, upon my marriage day, and—my mother!—how fat and hideous she grew before she died at last! Eh—"

She laughed toothlessly and looked about her amiably, and Yuan, seeing how placidly and honestly she spoke, took heart to know the truth, and so he asked her plainly, "Mother, is my father really ill?"

This recalled her to her purpose and she answered, hissing through her toothless gums as she must do when she talked, "He is ill, my son. I do not know how ill, but he sits there, for he will not go to bed, and he drinks and drinks and will not eat until he is yellow as a melon. I swear I never saw such yellowness. And no one dares go near him to say a single word, for he roars and curses beyond even what he ever did. He cannot live if he will not eat, be sure."

"Aye, aye, it's true—he cannot live if he will not eat," the serving woman echoed. She stood beside her mistress's chair, and shook her head and took a melancholy pleasure in her words, and then the two women sighed together and looked grave and watched Yuan secretly.

Then when he had thought a little while in great impatience Yuan said, for he knew he must go if it were true his father was so ill, although he doubted still and thought to himself that what his father said was true and women all were fools, "I will go then. Rest here a day or two, my mother, before you come back, for you must be weary."

Then he made sure for her comfort, and saw her in the quiet room which seemed now his own so that he left it sadly, and when she had eaten, he put from him the memory of the pleasant, lovely days and mounting on his horse once more, he turned his face to the north and to his father and again he wondered at these two women, for they seemed too cheerful at his going, more cheerful than they should be if the lord of the house lay ill.

Behind him went a score or so of his father's soldiers. Once hearing them guffaw together at some coarseness he could not bear them any more, and he turned on them in anger, hating the familiar clatter of them at his horse's heels. But when he asked them fiercely why they followed him, they answered sturdily, "Sir, your father's trusty man bade us follow you lest some enemy

take this chance and seize you for a ransom or even kill
you. There are many robbers through the countryside,
and you are an only, precious son."

And Yuan answered nothing. He groaned and turned
his face northwards steadily. What foolishness had made
him think of freedom? He was his father's only son,
most hopelessly his father's only son.

And of the villagers and country folk who watched
him passing there was not one who was not rejoiced to
see him go away again, because they did not understand
him or believe in him at all, and Yuan could see their
great content that he must go, and this sight remained
a darkness in the pleasure of those free days.

So Yuan rode against his will to his father's gates, the
guard behind him. They did not leave him the whole
way and he soon perceived they guarded him not so
much from robbers as from himself, lest he escape them
somewhere. It was on his lips a score of times to cry at
them. "You need not fear me—I will not run from my
own father—I come to him of my own will!"

But he said nothing. He looked at them in scorn and
silence and would not speak to them, but rode on as fast
as he could taking a haughty pleasure in his quick horse
that kept so easily before their common ones that they
must press their poor beasts on and on. Yet he knew
himself a prisoner, however he might go. No verse came
to him now; he scarcely saw the lovely land.

At evening of the second day of this forced riding he
reached his father's threshold. He leaped from his horse
and suddenly weary to his very soul he went slowly towards the room in which his father commonly slept,
not heeding all the secret stares of soldiers and of serving men, and answering no greeting.

But his father was not in his bed, although it was
night by now, and a lounging guard said when Yuan
asked him. "The general is in his hall."

Then Yuan felt some anger, and he thought to himself that after all his father was not very ill, and it was
only a ruse to win him home. He nursed his anger at

the ruse, so that he would not fear his father, and when
he remembered the pleasant lonely days upon the land,
he could keep his anger lively against his father. Yet
when he entered the hall and saw the Tiger, Yuan forgot some of his anger, for eye could see here was no
ruse. His father sat in his old chair, the tiger skin flung
across the carved back of it, and before him was the
glowing brazier full of coals. He was wrapped in his
shaggy sheepskin robe, and on his head was set his high
fur hat, but still he looked as cold as death. His skin
was yellow as old leather, and his eyes burned dry and
black and sunken, and the unshaved hair upon his face
was grey and harsh. He looked up when his son came
in, and then down again into the coals and gave no greeting.

Then Yuan came forward and bowed before his father,
saying, "They told me you were ill, my father, so I
came."

But Wang the Tiger muttered, "I am not ill. It is
woman's talk." And he would not look at his son.

Then Yuan asked, "Did you not send for me because
you were ill?" And Wang the Tiger muttered again, "I
did not send for you. They asked me where you were,
and I said, 'Let him stay where he is.'" He looked
down steadfastly into the coals and stretched his hands
above their shimmering heat.

Now these words might have angered anyone and
especially a young man in these days when parents are
not honored, and Yuan might easily have hardened himself more and gone away again to do as he liked in his
new willfulness, except he saw his father's two hands
stretched out, pale and dry as old men's hands are, and
trembling and seeking for some warmth somewhere, and
he could not say a word of anger. It came to him now,
as the moment must come to any gentle-hearted son, that
his father in his loneliness was grown a little child again,
and one to be dealt with as a child, with tenderness and
no anger, in whatever petulance he spoke. This weakness in his father struck at the roots of Yuan's anger, so
that he felt unusual tears come to his eyes, and if he

had dared he would have put his hand out to touch his father except some strange natural shame restrained him. Therefore he only sat down sidewise on a chair nearby and gazing at his father, waited silently and even patiently for what he might say next.

But there was this freedom that the moment gave him. He knew his fear of his father was forever gone. Never more would he be afraid of this old man's roarings and his darkening looks and his black brows drawn down and all the tricks the Tiger used to make himself fearful. For Yuan saw the truth, that these tricks were only weapons his father used; though he had not known it he had used them as a shield, or as men will take a sword and brandish it and never mean to bring it down on any flesh. So those tricks had covered the Tiger's heart, which never had been hard enough nor cruel enough nor merry enough to make of him a truly great lord of war. In this moment and its clearness Yuan looked upon his father and he began to love him fearlessly.

But Wang the Tiger, not knowing anything of this change in his son, sat brooding on, silent and seeming to forget his son was there. He sat long without moving and at last Yuan, seeing how ill his father's color was and how his flesh had dropped from him these last few days, so that the bones of his face stood out like rocks, said gently, "And would it not be better if you went to bed, my father?"

When he heard his son's voice again, Wang the Tiger looked up slowly as a sick man will, and he fixed his gaunt eyes upon his son and stared at him awhile and after another while he said hoarsely and very slowly, word for word, "For your sake once I did not kill an hundred and seventy-three men who deserved to die!" He lifted his right hand as though he would have held it over his mouth in a way he had, but the hand dropped of its own weight, and he let it hang and he said to his son again, still staring at him, "It is true. I did not kill them for your sake."

"I am glad, my father," said Yuan, moved not so much

by the living men, although he was glad to know they lived, as by the childish longing he discerned in his father to please him. "I hate to see men killed, my father," he said.

"Aye, I know it; you were always squeamish," answered Wang the Tiger listlessly, and fell to silent staring at the coals again.

Once more Yuan thought how to urge his father to his bed, for he could not bear the look of illness on his face and in the dry and drooping mouth. He rose and went to where the old trusty hare-lipped man sat on his haunches by the door, nodding as he sat, and whispered to him, "Cannot you persuade my father to his bed?"

The man started up and staggered to his feet, awake at this, and answered hoarsely, "And have I never tried, my little general? I cannot persude him even to go to his bed at night. If he lies down he rises up again within an hour or so and comes back to this chair to sit and I can only sit here, too, and I am so filled with sleep now I am as good as dead. But there he sits, always awake!"

Then Yuan went to his father and coaxed him and he said, "Father, I am weary, too. Let us go and lie upon a bed and sleep, for I am so weary. I will lie near you, and you can call me and know that I am there."

At this the Tiger moved a little as though he would rise; then he sank back and shook his head and would not rise and he said, "No, I am not finished what I have to say. There is something else—I cannot think of it all at once—two things I counted on my right hand that I must say. Go sit somewhere and wait until my thought comes out."

The Tiger spoke with his old vehemence now, and Yuan felt the habit of his childhood on him to go and sit. And yet there was this new fearlessness in him too, so that now his heart cried out against its duty. "What is he but a very tiresome old willful man, and here must I sit and wait for his humors!" And his willfulness shone out of his eyes and almost he was about to speak when the trusty man saw him and hastened forward to coax

him and said, "Let him have his way, little general, since
he is so ill, and bear what he says as we all must do."
So Yuan against his will, yet fearing it might indeed
make his father worse if he were opposed at such an
hour, who never had known opposition, went and sat
down sidewise on a chair and sat now less patiently
until the Tiger said suddenly, "It has come back to me.
The first thing is that I must hide you somewhere, for
I remember what you told me when you came home
yesterday. I must hide you from my enemies."

At this Yuan could not forbear crying out, "But, father,
it was not yesterday—"

Then the Tiger darted one of his old angry looks at
his son and he clapped his dry palms once together and
he cried, "I know what I say! How was it not yesterday
when you came home? You did come home yesterday!"

And again the old trusty man stood between the
Tiger and his son and called out pleadingly, "Let be—let
be—it was a yesterday!" And Yuan turned sullen, and
hung his head because he must be silent. For now it
was a strange thing, but the first pity he had for his
father was gone like a little quick mild wind passing
over his heart, and these angry old looks his father gave
him roused some deeper feeling in him than the pity.
His resentments rose in him, he told himself he would
not be afraid again, but he must be willful lest he be
afraid.

And in his own willfulness the father waited yet
longer before he would speak on, he thought because
he did not like his son to break into what he said, and so
he waited longer than he would have otherwise. But
the truth was the Tiger had something to say he did not
like to say, and he waited. In that time of waiting Yuan's
anger against his father leaped up more strongly than it
ever had. He thought of all the times he had been cowed
to silence by this man, and he thought of all the hours
he had spent at weapons which he hated, and he thought
of his days of freedom cut off once more, and suddenly
he could not bear the Tiger. No, his very flesh shrank
back from this old man and he loathed his father sud-

denly because he was not washed or shaven, and because he had let his wine and food dribble down upon his robe. There was not anything about his father that he loved, at least for this moment.

The Tiger not dreaming of all this hot loathing in his son's heart went on at last with what he had to say and it was this, "But you are my only precious son. What hope have I except in your body? Your mother for once has said a wise thing. She came and said to me, 'And if he is not wed, from whence will come our grandsons?' I told her then, 'Go and search out a good hearty maid somewhere, and it does not matter what she is except she be lusty and quick to bear, for women are all alike and one is not better than another. And bring her back and wed him, and then he can go out to hide in some foreign country until this war is over. And we shall have his seed.'"

This the Tiger said very carefully, each word what he had thought before, and he gathered up his weary wits to do this duty for his son before he let him go. This was no more than any good father ought to do, and what every son must in reason expect, for any son should accept the wife so chosen for his parents' sake, and wed her and give her child, and then he is free to find his love elsewhere as he will. But Yuan was not a son like this. He was filled with the poison of new times and full of secret willful freedoms that he did not know himself, and full, too, of his father's hatred against women, and what with his hatred, and what with his willfulness, he felt all his anger burst out of him now. Yes, his anger at this hour was like a checked flood in him, and all his life was gathered to its crisis now.

At first he could not believe his father truly said these words, for all his life he had been so used to hear the Tiger speak only of women as fools, or if not fools, then traitors and never to be trusted. But there the words were, spoken, and the Tiger sat and stared into the coals as before. Now Yuan knew suddenly why his mother and her serving woman had been so eager secretly to get him home, and pleased when he made ready to return, for such women think of nothing but of matches and of weddings.

Well, and he would not yield to them! He leaped up, forgetting that he ever had feared or loved his father, and he shouted, "I have waited for this—yes, when my comrades told me how they were forced to marriage—and many of them left their homes for this very cause —I used to doubt my own good fortune—but you are like all the others, all these old people who would keep us tied forever—tied through our bodies—forcing us to the women you choose—forcing us to children—well, I will not be tied—I will not have my body used like this to tie my life to yours—I hate you—I have always hated you—I know I hate you—"

Out of Yuan rushed such a stream of hatred now that he began to sob wildly, and the trusty man, in terror at such anger, ran and held him around the waist and would have spoken and could not, because his split lip was all awry. Yuan stared down and saw this man, and he was beside himself. He lifted up his hand and beat it down clenched upon that old hideous face, so that the man lay felled to the floor.

Now the Tiger rose tottering, not to his son—no, he had stared in a daze at Yuan, as though he could not comprehend what these words were, his eyes dazed and staring. When he saw his old servant fall, he went to lift him up.

But Yuan turned and fled. Not waiting once to see what was done, he ran through the courts and found his horse tied to a tree and ran through the great outer gate and past the staring soldiers there and leaped upon his horse and rode out of that place and to himself he cried it was forever.

Now Yuan had run out of his father's house in wildest anger, and this anger must cool from its very heat or he would die. And it did cool. He began to think what he could do, a lone young man, who had cut himself away from comrades and from father. The very day helped him to coolness, for the winter sunshine, which seemed so endless in the days Yuan spent in the earthen house, now was not endless. The day was turned to greyness, and the wind blew from the east, very chill and bitter, and the land through which Yuan's horse went slowly, for the beast was wearied with the days of travel, turned grey, too, and in its greyness Yuan felt himself swallowed up and cooled. The very people on the land took on this same greyness, for they were so like the earth upon which they lived and worked that their looks changed with it and their speech and all their movements quieted. Where in the sunshine their faces were live and often merry, now under the grey sky their eyes were dull and their lips unsmiling, and their garments dun-colored and their bodies slow. The little vivid colors of the land and hills, the blue of garments, the red of a child's coat, the crimson of a maiden's trousers, all these huts which commonly the sun would choose out and set alive, were now subdued. And Yuan, riding now through this dun country, wondered how he could have loved it so before. He might have turned back to his old captain and the cause, except he remembered the villagers and how they had not loved him, and these people whom he passed this day seemed so sullen that he cried to himself bitterly, "And shall I go and throw my life away for them?" Yes, on this day even the land seemed to him unsmiling. And as if that were not enough, his horse began to hobble and when he descended near a certain small city that he passed, he found the beast stone-bruised and lame and useless.

Now as Yuan had stopped and bent to look at the horse's hoof he heard a great roaring noise, and he looked up and there rushed past him a train, smoking mightily and full of haste. But still it did not pass too quickly for Yuan to see the many guests within, because he was so near and kneeling by his horse. There they sat so warm and so secure and thus went with such speed that Yuan envied them, and felt his own beast too slow and now useless and he cried to himself, and it seemed to him a quick clever thing to think, "I will sell this beast inside the city and take that train and go far away—as far as I can—"

On that night he lay at an inn, a very filthy inn it was, inside that little city, and Yuan could not sleep, the vermin crawled so on him, and he lay awake and while he lay he planned what he could do. He had some money on him, for his father always made him wear a belt of money next his body, lest he be too short sometime or other, and he had his horse to sell. But for a long time he could not think where he must go and what he must do.

Now Yuan was no common and untutored lad. He knew old books of his own people, and he knew the new books of the west, for so his tutor had taught him. From his tutor, too, he had learned to speak very well a foreign tongue, and he was not helpless and untaught as he might have been. So while he tossed his body on the hard boards of that inn bed, he asked himself what he should do with the silver that he had, and with his knowledge. To and fro in his own mind he asked himself if he had better go back to his captain. He could go and say, "I have repented. Take me back." And if he told that he had left his father and struck down the trusty man, it would be enough, since among this band of revolutionists it was a passport if a parent were defied and always proof of loyalty, so that some of these young, both men and women, even killed their parents to show their loyalty.

But Yuan, even though he knew he would be welcome, somehow did not want to go back to that cause. The memory of the grey day was still melancholy in him, and he thought of the dusty common people and then he did not love them. He muttered to himself, "I have never in all my life long had any pleasure. All the little joys that other young men have I have not had. My life has been filled with my duty to my father and then this cause I could not follow." And suddenly he thought he would like some life he had not yet seen, a merrier life, a life with laughter in it. It seemed to Yuan suddenly that all his life he had been grave and without

playmates, and yet there must be pleasure somewhere
as well as work to do.

When he thought of play he remembered into his
very early childhood, and he thought of that younger
sister he once knew and how she used to laugh and
patter here and there upon her little feet and how he
used to laugh when he was with her. Well, and why
should he not seek her out again? She was his sister,
they were one blood. He had been so knotted into his
father's life all these long years that he had forgotten
he had others too to whom he belonged.

Suddenly he saw them all in his mind—he had a score
of kin folk. He might go to his uncle, Wang the Merchant. For a moment he thought it might be pleasant
to be in that house again, and he saw in his memory a
hearty merry face, which was his aunt's, and he thought
of his aunt and of his cousins. But then he thought will-
fully, no, he would not go so near his father, for his
uncle surely would tell his father, and it was too near. . . .
He would take the train and go far away. His sister was
far away, very far in the coastal city. He would like to
live awhile in that city and see his sister and take pleasure in the merry sights, and see all the foreign things
he had heard of and never seen.

His heart hurried him. Before dawn came he rose
leaping up and shouted for the servant in the inn to
fetch him hot water to wash himself and he took off his
clothes and shook them well to rid them of the vermin,
and when the man came he cursed him for such filth
and was all eagerness to be gone.

When the serving man saw Yuan's impatience he knew
him for a rich man's son, for the poor dare not curse so
easily, and he grew obsequious and made haste, and so
by dawn Yuan was fed and off, leading his red horse to
sell. This poor beast he sold for very little at a butcher's
shop. A moment's pang Yuan had, it is true, for he shrank
a little to think his horse must be turned into food for
men, but then he hardened himself against this softness.
He had no need for horses now. He was no longer a
general's son. He was himself, Wang Yuan, a young man

free to go where he would and do what he liked. And that very day he mounted into the train that took him to the great coastal city.

It was a lucky thing for Yuan that he had sometimes read to his father the letters which the Tiger's learned wife sent him from that coastal city where she had gone to live. The Tiger as he was older grew more indolent about reading anything, so that, although as a youth he had read very well, in his age he had forgotten many letters and did not read with ease. Twice a year the letters came from this lady to her lord, and she wrote a very learned sort of writing which was not easy to read, and Yuan read the letters to his father and explained them. Now remembering, he could remember where she said she lived, in what street and in what part of that great city. So when at the end of a day and a night Yuan came down off that train, having crossed a river on the way and skirted by a lake or two and passed through many mountains and through much good planted land whereon the spring wheat was sprouting, he knew where he must go. It was not very near to where he was and so he hired a ricksha to pull him there, and thus he went through the lighted city streets alone and to his own adventure, and as he went he stared about him as freely as any farmer might, since no one knew him.

Never had he been in such a city as this was. For the houses rose so high on the sides of the streets that even with all the blazing lights he could not see their tops which ended somewhere in the darkness of the sky. But at the foot of the towering houses where Yuan was it was bright enough, and the people walked as though in the light of day. He saw the people of the world here, for they were of every race and kind and color; he saw black men from India and their women wrapped about with cloth of gold and with pure white muslin and with scarlet robes to set off their dark beauty. And he saw the swift-moving shapes of white women and their men with them all dressed the same always, and all their noses long, so that Yuan looking at the men wondered

how these women told their husbands from other men,
they looked so much the same except some were big-
bellied or hairless on their scalps or had some other such
lack in beauty.

Still most of the people were his own kind, and
Yuan saw every sort of countryman of his upon these
streets. There were the rich, who came riding in great
machines to the door of some pleasure house, and they
drove up with the great shrieking noise of horns, and
Yuan's ricksha man must draw aside and wait until they
passed, as in the old days kings might have passed. Where
the rich were, there were the poor beside them, the beggars and the maimed and the diseased who made much
of their woes to gain a little silver. But it was hardly
gained, and the silver leaked from the purses of the rich
in very small scanty pieces, for usually the rich passed
on their way, their noses high and their eyes unseeing.
In all his eagerness for pleasure, Yuan could feel a moment's hatred of these haughty rich, and he thought
they ought to give a little to the beggars.

Through all this moving multitude Yuan went obscure
enough in his humble vehicle until the man stopped
panting before a certain gate set in a long wall, and like
a score of other gates on either side. This was the place
Yuan sought and so he came down and fetched out the
coins he had promised to the man and gave them to
him. Now Yuan had seen with indignation how little
those rich men and ladies had heeded the cries of the
beggars and how they had pushed past the scrawny
hands thrust out before them. Yet when this working
man cried humbly, trembling and sweating with his
running, "Sir, add a little out of the kindness of your
heart," for he had noted Yuan's robe of silk and his
well-fed looks, it did not seem the same thing to Yuan at
all. He did not feel himself rich and it is known that
these men who pull at rickshas never are content. So he
cried stoutly, "Is not the price agreed?" And the man answered, sighing, "Oh, aye, it is the price agreed—but I
thought from your kind heart—"

But Yuan had forgotten the man. He turned to the

gate and pressed a bell he saw there. Then the man seeing himself forgotten, sighed again and wiped his hot face with a filthy cloth he had about his neck and wandered down the street, shivering in the keen night wind which turned his sweat to ice upon his flesh.

When the manservant came to open the gate, he stared at Yuan as at a stranger and for a while would not let him in, because in that city there were many well-dressed strangers who rang at gates and said they were friends and relatives of those who lived there, and when they were bidden to come in they drew out foreign guns and robbed and killed and did what they would, and sometimes their fellows came and helped them and they seized a child or man and took him away to hold for ransom. So the servant quickly barred the gate again, and although Yuan cried out what his name was, there he must wait awhile. Then once more the gate opened, and this time he saw a lady there, a quiet, grave-faced lady, large and white-haired, her robe of some dark plum-hued satin. Yuan looked at her as she looked at him, and he saw her face was kind, a full pale face, not wrinkled much, but never beautiful, since the mouth was too large and the nose large and flat between the eyes. Still the eyes were kind and comprehending and Yuan took courage, and he smiled a little in shyness and he said, "I need to ask your pardon that I come like this, lady, but I am Wang Yuan, the Tiger's son, and I have left my father. I ask nothing from you except, since I am alone, that I may come in and see you and my sister."

The lady had been looking at him very closely as he spoke, and she said mildly, "I could not believe the man when he said it was you. It has been so long since I saw you that I would not know you, except you are so like your father. Yes, none could fail to see you are the Tiger's son. Come in, then, and be at home."

And though the servant looked still doubtful the lady urged Yuan to come in and she was so mild and placid that she seemed not surprised at all, or in truth as though anything on this earth could surprise her now. No, she

led him into a narrow hall, and then she bade the servant
make a room ready with a bed in it, and asked Yuan if
he had eaten and she opened a door into a guest hall,
and asked him to be seated there and at his ease while
she went to fetch certain things for his comfort in the
room the servant made ready for him. All this she did
so easily and with such ready welcome that Yuan was
pleased and warmed and felt himself a welcome guest
at last, and this was very sweet to him, wearied as he
was with what had come about between his father and
himself.

In this guest hall he sat himself down upon an easy
chair and waited wondering, for it was not such a room
as he had ever seen, but, as his way was, showing no
wonder or excitement on his grave face. He sat quietly,
wrapped in his long robe of dark silk, looking a little
about the room, yet looking not so much that if one
came in he would be surprised at such a thing, for he
was of a nature which hated to seem strange or ill at
ease in any new place. It was a small, square room and
very clean, so clean that on the floor a flowered woolen
cloth was spread, and even this had no soil upon it. In
the center of this cloth a table stood, and on the table
another cloth of red velvet, and in this center a pot of
pink paper flowers, very real to see, except the leaves
were silver and not green. There were six chairs such
as the one he sat on, soft in the seat and covered with
pink satin. At the windows were hung white strips of
fine cloth, and on the wall was hung a picture of a foreign sort behind a pane of glass. This picture showed
high mountains very blue, a lake as blue, and on the
mountains foreign houses such as he had not seen. It was
very bright and pretty to the eye.

Suddenly a bell rang somewhere, and Yuan turned his
head to the door. He heard quick footsteps, and then a
girl's voice high and full of laughter. He listened. It
could be perceived she spoke to someone, although he
heard no answering voice, and many words she used he
scarcely understood, ripples interspersed of some foreign
tongue

"Ah, it is you?—No, I am not busy— Oh, I am tired today, I danced so late last night— You are teasing me— She is much prettier than I— You laugh at me— She dances much better than I do—even the white men want to dance with her— Yes, it is true I did dance with the young American— Ah, how he can dance— I will not tell you what he said!—No, no, no!— Then I will go with you tonight—ten o'clock! I will have dinner first—"

He heard a pretty rill of laughter and suddenly the door opened and he saw a girl there, and he rose to bow, his eyes dropped down in courtesy, avoiding a direct look at her. But she ran forward swiftly, graceful as a darting swallow and as quick, her hands outstretched. "You are my brother Yuan!" she cried gaily in her little soft voice, a voice high and floating seemingly upon the air. "My mother said you were here all of a sudden—" She seized his hands and laughed. "How old-fashioned you are in that long robe! Shake hands like this—everybody shakes hands now!"

He felt her small smooth hand seize his, and he pulled his own away, too shy to bear it—staring at her while he did it. She laughed again and sat down on the arm of a chair and turned her face up at him, the prettiest little face, three-cornered as a kitten's, the black hair smooth and curled upon her rounded cheeks. But it was her eyes that held him, the brightest, blackest eyes shot through with light and laughter, and beneath them was her red little mouth, the lips very full and red and yet small and delicate.

"Sit down," she cried, a little imperious queen.

He sat then, very carefully upon the edge of a chair, not near her, and she laughed again.

"I am Ai-lan," she went on in her light fluttering voice. "Do you remember me? I remember you so well. Only you have grown up better than you were—you used to be an ugly little boy—your face so long. But you must have some new clothes—all my cousins wear foreign clothes now—you would look nice in them—so tall! Can you dance? I love to dance. Do you know our cousins? My eldest cousin's wife dances like a fairy! You should

see my old uncle! He'd like to dance, but he is so old
and hugely fat, and my aunt won't let him. You should
see him when she scolds him for staring at pretty girls!"
Again she laughed her restless, flying laughter.

Yuan stole a look at her. She was slighter than any
creature he had ever seen, as small as any child about
the body, and her green silk robe fitted as tightly to
her as a calyx to a bud, the collar high and close about
her slender neck, and in her ears were little rings of
pearls and gold. He looked away and coughed a little
behind his hand.

"I came to pay my respects to our mother and to you,"
he said.

She smiled at this, mocking his sedateness, a smile
that set her face twinkling, and she rose and went to the
door, her step so swift it seemed like a light running.

"I'll go and find her, brother," she said, making her
voice solemn to mock his. Then she laughed again and
flung a teasing look at him from out her black kitten's
eyes.

The room was very quiet with her going, as though a
little busy wind had suddenly ceased to blow in it. Yuan
sat astonished, not able to comprehend this girl. She was
not like anyone he had ever met in all his soldier's life.
He set his brain to remember how she was when they
were small together before his father made him leave
his mother's court. He remembered this same swiftness,
this prattle, this darting of her great black eyes. He remembered, too, how dull his days had seemed at first
without her, how lifeless were his father's courts. Remembering it, even now this room seemed too quiet
and lonely and he wished she would come back to it,
and he was eager to see her more, because he wanted
more of laughter like hers. Suddenly he thought again
how his whole life long had been without laughter, always filled with a duty of some kind or other, and how
he had never play and merriment such as any poor child
has upon the street and such as any crowd of laboring
men has if they stop a moment to rest in the sunshine
of noon and eat their food together. His heart beat a

little quickly. What had this city for him, what laughter and what gaiety such as all young men must love, what new shining life?

When the door sounded again, therefore, he looked eagerly towards it but now it was not Ai-lan. It was the lady, and she came in quietly and as one who made her house ready and full of good ease and comfort for all. Behind her came the serving man bearing on a tray some bowls of hot food, and she said, "Set the food here. Now, Yuan, you must eat a little more if you would please me, for I know the food upon the trains is not like this. Eat, my son—for you are my son, Yuan, since I have had no other, and I am glad you have sought me out, and I want you to tell me everything and how you are come here."

When Yuan heard this good lady speak kindly and when he saw her face honest in its look and meaning and when he heard her comfortable voice and saw the inviting look her little mild eyes had when she put a chair for him beside a table, he felt foolish tears come to his eyes. Never, he thought passionately within himself, had such gentle welcome been made for him anywhere—no, no one was so kind to him as this. Suddenly the warmth of this house, the gayness of the colors of the room, the remembered laughter of Ai-lan, the comfort of this lady, rose up and wrapped him round. He ate eagerly, for he found himself very hungry and the food was seasoned carefully and not scant of fat or sauces as foods are when they are bought, and Yuan, forgetting how once he had eaten eagerly of country fare, thought now this was the best, most heartening food he ever ate, and he ate his fill. Yet he was quickly satisfied because the dishes were so fat and highly seasoned, and he could eat no more in spite of all the lady's urgings.

When it was over and the lady waited while he ate, she bade him sit in the easy chair again, and then warmed and fed and comforted, Yuan told her everything and even things he scarcely knew himself. Now he met the lady's gaze, a full, waiting gaze, and suddenly his shyness dropped from him and he began to speak and tell her all he wanted—how he had hated war and how he wanted to live upon the land, not ignorantly, as the peasants did, but as a wise husbandman, one learned enough to teach the peasants better ways. And he told how for his father's sake he ran from his captain secretly and now in some new understanding of himself those wise eyes gave him while they rested on him, he said, troubled, "I thought I ran because I would not go against my father, but now as I tell it, lady, I see I went partly because I hate the killing my comrades must do some day even in their good cause. I cannot kill —I am not brave, I know. The truth is I cannot hate wholly enough to kill a man. I always know how he feels, too."

He looked at the lady humbly, ashamed to show his weakness. But she answered tranquilly, "Not everyone can kill, it's true, else would we all be dead, my son." And after a while she said more kindly still, "I am glad you cannot kill, Yuan. It is better to save life than take it, and so I think, although I serve no Buddhist god."

But it was not until he told haltingly and half ashamed how the Tiger would have him wed anyhow to any maid that the lady was fully moved. Until now she had listened to him kindly and full of comprehension, murmuring small assents now and then when he waited for a moment. But when he hung his head and said, "I know he has the right to do it—I know the law and customs—but I could not bear it. I cannot—I cannot— I must have my body for my own and free—" And then troubled by his own memory of his hatred against his father and needing to confess it somehow he said further, for he wanted to tell everything, "Almost I understand how sons kill their fathers in these days—not that I could really do it, but I understand the feeling in those with a readier hand than mine."

He looked at the lady to see if this were too hard for her to bear, but it was not. She said with a new force and with more certainty than she had yet spoken, "You are right, Yuan. Yes, I always tell the parents of the youth nowadays, the fathers and the mothers of Ai-lan's friends, and even your uncle and his lady, who complain unceasingly against this generation, that in this at least the young are right. Oh, I know very well how right you are. I will never force Ai-lan to any marriage—and I will help you, if need be, against your father in this thing, for here I am sure you are truly right."

This she said sadly, but with some secret passion gathered from her own life, and Yuan wondered to see her small quiet eyes change and sparkle so, and her whole placid face grow moved. But he was too young to think long of any other than himself and the comfort of her words joined to the comfort of this quiet house, and he said longingly, "If I could stay here for a while until I can see what I must do—"

"And so you shall," she answered warmly. "You shall stay here as long as you have need. I have ever wanted a son of my own and here you are."

The truth was the lady suddenly loved this tall dark youth and she liked the big honest look upon his face and she liked the slow way he moved, and though he might not be pretty by the measure of the usual guess, being too high-cheeked and his mouth too big, still he was taller than most young men are, and she liked a certain shyness and delicacy he had about him when he spoke, as though even if he were willful he was not too sure of his own abilities. Yet this delicacy was only in his speech, for his voice was deep and good and a man's voice.

And Yuan saw her liking and was yet more warmed by it and it made this house his home. When they had talked a little more, she led him to a small room which was to be his own. It was up a stair and then up another smaller winding stair, and under the roof it stood, clean and with all the things he needed. When she was gone and he was alone, he went and looked out of the window and there was the light upon the many streets and all the city lay glittering and shining and in the high darkness he seemed looking into a new heaven of some sort.

Now began for Yuan a new life indeed, a full new life such as he had never dreamed for himself. In the morning when he rose and washed and clothed himself, he went down the stairs and there the lady waited for him, and she had her same beaming look this morning to set him at fresh ease. She led Yuan in to where the breakfast was upon the table, and at once she began to tell him what her plans were for him, but always very carefully too, so that she might not say a thing against his will. First, she said, she must buy him some garments, since he came forth in only what he had upon him, and then she must send him to a school for young men in that city. She said, "There is no great haste, my son, for you to work. It is better in these days to have your fill of this new learning, or else what you will earn will be very little. Let me treat you as my son. Let me give you what I had planned for Ai-lan if she would have had it. You shall go to this school here until it is clear what your place is in your books, and when you are finished here, then you may work, or you may even go to some foreign country for a while. Nowadays the young men and women are all zealous to go abroad, and I say it is a good thing for them to go. Yes, though your uncle cries out it is a waste and that they all come back too full of their own skill and abilities so that there is no living with them, I say still it is well for them to go and learn what they can and come back and give it to their own country. I only wish Ai-lan—" Here the lady stopped and looked sorrowful for a while and as though she had forgotten what she spoke of because of some inner trouble of her own. Then she made her face clear again and said resolutely, "Ai, I must not try to shape Ai-lan's life— If she will not, then she will not—and do not let me shape you, either, son! I only say that if you would—if you will—why, then I can think of a way to do it."

Now Yuan was so dazed at all this newness that he could scarcely take it all into him, and he stammered forth joyfully. "Be sure I can only thank you, lady, and I do most gladly what you say—" And he sat down and in his young new hunger and in all the joyfulness of a heart

at rest and a place to be his home he ate a mighty breakfast, and the lady laughed and was pleased and said, "I
swear I am glad you are come, Yuan, if for nothing else
than that I shall see you eat, for Ai-lan is so fearful lest
she put a little flesh upon her bones she dares not eat
at all, scarcely, and not more than a kitten does, and she
will not rise from her bed in the morning lest seeing
food she crave it. She cares for beauty more than for
anything, that child of mine. But I like to see the young
eat!"

So saying she took her own chopsticks and searched
out the best bits of the fish and fowl and condiments
for Yuan, and took far greater pleasure in his healthy
hunger than in anything she ate herself.

So began Yuan's new life. First this lady went out to
great shops of silks and woolen stuffs sent from the foreign countries, and she called tailors to the house and
they cut and measured all the stuffs and made robes for
Yuan according to the city fashions. And the lady hastened them, because Yuan still had his old robes on, and
they were cut too wide and in a country style and she
would not let him go to see his uncle and cousins while
he wore them, and when they heard he was come, for
be sure Ai-lan must tell them that he was there, they
bid him come to a feast of welcome. But the lady held
them off a day until his best robe was finished, a robe of
satin peacock blue and flowered in the same color and a
short jacket, sleeved, of black satin. And Yuan was glad
she did, for when he clothed himself in the new garment and had called a city barber to come and cut his
hair and shave the young soft hairs from off his face and
when he had put on his feet the new leather shoes the
lady bought for him, and had drawn on the black short
silken jacket and put on his head a foreign hat of felt
such as every young man wore, he could not but know,
as he stared into the mirror on the wall in his own room,
that he looked a very fine young man, and like all the
young men in the city, and it was only nature to be glad
of this.

Yet this very knowledge made him shamefaced, and

he went down very shyly to the room where the lady waited for him, and Ai-lan was there, too, and she clapped her hands to see him and cried out, "Ah, you are a very beautiful young man now, Yuan!" And she laughed so teasingly that Yuan felt the blood rush up to make his face and neck red, so that she laughed again. But the lady rebuked her mildly and turned him about to see that all was right, and it was, and she was pleased again with him, because his body was so straight and strong it paid her to see how well her pains were rewarded in his better looks.

On the second day after this one the feast was set, and Yuan went with his sister and with the lady whom already he called mother—and the word came to his tongue more easily than it did for his own mother, somehow—to his uncle's house. They went in a vehicle not drawn by horses, but forced by an engine in its vitals and driven by a serving man, and Yuan had never sat in such a thing before, but he liked it very well because it ran as smoothly as though it went on ice.

While they went and before they ever reached his uncle's house Yuan knew much about his uncle and his aunts and cousins, for Ai-lan chattered of them, telling this thing and another, laughing as she told, and with such sly looks and twistings of her little round red mouth as added point to every word. And as she talked Wang Yuan could see the very pictures of their kin and in spite of his decorum he laughed, she was so witty and so mischievous. He saw his uncle as she told him off, "A very mountain of a man, Yuan, holding such a paunch before him I swear he needs to grow another leg to carry it on, and jowls down to his shoulders, and bald as any priest! But far from any priest, Yuan, and only sore against his fat, because he cannot dance as his sons do—though how he thinks to clasp a maid and have her near him—" At such a thought the maid burst into laughter and her mother cried out mildly, but her eyes twinkled, too, "Ai-lan, take care of your words, my child. He is your uncle."

"Yes, and so I say what I like," she answered pertly.

"And my aunt, Yuan, his first lady, she hates it here and longs to go back to the country. And yet she fears to leave him lest some maid catch him for his money, and being modern will not be his concubine but his true wife, and so push her to one side. His two ladies join in this one thing at least, they will not let him take a third —a sort of women's league these days, Yuan— And my three cousins— Well, the eldest is wed as you know, and my cousin's wife is the man there and rules him furiously, so that my poor cousin must take his pleasure all secretly and then she is so clever that she smells a new perfume on him, or finds a dash of powder on his coat, or hunts his pockets for a letter, and he is his own father over again. And our second cousin Sheng—he is a poet, a pretty poet, and he writes verses for the magazines and stories about death for love, and he is a rebel of a sort, a gentle, pretty, smiling rebel, always newly in some love. But our third cousin is the real rebel, Yuan. He's a revolutionist—I know he is!"

At this her mother cried out in earnest, "Ai-lan, be careful what you say! Remember he is our kin, and that word is dangerous in this city in these days."

"He told me so himself," said Ai-lan, but she put her voice low, and glanced at the man's back who drove the vehicle.

So much she said and much more, and when Wang Yuan went in his uncle's house, he knew each one there because of what his sister said.

It was a different house indeed from the great house Wang Lung had bought and left his sons in that old northern country town. That house was aged and great, and the rooms were vast and deep and dark, or small and dark and set about the courts, and there was no upper story to it, but room upon room sprawled out, and space was plenty and the roofs were high and beamed and old, and the windows latticed with a sort of shell sent from the south.

But this new house in this new foreign city stood in a street with others like it which pressed hard against it. They were foreign houses, tall, high, narrow, without a single court or garden, and the rooms were close together, small, and very bright with many glass windows without lattices. The sunlight poured into the rooms, hard and shining and lightening every hue and color on the walls or on the flowered satin-covered chairs and tables, and the bright silks of women's clothes and the vermilion of their painted lips, so that when Yuan entered the room where all his kin folk were, he felt a glitter there which was too much for beauty.

Now his uncle rose, his hands lifting his huge belly from his knees, and from it his brocaded robes hung down like curtains, and he gasped out to greet his guests, "Well, sister-in-law, and my brother's son, and Ai-lan! Well, eh, this Yuan is a great tall black lad, too, like his father—not like, no, I swear—gentler than a tiger somewhat, perhaps—"

He laughed his rolling gasping laugh and heaved himself into a seat again, and his lady rose and Yuan looking sidewise saw her a neat, grey-faced lady, very plain and proper in her black satin coat and skirt, her hands crossed into her sleeves, and her little bound feet holding her unsteadily. She gave greeting to them, and she said, "I hope I see you well, sister-in-law, and brother's son. Ailan, you are grown thin—too thin. These maids nowadays will starve themselves and wear their little straight-cut dresses that are bold as men's robes. Pray sit down, sister—"

Near her stood a woman Yuan did not know at all, a woman with a scrubbed rosy face, her skin shining with soapy washing and her hair drawn straight from her brow in a country fashion, and her eyes very bright but not too wise. No one thought to say this woman's name, and Yuan did not know if she were a servant or not, until his lady mother said a kind greeting to her and from it Yuan knew this was his uncle's concubine. He moved his head a little then and the woman blushed and bowed as country women will, her hands folded in her sleeves, but she said nothing.

Then when greetings were all given, the cousins called out to Yuan to come and drink his tea aside in another room with them, and he and Ai-lan did, glad to be free of their elders. And Yuan sat silently and heard the chatter of those who know each other well, to whom only he was stranger, though he was their cousin.

Very well he marked them one by one, his eldest cousin not young any more, not slender either, but his belly growing as his father's did. He was half foreign in his dark woolen foreign garb, and his pale face was handsome still, his soft hands smooth-fleshed, and his wandering restless glance lingered over-long even on his girl cousin, so that his pretty sharp-voiced wife recalled him with a little sneer she slipped sidewise into something else she said. And there was Sheng the poet, his second cousin, his hair straight and long about his face, his fingers long and pale and delicate, his face studied in its look of smiling meditation. Only the young third cousin was not smooth in his looks and ways. He was a lad of sixteen years or so, clad in a common school uniform of grey, buttoned to the neck, and his face was not beautiful at all, shaped anyhow and pimpled, and his hands were angular and loose and hung too long from out his sleeves. He only said nothing while the others chattered, but he sat eating peanuts from a dish nearby, eating hungrily and yet with such a look of young gloom upon his face that one would say he ate them against his will entirely.

About the room and among the feet of all of them ran younger children, a lad or two of ten and eight, two little girls, and there was a screaming two-year-old looped in a band of cloth held by a serving woman, and a babe in arms suckling at the breast of a wet nurse. These were the children of Yuan's uncle's concubine, and of his elder cousins, but Yuan was shy of children and he let them be.

At first the talk was among them all, and Yuan sat silently, for while they bade him eat as he would from varied sweetmeats that stood near in dishes on small tables, and while his elder cousin's wife called to a serving maid to pour out tea, they forgot him seemingly, and paid no heed to courtesies in which he had been taught. So he cracked a few nuts noiselessly and sipped his tea and listened, and now and then he shyly gave a nut meat to a child who gobbled it gracelessly and with no word of thanks.

But soon the talk fell quiet among the cousins. The elder cousin, it is true, asked Yuan a thing or two, such as where he would go to school, and when he heard Yuan might go abroad he said enviously, "I wish I might have gone, but my father never would spend the money on me." Then he yawned and put his finger in his nose and fell to moody thinking, and at last he took his youngest lad upon his knee and fed him sweets and teased him for a while and laughed to hear him grow angry and laughed yet more when the child beat him with little furious fists. Ai-lan fell to talking in a low voice with her cousin's wife, and the cousin's wife spoke in an angry tone which she made low, but still Yuan could hear her and perceive the speech was of her mother-in-law and how she demanded things no woman nowadays would give another.

"With this house full of servants she will call to me to pour her bowl of tea, Ai-lan—and she blames me if a measure more of rice is used this month than last! I swear I cannot bear it. Not many women nowadays will live in the house with their husband's parents, and no more will I!" And much more of such women's talk.

Of all of them Yuan looked most curiously at his second cousin, Sheng, whom Ai-lan called the poet, and this was partly because Yuan himself loved verses and partly because he liked the grace about the youth, a slender grace, made quicker and more marked because he wore the dark and simple foreign garb. He was beautiful, and Yuan loved beauty very well, and he could scarcely keep his eyes from Sheng's golden, oval face and from his eyes, as apricot in shape as any maid's, and soft and black and dreaming, for there was some feeling in this cousin, some look of inner understanding, which drew the heart of Yuan and made him long to speak with Sheng. But neither Sheng nor Meng said anything and soon Sheng read a book, and when the nuts were gone Meng went away.

But in this crowded room no speech was easy. The children wept at anything, and the doors squeaked with constant passing of the servants coming in with tea and titbits and there was the whispering of his elder cousin's wife, and Ai-lan's laughter and mocking interest in the tales she heard.

So did a long evening pass. There was a mighty dinner at which the uncle and the elder cousin ate beyond belief, complaining together if some dish fell below their hopes, and comparing the cooking of meats and sweets, and praising loudly if a dish were good, and calling for the cook to come and hear their judgments. The cook came, his apron very foul and black with all his labors, and he listened anxiously, his oily face all smiles if he were praised and he all promises and hanging of his head if he were blamed.

As for the lady, Yuan's uncle's wife, she was distraught on her own account to find out if any dish were meat or cooked with lard or had an egg in it, for now that she was old she took the Buddhist vow against all flesh, and she had her own cook, who served up vegetables in every sort of cunning shape of meats, so that a dish that one would swear was pigeons' eggs in soup, would have no pigeon egg at all, or a fish would come so like a fish with eyes and scales in such cunning imitation that one must believe it was a fish until he cut and saw there were no flesh and bones. The lady kept her husband's concubine busy to see to all this, and she did it ostentatiously, saying, "Lady, it ought to be a task my son's wife does for me, but in these new days the son's wives are not what they were. I have no daughter-in-law at all or good as none."

And her son's wife sat straight and stiff, very pretty but cold in looks and pretended she heard nothing of all this talk. But the concubine, being easy in her temper and one to keep the peace always, answered amiably, "I do not mind, lady. I like to be busy."

So she did busy herself about a score of little things

and kept the peace for all, a ruddy, plain woman, healthy and sound and always smiling, whose great happiness was to be left for a little while to do embroideries upon her shoes or upon the shoes of her children. She kept by her always her bits of satin, her fine-cut paper patterns for flowers and birds and leaves, and all her many colored silks she hung ready about her neck, and around her middle finger always was her brass ring thimble, so always there, that many times at night she forgot and slept with it, or she would search for it and wonder and then find it still on her finger and burst into loudest merry childlike laughter at herself until all must laugh who heard her.

In all this family talk and noise, the whines of children and the bustle of the food, the learned lady maintained her quiet dignity, answering if one spoke to her, eating delicately but without undue heed to what she ate, and courteous even to a child. Her mild grave eye could by its very meditative gravity check Ai-lan's too quick tongue and too shining eyes that must see any cause for laughter, and somehow in this whole company her presence sat, beneficent and kind, and made them all more kind and courteous. Yuan saw it and respected her the more and was proud to call her mother.

For a little time Yuan lived carefree as he never had dreamed a life could be. He trusted everything to the lady and obeyed her as though he were her little child, except he obeyed her joyfully and eagerly, because she never laid a command on him at all but always asked him if a certain plan she had was what he liked best to do, and she put it so kindly that to Yuan it seemed always what he would have chosen himself if he had thought of it first. She said to him one early day, when they sat alone at the morning meal to which Ai-lan never came, "My son, it is not kind to leave your father ignorant of where you are. If you like it, I will write a letter to him myself and tell him you are safely with me, and that you are safe from his enemies, since here in this coastal city we are under the government of foreigners, and they do not let wars come here. And I will beg him to let you free from this marriage and let you choose some day for yourself as the young do nowadays, and I will tell him that you are to go to school here and that you are well and that I will care for you, for you are my own son."

Yuan had not been all at ease about his father. In the daytime, when he went here and there upon the streets to see the sights, when he was swept among the strange city people or when he was in this clean and quiet house and busy with the books he had bought to go to the new school, he could remember to be willful and he could cry out it was his right to live this free life and his father could not force him to come back. But in the nights or when in the dark morning he awoke, not being used yet to the noise that came up early from the streets, then freedom seemed a thing impossible, and some of the old childhood fear came back on him and he cried to himself, "I doubt I can stay on here. What if he comes and fetches me back again with his soldiers?"

At such times Yuan forgot all his father's many kindnesses and much love, and he forgot his father's age and illness, and he only remembered how his father often was angry and that he was always bent upon having his own will, and then Yuan felt the old sad careworn fears of childhood come on him again. Many times already he had planned how to write his father, and how to make the letter pleading, or if his father came, how he could hide again.

So now when the lady said this, it seemed the easiest, surest way, and he cried gratefully, "It is the best thing, mother, to help me." And when he had thought a little while as he ate, his heart released itself, and he dared to be a little willful and he said, "Only when you write, write very plainly, because his eyes are not so good as they were, and be sure you make it plain I will not come back to be wed by him. I will never go back again, not even to see him, if I am to be in danger of such slavery."

The lady smiled peaceably at his passion, and she said mildly, "Aye, I will say it, but more courteously,"

and she seemed so calm and sure that Yuan let his last
fears go and trusted her as he might have had he been
born of her own flesh. He feared no more, but felt his
life here safe and sure, and he turned ardently to all its
many parts.

Hitherto Yuan's life had been most simple. In his
father's courts there were but the few things he could
do that he had always done, and in the school of war,
the only other place he knew, there had been much the
same simplicity of books and studied warfare, and the
bickering and friendship of the lads he knew in the
few short hours they had for play, for there they were
not allowed to wander at their will among the people,
but were schooled most sternly for their cause and the
coming warfare for it.

But in this great noisy hurried city Yuan found his
life like a book whose pages he must read all at once,
so that he lived a score of different kinds of life, and he
was so greedy and so kindled and so eager that he could
not bear to let any of them pass him by.

Nearest to him in this house was the merry life he
craved. Yuan, who had never laughed with other children or played or forgot his duty, now found a new late
childhood with his sister Ai-lan. These two could bicker
without anger and could play at some game or other of
their own and set each other laughing until Yuan forgot
everything except his laughter. At first he was shy with
her, and only smiled instead of laughing, and his heart
was hindered so it could not come out freely. He had
been so long taught that he should be sober and should
move with dignity and slowness and keep his face grave
and straight and answer with full thought, that he did
not know what to do with this teasing maid who mocked
at him and copied his grave looks upon her little shining face, and made it look so like his own long one that
the lady could not but smile, and even Yuan must laugh,
although at first he did not quite know if he liked to be
so mocked or not, since no one had ever done it before.
But Ai-lan would not have him grave at all. No, she
would not rest until she had him answering her wit, and

she was just enough to cry applause when he said a good thing, too.

One day she cried, "Mother, this old sage of ours is growing young again, I do declare! We'll make a boy of him again. I know what we must do—we must buy him some foreign clothes, and I will teach him to dance and he shall go with me sometimes to dance!"

But this was too much for Yuan's new-found merriment. He knew that Ai-lan went out often for this foreign pleasure called dancing, and he had seen it sometimes at night in passing by some gay lighted house, but it always made him look away, it seemed so bold a thing to do that a man should clasp a woman to him closely, who was not his wife, and even though she were his wife it seemed a thing not to be done thus publicly. But when Ai-lan saw his sudden gravity, she grew very willful and persisted in her notion, and when he said shyly in excuse, "I could never do it. My legs are too long," she answered, "The legs of some foreign men are longer than yours are and yet they do it. The other night I danced with a white man at Louise Ling's house, and I swear my hair kept catching on his waistcoat button, and yet he danced like a tall tree in the wind. No, think of some other reason, Yuan!"

And when he was too shy to speak the real reason, she laughed and shook her little forefinger in his face and said, "I know why it is—you think all the maids will fall in love with you and you are afraid of love!"

Then the lady said gently, "Ai-lan—Ai-lan—not too bold, my child," and Yuan laughed in some discomfort and let the moment pass.

But Ai-lan would not so let it pass, and each day she cried at him, "You shall not escape me, Yuan—I'll teach you to dance yet!" Many of her days were so filled with hours for merry-making that when she ran in from school, she threw down books and changed her garments to some of gayer hue, and went out again to see a theatre or some picture made so like life that the people moved and spoke, and yet even in these days when she saw Yuan but a moment or two, she could tease him that she would begin tomorrow or tomorrow and he must harden himself to the thought of love.

What it might have come to between himself and Ai-lan, Yuan could not have said, because he was still afraid of the pretty chattering girls who came and went with Ai-lan and whom, though she told him their names and said to them, "This is my brother Yuan," he still did not know, they all looked so alike and all so pretty. And he was afraid too of something deeper in himself than even these pretty maids, some secret power in himself he feared their little careless hands might stir alive in him.

But one day there came a thing to help Ai-lan in her mischief. There was an evening when Yuan came out of his room to eat the evening meal and he found the lady whom he called his mother waiting for him alone at the table, and the room very quiet since Ai-lan was not there. This was no surprise to Yuan, for often these two ate alone while Ai-lan went to some merry-making with her friends. But this night the lady said in her quiet way, as soon as he had set himself at table, "Yuan, I have wanted for a long time to ask a thing of you, but knowing how busy you have been and eager to get on in all your books, rising early and needing all your sleep, I have not done it. But the truth is I am at the end of my own ability in a certain matter. I must have help, and since I have looked on you as son in truth, I can ask of you what I cannot ask of any other."

Then Yuan was in great surprise, for this lady was so sure and quiet always, very safe in her content and understanding, that one could not think she needed any sort of aid from anyone. He looked up at her from over the bowl he held and said wondering, "Be sure, mother, I am ready to do anything, because you have been more than own mother to me since I came here. There is not any kindness I have not had from you."

At the plain goodness in his voice and look, some gravity in the lady broke. Her firm lips trembled and she said, "It is your sister. I have given my life to this girl of mine. I suffered first because she was not a boy. Your own mother and I conceived near together, and

then your father went away to a war, and when he came
back, we both had given birth. I cannot tell you how
much I wanted you, Yuan, to have been mine. Your
father never—he never looked at me. I always felt a
power for some feeling in him—a strange, deep heart
he has, but none has ever had it that I know, except you.
I do not know why he hates women so. But I used to
know how he longed for a son, and all the months he
was away I used to tell myself that if I bore his son—I
am not foolish, Yuan, as most women are—my father
taught me all his learning. I always thought that if your
father would only look at what I really am, see what
my heart is, he might have taken comfort in me for the
little wisdom I have had. But no, to him I was ever no
more than a woman who might bear a son for him—and I
bore no son, only Ai-lan. When he came home from war
and victory he looked at you, Yuan, in your country
mother's arms. I had dressed Ai-lan as bravely as a boy
in red and silver, and she was the prettiest babe. But he
never saw her. Time and time again I sent her to him
on some pretext or took her to him, for she was so
clever and so forward for her age, I felt he must see
what she was. But he has the strangest shyness toward
all females. He only saw she was a girl. At last in my
own loneliness, Yuan, I told myself I would leave his
courts—not openly, but with the excuse of schooling for
my daughter, and I was sure that I would let Ai-lan
have everything a son would have, and do my best
against this bondage of a woman's birth. And he was
generous, Yuan—he has sent me money—there has been
nothing lacking except he did not care if I were dead
or living, or my daughter either. . . . I help you, not
for his sake, but for your own, my son."

She cast a deep look at him when she said this, and
Yuan caught the look, and was confused because he saw
thus into this lady's life and thoughts, and he felt shy
and speechless at such knowledge because she was his
elder. Then she went on, "So have I spent myself for
Ai-lan. And she has been a lovely, merry child. I used
to think she must one day be great, perhaps, a great

painter or poet, or best of all a doctor as my father was,
for there are women doctors nowadays, or at least
some leader in this new day for women in our land. It
seemed to me this one child I have given birth to must
be great and all that I would have been—learned and
wise in everything. I never had the foreign learning as I
craved to have it. I read her school books now that she
has thrown by, and I grieve to see how much there is
in them that I can never know. . . . But I have come
to understand now that she will never be very great.
Her only gift is in her laughter and in her mockery and
in her pretty face and in all her winning ways of gaining
hearts. She will not work much at anything. She loves
nothing very well except her pleasure—kind she is, but
without any depth to kindness. She is kind because life
is more pleasant when she is kind than not. Oh, I know
my child's measure, Yuan—I know the stuff I have had to
shape. I am not deceived. My dreams are gone. Now all
I ask is that she wed wisely somewhere. For she must
be wed, Yuan. She is such a one as must be in a man's
care. And she has been bred in such freedom that she
will not wed where I might choose, and she is willful,
and I live in misery lest she cast herself away on some
lad or on some foolish man too old for her. There is
even some perverseness in her that for a while made her
even look twice at a white man and think it an honor
to be seen with him. But I do not fear this now. She
has taken another turn. I fear rather a man she is with
continually. I cannot always follow her and I do not
trust these cousins nor the cousin's wife. Yuan, to please
me, go with her sometimes at night and see if she is
safe."

At this instant while her mother talked so long, Ai-lan
came into the room dressed for her merry-making. She
wore a long straight robe of deep rose bound about with
silver and on her feet were silver shoes, foreign and
high at the back, and the collar was cut away from her
gown in the newest fashion and her soft neck showed as
slim and smooth and golden as a child's, and the sleeves
were cut away, too, just below the shoulder and left

bare her pretty arms and hands, slender, yet with no bones to be seen and covered with the softest and most delicate of flesh. Upon her wrists, slight as a child's yet round as any woman's, she wore carved silver bracelets, and on each middle finger of her hands were rings of silver and of jade, and her hair was curled about her lovely painted face, as smooth and black as jet. About her shoulders, but not fastened, was a cloak of softest whitest fur, and when she came in she threw this back, and looked smiling, first at Yuan and then at her mother, knowing very well how fair she was and innocently proud in all her beauty.

Both of them looked at her and could not move their eyes away and this Ai-lan saw too, and laughed a little cry of pure delighted triumph. This broke the mother's gaze and she said quietly, "Whom do you go with to-night, my child?"

"With a friend of Sheng's," she answered gaily. "A writer, mother—and famous for the tales he writes too, —Wu Li-yang!"

It was a name that Yuan had heard of sometimes—a man in truth famous for his tales written in the western manner, tales very bold and free and full of talk of love between man and maid, and ending very often in death somewhere, and Yuan was not a little curious to see him, although his tales were such that Yuan read them secretly and even so he was ashamed to read them.

"Some time you might indeed take Yuan," the mother said mildly. "He works too hard, I tell him. He ought to have a little pleasure sometimes with his sister and his cousins."

"So you should, Yuan, and I have been ready for a long time," cried Ai-lan, smiling lavishly and looking at him from her great black eyes. "But you must buy the clothes you need. Mother, make him buy foreign clothes and shoes—he will dance better with his legs free from those robes. Oh, I like to see a man in foreign clothes—let's go tomorrow and buy him everything! You're not ugly, you know, Yuan. You'd look as nice as any man in foreign clothes. And I'll teach you to dance, Yuan. I'll begin to-morrow!"

At this Yuan blushed and shook his head, but not with his first decision, for he felt what the lady had been telling him, and he could not but think how kind she had been to him, and this was a way to repay her. Then Ai-lan cried, "What will you do if you cannot dance? You can't sit keeping alone at a table—we all dance, we younger ones!"

"It is the fashion, true enough, Yuan," the mother said, half sighing, "a very strange and dubious fashion, I know, brought over from the West, and I hate it and I cannot think it wise or well, but so it is."

"Mother, you are the oddest, old-fashioned soul, and yet I love you," said Ai-lan, laughing.

But before Yuan could speak the door opened and Sheng came in, dressed in the black and white of foreign clothing, and with him another man, whom Yuan knew was the story teller, and with them was a pretty girl, dressed exactly like Ai-lan except in green and gold. But to Yuan all girls looked the same these days, all pretty, all slight as children, all painted, and all with tinkling voices and little constant cries of joy or pain. He did not see the maid, therefore, but he looked at the famous young man, and he saw a tall smooth man, his face large and smooth and pale and very beautiful with narrow red lips and black and narrow eyes and straight narrow black brows. But the man was notable most for his hands which he moved incessantly even when he did not speak; large hands they were, but shaped like a woman's hands, the fingers pointed at the ends and thick and soft at the base, and the flesh smooth and olive and oiled and fragrant,—voluptuous hands, for when Yuan took one in his own for greeting, it seemed to melt and flow warmly about his fingers and Yuan hated suddenly the touch of it.

But Ai-lan and the man drew together intimately in their looks and his eyes told her boldly what he thought of her beauty and seeing it the mother's face was trou-led.

Then they were suddenly gone, like a flower-laden wind, the four of them, and in the quiet room Yuan sat alone again with the mother, and she looked at him straightly.

"You see, Yuan, why I ask you?" she said quietly. "That man is already wed. I know. I asked Sheng to tell me, and at first he would not, but at last he made light of it and told me it was not thought now, if the man's wife were old-fashioned and chosen by his parents, a dishonor if he walked with other maids. But I wish it were not my maid, Yuan!"

"I will go," Yuan said, and now he could forget what had seemed wrong to him, because he did it for this lady's sake.

Thus it came about that Yuan was bought the foreign clothes and Ai-lan and her mother went with him to the foreign shop and there a tailor measured him and stared at his shape, and fine black cloth was chosen for one suit and a dark brown rough stuff for a suit to wear by day. And leather shoes were bought and a hat and gloves and such small things as foreign men may wear, and all the time Ai-lan was chattering and laughing and putting out her pretty fluttering hands to pull at this or push that away, and she put her head on one side and looked at Yuan to see what would make him prettiest, until Yuan, half shy and shamed, was laughing too, and merrier than he had ever been his life long. Even the clerk laughed at Ai-lan's talk and glanced at her secretly, she was so very free and pretty. Only the mother sighed while she smiled, for this maid did not care what she said or did, and thought only to make people laugh at her and she searched, not knowing it, to see what was in anyone's eyes and if he found her pretty, and he always did, then she grew more merry still.

So Yuan was garbed at last, and the truth was that once he was used to a certain feeling of nakedness about his legs, where he had been accustomed to his swinging robes, he liked the foreign clothing very well. He could walk freely in it, and he liked the many pockets where he could store small things he needed every day. It was true, too, that it was pleasant to him the first day he put his new garb on himself to see Ai-lan clap her hands and hear her cry, "Yuan, you are handsome! Mother, look at him! Doesn't it become him? That red tie—I knew it would sit well beneath that dark skin of his and so it does— Yuan, I'll be proud of you!— Look, here we are— Miss Ching, this is my brother Yuan. I want you to be friends. Miss Li, my brother!"

And the maid pretended so to introduce him to a row of pretty girls and Yuan did not know how not to yield to his shyness and he stood smiling painfully, the dark blood in his cheeks as red as the new tie. But still it was somehow sweet, too, and when Ai-lan opened a music machine she had and set the music beating through the room, and when she seized him and laid his arm about her and took his hand and gently forced him to a movement, he let her do it, half confused, and yet finding it very pleasant. He found a natural rhythm in himself, so that before very long his feet were moving of their own accord to the pace the music set, and Ai-lan was delighted at the ease with which he learned how to move himself to music.

Thus Yuan began this new pleasure. For he found it was a pleasure. Sometimes he was ashamed of a craving it aroused in his blood, and when this craving came, he must restrain himself because he longed to seize closer the maid he held, whatever maid it was, and give himself and her to the craving. Indeed it was not an easy thing for Yuan, who until this hour had never touched even a maid's hand, nor spoken to any maid who was not his sister or his cousin, to move to and fro in warm lighted rooms to the strange twisting foreign rhythms of music, and in his very arms a maid. At first, the first evening, he had been so torn with fear lest his feet betray him and go astray that he could not think of anything else except how to set them properly.

But soon his feet moved of their own accord and smoothly as any other pair of feet, and the music was

their guide, so Yuan did not need to think of them again.
Among the people of every race and nation who gathered in the pleasure houses of that city, Yuan was only
one, and he was lost among their strangeness, who did
not know him. He was alone, and he found himself alone
and with a maid against his body and her hand in his.
He saw no maid better than another, in these first days,
and they all were pretty and they all were friends of
Ai-lan's and willing enough, and anyone did as well for
him as any other, and all he wanted was a maid to hold
and to set his heart burning with a slow sweet smoth-
ered fire to which he dared not yield.

If afterwards he was ashamed, when he was cooled by
daylight and the soberness of school rooms, still he need
not tell himself the thing was dangerous for him and he
should avoid it, because there was his duty to the lady,
and he could say he was helping her.

It was true he did most carefully watch his sister,
and at the end of every evening's pleasure he waited
until Ai-lan was ready to come home, and he never
asked another maid to go with him, lest he must take
her home and leave Ai-lan. Especially was he so careful
because he must justify to himself these hours he spent
thus, and he was very zealous and the more because it
was true that the man Wu did meet Ai-lan very often.
This one thing could make Yuan forget the sweet sickness that stole into him sometimes when the music
swayed too much and the maid he held clung closely
to him, and it was if he saw Ai-lan turn aside to any
other room with that one named Wu, or if she sought
a balcony for the coolness. Then he could not rest until
the dance was ended and he could go and find her and
stay near her.

But be sure Ai-lan did not always bear it. Often she
pouted at him, and sometimes she cried in anger, "I
wish you would not stick so close to me, Yuan! It is
time you went alone now and sought out maids for yourself. You do not need me any longer. You dance as well
as anyone. I wish you would let me be!"

To this Yuan answered nothing. He would not say out

what the lady had told him and Ai-lan would not press the thing too plainly, either, not even in her anger. It was as though she feared to tell something she did not want told, but when she was not angry she could forget and be as merry a play-fellow as ever with him.

At last she grew cunning and even was not angry with him. Rather she laughed and let him follow her as he would, as though she wanted to keep him friendly to her. For everywhere Ai-lan went, the story teller was. He seemed to know the maid's mother did not like him, for now he never came to her house. But always at other houses, whether public or of friends, there he was near Ai-lan, as if he knew where Ai-lan was to be. And Yuan began to watch Ai-lan dancing with this man, and he saw at these times her little face was grave. This very gravity sat so strangely on her that Yuan was troubled by it often, and once or twice he was about to tell the lady of it. Yet there was nothing true to tell, for Ai-lan danced with many men, and one night when they came home together Yuan asked her why she was so grave with that one man, and she said lightly, laughing while she spoke, "Perhaps I do not like to dance with him!" And she drew down her mouth and thrust out her little red painted lips to Yuan to mock at him.

"Then why do it?" Yuan put to her bluntly, and she laughed and laughed at this, some hidden mischief in her eyes and at last she said, "I can't be rude, Yuan." So he let it pass from his mind, though doubtfully, and it remained a darkening on his pleasure.

There was another thing to mar his pleasure, too, a small thing and usual, and yet there it was. Each time Yuan came out of the heated brilliant midnight rooms where flowers were and food and wine spilled out and more than anyone had needed, he seemed to step out into that other world he wanted to forget. For in the darkness or in the grey dawn, the beggars and the desperate poor stood huddled by the doorways, some to try and sleep, but some to steal, like street dogs, into the pleasure houses after the guests were gone, and grovel under tables to snatch at the broken bits of food that were thrown there. It could be but a brief moment only, for the serving men roared and kicked at them and dragged them out by the legs and barred the gates against them. These piteous creatures Ai-lan and her playmates never saw, or if they saw they paid no heed to them and were as used to them as to stray beasts, and they went laughing and calling to each other from their vehicles, and so went gaily to their homes and beds.

But Yuan saw. Even against his will he saw them, and it came to be that even in the midst of the night's pleasure, in the midst of music and of dancing, he remembered with great dread the moment when he must go into the grey street and see the cringing figures and the wolfish faces of the poor. Sometimes one of these poor stretched out a hand in despair at such deafness as these merry rich people had, and the hand would lay hold upon a lady's satin robe and cling to it.

Then a man's lordly voice would shout out, "Your hand away there! How can you lay your filthy hand upon my lady's satin robe and soil it?" And a policeman of those who stood there would rush forth and beat the taloned filthy hand away.

But Yuan shrank and bent his head and hurried on, because he was so formed in spirit that he felt as upon his own flesh the beating of the wooden club, and it was his own starved hand that winced and fell down broken. At this time of his life Yuan loved pleasure, and he was unwilling to see the poor, and yet he was so shaped within that he saw them all even while he wished he did not.

But there were not only such nights in Yuan's life now. There were the sturdy days of work in school among his fellows, and here he came to know better his cousins Sheng and Meng, whom Ai-lan called the Poet and the Rebel. Here in the school these two were their true selves, and in the classrooms or in throwing a great ball about upon the playground, they all, these three young cousins, could forget themselves. They could sit in the decorous listening rows of desks, or leap and shout at their fellows and roar with laughter at some faulty play, and Yuan came to know his cousins as he never did at home.

For as young men at home among their elders are never their true selves, so were not these two, Sheng always being silent and too good for everybody, and secret as to his poems, and Meng always sulky and prone to knock against some small table or other too full of small toys and bowls of tea, so that his mother cried constantly against him, "I swear no son of mine has ever been so like a young buffalo in my house. Why can you not walk smooth and silent as Sheng does?" And yet when Sheng came home so late from pleasure that he could not rise in time the next morning for his school she would cry at Sheng, "I ever say I am the most suffering mother in the world, and all my sons are worthless. Why can you not stay decently at home at night as Meng does? I do not see him slipping out at night dressed like a foreign devil and going I do not know to what evil place. It is your elder brother leads you wrong, as his own father did lead him. It is your father's fault at bottom and I always said it was."

Now the truth was that Sheng never went to the same pleasure houses as his elder brother did, for Sheng liked a daintier sort of pleasure, and Yuan saw him often in the pleasure houses where Ai-lan was. Sometimes he went with Yuan and Ai-lan, but often he went alone with some maid he loved for the time, and they two would dance together the whole evening through in silence and in perfect pleasure.

Thus the brothers went their own ways, each absorbed in some secret life of this great multitudinous city. But, although Sheng and Meng were two such diverse souls that they might easily have quarrelled, more easily than either with the elder brother, who was too far older than they were, since there were two between, one dead by hanging himself in his youth, and the other given to the Tiger, yet they did not quarrel, partly because Sheng was a truly gentle laughing youth who held nothing worth a quarrel, and he let Meng have his way, but also

because each was in the other's secret. If Meng knew
Sheng went to certain places, Sheng knew Meng was a
secret revolutionist and had his own certan hidden meeting places, too, though in a different cause, yet in a more
dangerous one. And so the two kept silence for each
other and neither defended himself before the mother
at the expense of the other. But each, as time went on,
came to know Yuan and to like him the more, because
he told to neither of them what one might tell to Yuan
alone.

And now this school began to be the great pastime of
Yuan's days, for he truly did love learning. He bought his
great heap of new books and held them piled beneath
his arms, and he bought pencils and at last he proudly
bought a foreign pen such as all the other students had,
and fastened it upon his coat's edge, and he laid aside
forever his old brush, except when he wrote to his
father once a month.

All the books were magic to Yuan. He turned their
clean, unknown pages eagerly, and he longed to print
each word upon his mind, and learn and learn for very
love of learning. He rose at dawn if he could wake and
read his books, and he memorized the things he did not
understand; whole pages he put to his memory like
this. And when he had eaten his early breakfast—solitary,
because neither Ai-lan nor his mother rose as soon as
he did on school days, he rushed off, walking through
the still half-empty streets and was the first to reach his
classrooms always. And if a teacher came a little early,
too, then Yuan took it as a chance for learning and he
overcame his shyness and put what questions that he
could. If sometimes a teacher did not come at all, then
Yuan did not, as the common students did, rejoice in an
hour for holiday. No, rather he took it as a loss he could
not happily bear and spent the hour in studying what
the teacher might have taught.

This learning was the sweetest pastime therefore to
Yuan. He could not learn enough of history of all the
countries of the world, of foreign stories and of verses,

of studies of the flesh of beasts; most of all he loved to study the inner shapes of leaves and seeds and roots of plants, to know how the rain and sun can mould the soil, to learn when to plant a certain crop, and how select its seeds, and how increase its harvest. All this and much more did Yuan learn. He begrudged himself the time for food and sleep except that his great lad's body was always hungry, too, and needing food and sleep. But this the lady mother watched, and while she said nothing, yet she watched him, although he scarcely knew it, and she saw to it that certain dishes which he loved were often set before him.

He saw his cousins often, too, and they were daily more a part of Yuan's life, for Sheng was in a classroom with him, and often had his verses or his writing read aloud and praised. At such times Yuan looked with humble envy at him, and wished his verses were as smoothly rhymed, although Sheng looked down most modestly and pretended it was nothing to him to be praised. And he might have been believed, except that on his pretty mouth a little smile of pride sat very often and betrayed him when he did not know it. As for Yuan, at this time he wrote very little verse, because he lived too occupied for any dreaming, and if he did write, the words came roughly and he could not make them grouped and as they used to be. It seemed to him that his thoughts were too big for him, unshaped, not easily to be grasped and caught into a form of words. Even when he smoothed and polished and wrote them over many times, his old scholar teacher often said, "It interests me, it is fair enough, but I do not catch just what you mean."

Thus he paused one day when Yuan had written a poem about a seed, and Yuan could not say what his meaning was exactly, either, and he stammered out, "I meant—I think I meant to say that in the seed, in that last atom of the seed, when it is cast into the ground, there is an instant, a place perhaps, when seed becomes no longer matter, but a sort of spirit, an energy, a kind of life, a moment between spirit and material, and if we could catch that transmuting instant, when the seed begins to grow, understand the change—"

"Ah, yes," the teacher said, doubtfully. A kindly, aged man he was who kept his spectacles low on his nose and stared across them now at Yuan. He had taught so many years he knew exactly what he wanted and so what was right, and now he laid Yuan's verses down and he pushed his spectacles and said half-thinkingly, and picking up the next paper, "Not very clear, I fear, in your mind. . . . Now, here's a better one, called 'A Walk on a Summer Day'—very nice—I'll read it." It was Sheng's verse for that day.

Yuan fell to silence and kept his thoughts to himself, listening. He envied Sheng his pretty, swiftly running thoughts and pure rhymes; yet it was not bitter envy, either, but very humble and admiring envy, even as Yuan loved secretly his cousin's handsome looks, so much more clearly handsome than his own.

Yet Yuan never knew Sheng's self, for with all his smiling courteous seeming openness, none ever knew Sheng well. He could give anywhere the gentlest words of praise and kindness, but though he spoke often and easily, yet what he said never told his inner thought. Sometimes he came to Yuan and said, "Let us go and see a picture today after school—there is a very good foreign picture at the Great World Theatre," yet when they both had walked there together and sat three hours through and come away again, and though Yuan had liked being with his cousin, still when he thought of it he could not remember that Sheng had said anything. He only could remember in the dim theatre Sheng's smiling face and his shining, strangely oval eyes. Only once Sheng said of Meng and his cause, "I am not one of them—I never shall be a revolutionist. I love my life too well, and I love only beauty. I am moved only by beauty. I have no wish to die in any cause. Some day I shall sail across the sea, and if it is more beautiful there than here, it may be I shall never come back again—how do I know? I have no wish to suffer for the common people.

They are filthy and they smell of garlic. Let them die. Who will miss them?"

This he said in the most tranquil pleasantness while they sat in the gilded theatre and looked about upon the well-dressed men and women there, all eating cakes and nuts and smoking foreign cigarettes, and he might have been the voice of all of them speaking. Yet though Yuan liked his cousin very well, he could not but feel a coldness in him at the calmness of these words, "Let them die." For Yuan still did hate death, and though at this time in his life the poor were not near him, he did not want them to die, nevertheless.

But these words of Sheng's that day prompted Yuan to ask another time more concerning Meng. Meng and Yuan had not talked very often together, but they played on one side of the game of ball, and Yuan liked the fierceness of Meng's thrust and leaping. Meng had the hardest tightest body of them all. Most of the young men were pale and slackly hung and they wore too many clothes they did not take off easily, so that they ran anyhow as children do, and fumbled at the ball, or threw it sidewise as a girl might, or kicked it mildly so that it rolled along the ground and stopped very soon. But Meng sprang at the ball as though it were his enemy and he kicked it with his hard leather-shod foot, and up it soared and came down with a great bound and flew up again, and all his body hardened at the play, and Yuan liked this as well as he liked Sheng's beauty.

So one day he asked of Sheng, "How do you know Meng is a revolutionist?" and Sheng answered, "Because he tells me so. He has always told me something of what he does, and I am the only one he tells, I think. I live in a little fear for him, too, sometimes. I dare not tell my father or my mother, nor my eldest brother even, what he does, for I know they would accuse him, and he is so fiery and so angry in his nature that he would run away forever. He trusts me now and tells me very much and so I know what he is doing, although I know there are secrets that he will not tell, for he has taken some wild oath of patriotism, and he has cut his arm and let his blood and written down his oath in blood, I know."

"And are there many of these revolutionists among our schoolmates?" Yuan asked, somewhat troubled, for he had thought that here he was safe enough, and now it seemed he was not safe, for this was the very thing his comrades in the school of war did, and still he did not want to join them.

"Many of them," answered Sheng. "And there are maids among them, too."

Now Yuan stared indeed. For there were maidens among the students in his school, this being the custom in this new and forward coastal city, that in many schools for men the law allowed young women to come also, and though there were not many maids yet who dared to be learned, or whose fathers let them be, yet there were a score or two in this one school, and Yuan had seen them here and there about the classrooms, but had paid no heed to them, nor counted them as any part of his life there, since they were not often beautiful and were always bent on books.

But after this day being troubled at what Sheng had said he looked at them more curiously, and now every time he passed a maid, her books beneath her arm and her eyes downcast, he wondered if so demure a creature could be part of all the secret plotting. One especially he noted, for she was the only one of her kind in the class which he and Sheng shared. She was a slender creature, bony as a little hungry bird, her face delicate and peaked, the cheek bones high, and the narrow lips pale and fine beneath the straight nose. She never spoke in class and what her thoughts were none knew, because she wrote neither good nor ill, and drew no comment from the teacher. But she was always there and sat listening to every word he said, and only in her narrow sombre eyes her interest seemed to shine sometimes.

Yuan looked at her curiously, until one day the maid felt his stare and looked back, and thereafter when Yuan looked at her he found her always watching him with her secret steady eyes, and so he looked no more. But he asked Sheng about her, since she moved withdrawn from anyone, and Sheng laughed and answered, "That one! She is one of them. She is a friend of Meng's— she and Meng are always in some secret talk and planning—look at her cold face! The cold ones make the steadiest revolutionists. Meng is too hot. He is all hot today and in despair tomorrow. But this girl, she is always cold as ice and same as ice and hard as ice. I hate girls to be so same and cool. But she cools Meng when he is hot and makes some too early showing of the plans, and when he despairs, her sameness pulls him up again. She comes from an inland province where there is revolution already."

"What do they plan?" asked Yuan curiously, his voice made low.

"Oh, when the army comes they plan to meet it triumphantly," said Sheng and he shrugged himself and walked with seeming indolence away from any who might hear them. "Most of all they work among the mill folk here who get a few pence only for their daily wage, and they tell the pullers of the rickshas how downtrodden they are and how these foreign police oppress them cruelly and all such things, so that if this day of triumph comes these low people will be ready to rise and seize what they may wish. But wait, Yuan,—they'll come and see if they can win you. Meng will come and see you some day. He asked me only the other day what sort you were, and if you were a revolutionist at heart."

At last one day Yuan perceived that Meng did seek him out, and he laid his hand on Yuan and caught him by his clothes and said in his usual sulky way, "You and I are cousins, yet we seem strangers still, never meeting much alone. Come with me to the tea shop at the school gate, and let us eat together."

Now Yuan could not well refuse, for it was the last class hour of that day, and all were free now, and so he went with Meng. They sat awhile, speechlessly, but after all it seemed Meng had nothing he cared to say, for he only sat and stared out into the street and watched the passers-by, and if he spoke at all it was to make a bitter joke at something that they saw. He said, "Look at that great fat lord in that motor car! See how he eats and how he lolls! He is an extortionist—a usurer or a banker or he has a factory. I know the very look! Well, he does not know he sits upon a hidden fire!"

And Yuan, knowing what his cousin meant, said nothing, though in honesty he thought to himself that Meng's own father was somewhat fatter still than this man was.

Or Meng said, "See that man toiling at his ricksha— he is half-starved—look, he has broken some little law. He's newly come from the country and he does not know he must not cross the street when that policeman holds his hand so. There, see what I said! Look at that policeman beat him—see him force the ricksha down and seize its cushions! Now that poor man has lost his vehicle and his day's earnings. And yet he must pay out just the same tonight at the place where he hires the ricksha!"

And when he saw this thing and watched the ricksha man turn away drooped in despair, Meng's voice grew shaking and Yuan looked and to his wonder he saw this strange lad was weeping angrily and struggling against his tears uncouthly. When Meng saw Yuan looking at him with such sympathy, he said, half choking, "Let's go where we can talk. I swear I cannot bear it if I do not talk. I swear I could kill these stupid folk for bearing their oppression so patiently."

And Yuan to soothe him took him to his own room and shut the door and let the lad talk.

This talk with Meng stirred deep in Yuan a sort of conscience that he wished not to remember. Yuan loved so well the ease of these days, the merriment and stir, the rest from duty, the doing only what he liked to do. These two women in the house, the lady and his sister, gave him lavishly their praise and tenderness, and he lived in warmth and friendliness. He would have forgotten that there were others who were not warmed or fed. He was so happy that he would not think of any sorrowful thing, and if sometimes in the dark dawns now he remembered that still his father might have power over him, he put the thought away, because he trusted to the lady's resourcefulness and care for him. Now these poor of whom Meng must talk brought an old shadow over him again, and he drew away from shadows. . . . Yet through such talk Yuan learned to see his country as he had not. In those days in the earthen house he saw it as spreading, lovely lands. He saw the fair body of his country. Even then he had not deeply felt the people. But here in these city streets, Meng taught him how to see the country's soul. Through the younger lad's angry notice of every smallest slight put on any lowly man or laborer, Yuan learned to notice, too. Since always where the very rich are there are the very poor, too, Yuan as he came and went upon the streets saw many more of these, for most were poor —the poorest starving children, blind and foul with disease and never washed, and in the fairest brightest streets, faced on both sides with great shops of every sort of merchandise, and fluttering silken banners overhead and hired musicians to play in balconies and draw their crowds of purchasers, even on these streets the filthiest beggars whined and wailed, and most faces were too pale and thin, and there were scores of prostitutes who came out even ahead of night to ply their hungry trade.

He saw everything and in the end this notice went far deeper in him than it could in Meng, for Meng was one of those who must serve some cause, who bend everything to serve the cause. Whenever he saw a starved man, or if he saw the poor clustered at the gate where rotten eggs are thrown outside the gates of factories where eggs are sent in ships to foreign lands, and these poor buying bowlfuls for a penny and drinking down the stuff, or if he saw men straining at great loads too heavy even for beasts, or if he saw rich and idle men and silk-clad painted women, laughing and taking pleasure while the poor begged, then his anger burst from him, and for everything he felt, he had this cry for cure, "These things will never be better until our cause is gained. We must have revolution! We must have all

the rich thrown down, and these foreigners who force
us cast out again, and the poor shall be lifted up, and
only revolution can do it. Yuan, when will you see this
light and join our cause? We need you—our country
needs us all!"

And Meng turned his burning, angry eyes on Yuan as
though he would fasten them in him until he gave his
promise.

But Yuan could not promise because he feared the
cause. It was the same cause, after all, from which he
had escaped.

And Yuan could not somehow trust to any cause to
cure these ills, nor could he hate a rich man hot and
properly as Meng could. The very plumpness of a rich
man's body, the ring upon his finger, the fur lining of
his coat, the jewels in his lady's ears, the paint and
powder on her face, could send Meng wildly deeper in
his cause. But even against his will Yuan must see a
kindly look if it were on a rich man's face, or he could
see a look of pity in a painted woman's eyes, who gave
a bit of silver to a beggar, even though she wore a satin
coat, and he liked laughter, whether it was from rich or
poor; he liked the one who laughed even if he knew
him evil. The truth was, Meng must love or hate men
for being white or black, but Yuan could not for his life
say, "This man is rich and evil, and this man is poor and
good," and so he was spoiled for any cause-making, however great the cause.

He could not even hate as Meng hated them the
foreigners who mingled with the city crowds. For the
city, being very great in trade with all parts of the
world, was filled with foreigners of every hue and
tongue, and anywhere upon the streets Yuan saw them,
some gentle, but some loud and evil and often drunken,
and many poor and rich among them. If Meng hated
any rich men worse than others it was rich foreigners;
he could bear any cruelty better than this, if he saw a
drunken foreign sailor kick a ricksha puller or a white
woman buying something from a vendor and bent on
paying less than she was asked, or any of those common

sights that may be seen in any coastal city where men of many-nations meet and mingle.

Meng grudged these foreigners the very air they lived upon. If he passed one, he would not give way a foot of path before him. His long sour lad's face grew darker still and he would thrust his shoulders out, and if he pushed the foreigner, even though a woman, from his way, then so much the better, and he muttered full of hate, "They have no business on our land. They come to rob and plunder us. With their religion they rob our souls and minds, and with their trade they rob us of our goods and money."

One day Yuan and Meng walking home from school together passed upon the street a slight slender man whose skin was white and his nose high as white men's are, but his eyes and hair were very black and not like white men's. Then Meng cast the man a furious look and he cried to Yuan, "If there is a thing I hate above another in this city, it is such men as these who are nothing wholly, but are mixed in blood and untrustworthy and divided in their hearts! I never can understand how any of our race can so forget himself, man or woman, as to mix his blood with blood of foreigners. I would kill them all for traitors and kill such fellows as the one we passed."

But Yuan must remember the man's gentle look and how his face was patient in spite of paleness and he said, "He looked kind enough. I cannot think he must be evil only because his skin is pale and his blood mixed. He cannot help what his parents did."

But Meng cried out, "You ought to hate him, Yuan! Have you not heard what white men have done to our country, and how they hold us hard as any prisoners with their cruel, unjust treaties? We cannot even have our laws—why, if a white man kills a countryman of ours, he is not punished scarcely—he will not go before our court—"

While Meng cried out thus, Yuan listened, smiling half in apology, because he was so mild before the other's heat, and feeling perhaps it was true he ought to hate for country's sake, but he was not able.

Therefore Yuan could not yet join Meng's cause. He said nothing when Meng begged him, smiled in his shy way, and could not say he would not, but he put forth the reason that he was so busy—he had no time for even such a cause, and at last Meng let him be and even ceased to talk with him, and gave him but a surly nod or two in passing. On holidays and patriotic days when all must go forth with flags and singing, Yuan went too, as they all did, lest he be cried a traitor, but he joined no secret meetings and he made no plots. Sometimes he heard some news of those who plotted, how this one had been found with a bomb hidden in his room to throw at some great man, and once a band of plotters went and beat a certain teacher whom they hated for his friendship with the foreigners, but when he heard such things Yuan turned more steadfastly to his books and would not lend his interest elsewhere.

The truth was at this time Yuan's life was pressed too full for him to know what any one thing was at bottom. Before he could think clearly to the end of rich and poor, or before he could comprehend the meaning of Meng's cause, or even take his fill of gaiety, some other thing came to his mind. There was all he knew at school, the many things he learned and did, the strange lessons that he had, the magic of a science opening to him in a laboratory. Even in the chemistry he hated because its stinks offended the delicacy of his nose, he was charmed by the hues of potions that he made and wondered at the way two mild passive fluids cast together could suddenly foam up into a new life, new color and new odor, and so make a different third. Into his mind these days there poured every sort of thought and perception of this great city where the whole world met, and there was not time in day and night to see what each one meant. He could not give himself to any single knowledge because there were so many, and in his heart sometimes he envied his cousins and his sister very much, for Sheng lived in his dreams and loves, and Meng lived in his cause, and Ai-lan in her prettiness and pleasure, and to Yuan this seemed easy living, since he lived in such diversity.

Even these city poor were so unlovely in their poverty that Yuan could not feel them wholly pitiful. He did pity them, and he did want them fed and clothed, and nearly always if he had a penny and a beggar laid his claws upon Yuan's arm, he gave the penny. But he feared he gave it not all in pity either, but partly to buy his freedom from that filthy clinging hand and from the whining voice beside his ear, "Have a kind heart, young sir—a kind heart, sir, lest I starve, I and my children!" There was only one more hideous sight than a beggar in this city, and it was their children. Yuan could not bear the puling children of the very poor, their little faces set already in the whining look of beggary, and worst of all were starveling babes half-naked and thrust into the naked skinny bosoms of the women. Yes, Yuan drew shudderingly from them all. He threw his pennies at them and averted his eyes and hastened on his way. And to himself he thought, "I might join Meng's cause if they were not so hideous, these poor!"

Yet there came something, too, to save him from complete estrangement from these of his own people, and it was his old love of lands and fields and trees. In the city during the winter that love receded and Yuan often forgot it. But now as spring drew on, he felt a restlessness come on him. The days grew warm, and in small city gardens the trees began to bud and leaf, and on the streets came vendors carrying on their poles' ends baskets of blossoming plum trees, twisted into dwarfish shapes, or great round bunches of violets and spring lilies. Yuan grew restless in the mild spring winds and these winds made him remember the little hamlet where the earthen house stood, and he had a craving in his feet to stand on earth somewhere instead of on these city pavements. So he entered his name in the new spring term into a certain class of that school where teachers taught of cultivation of the land and Yuan, among others, was apportioned a little piece of earth outside the city, for practice at the land to test what they had learned in books, and in his bit of land it was part of Yuan's task that he must plant seeds and keep the weeds out and do labor of this sort.

It so happened that the piece Yuan had was at the end of all the others, and next to a farmer's field, and the first time Yuan came out to see his plot of land he went alone, and the farmer stood there staring, his face alight with grinning, and he shouted, "What do you students here? I thought students only learned in books!"

Then Yuan answered, "In these days we learn in books of sowing and reaping too, and we learn how to make the land ready for the sowing, and that is what I do to-day."

At this the farmer laughed loudly and said with a mighty scorn, "I never did hear of such a learning! Why, farmer tells his son and his son tells his son—one looks only at his neighbor and does what his neighbor does!"

"And if the neighbor is wrong?" said Yuan, smiling.

"Then look at the next neighbor and a better one," said the farmer and then he laughed over again and fell to hoeing in his own field and he muttered to himself and stopped to scratch his head and shake himself and laugh again and cry out, "No, I never did hear such a thing in all my days! Well, I'm glad I sent no son of mine to any school, to waste my silver to have him learn of farming! I'll teach him more than he can learn, I'll swear!"

Now Yuan had never held a hoe in his two hands in all his life, and when he took up the long-handled clumsy thing it felt so heavy that he could not wield it. However high he lifted it he could not bring it down in such a way as to cut the packed soil and it always came down sidewise, and he sweat most fearfully and still he could not do it, so that although the day was cold for spring and biting windy, his sweat was pouring down him as though it were summer.

At last in despair and secretly he glanced at the farmer to see how he did it, for the farmer's steady strokes went

up and down and made a mark each time the hoe's point
fell, although Yuan hoped the farmer would not see him
glance, for indeed he was a little proud. But soon he
saw that the farmer did see him, and had seen him all
along and was laughing in himself to see the wild way
Yuan flung his hoe about. Now catching Yuan's glance
he roared with fresh laughter and striding over clods
he came up to Yuan and cried, "Never tell me you are
watching what a neighbor farmer does, when you have
learned it all in books!" And he laughed and cried again,
"Has not your book told you even how to hold the hoe?"

Then Yuan struggled a little over a petty anger, for
to his own surprise he found it was not easy for him to
hear the laughter of this common man, and he had his
own rueful knowledge that indeed he could not even
dig this bit of land, and how could he hope to plant the
seed in it? But his reason overcame his shame at last and
he let his hoe drop and he grinned, too, and bore the
farmer's laughter and wiped his dripping face and said
sheepishly, "You are right, neighbor. It is not in the book.
I'll take you for my teacher if you'll let me learn of you."

At this simple speech the farmer was very pleased and
he liked Yuan and he stopped his laughing. In truth he
was secretly proud that he, a humble farmer, had something he could teach this young man, a youth from the
schools, as anyone could see, and learned in his speech
and looks. And so, importantly and with a sort of pom-
pousness upon him, the farmer eyed the young man
and said seriously, "First, look at me and at yourself, and
ask which one is free to wield the hoe without such
sweating."

And Yuan looked and saw the farmer, a man strong
and brown, stripped to the waist, his legs bare to his
knees, his feet in sandals, his face brown and red with
winds and weather, his whole look good and free. Then
Yuan said nothing, but he smiled and without a single
word he took off his outer heavy coat and then his inner
coat, and rolled his sleeves up to his elbow and stood
ready. This the farmer watched, and suddenly he cried
again, "What woman's skin you have! Look at this arm of

mine!" And he put his arm by Yuan's and outstretched his hand. "Put out your hand!—Look at your palm all blisters! But you hold your hoe so loosely it would have rubbed a blister even on my hand."

Then he picked up the hoe and showed Yuan how to hold it in his two hands, the one hand firm and close to keep the handle sure, and the other farther on, to guide the swing of it. And Yuan was not ashamed to learn, and he tried many times until at last the iron point fell true and hard and clipped away a piece of earth each time it fell, and then the farmer praised him and Yuan felt as glad as he did if he had a verse praised by his teacher, although he wondered that he did, seeing the farmer was but a common man.

Day after day Yuan came to work upon his plot of land, and he liked best to come when all his fellows were not there, for when they came the farmer would not draw near at all, but worked in some more distant field of his. But if Yuan were alone he came and talked and showed Yuan how to plant his seed and how to thin the seedlings when they sprang up, and how to watch for the worms and insects that were eager and ready always to devour each seedling as it came.

And Yuan had his turn in teaching, too, for when such pests came he read and learned of foreign poisons that would kill them and he used these poisons. The first time he did this the farmer laughed at him and cried out, "Remember how you watched me, after all, and how your books have not come true nor showed you how deep to lay your beans or when to hoe them free of weeds!"

But when he saw worms shrivel up and die upon the bean plants under the poison then he grew grave and wondering and said in a somewhat lower tone, "I swear I would not have believed it. So it is not a thing willed by gods, these pests. It is something man can do away with. Something there is in books, after all—yes, more than a little even, I can say, because planting and sowing are of no use if worms devour the plants."

Then he begged some poison for his own land, and

Yuan gave it gladly, and in such giving these two became friends after a fashion, and Yuan's plot was best of all, and for this he thanked the farmer, and the farmer thanked Yuan that his beans throve and were not eaten as his neighbors' fields were.

It was well for Yuan to have this friend and to have this bit of land to work upon. For often in the springtime as he bent himself upon the earth, some content rose up in him which he had never known. He learned to change his clothes and wear a common garb such as the farmer wore, and even to change his shoes to sandals, and the farmer let him be free in his home, for he had no unwed daughter, and his wife by now was old and ugly, and Yuan kept his clothes for work there. So every day he came he changed himself into a farmer, and he loved the earth more even than he thought he would. It was good to watch for seeds to sprout, and there was a poetry in it too, a thing he scarcely could express, although he tried to do it and made a verse about it. He loved the very labor of the land, and when his own was done, he often went and labored on the farmer's land, and sometimes at the farmer's asking he would eat a meal on the threshing floor where as the days grew warmer the farmer's wife would spread the table. And he grew hard and brown until Ai-lan cried at him one day, "Yuan, how is it you grow blacker every day? You are black as any farmer!"

Then Yuan grinned and answered, "So I am a farmer, Ai-lan, but you never will believe me when I say so!"

For often at his books or even in the midst of an evening's pleasure, when he was far away from that bit of land, it came suddenly to his mind and while he read or while he played, he planned some new seed he could sow or he would wonder if perhaps a vegetable he had would be fit for gathering before the summer came, or he would be troubled because he remembered a yellow withering beginning upon a plant's tip.

To himself Yuan thought sometimes, "If all the poor were like this one man, then I might be willing to join Meng's cause and make it mine."

It was well that Yuan had this solid and secret content in this little plot of land lent him. It was secret, for not if he would could he have told anyone why he liked to work on land, and at this time of his youth he was even a little ashamed of this liking, because it was the fashion of these city youths to laugh at country men and call them louts and "big turnips" and many names like these. And Yuan cared what his fellows said. Not even to Sheng therefore could he speak of this, though with Sheng he could talk of many things, such as a beauty they both saw in a sudden color or shape somewhere; still less to Ai-lan could he have told what strange deep solid pleasure he had in this bit of land. He might have spoken if there had been need to tell, to this one whom he called his mother, for though they did not speak much of inward things, still at the mealtimes they had alone in the house, the lady did talk often, in her grave way, of things she liked to do.

For this lady was full of quiet good works, and did not give herself over completely to gaming or feasting or going to see running horses and dogs, as many ladies did in this city. These were not pleasures to her, although if Ai-lan wished it, she went with her and sat and watched it all, apart and elegant, and as though it were a duty and nothing to be done for its own sake. Her real pleasure was in a certain good work she did for children, those female children, newly born, who are cast away unwanted by the poor. These when she found them she gathered into a home she kept and she hired two women to be mothers to them, and she herself went there daily, too, and taught them and watched to see those who were ill or wasted, and she had nearly twenty of these little foundlings. Of this good work she talked to Yuan sometimes and how she planned to teach these girls some good honest livelihood and wed them to such honest men as might be found, farmers or tradesmen or weavers, or whatever man might want good, working maids.

Once Yuan went with her to the home, and he was amazed to see the change that came upon this grave staid lady. It was a poor plain place, for she had not much money to spend there, since even for these she would not rob Ai-lan of any pleasure, but once within the gate the children fell upon her, crying out she was their mother, and they pulled her dress and hands and loved her eagerly, until she laughed and looked shyly at Yuan, and he stood staring, for he had not seen her laugh before.

"Does Ai-lan know of them?" he asked.

At this the lady was suddenly grave again, and nodded, saying only, "She is busy with her own life now."

And then she led Yuan here and there about the plain home; from court to kitchen all was clean though poor, and she said, "I do not want much money for them, for they are to be the wives of working men." To this she added presently, "If I find one, even one, among them, who might be what I planned for Ai-lan . . . I will take her apart then to my own home and spend myself upon her. I think there is this one—I do not know yet—" She called and a child came out to her from another room, a child older than the rest, a child of a certain gravity of look, although not more than twelve or thirteen years of age. She came with confidence and put her hand into the lady's hand and looked at her and said in a clear voice, "Here I am, my mother."

"This child," the lady said, most earnestly, looking down into the child's upturned face, "has some spirit in her but I do not yet know what it is. I found her my own self, laid at this door, when she was newborn, and I took her in. She is the eldest and the first I found. She is so quick at letters, so true to every teaching, so to be depended on, that if she continues thus, I shall take her to my own home within a year or two. . . . So, Mei-ling, you may go."

The child gave her a smile, a quick, lighting smile, and she threw Yuan a deep look, and though she was only yet a child Yuan did not forget the look, it was so clear and questioning, straightly put, not as though to him more than to another. Then she went away again.

To such a lady, then, Yuan might have spoken but

there was no need for speech after all. He only knew he liked the hours he put upon the land. They joined him to some root he had, so that he was not, as were many others, rootless and floating upon the surface of the life in this city.

Again and yet again Yuan, when he suffered unrest or questioning of some sort, went to this bit of land, and there sweating in the sun or wet with cool rain, he worked in silence or talked quietly of common things with his neighbor farmer. Although such work, such talk, seemed nothing or of no great import of any kind while it was being done, yet when night came Yuan could go home and he was cleansed and freed of all inward impatience. He could read in his books and meditate upon them happily, or he could go with Ai-lan and her friends and spend the hours in noise and light and dancing, and not be disturbed having in himself some quietness he learned upon his land.

And he well needed this quietness the land gave him, the steadiness and root it gave him. For in this spring his life was given a twist he had not dreamed it could be given.

In one thing Yuan was very far behind Sheng and very far behind Ai-lan and behind even Meng. These three lived in a warmer air than Yuan ever had. In this great city they had spent their youth, and all its heats poured into their blood. There were here a hundred hundred heats for youth; the pictures of love and beauty painted on the walls, the pleasure houses where the pictured loves of strange men and women in foreign lands were shown, the halls of dancing where for a little silver a woman may be bought for a night, these were the crudest heats.

Above these somewhat were the printed tales and stories and verses of love that could be found for sale in any little shop. In the old days these were counted all for evil, and understood for what they were, a torch to light the fires in man or maid, and none would read them openly. But now in this day, the subtlety of outer nations had crept in and under guise of art and genius and such fair names the young read these writings everywhere and studied them; yet for all the fairness of the names, the torch was there still and the old fires were lighted.

Young men grew daring and maids, too, and old modesties were gone. Hands touched, and it was not counted evil as it used to be, and a youth himself might ask a maid to be betrothed to him, and her father did not sue his father at a court of law as once he might and still would in an inland city where the evil ways of foreigners were unknown. And when the two were openly betrothed, they came and went as freely as though they were savages, and if sometimes, as it must happen, blood ran too hot and high and flesh met flesh too soon, then the two were not killed for honor's sake, as would have happened in their parents' youth. No, only the marriage day was hastened forward, and so the child was born in wedlock, and the young pair were as careless as though they both were honorable, and parents, if they were miserable, could but look at each other in sick privacy and bear it as they could, for this was the new day. But many a father cursed the new day for his son's sake and the mother for her daughter's sake. But still this was the new day and none could turn it back.

In this day Sheng had lived and Meng his brother, and Ai-lan, too, and they were part of it and did not know another. But Yuan was not so. Him the Tiger had reared in every old tradition and in his own added hatred of all women. And Yuan had never dreamed of women, even. Or if inadvertently he did dream in his sleep he woke in hottest shame at it, and sprang out of bed and fell to furious labor on his books or else he walked the streets awhile or did some such thing to clear his mind of evil. Some day, he knew, he must wed as all men did and have his sons in decency, but it was not a thing to think of when he had so much to learn. He craved learning only now. He had plainly told his father and he was not changed yet.

But in the spring of this year, he was harassed with nightly dreaming, plagued by dreams. It was the strangest thing, for by day he never let his thoughts go to love or women. Yet his thoughts asleep were filled with such lewdness that he awoke and sweat with shame, and he was cleansed only when he went striding to his bit of land and worked there desperately, and on the days when he could work there longest, in the nights of such days, he dreamed the least and slept the sweetest. So he turned yet more ardently to labor there.

Now although he did not know it Yuan was as hot as any youth within, and hotter far than Sheng, who diffused his heart into a hundred pretty languors, and hotter, too, than Meng, who had his cause to burn for. And Yuan had come out of the cold courts of his childhood into this heated city. He who had never even touched a maid's hand could not yet put his arm about a maid's slight body and hold her hand in his with no rebuke, and feel her breath upon his cheek, and move her as he would to sounds of music, without the sweet sickness in him which he loved and feared. And though he was decorous, until Ai-lan teased him without pity, and he scarcely touched the hand he held, and never rested the maid's body against his own, as many men were eager to do, and did it unreproved, too, still Ai-lan's very teasing set his thoughts moving as they would not have dared to move and as he wished they would not.

She cried sometimes, pursing out her pretty lips, "Yuan, you are so old-fashioned! How can you dance well if you push the girl away from you like that? Look, this is the way to hold a maid!"

And there in the room where they all sat in the rare evenings when she was home with her mother, she set the music going in its box and she pressed herself into his arms and let her body follow all the lines of his, her feet weaving in and out with his. And she did not fail to tease him with the other maidens by, too, and she cried, laughing, if one were there, "If you would dance with my brother Yuan you must force him to hold you rightly. What he would like best would be to set you up against a wall somewhere and do his dancing all alone!" Or she would say, "Yuan, you are handsome, we all know, but not so fearfully handsome you need to fear every maid! Doubtless there are some of us who have our loves already set!"

And with such raillery before her friends she set them all to merriment so that bold maids grew bolder and pressed themselves against him shamelessly, and though he would have stopped their boldness he feared the sharp merriment of Ai-lan's further speech, and bore it as he could. And even timid maids grew smiling when they danced with him and bolder than they were with bolder men, and they, too, added upturned eyes and smiles and warmer handclasps and the touch of thigh to thigh and all those wiles which women know by nature.

At last he grew so troubled by his dreams and all the freedom of the maids he knew for Ai-lan's sake, that he would never have gone with her again except that the mother still said so often, "Yuan, it comforts me to know you are with Ai-lan; even though she has another man to take her where she goes, I feel the better if I know you are there, too."

And Ai-lan was willing enough for Yuan to go with her, for she was proud to show him off, for he was a tall youth, and not ill at look at, and there were maids she knew to whom it was a favor that she brought him with her. Thus were the fires ready in Yuan against his will but he laid no torch to them.

Yet was the torch laid and in no way he could foresee, nor, indeed, that any could foresee.

And thus it was. One day Yuan lingered in the classroom to write down a foreign poem which his teacher had set upon the wall for a task, and he lingered until every other one was gone, or so he thought. It so happened that this was the class that he and Sheng sat together in, and also that pale maid who was a revolutionist. Now as Yuan finished what he wrote and closed his book and put his pen into his pocket and stirred himself to rise, he heard his name called and one spoke thus, "Mr. Wang, since you are here, will you explain to me the meaning of those lines set there? You are more clever than I am. I thank you if you will."

This Yuan heard said in a very pleasing voice, a maid's voice, but not tinkling with affectation as even Ai-lan's voice was, or those of her friends. It was rather somewhat deep for any maid, very full and thrilling in its tone, so that any casual word it spoke seemed to take on more meaning than the mere word had. Yuan looked up in haste and great surprise, and there beside him stood that maid, the revolutionist, her pale face paler still than he remembered it, but now that she stood near him, he saw her dark narrow eyes were not cold at all but filled with inward warmth and feeling, and they belied the set coldness of her face, and burned there in its paleness. She looked at him steadfastly, and then with calmness set herself beside him and waited for him to answer, as cool as though she spoke on any day to any man.

He somehow answered, stammering while he did, "Ah, yes, of course—only I am not sure. I think it means—foreign verse is always difficult—it is an ode—a sort of—" and so he stammered on, speaking something, somehow, and conscious always of her deep and steadfast look, now on his face, now on the words. And then she rose and thanked him, and again she spoke the simplest words and yet somehow her voice freighted them with a great load of gratitude, far more, Yuan thought, than any service could deserve. Then naturally they drew together as they left the room and walked together down the silent halls, for it was late afternoon and every student eager to be gone, and so they walked out to the gate and the maid seemed content to be silent until Yuan asked a thing or two for courtesy's sake.

He asked, "What is your honored name?" and he asked in the old-fashioned courteous way he had been taught. But she answered crisply, the words short and curt seemingly, and without the return courtesy, except that voice of hers gave meaning to everything she said.

At last they reached the gate, and Yuan bowed deeply. But the maid gave a quick nod and went her way, and

Yuan looking after her, saw her a little taller than most women as she walked sure and swift among the crowds until he lost her. Then he leaped wondering into a ricksha and went home, and he wondered what she really was, and wondered at the way her eyes and voice said other things than did her face and words.

On this slight beginning a friendship grew. Now Yuan had never had a maid for friend, nor in truth had he many friends, for he had not, as some did, a little special group in which he took a natural place. His cousins had their friends, Sheng his friends among young men like himself, who fancied they were the poets and the writers and the young painters of a modern day, and they followed zealously after leaders such as the one surnamed Wu, at whom Yuan glanced sidewise while he danced with Ai-lan. And Meng had his secret group of revolutionists. But Yuan belonged to none, and though he spoke to a score or so of young men as he passed them, and though he knew this maid or that of Ai-lan's friends to talk lightly with a little while, he had no bosom friend. Before he knew it this maid came to be his friend.

And thus it came about. At first it was always she who pressed the friendship, coming as any wilier maid might do to ask his explanation or his advice on something or other, and he was deceived as all men easily are by even such simple wile as this, for after all he was a man and very young and it was pleasant to him to advise a maid, and he came to helping her to write her essays and at last it came about that with one excuse or another they met somehow every day, although not openly. For if any had asked Yuan what he felt for this maid he would have said he felt friendship only, nothing more. She was in truth a very different maid from any he thought fair—thought even a little fair, because there was no maid to whom he gave a real thought yet in his life, and to himself if he meditated on any maid at all it was to see some pretty flowery maid like Ai-lan, with little pretty hands and lovely looks and dainty ways, and all these qualities he saw in Ai-lan's friends. Yet he had not

loved one of them—he had only said in his heart that did
he ever love, the maid must be pretty as a rose is
pretty, or a budded plum flower or some such delicate
useless thing. So had he written secret verses sometimes
to such maids, a line or two and always unfinished, because the feeling was so slight and vague and there was
no one single maid who stood enough to him as the
one to write to above all others. It was rather that his
love was diffused like a dim coming light before the
sunrise.

Certainly he never thought of one to love like this
maid, severe and earnest and clothed always in her
dark straight robes of blue or grey, and wearing leather
shoes, and bent always on her books and cause. Nor did
he love her now.

But she loved him. At which hour he found this out
he scarcely knew. Yet he knew, too. One day they met
at a distance to walk upon a quiet street along a canal's
edge, and it was evening and the time of twilight, and
they were about to turn homeward, when suddenly he
felt her looking at him and he caught her look and it
was changed, a deep clinging burning look it was, and
then her voice, her lovely voice that never seemed a part
of her, came forth and said, "Yuan, there is one thing I'd
rather see than anything."

And when he faltered out to know what it was, his
heart beating very thickly of a sudden, although he had
not thought of loving her, she said on, "I want to see
you in our cause. Yuan, you are my very brother—I want
to call you comrade, too. We need you—we need your
good mind, your strength. You are twice what Meng
can ever be."

Suddenly Yuan thought he saw why she had come to
friendship with him, and he thought angrily that she
and Meng had planned it, and his rising feeling checked
itself.

But then her voice said again, very soft and deep-
sounding in the twilight, her voice said, "Yuan, there is
another reason."

And now Yuan dared not ask her what it was. But a

faintness in him rose and choked him nearly, and he felt his body tremble, and he turned and said, half whispering, "I must get home—I promised Ai-lan—"

And so with no other word they both turned and walked homeward. But when they parted they did that they never had done; scarcely meaning it, and certainly not planning so to do. They clasped their hands together, and with that touch some change came into Yuan, and he knew they were no more friends, not now friends any more, though still he did not know what they were.

But all that evening when he was with Ai-lan, when he spoke to this maid, danced with that one, he looked at them as he never had and puzzled over how maids in the world can be so differing, and that night when he went to bed he lay a long time pondering on this, the first time he had even thought of any maid. For now he thought long of this one maid and he thought about her eyes, how he had once thought them cold like dull onyx in the paleness of her face. But now he had seen them brighten into warm beauty of their own when he spoke to her. Then he remembered how her voice was always sweet, and how its richness seemed unsuited to her quietness and seeming coldness. And yet it was her own voice. So pondering he wished that he had had courage to ask her what that other reason was. He would have liked to hear her voice tell him such a reason as he guessed.

But still he did not love her. He knew he did not love her.

And last he came to the memory of that touch of her hand to his, the heart of her hand pressed against his hand's heart; so, palm to palm, they had stood an instant in the darkness of the unlit street, so fixed a ricksha swerved to pass them, and they did not see it until the man cursed them, and still they did not care. It had been too dark for him to see her eyes, and she had said nothing, nor had he. There was only that close touch to think on. And when he thought of it the torch was lit. Something flamed inside him, though what it was puzzled him no little, for still he knew he did not love her.

Now if it had been Sheng who touched this maid's hand he would have, if he liked, smiled and forgotten it, for he had touched many maids' hands warmly for a moment, or if he liked he would have touched it again and yet again, as often as he would if he found the maid loved him, or at least until he wearied of it and he would have written a tale or two or made a verse and then forgot her the more easily. And Meng would not have dreamed long of it either, for in this cause of his were maids enough, and they made it a purpose, youths and maids, to be bold and free together, and to call each other comrade, and Meng heard much talk and made some talk, too, about men and women being equal always and free to love each other as they would.

Still, with all this freedom, there was not overmuch true freedom, for these maids and youths, as Meng did, burned with another cause than lust, and the cause burned them clean. And Meng was cleanest of them all, for he had grown so filled with loathing of lust, having seen his own father's heats and his elder brother's wandering eyes, that he scorned all vain pastime spent with women, because to him it seemed they wasted mind and body that should be spent for cause. As yet Meng had never touched a maid. He could speak as well as any on free love and rights of love without a rule of marriage, but he did none of it.

But Yuan had no burning cleansing cause. He had not the safety of Sheng's idle, pleasant ways with maidens either, and so when this one maid touched Yuan's hand as none had ever touched it he could not forget it. Here was a thing to wonder at, too, that this hand of hers, when he remembered it, was hot and moist in the palm. He had not thought her hand could be hot. Thinking of her pale face, of her cool pale lips that moved so little when she spoke, he would have said, if he had thought of it before, that her hands would be dry and cool and the fingers loose to hold. But this was not true. Her hand had held to his hand, close and hot and clinging. Hand and voice and eyes—those spoke of her hot heart. And when Yuan began to think what her heart might be, the heart of this strange maid who was so bold and calm, yet shy as he could know her shy through his own shyness, then he tossed upon his bed and longed to touch her hand again and yet again.

Nevertheless, when at last he fell asleep and woke in the cool morning of the spring, he knew he did not love her. He could think in the cool morning and remember how hot her hand was, and say to himself that even so he did not love her. And on that day in the school in great shyness he avoided every glance at her, and he did not linger anywhere and at the earliest hour after noon he went out to his land and worked there feverishly, and to himself he thought, "This feel of earth upon my hands is better than the touch of any maid's hand." And he remembered how he had lain and thought in his bed the night before and he was ashamed and glad his father did not know.

Before long the farmer came by and he praised the clever way Yuan felled the weeds about his turnips and he laughed and said, "Do you remember that first day you hoed? If it had been today, you would have felled each turnip with the weeds!" And he laughed mightily, and then he said to comfort Yuan, "But you will make a farmer yet. It is told in the muscle of your arm and in the bigness of your back. Those other students—such a puny lot of pale weeds I never saw—their spectacles and dangling little arms and their gold teeth and their sticks of legs stuck into foreign trousers—if I had such bodies as they have I swear I'd wrap me in robes somehow and hide myself." And the farmer laughed again and shouted, "Come and smoke awhile and rest yourself before my door!"

And so Yuan did, and he listened, smiling, to the farmer's loud constant voice and to all the farmer's scorn of city men and especially did the farmer hate the young men and the revolutionists, and he cried down every mild good word Yuan said for them and he shouted, "And what good can they do me, then? I have my bit of land, my home, my cow. I want no more land than I have, and I have enough to eat. If the rulers would not tax me so hard, I would be glad, but men like me have always been so taxed. Why should they come and talk to me of doing good to me or mine? Whoever heard of good coming out of strangers? Who will do good for any man except these of his own blood? No, I know they have something they want for themselves—my cow, perhaps, or else my bit of land."

And then he cursed awhile, and cursed the mothers who could bear such sons and grew merry at the expense of all who were not like himself and praised Yuan for working on the land so well, and then he laughed and Yuan laughed and they were friends.

From this robustness and from the cleanness of the earth Yuan went home again and to his bed, and he would not go out that night for any pleasure even, because he wanted nothing of any maid, and he desired to touch no maid at all, but only to do his work and learn his books, and so this night he slept. In this way the land healed him for a time.

Yet in him were the flames already lit. Another day or two and his mood changed itself again, and he was restless and he turned his head secretly one day to see if that maid were in the schoolroom, and she was, and between the heads of others their eyes met, and her eyes clung to his although he turned back quickly. But he could not forget her. In a day or two again he said in passing through the door, although he had not planned it, "Shall we walk together again today?" And she nodded, her deep eyes looking down.

That day she did not touch his hand and it seemed to him she walked farther from him than she used to do, and was more silent, and talk came harder than it did. And here was something contrary in Yuan, which surprised himself. He would have sworn he would be glad not to be touched and that he did not want her very near. And yet when they had walked awhile he wished that she had touched him. He would not even at parting put out his hand, and yet he watched and longed to see her hand come forth, so he must meet it. But it did not, and he went home defrauded somehow, and yet angry that he felt so, and he was ashamed and swore he would not walk with any maid, and that he was a man with work to do. And he astonished a certain mild old teacher that day with his bitter writing of how men ought to live alone and strive after learning and keep away from women, and that night he told himself a hundred times that he was glad he did not love this maid. Each day thereafter for a while he went dogged to his land and would not let himself remember that he wanted any touch.

Then one day, some three days after that, he had a letter written in a small square writing that he did not know. Now Yuan had not many letters, and only one sometimes from a comrade he had loved in the school of war who loved him still. And this letter was not the hasty writing of his friend. He opened it, and there within he found a page from the maid he did not love— a single page, very short, and saying these words clearly, "Have I done something to make you angry with me? I am a revolutionist, a modern woman. I have no need to hide myself as other women have. I love you. Can you then love me? I do not ask or care for marriage. Marriage is an ancient bondage. But if so be you need my love, you have it when you will." And then, very small and cryptic, she twisted close together the shaping of her name.

So was love first offered to Yuan. Now must he think of love, sitting in his room alone, this letter in his hand, and he must wonder of all that love could mean. Here was a maid ready for his taking if he would take her. And many times his blood cried out that he might take her. He began to lose his childish youth in those few hours, and manhood grew in him in rushing heartbeats and in his ardent blood. His body was no more a lad's body now. . . .

In a few days the heats within him ripened him and he was full-grown and a man in his desires. But still he wrote no answer to the maid, and at the school he avoided every sight of her. Twice on different nights he sat down to write, and twice beneath his pen the words rose up,

"I do not love you," but yet those words he would not write because his curious body pressed him to let it know what it desired. So in this dark confusion of his blood and heart he wrote no answer and he waited for himself.

But he was sleepless and more nearly angry and full of impatience than he had ever been before, so that the lady, his mother, looked at him most thoughtfully, and Yuan felt her questioning. Yet he would say nothing, for how could he say that he was angry because he could not take a maid he did not love, and that he was angry because he could not love her since he wanted what she offered him? So he let the struggle wage itself in him and was as moody as his father ever was when any war was to be waged.

Now out of all this mingled life of Yuan's, wherein he was caught a little in everything and in nothing wholly, the old Tiger suddenly forced a clarity, and this without knowing at all what he did. These many months since the lady had written him first the Tiger had not answered anything. He sat there in his distant halls, silent and sulky against his son, and no word came out of him. Once again the lady wrote, and yet again, without telling Yuan she did, and if Yuan asked sometimes why she had no answer from his father, she answered soothingly, "Let be. As long as he says nothing, there can be no ill news." And indeed Yuan was very willing to let be, and every day his mind was more swallowed in his life, and at last he almost forgot that he had anything to fear at all from his father, or that he had run away from his father's power, it seemed so much his life here.

Then one day in the later passing spring the Tiger put forth his power again upon his son. He came out of his silence and he wrote a letter not to the lady, but to his own son. This letter he did not bid a letter writer write for him, either. No, with his own brush which he had not for long used the Tiger put down a few words to his son, and though the letters were sharply, rudely made, the meaning of them was very plain. They said,

"I have not changed my will. Come home and be wed. The day is set for the thirtieth of this moon."

This letter Yuan found waiting for him in his room one night when he came in from an evening's pleasure. He came in all languorous and roused with pleasure, so that almost, while he swayed to this music and to that, he had made up his mind that night to take the love the maid had offered to him. He came in filled with this excitement, that the next day perhaps, or the next day but one, he would go with her where she would and do as she was willing—or at least he played with the thought that so perhaps he would. Then his eye fell on the table, and there the letter was, and very well he knew the superscription, and who had written it. He seized it and tore the tough old-fashioned paper of its envelope, and drew the inner paper forth, and there the words were, plain as though he heard the Tiger's shout. Yes, the words were like a shout to Yuan. When he had read them, the room seemed suddenly filled with silence as though after a great roar of noise. He folded the paper again and thrust it in the envelope again and sat down breathless in the silence.

What should he do? How answer this command his father laid upon him? The thirtieth? It was less than twenty days away. And then the old childhood fear fell on him. Despair crept up into his heart. After all, how could he withstand his father? When had he ever withstood his father?? Always somehow in the end his father had his way, by fear or love, or some such equal force. The young never could escape the old. It came to Yuan weakly that perhaps it would be better if he did go back and yield to his father in this one thing. He could go back and wed the maid and stay a night or two and do his duty and come away and never go home again. Then might he by any law do as he pleased and it would not be counted to him for a sin. He could wed whom he pleased after he had obeyed his father. So thinking back and forth he lay down to sleep at last, and yet he could not sleep. All the warm flush of pleasure was gone clean out of him. When he thought of lending his body to his father, to the woman chosen now and waiting, he was as cold as though he lent a beast to breed.

In this mood of weakness he arose early, having not slept at all, and he went to find the lady and he roused her at her door and when she came to open it, he gave the letter to her mutely and waited while she read it. Her face changed at the words. She said quietly, "You are exhausted. Go and eat your breakfast. And force the food a little, son, for its heat will restore you, even though I know now you think you cannot swallow. But eat. I will come quickly."

Yuan did obediently what she said. He set himself before the table, and when the serving maid had brought the hot morning gruel of rice and the condiments and the foreign breads the lady liked to eat, he did force himself. Soon the hot food sent its heat into him, and he began to feel more cheered, and less hopeless than he had been in the night, so that when the lady came he looked at her and said, "Almost I am ready to say I will not go."

The lady sat down then, too, and took up a little loaf and ate it slowly, thinking while she ate, and then she said. "If so be you can say this, Yuan, I will stand by you. I will not put strength into you, to force your decision, for it is your own life and he is your father. If you feel your old duty to him stronger than the duty to yourself, then return to him. I will not blame you. But if you will not go back, then stay on, and I will help you somehow at every step. I am not afraid."

At these words Yuan felt courage coming into him again, a good rising courage, almost enough to make him dare against his father. But still it needed Ai-lan's recklessness to finish out his courage. When he came home that noon there Ai-lan was, playing in the parlor with a little dog she had had given her by the man Wu, a tiny furry black-nosed toy which she loved very well. When Yuan came in she looked up and cried out, "Yuan, my mother told me something today and bade me talk with you because I am young, too, and she thought it would be only just that you know what a maid would

say these days. Why, Yuan, you would be a fool to listen
to that old man! What if he is our father? How can we
help that? Why, Yuan, not I nor any of my friends
would think of such a folly as to go and wed a person we
had never seen! Say you will not—what can he do?
He cannot come and fetch you here with his armies. In
this city you are safe—you are not a child—your life
belongs to you—some day you will wed rightly as you
like. You are too good for an ignorant wife who cannot
write her name—and even she might have her feet
bound! And do not forget these days that we new
women will not be concubines. No, that we will not. If
you marry such a woman as your father chooses, you
are married to her. She is your wife. I would not bear to
be a second wife. If I chose a man already married,
then he must turn away his first wife and live with her
no more, and I must be the only one. I have so sworn
it. Yuan, we have a sisterhood, we new women, and we
have so sworn that we will never marry rather than marry
to be concubines. Better then if you do not obey your
father now, for it will not be easier in the end."

These words of Ai-lan's did what Yuan could not do
for himself. Listening to her voice, now made so earnest
for all its soft willfulness, and thinking of the many like
her in this city, he came to think under the magic of
her brilliant, willful beauty, "It is true I do not belong to
my father's time. It is true he has not this right nowadays
over me. It is true—it is true—"

And under this new strength he went straight to his
room and he wrote quickly while he felt courageous,
"I will not come home for such a thing, my father. I
have my right to live these days. These are the new
times." And then Yuan sat and thought awhile, and
doubted perhaps that the words were too bold, and he
thought it might help them if he added a few milder
ones and so he added, "Besides, it is the end of the
term of school, and it is a very ill time for me to come,
and if I come I miss the examinations, and my work
of many moons is lost. Release me, therefore, my father,
though the truth is I do not want to wed." So though

he put at the first and last of the letter the proper courteous words, and he added these few mild words, still Yuan wrote his meaning plain. And he would not trust the letter to a serving man. He put the stamp on and himself went down the sunlit city street and thrust the letter in the box for it.

Once it was gone he felt stronger and at ease. He would not recall what he had written, and going homeward again he was glad, and among all these modern men and women walking to and fro upon the streets he felt yet stronger and more sure. It was true that in these times what his father had required of him was an absurdity. These people on these streets, if he told them, would only laugh at such old dead ways, and cry him for a fool to feel any fear. Mingling thus among them Yuan felt suddenly very safe. This was his world—this new world—this world of men and women free and free to live in each his own way. He felt a darkness lifted from him, and suddenly he thought he would not go home yet to sit and study. He would be amused awhile at something. There beside him on the street was the great glitter of a pleasure house, and in letters of many languages a sign said, "Showing Today the Greatest Film of the Year, 'The Way of Love.'" And Yuan turned and joined the many who went into that wide-flung door.

But the Tiger was not so easily denied as this. In less than seven days he had written his answer back, and this time he wrote three letters, one to Yuan, one to the lady, and the third one to his elder brother. But they all said the same thing in different ways, although he had not written the letters himself, so the language was more smooth. Yet the very smoothness seemed to make the words more cold and angry. What they said was this, that his son Yuan would be wed on the thirtieth of that same moon, for the geomancer had said this was the lucky day to wed him. Because the young man his son could not return to his home on that day, since the examinations of the school were set for then, the parents had decided that he must be wed by proxy, and so a cousin would stand up for him who was Wang the Merchant's eldest son and who could answer in his place. But Yuan would be truly wed upon that day, as truly as though he came himself.

These words Yuan read in his letter. So did the Tiger have his will, and Yuan knew his father never could have been so cruel except that he was forced to it by anger, and Yuan felt that anger and was afraid of it again.

And now indeed the thing was too strong for Yuan. For by the old law the Tiger did no more than he had right to do, and no more than many fathers have done always. Yuan knew this very well, and that day when he had this letter, and the servant had given it to him as he came within the door, so that he stood there in the little hall alone and read it, he felt all his courage ebb away from him. What was he, one lone youth, to do against the gathered power of all these old centuries? He turned slowly and went into the parlor. Ai-lan's little dog was there and came and rubbed against him, snuffling, and when Yuan paid no heed to it, barked a short high bark or two. Still Yuan did not heed it, though commonly he could laugh at this little fierce lion of a dog. He sat down and leaned his head in his hands and let the dog bark on.

But the barking called the lady, and she came in to see what was wrong and if a stranger had come in, and when she saw Yuan, very well she knew what was wrong. She said soothingly, for she had her letter earlier, "You are not to give up, son. This is more than a matter for you now. I will ask your uncle here and your aunt and your elder cousin, and we will talk it over in a council to see what shall be done. Your father is not the only one in this family, nor even the eldest one. If your uncle will be strong, it may be we can divert your father's will by some persuasion."

But Yuan could only cry out when he thought of that old fat pleasure-loving lord who was his uncle, "And when was my uncle ever strong! No, the only strong men in this country, I swear, are those who have armies and guns—they force all the others to their will, and

who knows it better than I? I have seen my father force
his will by threat of death a hundred times—a hundred
hundred times. Everybody fears him because he has
swords and guns—and now I see he is right—it is such
force as this which rules at last—"

And Yuan began to sob, because he felt so helpless.
All his running away and all his willfulness were of no
use now.

But after a while he yielded to the lady's urging and
her comforting, and that very night she made a sort of
feast and bid all the family there, and they all came,
and when the feast was eaten, the lady told the matter
forth, and they all waited to hear what was to be said.

Now Sheng and Meng and Ai-lan were there too, although they were given lower seats, since they were
young, for at this time the lady had taken care to seat
everyone as old custom taught, since this was a family
gathering for counsel. But the young ones were silent
and waited as they should. Even Ai-lan was silent, though
her eyes sparkled to show she inwardly derided all this
gravity, and would make a joke of it afterwards, and
Sheng sat as though he thought inwardly of other pleas-
anter things. But Meng sat silentest of all and stillest.
His face was fixed and very red and angry, and he
thought of nothing but this thing and he suffered because he could not speak. . . .

It was Wang the Eldest's duty to speak first, but it
could be seen he wished it were not, and Yuan, looking
at him, gave up any little scanty hope he might have
had that this man would say anything to help him. For
Wang the Eldest was afraid of two. He was afraid of the
Tiger, his youngest brother. He remembered how he
used to be a fierce young man, and he remembered that
his own second son was in a very soft good life in a
great inland city holding it almost as a governor in the
Tiger's name, and this son was nearly always ready to
send his father silver now and then when Wang the Eldest had such need, and when had he not this need in
this foreign city where there was every sort of way to
spend it? So Wang the Eldest had no desire to make

the Tiger angry. Beyond this one he feared his own
wife, the mother of his sons, and she had told him
plainly what he must say. Before they left their home
she called him to her room and said, "You shall not take
sides with the son. In the first place we older ones must
stand together, and in the second place it may be we
shall need your brother's help some future time if this
talk of more revolution comes to anything. We still have
lands in the north to take thought of, and we cannot
forget what we owe ourselves. Moreover the law is on
the father's side, and the young man should obey."

These words she said so positively that now the old
man sweat to meet her eyes she kept fixed on him, and
he wiped his shaved head before he spoke, and drank a
little tea, and coughed and spat once or twice and did all
he could to put off what must come, but still they all
waited, and so haltingly and gasping as he spoke, for he
was always hoarse these days because his fat pressed in-
wards on him, he said, "My brother has sent me a letter
and he says Yuan is to be wed. And I am told Yuan does
not wish to wed. And I am told—I am told—"

Here he wandered off and met his lady's eye and
looked away and sweat newly and wiped his head again,
and Yuan at the moment hated him with all his heart.
To such a one as this, he thought passionately, was his
life committed! Then suddenly he felt his eye commanded and he looked and Meng's eyes were fastened
upon him with great scornful question, and they said,
"Have I not told you there is no hope for us in the
old?"

But now the old man was forced on by his lady's
fixed cold gaze and he said very fast, "But I think—I
think—it is better for sons to obey—the Sacred Edicts say
—and after all—" Here the old man smiled suddenly, as
though here he did think of something of his own to
say, "After all, Yuan, my son, one woman is truly much
like another, and after it is over you will not mind much
and it will only be a day or two and I will write a letter
to the master of your school and beg him to excuse you
from your examinations, and if you please your father it

will be better, for he is such a fierce angry man, and after all, the time may come when we need—"

Here his eye wandered to his lady again, and she bade him in such silent fierceness to be still that he ended suddenly and in great weakness, "It is what I think," and he turned to his eldest son and said in much relief, "Speak, son, for it is your turn."

Then the eldest son spoke, and he spoke with more reason, but on both sides, because he wished no offense to anyone. Yet he said kindly, "I understand Yuan's wish to be free. I was so in my youth, and I remember that in my time I made a great pother about my marriage and would have whom I would." He smiled a little coolly, and he spoke with more daring than he might have used if his sharp and pretty wife had been there, but she was not, for she was near the moment of a birth, and very angry these days that she must have another child after four already born, and she swore day and night that she would learn the foreign ways of not conceiving any more. So since she was not there he looked at his father and laughed a little and he said, "The truth is I often wonder why I made such a noise about it then, for in the end it is true what my father says, that women are the same, and marriage is the same, and the end is the same and sure to come. It is as well to marry cool at first, because it ends cold always, and love does not last so well as reason."

And this was all. None other spoke. The learned lady did not speak, for where was the use before these two men? She kept her words for Yuan alone. And none of the young spoke, for to them speech was useless, too. These young ones as soon as could be slipped out one by one into another room, and there they talked to Yuan, each in his own way. Sheng thought the whole thing to be laughed at, and so he told Yuan. He laughed and smoothed his hair down with his pretty pale hands and he said, laughing, "If it were I, I would not even answer that summons, Yuan. I do feel for you, and I am glad I know my parents would not treat me so, for however they may rail against the new ways, they are used now to living in this city, and they would not truly force us to anything, and all their power spends itself in talking. Pay no heed—live your own life. Say nothing angry, but do as you please. You need not go home again."

And Ai-lan had cried out vehemently, "Sheng is right, Yuan! You shall not think of it again. You will live here with us always, and we all belong to the new world and you can forget everything else. There is enough here to keep us all happy and amused our whole lives long. I swear I do not ever want to go to anywhere else!"

But Meng kept silence until all the talk was over. Then he said with a slow dreadful gravity, "You all speak like children. By the law Yuan will be married on the day his father sets. By the law of this nation he will not be free again. *He is not free*—it does not matter what he says he is or thinks he is or how he amuses himself— he is not free. . . . Yuan, now will you join the revolution? Do you see now why we must fight?"

And Yuan looked at Meng and met his two burning savage eyes and caught the desperation of his soul. He waited for a moment and then from his own despair he answered quietly, "I will!"

So did the Tiger drive his son to be his enemy.

Now Yuan said to himself he could throw all his heart into this cause to save his country. Before this time, when it was cried to him, "We must save our country," though his heart was always stirred because it seemed something which ought to be done, yet he was checked because he never could wholly see how the country must be saved, or if saved, then from what, or even what this word country meant. Even in his early childhood days in his father's house when his tutor had so taught him he felt this impulse to save, and yet this bewilderment, so that while he would do something he did not know what to do. In the school of war he had heard of much evil done his country by foreign enemies, and yet his father was an enemy too and he could see nothing clearly still.

At this school it had been so also. He listened often to

Meng's talk of the same thing, how the country must be saved, for Meng had no other thing to talk of, if he did not talk of his cause, and he scarcely heeded his books at all these last days he was so busy in his secret meetings, and he and his comrades were always shaping protests against some authority in school or city and they made parades and marched along the streets carrying banners to cry against their foreign enemies and against evil treaties and against the laws of the city and of the school and against anything which was not in accordance with their own wish. They forced many to parade with them, even though these went sometimes against their will, for Meng could force his fellows by looks as black as any war lord's, and he could roar and shout at a reluctant schoolmate, "You are no patriot! You are the running dog of foreigners—you dance and play while our country is destroyed by enemies!"

So Meng had even cried to Yuan one day when he pleaded he was busy and had no time for such parades. Sheng could laugh and jeer a little in his pleasant way if Meng came near him with his furious talk, for Meng was his younger brother first before he was the leader of young revolutionists, but Yuan was only cousin and he must evade the angry youth as best he could. And to this time the best hiding place had been his plot of land, for Meng and his comrades had no time for steady stupid plodding toil on land, and there Yuan was safe enough from them.

But now Yuan knew what it meant to save his country. Now he saw why the Tiger was an enemy. For, now, to save his country meant to save himself, and now he saw how his father was his enemy, and none could save him if he did not save himself.

Into the cause he threw himself. There was no need to prove his own sincerity since he was Meng's cousin and Meng swore for him. And Meng could swear him true, because he knew Yuan's reason for anger, and he knew the only surety of zeal for a cause is ever in such deep personal anger as Yuan now felt. Yuan could hate the old because the old was now his particular enemy.

He could fight to make his country free because only so could he be free. He went with Meng that same night, therefore, to a secret meeting held in a certain room in an old house at the end of a winding street.

This street was known as a street of prostitutes for poor men, and many men came and went there who were dressed anyhow and many young working men could come and go there and none remark them, because it was known what the place was. Down this street then Meng led Yuan. To the calls and noises of the place he paid no heed. He knew it well and did not even see the women who ran out from one door and another in search of trade. If one plucked at his sleeve too long he shook her hand away as though it were some senseless insect which annoyed him. Only when one laid too long a hold on Yuan did Meng shout out, "Let go of him! We have a certain place already—" He strode on, and Yuan beside him glad to be released, because the woman was so coarse and beastly in her looks and not young, so that she was very fearful in her leering fondness.

Then into a house they went where a woman let them in, and Meng turned up a stair and then into a room, and there were some fifty and more young men and women waiting. When they saw Yuan follow their leader in, the low talking ceased and there was an instant's doubting silence. But Meng said, "You need fear nothing. This is my cousin. I have told you how I hoped he would join our cause because he has much help to give us. His father has an army even that one day might be for our use. But he was never willing. He never felt the cause clearly until today he knows what I have told him is the truth, that his own father is his enemy—as all our fathers are our enemies. Now he is ready—he hates enough to be ready."

And Yuan, in silence listening to these words, looked round about on all those fiery faces. There was not one face there which was not somehow fiery, however pale it might be or however it was not beautiful, and the eyes of all looked the same. At these words Meng said,

and at these eyes, his heart stopped a little. . . . Did
he truly hate his father? Suddenly it was hard to hate
his father. He wavered, stammering in his mind at that
word hate—he hated what his father did—well enough
he hated much his father did. At that very moment
while he wavered someone rose out from a certain shadowed corner and came to him and put out a hand. He
knew the hand and turning he looked into a face he
knew. It was that maid, and she said in her strange
lovely voice, "I knew some day you must join us. I knew
there would be a thing to make you join us."

At this sight and this touch, at the hearing of her voice,
Yuan was so warmed and welcomed that he remembered
freshly what his father did. Yes, if his father could do
such a hateful thing as make him wed a woman he had
never seen, then he did hate his father, too. He grasped
the maid's hand in his own. It was most wild and sweet
to know she loved him. Because she was here and
held his hand, he suddenly felt one of them. He looked
quickly about the room. Why, they were all free here,
free and young together! Meng was still talking. No
one thought it strange that they two stood, a man and
a maid, hand in hand, for here all were free. And Meng
ended, saying, "I stand his guarantor. If he be traitor
then I will die too. I swear for him."

And the maid, when he had finished speaking, led
Yuan out a few steps still holding fast his hand, and she
said, "I, too—I swear for him!"

So she bound him to her and to her fellows. Without
a word against it then Yuan took his pledge. Before them
all and in the silence of all, his own blood was let a little
with a small knife Meng drew across Yuan's finger. Meng
dipped a brush in the blood and Yuan took the brush
and set his name in writing to the written pledge. Then
they all rose together and received him and swore the
pledge together, and gave a certain sign to Yuan to keep
for proof of brotherhood and so was he at last their
brother.

Now Yuan discovered many things he had not known. He found that this one brotherhood was netted to many scores of others everywhere and this net ran over very many provinces of that country and into many cities, and especially it ran southward, and the center of it all was in the great southern city where that school of war was. From that center there were given forth commands by secret messages. These messages Meng knew how to receive and read and he had his helpers who called together all the band, and then Meng told them what must be done, how a strike must be called or how a declaration must be written, and at the same time that he did this, in scores of cities was the same thing done, for thus were many young banded secretly in that whole country.

Every meeting of these brotherhoods was a step forward in the carrying out of a great plan of the future, and this plan was not so new to Yuan in truth, because he had heard of something much the same his whole life long. From his childhood his father had been used to say, "I will seize the seat of government and make a great nation. I will make a new dynasty," for the Tiger had these same dreams in his youth. Then Yuan's tutor had taught him secretly, "Some day we must seize the seat of government and make a new nation—" And in the school of war he heard it, and now he heard it still. Yet to many it was a new cry. To sons of merchants, sons of teachers, sons of quiet usual people, those sons who were beset with dull ordinary life, it was the mightiest cry that ever was. To speak of making a nation, of seeing the country rise to new greatness, of waging mighty wars against foreign peoples, made every common youth among them dream great dreams and see himself a ruler or a statesman or a general.

But Yuan was not so new to the cry, and often he could not shout so loudly as the others did, and sometimes he wearied them by asking overmuch, "How shall we do this thing?" Or he would say, "How can it save the country if we do not go to classes and spend our time only in parades?"

But he learned after a while to keep silence, for the others would not bear such talk, and it fell hard on Meng and on the maid if he did not do as the others did, and Meng told him privately, "It is not your right to question the orders that come through to us from above. We must obey, for only thus can all be ready for the great coming day. I cannot let you question thus, for the others may not, and they will say I favor my cousin."

So Yuan must push down the question rising in him even then, which was to ask where the freedom was if he must obey what he did not understand. He told himself doubtless they would have freedom later and he told himself that there was no other way to go, for it was sure he had no freedom with his father, and he had cast in his lot now with these others.

Therefore he did his duty as it was appointed to him these days. He made flags ready for the days of parade, and he wrote out the petitions to teachers for this thing or that, because his writing was clear and better than most, and he made himself stay out of class on days of strike when teachers would not grant what had been asked, although he studied secretly that he might not miss the learning, and he went to certain laborers' houses and gave them sheets of paper whereon were written for them sayings which told them how abused they were in their labor and how they were given too little wage and how their masters grew rich from them, and all such things they knew already. These men and women could not read, and Yuan read to them, but they heard him gladly and they looked at each other aghast to hear how they were oppressed even more than they had thought, and one and another would cry out, "Aye, it is true our bellies are never so full as they ought to be—" "Aye, we do work all the day and in the night and our children are not fed—" "There is no hope ahead for such as us. What is today is the same tomorrow and forever, for each day we eat all we make," and they looked at each other fiercely and in despair when they found how cruelly they were used.

And Yuan looking at them and hearing them could

not but be sorrowful for them, for it was true they were used cruelly many times, and their children were not nourished but were starving pale and worked at looms and at foreign machinery for many hours every day and often died there and none cared. Not even their parents cared overmuch, since children are so easily made and born, and are always more than can be wanted in a poor man's house.

Yet with all his pity the truth was Yuan was glad when he could go away, because there was always such a stink about these poor and his nostrils were fastidious. Even after he went home and was cleaned and far away from them he seemed to have the smell about him. In his quiet room with his books alone, he lifted up his head and smelled that odor. Though he changed his coat he smelled it. Even if he went out to some house of pleasure he smelled it. Above the scent of the woman in his arms while he danced, above the fragrance of clean well-cooked foods he could discern the stink of the poor. It penetrated everywhere and he loathed it. There was in Yuan this old shrinking which still kept him from giving himself wholly anywhere, because in everything there was some small thing to strike too coldly on his senses, and although he was ashamed he was so small, he knew he was a little cold in the cause for the shrinking of his flesh from this stink.

There was another trouble, too, in this fellowship he now was in, and often this obscured the cause and made a cloud between him and the others. It was the maid. For since Yuan had joined the cause it seemed this maid felt it sure that he was hers, and she could not let him be. Now there were other pairs among these youths, who lived together boldly and it was taken as a thing which could be done, and no talk made of it among the others. They were called comrades, and the bond between any two held only as long as the two wished it. And this maid so hoped that Yuan would live with her.

But here was a strange thing. If Yuan had not joined the cause, and had lived on his old pleasant dreaming life, not seeing the maid much, and only in the schoolroom, and only sometimes walking alone with her, then her boldness and her lovely voice and her frank eyes and hot-hearted hand might have in the end enticed him by strangeness and difference from the other usual maids he knew and saw more often who were friends of Ailan's. For Yuan was very shy with maids, and so shy that boldness could seem enticing to him.

But now he saw this maid every day and everywhere. She marked him for her own and waited for him after every class and walked away with him, so that others saw it and many of his fellows jeered at Yuan and cried out at him, "She waits—she waits—you cannot escape—" and such ribaldry was always in his ears.

At first Yuan feigned not to hear it, and then when he must hear it he smiled in a sickly fashion, and then he grew ashamed and tried to linger long or to go out by some other unexpected way. And yet he could not face her bravely and say to her, "I am weary of your always waiting." No, he could not but pretend to greet her, and when he went to the secret meetings, there she was, and always she had a place beside her saved for him, and all the others took it for a truth that they two were joined together in every fact.

And yet they were not, for Yuan could not love this maid. The more he saw her and the more she touched his hand, and now she took his hand often and held it long and made no secret at all of her longing, the less Yuan could love her. And yet he must value her because he knew her very faithful and truly loving to him, and though he was ashamed he did sometimes take advantage of this very faithfulness, for when he was commanded to do a thing he did not like to do, she was quick to see his reluctance and if it could be done, she cried out that it was what she wanted to do herself, and she managed it so that Yuan more often had what he liked best to do, some writing perhaps, or to go out to villages and talk to farmers there instead of to the city poor who did stink so vilely. So Yuan did not want to make her angry because he valued what she did for him, and yet he was man enough to be more than often ashamed because he took this service from her and still could not love her.

The more he denied her—though for long it did not come to words—the more passionate this maid's love grew, until one day it did come to words, as all such things must. It happened on that day Yuan had been sent to a certain village, and he had wanted to go alone and come back by his bit of land and see how it did, for he had been too busy with the added work of this cause to be there as often as he liked to be. It was a most beautiful day in the late spring of that year, and he had planned that he would walk to the village and sit and talk awhile with the farmer folk and give his little books out secretly, and then wind eastward by his own bit of land. He liked the talk with the farmers, and often he talked with them not to persuade them by force, but as he might talk to anyone and he listened to them when they said, "But whoever heard of such things as these, that the land is to be taken from the rich and given to us? We doubt it can be done, young sir, and we would rather it were not, lest afterwards we be punished somehow. We are better as we are. At least we know our troubles. They are old troubles and we know them." And among them often only those who had no land at all were those who thought the new times welcome.

But on this day when he had planned dreaming lonely pleasant hours, this maid found him and said in her sure way, "I will come with you and I will talk to the women."

Now there were many reasons why Yuan did not want her. He felt constrained before her to speak more violently for the cause, and he did not love such violence. And he feared her touch upon him if she were alone with him. And he could not go by his own bit of land, lest that good farmer be there, and he had never yet told that farmer he now was joined to the cause, and he did not want that man to guess it, and so he did not want to go there with this maid. Yes, and more, he did not want this maid to see he cared how the plants grew whose seed he had sown himself. He did not want her to see the strange old close love he felt for such things, lest she be amazed at him. He did not fear her laughter, for she was one who never saw a thing to laugh at, but he feared her surprise and lack of understanding and her swift contempt for all she did not understand.

Still he could not shake her off, for she had so contrived that Meng had given her the command, and she must go. Therefore they set off together, Yuan silent and keeping to his own side of the road, and if she came over to him, he in a little while found an excuse to seek a smoother walking on the other side, and he was glad when the city road changed to the smaller country one and then this changed to a little path where they two must walk one behind the other, and Yuan went first so that he could look about him and not see her before him.

But be sure this maid understood before long how he felt. She made her talk at first very quietly, and as though she would not heed his short replies, and then she fell into silence, and at last they walked only in silence. And all the time Yuan felt her feelings rising in her and he dreaded her, and yet must go doggedly on. Now they came to a certain turn of road where willow trees had been planted long ago, and they were very old and the branches had been often cut and so often that the new branches of each year grew thick and tufted as brushes and met above the path and made a deep green hiding shade. Then as they passed through this quiet lonely place Yuan felt his two shoulders laid hold on from behind, and this maid twisted him about and cast herself against him and she burst into dreadful weeping and she cried, "I know why it is you cannot love me—I know where you go of nights—I followed you the other night and saw you with your sister, and how you went into that great hotel and I saw the women there. You like them better than you do me—I saw the one you danced with—that one in the peach pink gown —I saw her shamelessness the way she hung herself upon you—"

It was true that Yuan still went sometimes with Ai-lan,

for he had never told his sister or the lady that he joined
this cause, and though he often made excuse that he
was busy and so could not go for pleasure so much as
she did, yet he must go sometimes or Ai-lan would
wonder, and that lady still hoped to have him go and
keep her eased. When this maid wept out these words
he remembered that a night or two gone by he had
gone with Ai-lan to a party given for her nearest friend's
birthday at a great foreign hotel there in that city, and
he had danced with this friend and there were vast
glass windows in that hall which showed out upon the
street, and doubtless it was true he could have been
noted out from among the others by this maid's searching knowing eyes.

He stiffened his body now and was angry and he said
resentfully, "I went with my sister, and I was a guest
and—"

But the maid had felt him turn cold under her hot
hands and she flung herself back and cried in anger
greater than his, "Yes, I saw you—you held her and did
not fear to touch her, but you draw from me as if I were
a very snake! And what do you think would come to
you if I should tell the others that you spend your time
with the very people whom we hate and against whom
we all work? Your life is in my hands!"

Now this was very true, and Yuan knew it. But he
only answered quietly and with scorn, "Do you think
it is a way to make me love you, to speak to me like
that?"

Then she fell against him again, weakened, and she
sobbed softly against him, and lifted up his two arms
and by her own strength held them about her and so
they stood, and Yuan after a moment could not but be
moved by her sobbing, and be sorry for her, and when at
last she said, "You have so won me, and if it is against
your will it is against mine, too, for I did not want to
be won by any man—yet I know I would leave the
cause before I could leave you—I am so wicked and so
weak—" he felt his pity rise very swiftly, and then,

though unwillingly, he held his arms where she had put them.

After a while she quieted herself and moved away and wiped her eyes and they went on again and now she was very sad and quiet, and they did their work and she spoke no more on that day.

But Yuan knew and she knew how the matter was between them. And here was the perversity in Yuan, that until this time he never had looked twice at any friend of Ai-lan's, and they all looked alike to him, these pretty daughters of the rich, all with their high light merry voices and their tinkling laughter and their varied pretty clothes and jewels in their ears and smooth skin and painted fingernails and all such likenesses one to the other. He loved the rhythms of music and a maid added to the music and now he was not so disturbed as he had been at first by maids.

But this other maid's incessant jealousies drove him strangely to look at the very ones against whom she complained, and their merriment was sweet to him because she was never merry, and he found a sort of pleasure in their gaiety and lack of any cause except to find pleasure anyhow. He began to single out two or three maids he liked above others, one the daughter of an old prince who had lived for refuge in this city since the empire had fallen down, and she was the smallest pretty maid he had ever seen, so perfect in her little beauty that Yuan liked to see her now he had taken thought to do it, and another older maid, who liked his youth and looks and while she swore she would not wed and would do her business all her life, which was to own and manage a shop for women's garments in that city, still she liked to dally and Yuan pleased her, and he knew he did, and he found her sharp beauty, sword slender as she was, and her short black hair smooth as paint upon her head, a teasing prodding pleasure to him.

This little passing thought he took for these two maids and one or two more made him feel guilty when the other maid reproved him as she often did, and one day she was hot and pleading in her anger and another she was cold and hateful and Yuan was bound to her in strange comradeship, so that he felt tied, and yet he could not love her.

One day a few days before the day his father was to wed him in that far-off town he was thinking of it, and he stood melancholy and alone before the window in his room and looked down upon the city streets and thought distastefully that he must see that maid today, and then he thought, "I cry against my father, because he binds me, and yet what a fool am I that I have let her bind me, too!" And he was so struck that he had not thought of this before, how he had let his freedom go again, that he sat down and planned swiftly of what escape he now could have and how he might be free once more by some means from this new bondage, which in its way was as heavy as the other because it was so secret and so close.

Then suddenly he was freed. For all this time the cause had been strengthening itself in the south, and now the hour was struck, and out of the southern city the armies of the revolution marched swiftly through the very heart of that country. Suddenly as a great typhoon wind springs up the coast from the southern seas, those armies took on flesh and blood and truth, and they were filled with a power which made them more than human, almost, so that all about the country and into every city there ran ahead of them and behind them and on every side of them the tales of their strength and power and never-failing victories. For these armies were all young men, and among them were maids, too, all filled with secret power, so that they did not fight as soldiers do who only fight for pay. They fought for a cause which was their life, and so they were invincible, and the soldiers of the rulers, who were hirelings, ran before them like leaves before a bitter wind. Before them like a vanguard ran tidings of the terror of their strength and fearlessness and how death could not touch them, since they did not fear to die.

Then the rulers of the city were so much afraid they fell upon every revolutionist they knew within that city, lest these plot from within to join those who were to come, and there were many in other schools like Meng and Yuan and like that maid. This happened in three little days, that these rulers sent burly soldiers into every room where any student lived, and if anything were found, a book, a bit of paper, a flag or any symbol of the cause of revolution, then he was shot, and if it were a maid, then she was shot. In those three days there were so shot in that one city hundreds of such youths and maidens, and no one dared to say a word against it, lest he be held a friend of them and so lose his own life. And there were killed among the guilty many innocent, for there were evil men who had enemies who would not die, and these went and told secretly the names of those they hated and gave false witness of their being revolutionists, and on such bare word even were many killed, so great was the fear among the rulers that the revolutionists within the city would join the cause of those who came from outside to attack.

Then one day this thing took place without a warning. On a morning when Yuan sat in his class and at a very moment when he swore to himself he would not turn his head because he knew that maid was looking at him, and half he was about to turn because he felt somehow constrained to do it, suddenly there came into the room a band of soldiers and the captain of them shouted, "Stand and be searched!" Then every one of them stood dazed and wondering and frightened while soldiers passed their hands over their bodies and looked at their books, and one took down into a book the names of where they lived. In utter silence was this done, the teacher standing silent, too, and helpless. There was no sound except the clanking of the soldiers' swords against their leather heels and the sound of their thick shoes upon the wooden floor.

Out of that silent, frightened roomful three were singled out because something was found upon their persons. Two were lads, but the third one was that maid, who had a guilty paper in her pocket. Those three the soldiers held before them, and when they turned to go, they prodded them with bayoneted guns to hasten them. This Yuan watched, staring dazed and helpless to see the maid go out like this. And at the door the maid turned back her head and gave him one look, one long, imploring, speechless look. And then a soldier touched her sharply with his pointed gun and pushed her on, and she was gone, and Yuan knew he would never see her any more.

His first thought was, "I am free!" and then he was half ashamed because he could not but be glad, and yet he could not but remember, too, that great tragic look the maid had given him as she went, and somehow he felt himself guilty for that look, because though with her whole heart she loved him, he had not loved her. Even while he justified himself and cried in his silent self, "I could not help it—could I help it if I did not want her?" there was another smaller weaker voice which said, "Yes, but if I had known she was to die so soon —could I have comforted her a little?"

But his questionings were soon stopped, for there could be no more work that day, and the teacher gave them dismissal and they all hastened away from that room. But in the hastening Yuan felt his arm taken and he looked and there was Sheng, and Sheng led him secretly aside where none could hear and he whispered, his smooth face for once all in a disarray of fright, "Where is Meng?—he does not know of this raid today and if he is searched—my father will die of it if Meng is killed."

"I do not know," said Yuan, staring back. "I have not seen him these two days—"

But Sheng was gone, his agile body slipping swiftly in and out among the throngs of silent, frightened students pouring now from every room.

Then Yuan went by small quiet streets to his own home and there he found the lady and he told her what had come about, and he said to ease her at the end, "Of course I have nothing I need fear."

But the lady's mind went more deeply than did Yuan's,

and she said swiftly, "Think—you have been seen with Meng—you are his cousin—he has been here. Has he not left a book or paper or any least thing in your room? They will come here to search. Oh, Yuan, go you and look while I think what I am to do with you, for your father loves you, and if you should suffer anything it would be my fault because I did not send you home when he commanded it!" And she was in more fear than Yuan had ever seen upon her.

Then she went with him to his room to look at all he had. And while she looked at every book and in each drawer and on each shelf, Yuan bethought him of that old letter of love the maid had sent which he had never torn to pieces. He had kept it between the pages of a book of verse, not that he valued it but at first it was precious to him because after all it spoke of love—the first word of love in his whole life and so for a while magic for its own sake and then he had forgotten it. Now he took it out while the lady's back was turned, and he crushed it in his hand and made some excuse and left the room and slipped into another room and set a match to it. While it burned between his thumb and finger, he remembered that poor maid and how she had looked at him, the look a hare might give before the wild dogs fell upon it to devour it. And Yuan was filled with a great sadness when he thought of her, a sadness strangely deeper somehow, because even now, now more than ever, he knew he did not love her and that he never could have loved her, and he was not even sorry for her death, though he felt guilty that he was not. So the letter fell to ash between his fingers and then was dust.

Yet even if Yuan had had a mind to grieve, he had not time for it, for scarcely was the letter burned before he heard the noise of voices in the hall, and the door opened and his uncle came in and his aunt and elder cousin and Sheng, and they all cried out to know if Meng had been seen. And the lady came in from Yuan's room, and they all put questions at each other and were frightened and the uncle said, his fat face trembling with fright and weeping, "I came here to be safe from those tenants on my land who are the cruelest wildest savages, and I thought here I would be safe with foreign soldiers to protect us, and I do not know what these foreigners are about that they allow such things to be, and now here is Meng gone, and Sheng says he was a revolutionist, although I swear I did not know it. Why was I not told of it? I would have seen to it long ago!"

"But, father," answered Sheng in a low, troubled voice, "what could you have done except to talk and noise it more about?"

"Aye, that he would have," said Sheng's mother sourly. "If anything is to be kept it is only I who keep it in our house. But I take it hard I was not told, either, and Meng my own favorite son!"

And the elder son, whose color was as pale as willow ashes, said anxiously, "For this one foolish boy's sake we are all in danger, for the soldiers will come and question us and suspect us."

Then the lady, Yuan's mother, said quietly, "Let us all think what we must do in such a danger. I must think of Yuan, since he is in my keeping. I have thought of this. He is to go abroad sometime anyway to foreign schools, and I will send him now. As quickly as it can be done and all the papers signed, I will send him, and in foreign parts he will be safe."

"Then we will all go," cried the uncle eagerly. "In foreign parts we will all be safe!"

"Father, you cannot," said Sheng patiently. "The foreigners will not let men of our race on their shores unless it be for study or some such special thing."

At this the old man swelled himself out and opened up his little eyes and said, "And are they not here upon our shores?"

But the lady said to soothe them all, "It is scarcely useful now to talk of ourselves. We old ones are safe enough. They will not kill such old staid folk as we are for revolutionists and scarcely you, eldest nephew, who have wife and children and are no longer young. But Meng is known and through him Sheng is in danger

and so is Yuan, and we must somehow get them from
the country to foreign parts."

So they planned how this could be done, and the lady
bethought herself of a foreign friend whom Ai-lan knew,
and how through him the many papers to be written
and signed and hastened on could be written, and the
lady rose and put her hand upon the door to call a servant
to go fetch Ai-lan home from a friend's house where she
had gone for a morning's gaming, for she was not willing
to go to school these days of disturbance, because it
made her sad, and she could not bear sadness.

Even as the lady put her hand upon the door a mighty
noise rose up from the lower rooms, the noise of a bold
rough voice shouting, "Is this where one Wang Yuan
lives?"

Then they all looked at each other, and the old uncle
turned as pale as the fat upon a butchered beef and
looked about to hide himself. But the lady's quick
thought was for Yuan first, and then for Sheng.

"You two," she gasped—"quick—into the little room
beneath this roof—"

Now this room had no stairway to it, and its entrance
was no more than a square hole let into the ceiling of this
very room where they were gathered. But the lady even
as she spoke had pulled a table beneath it and dragged
at a chair, and Sheng sprang forward, being ever a little
more quick than Yuan was, and then Yuan after him.

But none was quick enough. Even as they hastened,
the door was flung open as by a gale of wind, and eight
or ten soldiers stood there and the captain cried out,
looking first at Sheng, "Are you Wang Yuan?"

Now Sheng was very pale, too. He waited for one
instant before he answered, as though he took thought
for what he should say, and then he answered very low,
"No, I am not he."

Then the man roared out, "Then this other one is
he— Aye, I remember now the maid said he was tall
and very dark, and his brows were black above his eyes
—but his mouth soft and red—it is this one—"

Without one word to deny himself, Yuan let himself

be bound, his hands behind his back, and no one could
stay the matter. No, although his old uncle wept and
trembled and though the lady came up beseeching and
said in her grave sure way, "You are mistaken—this lad is
no revolutionist. I can swear for him—he is a studious,
careful lad—my son—who has never taken any part in
all this cause—"

But the men only laughed coarsely, and one great
round-faced soldier cried out, "Ah, lady, mothers never
know their sons! To know a man one must ask the maid
—never his mother—and the maid gave his name and
the number of this very house, and told his looks exactly—aye, she knew his looks very well, didn't she?—
I swear she knows his every look!—and she said he was
the greatest rebel of them all—yes, she was so bold and
angry at first, and then she grew silent for a while, and
then she gave his name of her own will, without a moment's torture for it!"

Then Yuan saw the lady look dazed at this, as at a
thing she did not understand at all. He could say nothing. He kept silent but in his heart he thought dully to
himself, "And so her love turned into hating! She could
not bind me by her love—her hate binds me fast enough!"
And thus must he let himself be led away.

Even at that moment Yuan feared with every certainty that he must die. These latter days, though it was
never public, yet he knew the end of all such as were
known to have been joined to the cause was death, and
no proof could be surer than this of his guilt, that the
maid herself had given his name. Yet though he told
himself so, that word death could not seem real to him.
Not even when he was thrust into a prison cell, full of
other youths like himself, and not when the guard
shouted at him when he stumbled on the threshold because it was so dark, "Aye, pick yourself up now, but
tomorrow others must do it for you—" even then he could
not understand the meaning of the word. The guard's
words struck into his heart like the bullets waiting in
the guns for tomorrow, and yet Yuan could take thought

to look through the dimness of that crowded cell, and
be eased because he saw none in it but men, and not
one woman. He could think, "I can bear to die better
than I could bear to see her here and have her know
I am to die, and have her know she has me after all."
This thing remained an ease to him.

All had come about so quickly Yuan could not but
believe that somehow he would be saved from here.
At first he thought that any moment he would be saved.
He trusted very much the lady his mother, and the more
he thought the more confident he was that she would
think how to save him. The first hours he so believed,
and the more because he felt, as he looked about upon
his fellows, that he was much better than any of them,
and they looked poor and less wise than he, and of families of less wealth and influence.

But after a while the darkness fell completely black,
and in the black silence they all sat or lay upon the
earthen floor. For none spoke, lest out of their own
mouths they be committed by some word which might
confirm their guilt, and each man feared the other and
so long as face could see even the dim shape of face,
there was no sound except the movement of a body
changing its position, or some such voiceless sound.

Then night fell, when none could see another's face,
and the darkness seemed to shut each into his own cell,
and a first voice cried softly, "Oh, my mother—oh, my
mother—" and broke into desperate weeping.

This weeping was very hard to bear, for each felt it
might be his own self weeping, and a louder voice cried
out, very loud and surly, "Be silent! What child is it who
cries for its mother? I am a loyal member—I killed my
own mother, and my brother killed our father, and we
know no parents but the cause—eh, brother?"

And another voice out of the darkness answered, twin
to that voice, "Yes, I did it!" And the first voice said,
"Are we sorry?" And the second sneered and answered
again, "Though I had a score of fathers I would gladly
kill them all—" And another cried emboldened, "Aye,
those old men and women, they only breed us to make

sure they have servants for their old age to keep them
warmed and fed—" But the first softest voice moaned
on most steadily, "Oh, my mother—oh, my mother—" as
though the one who cried these words heard nothing.

But at last as deep night wore on even such cries
must be stilled. Yuan had not spoken once while others
spoke, but after they were quiet the night stayed on and
on forever with its deep exhausted stillness, and he
could not bear it. All his hopefulness began to ebb
away. He thought the door must open any moment and
a voice shout forth, "Let Wang Yuan come—he is freed!"

But no voice called.

At last it seemed to Yuan some sound must be made
because he could not bear the stillness. He spent himself in thought. Against his will he thought of all his life
and how short it was and he thought, "If I had obeyed
my father, I would not now be here—" and yet he could
not say, "I wish I had obeyed him." No, when Yuan
thought of it, some stubbornness he had made him say
honestly, "Yet I do believe he asked a wrong thing of
me—" And again he thought, "If I had forced myself a
little and yielded to that maid—" And then again his
gorge rose and he thought honestly, "Yet I did not like
to do it—" And at last there was nothing else to do than
to think ahead to what was to come, since the past was
shaped and gone, and he must think of death.

Now did he long for any sound to come out of the
darkness, and he longed even to hear that lad calling for
his mother. But the cell was still as though it were
empty, and yet the darkness was not sleeping. No, it was
a living waiting wakeful darkness, full of terror and of
silence. He had not been afraid at first. But in the deep
night he grew afraid. Death, which had not been real
until this hour, now grew real. He wondered, breathless suddenly, if he would be beheaded or if he would
be shot. These days the gates of inland cities, he had
read, were decorated with the heads of the dead young
men and women who had joined the cause, for whom the
armies of deliverance had not come swiftly enough, so
that before the day of battle they were caught by the

rulers. He seemed to see his own head—and then it came to him like comfort, "But here in this foreign sort of city they will doubtless shoot us," and then he wondered at himself with a bitter sort of mirth, even, that it could matter to him that he could keep his head on his shoulders when he was dead.

Now even as he sat crouched in this agony these hours through, his back thrust between two walls into a corner and his feet dragged close to him, so he sat huddled, the door opened suddenly and a grey beam of early light fell into the cell and showed the prisoners curled among each other like a heap of worms. The light stirred them into moving, but before any could move to rise, a voice roared forth, "Out with you all!"

And soldiers came into the cell, and pushing and prodding with their guns they roused them all, and now roused, that lad began his wailing, "Oh, my mother—oh, my mother—" and would not leave off even when a soldier smote him hard across the head with his gun's butt, for he moaned these words as though he breathed them and could not help it, and must draw his life in so.

Now as these staggered forth, in silence otherwise than for this one, each knowing what was coming and yet dazed, too, a certain soldier held up a lantern that he had and flashed its light across each face. Yuan was the last of all, and as he came the light flashed across his face. This brightness blinded him suddenly after the long darkness of the night, and in that moment's blindness he felt himself pushed back into the room, and pushed so hard he fell upon the beaten earth. Then instantly he heard the door lock, and there he was, alone and still alive.

Three times did this thing happen. For during that day the cell was filled again with new young men, and again through that night and two more nights Yuan must hear them, sometimes silent and sometimes cursing and sometimes whimpering and sometimes crying out in their madness. Three dawns came, and thrice he was thrust back into the cell alone and the door locked on him. He was given no food, nor was any moment given him for speech or question.

The first day he could not but have hope. And on the second day he had a lesser hope. But by the third day he was so faint and weak with no food and no water even to drink, that it seemed a little matter to him if he lived or died. That third dawn he could scarcely rise to his feet at all and his tongue was dry and swollen in his mouth. Yet the soldier shouted at him and prodded him and made him rise, and when Yuan clung to the door-frame with his two hands, again the light flashed across his face. But this time he was not thrust into the cell again. Instead, the soldier held him, and when the others were all gone their doomed and certain way, the soldier led Yuan by another narrower passage to a place where a small barred door was set, and he drew back the bar and without a word thrust Yuan through the door.

Then Yuan found himself upon a small narrow street, such as wind through the inner, more secret parts of any city, and the street was still dim with early dawn and there was no one in sight, and out of his clouded mind Yuan could see this thing clearly, that he was free—somehow he had been freed.

Even as he turned his head this way and that to think how he could run, two came near out of the dusk, and Yuan shrank back against the door again. But one of the two was a child, a tall child, and she came running to him and came near and peered at him, and he saw her two eyes, very large and black and eager, and he heard this child call out in a low fervent voice, "It is he—here he is—here he is—"

Then the other came near, too, and Yuan saw her and knew it was his lady mother. But before he could speak, in spite of all his eagerness to speak and say it was he himself, he felt his body tremble on his feet and seem to melt away, and suddenly could not see anything and the child's dark eyes grew larger and blacker and then faded. From some very far distant place he heard a voice whisper, "Oh, my poor son—" and then he fell and heard and saw no more.

When Yuan awoke again he felt himself upon some moving swaying thing. He lay in a bed, but this bed rose and fell beneath him, and opening his eyes he saw he was in a small strange room where he had never been. Someone sat there watching him beneath a light set in the wall, and when Yuan summoned all his strength to look he saw this was Sheng, his cousin. And Sheng was watching Yuan, too, and when he saw Yuan looking he rose and smiled his old smile, but now it seemed to Yuan truly the gentlest sweetest smile a face could have, and he reached to a little table and fetched some hot broth in a bowl there and he said, soothing Yuan, "Your mother said the moment you awoke I was to give you this, and I have been keeping it hot these two hours on a little lamp she gave me—"

He began to feed Yuan as he might feed a child, and like a child Yuan said not a word, he was so weary and so dazed. He drank the broth down, too weak to wonder how he came here and what this place was, and like a child accepting all that was come about. He only felt the warm liquid very succoring and pleasant to his dry and swollen tongue and he swallowed it as best he could. But Sheng talked quietly as he dipped the broth up with the spoon, and he said, "I know you wonder where we are and why we are here. We are on a small ship,— a ship our uncle merchant has used to carry his goods back and forth to the nearest islands, and by his influence we are on it. We are to go across the nearest seas, and stay in the closest port and there we are to wait for papers we must have to go on to foreign parts. You are free, Yuan, but at a mighty price. Your mother and my father and my brother have laid hold on every sum they could and they borrowed much money of our second uncle, and your father was beside himself, and they said he kept groaning how he had been betrayed by a woman, too, and he and his son were done with women this time and forever. And he has given up your mar-

riage, and sent all the money for it and all he could get
and all these moneys together bought your freedom and
our escape on this ship. High and low money has been
paid—"

When Sheng said these words, Yuan listened, and yet
he was so weak he scarcely could perceive their meaning. He could only feel the ship rise and fall beneath him
and feel the good heat of the food slip down into his
starved body. Then Sheng said, suddenly smiling, "Yet
I do not know if I could have left happily even in such
a case if I had not known Meng was safe. Ah, he is a
clever one, that lad! Look here! I went grieving for him
and my parents were distracted between you and him,
and not knowing whether it was worse to know where
you were and that you were to be killed, or not know
where Meng was and that he might be safe or killed already. Then yesterday when I was on the street between your home and mine, someone thrust this bit of
paper in my hand, and on it is Meng's writing, saying,
'You are not to look for me or be anxious, and my parents need not think of me again. I am safe and where
I want to be.' "

Sheng laughed and set down the empty bowl and
struck a match to light a cigarette and he said gaily to
Yuan, "I have not even relished smoking these three
days! Well, that young rascal who is my brother is safe
enough, and I have told my father, and though the old
man is angry and swears he will not have Meng ever be
as his son again, still I know by now he has let down his
heart and gone to a feast tonight. And my elder brother
will be at the theatre to see a new piece put on with a
woman acting in her own right in this new fashion, and
not a man dressed as a woman, for he is all agog to see
the vileness in it. And my mother has been angry at my
father for a while and so we are all ourselves again, now
that Meng is safe and you and I are escaped." He
smoked a little and then he said, more gravely than his
wont was, "But, Yuan, I am glad that we are going to
other parts even though we go like this. I say little of it,
and I will not join in any cause and I take my pleasure

where I can. But I am weary of my country and its wars and though you all think me a smiling laughing fellow only thinking of my verses, yet the truth is I am very often sad and hopeless. I am glad to go and see another country and know how its people live. I feel my heart lift just to be going away!"

But even as he talked Yuan could listen no more. The comfort of the food and the softness of this narrow swinging bed and the knowledge of his freedom covered him with comfort. He could only smile a little, and he felt his eyes begin to close. Sheng saw it too, and he said very kindly, "Sleep—your mother said I was to let you sleep and sleep—and you may sleep better than you ever have, now you are free."

Yuan opened his eyes once more at this word. Free? Yes, he was free of everything at last. . . . And Sheng said once more, to finish out his thought, "And if you are like me, there is nothing much you do not want to leave."

No, Yuan thought, slipping into sleep—there was nothing he grieved to leave behind him. . . . At this instant of his sleep he saw again that crowded cell, those writhing forms—those nights—there was that maid turning to look at him before she went to die. He dropped his mind away and fell into sleep. . . . And then suddenly, in a great peace, he dreamed he was on his bit of land. There was the little piece of land he had planted. He saw it suddenly as clear as any picture; the peas were forming in their pods, and the green-bearded barley was coming to its height, and there was that old laughing farmer, working next upon his own fields. But here the maid was, too, and now her hand was very cold—very cold. Her hand was so cold he woke again a little—and remembered he was free. What had Sheng said, that he was not sorry. . . . No, the only thing he minded leaving was that little piece of land.

And then before Yuan slept there came this comfort to him, "But that land—it is one thing that will still be there when I come back—land is always there—"

II

WANG YUAN was in the twentieth year of his age when he went away from his own country, but in many ways a boy still and full of dreams and confusions and plans half begun which he did not know how to finish, or even if he wanted to finish them. He had all his life long been guarded and watched over and cared for by someone, and he did not know any other thing than such care, and for all his three days in that cell, he did not know what sorrow truly was. He stayed six years away.

When he made ready to return again to his country in the summer of that year he was near to his twenty-sixth birthday and he was a man in many things, though no sorrow had yet come to put the final shape of manhood on him, but this he did not know he needed. If any had asked him, he would have said steadfastly, "I am a man. I know my own mind. I know what I want to do. My dreams are plans now. I have finished my years at school. I am ready for my life in my own country." And indeed to Yuan these six years in foreign parts were like another half of his life. The early nineteen years were the first lesser half, and the six were the greater, more valuable ones, for these years had taken him and set him fast in certain ways. But the truth was, although he did not know it, he was set in many ways of which he was not himself aware.

If any had asked him, "How are you ready now to live your life?" he would have answered honestly, "I have a degree of learning from a great foreign college, and I took that degree above many who were native to the land." This he would have said proudly, but he would not have told of a certain memory he had that there were those among his fellows in this foreign people who muttered against him saying, "Of course, if a man wants to be nothing but a grind he can carry off the honors in grades, but we owe more to the school than that. This fellow—he grinds at his books and that is all—he takes no part in the life—where would the school be in football and in the boat races if we all did it?"

Yes, Yuan knew these pushing, crowding, merry foreign youths who so spoke of him, and they took no great pains to hide the words, but said them in the halls. But Yuan held his head high. He was secure in the praise of his teachers and in the mention he received at times of prize-giving, when his name often came the first and always it was said by the one who gave the prize, "Although he works in a language foreign to him, he has surpassed the others." So, although Yuan knew he was not loved for this, he had gone proudly on, and he was glad to show what his race could do, and glad to show them that he did not value games so high as children did.

If again one had asked him, "How are you ready now to live your man's life?" he would have answered, "I have read many hundreds of books, and I have searched to find out all I could from this foreign nation."

And this was true, for in these six years Yuan lived as lone as a thrush in a cage. Every morning he rose early and read his books, and when a bell rang in the house where he lived he went downstairs and took his breakfast, eating usually in silence, for he did not trouble to talk much to any other in that house, nor to the woman whose it was. And why should he waste himself in speech with them?

At noon he took his meal among the many students in the vast hall there was for this purpose. And in the afternoons, if he had not work in the field or with his teachers, he did what he loved most to do. He went into the great hall of books and sat among the books and read and wrote down what he would keep and pondered on many things. In these hours he was forced to discover that these western peoples were not, as Meng had cried so bitterly, a savage race, in spite of the rudeness of the common people, and they were learned in sci-

ences. Many times Yuan heard his own countrymen in
this foreign country say that in the use and knowledge
of materials these folk excelled, but in all the arts whereby men's spirits live, they lacked. Yet now, looking at
the rooms of books which were all of philosophy, or all
of poetry, or all of art, Yuan wondered if even his own
people were greater, though he would have died before he spoke such a wonder aloud in this foreign land.
He even found translated into western tongues the sayings of the earlier and later sages of his own people, and
books which told of arts of the East, and he was aghast at
all this learning, and half he was envious of these people
who possessed it and half he hated them for it, and he
did not like to remember that in his own country a
common man often could not read a book, and less often
could his wife.

Yuan had been of two different minds since he came
to this foreign country. When he grew well upon the
ship and felt his forces come back into him after those
three days of death, he was glad to live again. Then as
he grew glad to live he caught from Sheng his pleasure
in the travel and in all the new sights they would see
and in the greatness of the foreign lands. So Yuan had
entered upon the new shores as eager as any child to
see a show, and ready to be pleased by everything.

And he found everything to please. When first he
entered into the great port city on this new country's
western coast it seemed to him that all he ever heard
was more than true. The houses were higher than he had
heard and the streets were tiled and paved like floors
of houses and clean enough to sit on or to sleep on and
not be soiled. And all the people seemed most wonder-
fully clean. The whiteness of their skins and the cleanness of their garments were very pleasing to see, and they
all seemed rich and fed, and Yuan was glad because
here at least the poor were not mingled among the
rich. Here the rich came and went most freely on the
streets and no beggars plucked at their sleeves and cried
out for mercy and a little silver. It was such a country

as could be enjoyed, for all had enough, and one could eat with joy because all so ate.

Thus Yuan and Sheng together in those first days could not but cry at much beauty to be seen. For these people lived in palaces, or so it seemed to these two young men who had not seen such homes. In this city away from the shops the streets stretched wide and shaded by great trees and families needed not to build high walls about them, but each grassy garden ran into the next man's, and this was a marvel to Yuan and Sheng, because it seemed every man so trusted his neighbor that he needed not to build against him or his thievery.

Thus at first all seemed perfect in that city. The great square high buildings were cut so clean against the blue metallic sky that they seemed mighty temples, only there were no gods inside. And between these ran at great speed the thousand thousand vehicles of that city all filled with rich men and their ladies, although even the people who went on foot seemed to do it out of joy and not because they must. At first Yuan had said to Sheng, "There must be something wrong here in this city, that so many people go at such speed somewhere." But when he and Sheng had looked awhile they perceived that these people looked very gay and often laughed, and their high clacking speech was more merry than it was mournful, and there was no trouble anywhere, and they went quickly because they loved swiftness. Such was their temper.

And indeed there was here a strange power in the very air and sunshine. Where in Yuan's mother country the air was often somnolent and soothing, so that in summer one must sleep long and in winter one wished only to curl into a close space for sleep and warmth, in this new country the winds and sunshine were filled with a wild driving energy, so that Yuan and Sheng walked more quickly than their wont was, and in the beaming light the people moved like shining mingling motes driven through the sunshine.

Yet already in those earliest two days when all was strange to them, and all to be enjoyed, Yuan found his pleasure checked by a certain moment. Even now after six years were gone Yuan could not say he had forgot that moment wholly, though it was a small thing, too. The second day upon the shore he and Sheng went into a certain common restaurant where many ate, and there were people not rich as some, perhaps, but still well enough to eat as they chose. When Yuan and Sheng passed through the doors from the street, Yuan felt, or thought he did, that these white men and women stared somewhat at him and at Sheng, and he thought they drew a little off from them, though the truth was Yuan was glad they did, because there was about them a strange alien odor, a little like a certain curd of milk they loved to eat, though not so foul, perhaps. When they went into that place to eat, a maid standing at a counter took their hats from them to hang among many others, for so the custom was, and when they came back to claim them this maid put many hats out at a time, and a certain man before Yuan could stay him, reached out his hand and seized on Yuan's hat, which was of a brown hue like his own, and he pressed it on his head and ran out of the door. At once Yuan saw what was the mistake, and hastening after he said with courtesy, "Sir, here is your hat. Mine, which is the inferior one, you have taken by mistake. It is my fault, I was so slow." And then Yuan bowed and held forth the other's hat.

But the man, who was no longer young, and who wore an anxious, sharp look upon his thin face, listened with impatience to Yuan's speech, and now he seized his own hat, and with great distaste removed from his bald head Yuan's hat. Nor did he stop except to say two words, and these he spat forth.

Thus Yuan was left standing holding his hat and wishing he need not set it on his head again, for he had not liked the man's shining white pate—and most of all he did not like the hiss of the man's voice. When Sheng came up he asked Yuan, "Why do you stand as though you had been struck?"

"That man," said Yuan, "struck me with two words I did not understand, except I know they were evil."

At this Sheng laughed, but there was an edge of light
bitterness in his laughter. "It may be he called you foreign devil," he said.

"Two evil words they were, I know," said Yuan, troubled, and beginning to be less joyful.

"We are now foreigners," said Sheng and after a while
he shrugged himself and said again, "All countries are
alike, my cousin."

Yuan said nothing. But he was not again so joyful and
not so wholly pleased again with anything he saw. Inside he gathered steadfastly his own self, stubborn and
resistant. He, Yuan, son of Wang the Tiger, grandson of
Wang Lung, would remain himself forever, never lost
in any millions of white alien men.

That day he could not forget his hurt until Sheng saw
it again and laughed and said with a little smile of malice,
"Do not forget that in our country Meng would have
cried at that little man that he was a foreign devil, so
the hurt might have been the other way." And after a
while he told Yuan to look at this strange sight or that,
until he had diverted Yuan at last.

In the next days and in all the years to come when
there was so much to see and to make wonder over, he
would have said he had forgotten that small one thing,
except he had not. As clearly today, if he happened to
take thought of it, as he had six years ago, he saw that
man's angry look and he could still feel the wound,
which seemed to him unjust.

But if he had not forgotten, yet the memory was often
buried. For Yuan and Sheng together saw much beauty
in those first days in the foreign country. They rode on
a train which bore them through great mountains where,
although spring was warm upon the foothills, yet snow
was white and thick against the high blue skies, and between the mountains there were black gorges where
deep waters foamed and frothed and Yuan staring down
at all this mad beauty felt it almost too much and scarcely
real, but like some wild painter's picture hung there beneath the train, foreign and strange and too sharply col-

ored, and not made of earth and rocks and water of which his own country was compounded.

When the mountains were behind them, there were valleys as extravagant and fields big enough to be countries and machines straggling like huge beasts to make ready the fertile earth for gigantic harvests. Yuan saw it very clearly, and this was even more a marvel to him than the mountains. He stared at the great machines and he remembered how the old farmer had taught him to hold a hoe and fling it so it fell true to its set place. So did that farmer still till his land, and so did others like him. And Yuan remembered how the farmer's little fields were made, each neatly fitted to the other, and how his few vegetables grew green and heavy with the human wastes he saved and poured on them, so that every plant grew to its richest best, and every plant and every foot of land had its full value. But here none could take thought of single plants and any foot of land. Here fields were measured by the mile, and plants unnumbered, doubtless.

Thus in those first days everything except that one man's words seemed good to Yuan and better than anything in his own country could be. The villages were clean and very prosperous, and although he could recognize the different look of a man upon the land and a man who lived in any town, still the man upon the land did not go ragged in his coat, and the houses on this land were never made of earth and thatch, nor did the fowls and pigs stray as they would. These were all things to admire, or so Yuan thought.

Yet from those first days even Yuan felt the earth here strange and wild and not like his own earth. For as time passed and Yuan knew better what that earth was from walking often along country roads or tilling a piece for himself in the foreign school even as he had in his own country, he never could forget the difference. Though the earth which fed these white folk was the same earth which had fed Yuan's race, too, yet working on it, Yuan knew it was not the very earth in which his forefathers were buried. This earth was fresh and free of human

bones, and so not tamed, since of this new race not yet
enough were dead to saturate the soil with their essences
as Yuan knew the soil of his own country was saturated
with its own humanity. This earth was still stronger than
the people who strove to possess it, and they were wild
through its wildness and in spite of wealth and learning
often savage in their spirits and their looks.

For the earth was uncaptured. The miles of wooded
mountains; all the waste of fallen logs and rotting leaves
beneath great trees ungarnered; the lands let free to
grass and pasture for beasts; the carelessness of wide
roads running everywhere; these showed forth the un-
conquered land. Men used what they wanted, they
brought forth great groaning harvests, more than they
could sell, they cut down trees and used only the fields
that were best and left the others to waste, and still the
land was more than they could use, and greater still than
they.

In Yuan's own country the land was conquered and
men were the masters. There the mountains were
stripped of their forests in years long past, and in these
present times were shaven even of the wild grasses to
feed the fires of men. And men coaxed the fullest harvests from the tiny fields they had, and forced the land
to labor for them for its fullest and into the land again
they poured themselves, their sweat, their wastes, their
dead bodies, until there was no more virginity left in it.
Men made the soil out of themselves, and without them
the earth would have been long since exhausted, and but
an empty barren womb.

So Yuan felt when he mused over this new country
and what its secret was. On his own bit of land he
thought first of what he had to put in before he could
have hope of harvest. Here this foreign earth was en-
riched still by its own unused strength. For a little put
in, it gave forth greatly, leaping into life too strong for
men.

When did Yuan come to mingle hatred in this admiration? At the end of six years he could look back and
see the second step he took in hatred.

Yuan and Sheng parted early and at the end of that first journey on the train, for Sheng fell into love of a great city where he found others of his own kind, and he said the schools there were better for such as he was who loved to learn of verse and music and of philosophies, and he cared nothing for the land as Yuan did. For Yuan set his heart to do in this foreign country what he had always hoped to do, to learn how to breed plants and how to till the soil and all such things, and the more steadfastly because he soon believed this people owed their power to their wealth of harvest from the land. So Yuan left Sheng behind in that city, and he went on into another town and to another school where he could have what he wanted.

First of all Yuan must find himself a place to eat and sleep and a room to call his home in this strange land. When he went to the school he was met courteously enough by a grey-haired white man who gave him lists of certain places where he might be housed and fed, and Yuan set forth to find the best one. The very first door at which he rang a bell was opened to him, and there stood a huge woman, one no longer young, and wiping her great bare red arms upon an apron that she wore about her vast middle.

Now Yuan had never seen a woman shaped like this one, and he could not bear her looks at this first instant, but he asked very courteously, "Is the master of this house at home?"

Then this female set her two hands on her thighs and she answered in a very loud-mouthed heavy way, "It's my house, and there is no man who owns it." At this Yuan turned to go away, for he thought he would rather try another place than this, thinking there must not be many even in this land so hideous as this woman, and he would rather live in a house where a man was. For this woman was truly more than could be believed; her girth and bosom were enormous, and on her head was short hair of a hue Yuan thought could not have grown from human skin except he saw it. It was a bright reddish-yellow color, dulled somewhat with kitchen

grease and smoke. Beneath this strange hair her round
fat face shone forth, a red again, but now of a different
purplish red, and in this visage were set two small sharp
eyes as blue and bright as new porcelain is sometimes.
He could not bear to see her, and he let his eyes fall
and then he saw her two spreading shapeless feet and
those he could not bear either and he made haste away,
and after courtesy turned to go elsewhere.

Nevertheless, when he had asked at another door or
two where it was marked there were rooms for lodgers,
he found himself refused. At first he did not know the
reason why. One woman said, "My rooms are taken,"
although Yuan knew she lied, seeing that her sign of
empty rooms was there. And so it was again and yet
again. At last the truth was shown him. A man said
bluntly, "We don't take any colored people here." At first
Yuan did not know what was meant, not thinking of his
pale yellow skin as being other than the usual hue of
human flesh, nor his black eyes and hair what men's
hair and eyes might always be. But in a moment he understood, for he had seen black men here and there about
this country and marked how they were not held in high
respect by white ones.

Up from his heart the blood rushed, and the man,
seeing his face darken and glow, said half in apology,
"My wife has to help me out in making our way in these
hard times, and we have regular boarders, and they
wouldn't stay if we was to bring in foreigners. There's
places where they do take them, though," and the man
named the number of the house and street where Yuan
had seen the hideous female.

This was the second step in hatred.

He thanked the man therefore with deep proud courtesy and he went back again to that first house, and
averting his eyes from her dreadful person, he told the
woman he would see the room she had. The room he
liked well enough, a small upper room against the roof,
very clean, and cut off by a stairway. If he could forget
the woman, this room seemed well enough. He could
see himself there quietly at work, alone, and he liked the

look of the roofs sloping down about the bed and table
and the chair and chest it held. So he chose to stay in
it, and this room was his home for the six years.

And the truth was the woman was not so ill as her
looks and he lived in her house, year after year, while
he went to that school, and the woman grew kind to
him and he came to understand her kindness, covered
as it was by her hideous looks and coarse ways. In his
room he lived as sparsely and as neatly as a priest, his
few possessions always placed exactly and this woman
came to like him well and she sighed her gusty sigh
and said, "If all my boys was like you, Wang, and as little trouble in their ways, I'd be a different woman now."

Then he found, as a few days went by, that this burly
female creature was very kind in her loud way. Although Yuan cringed before the sound of her great
voice, and shivered at the sight of her thick red arms
bared to her shoulders, still he thanked her truly when
he found some apples put in his room and he knew she
meant kindness when she shouted at him across the
table where they ate, "I cooked some rice for you, Mr.
Wang! I reckon you find it hard eating without what
you're used to—" And then she laughed freely and
roared, "But rice is the best I can do—snails and rats
and dogs and all them things you eat I can't supply!"

She did not seem to hear Yuan's protest that indeed
he did not eat these things at home. And after a while
he learned to smile in silence when she made one of
her jokes and he remembered at such times, he made
himself remember, that she pressed food on him, more
than he could eat, and kept his room warm and clean
and when she knew he liked a certain dish she went to
some pains to make it for him. At last he learned never
to look into her face, which still he found hideous, and
he learned to think only of her kindness, and this the
more when he found as time passed by and he came
to know a few others of his countrymen, in this town,
circumstanced as he was, that there were many less good
than she in lodging houses, women of acrid tongues and

sparing of their food at table, and scornful of a race other than their own.

Yet when he thought of it here was the strangest thing of all to Yuan, that this gross loud-mouthed woman once had been wed. In his own land it might have been no wonder, for there youths and maidens wed whom they must before the new times came, and a man must take what was given to him, even though it were an ugly wife. But in this foreign land for long there had been choosing of maid by the man himself. So once then was this woman chosen freely by a man! And by him, before he died, she had a child, a girl, now seventeen or so in age, who lived with her still.

And here was another strange thing,—the girl was beautiful. Yuan, who never thought a white woman could be truly beautiful, knew well enough this maid, in spite of all her fairness, must be called beautiful. For she had taken her mother's wiry flaming hair and changed it by some youthful magic in herself into the softest curling coppery stuff, cut short, but winding all about the shape of her pretty head and her white neck. And her mother's eyes she had, but softer, darker, and larger, and she used a little art to tinge her brows and lashes brown instead of pale as her mother's were. Her lips, too, were soft and full and very red, and her body slender as a young tree, and her hands were slender, not thick anywhere, and the nails long and painted red. She wore, and Yuan saw it as all the young men saw it, garments of such frail stuff that her narrow hips and little breasts and all the moving lines of her body showed through, and well she knew the young men saw and that Yuan saw. And when Yuan knew she knew it, he felt a strange fear of her and even a dislike, so that he held himself aloof and would not do more than bow in answer to a greeting she might give.

He was glad her voice was not lovely. He liked a low sweet voice and hers was not low or sweet. Whatever she said was said too loudly and too sharply in her nose, and when he was afraid because he felt the softness of her look or if by chance when he took seat at table,

where she sat beside him, his eyes fell on the whiteness
of her neck, he was glad he did not like her voice. . . .
And after a while he sought and found other things he
did not like, too. She would not help her mother in the
house, and when her mother asked her at mealtimes to
fetch a thing forgotten from the table, she rose pouting
and often saying, "You can never set the table, ma, and
not forget something." Nor would she put her hands in
water that was soiled with grease or dirt, because she
valued her hands so much for beauty.

And all these six years Yuan was glad of her ways he
did not like and kept them always clearly before him. He
could look at her pretty restless hands beside him, and
remember they were idle hands that did not serve another than herself, and so ought not maid's hands to be,
and though he could not, roused as he once had been,
avoid the knowledge sometimes of her nearness, yet he
could remember the first two words he ever heard upon
this foreign earth. He was foreign to this maid, too. Remembering, he could remember that their two kinds of
flesh, his and this maid's, were alien to each other and
he was set to be content to hold himself aloof and go
his solitary way.

No, he told himself, he had had enough of maids,
he who was betrayed, and if he were betrayed here in a
foreign land, there would be none to help him. No,
better that he stay away from maids. So he would not
see the maid, and he learned never to look where her
bosom was, and sedulously he refused to go with her
if she begged it to some dancing place, for she was bold
to invite him sometimes.

Yet there were nights when he could not sleep. He
lay in his bed and remembered the dead maid, and he
wondered sadly, yet with a thrilling wonder, too, what it
was that burned so hot between a man and maid in any
country. It was an idle wonder, since he never knew her,
and she turned so wicked in the end. On moonlit nights
especially he could not sleep. And when at last he did
sleep he woke and then perhaps again, to lie and watch
the silent, dancing shadows of a tree's branch against

the white wall of his room, shining, for the moon was bright. He turned restlessly at last and hid his eyes and thought, "I wish the moon did not shine so clear—it makes me long for something—as though for some home I never had."

For these six years were years of great solitude for Yuan. Day by day he shut himself away into greater solitude. Outwardly he was courteous and spoke to all who spoke to him, but to none did he give greeting first. Day by day he shut himself away from what he did not want in this new country. His native pride, the silent pride of men old before the western world began, began to take its full shape in him. He learned to bear silently a foolish curious stare upon the street; he learned what shops he could enter in that small town to buy his necessities, or to have himself shaved or his hair cut. For there were keepers of shops who would not serve him, some refusing bluntly or some asking twice the value of goods, or some saying with a semblance of courtesy, "We have our living to make here and we do not encourage trade with foreigners." And Yuan learned to answer nothing, whether to coarseness or to courtesy.

He could live days without speech to anyone and it came to be that he might have been like a stranger lost in all this rushing foreign life. For not often did anyone even ask a question of him of his own country. These white men and women lived so enwrapped within themselves that they never cared to know what others did, or if they heard a difference they smiled tolerantly as one may at those who do not do so well from ignorance. A few set thoughts Yuan found his schoolfellows had, or the barber who cut his hair, or the woman in whose house he lodged, such as that Yuan and all his countrymen ate rats and snakes and smoked opium or that all his countrymen bound their feet, or that all his countrymen wore hair braided into queues.

At first Yuan in great eagerness tried to set these ignorances right. He swore he had not tasted either rat or snake, and he told of Ai-lan and her friends who danced as lightly free as any maidens could. But it was no use, for what he said they soon forgot and remembered only the same things. Yet there was this result to Yuan, that so deep and often his anger rose against this ignorance that at last he began to forget there was any rightness or truth in anything they said, and he came to believe that all his country was like the coastal city, and that all maidens were like Ai-lan.

There was a certain schoolfellow he had in two of his classes where he learned of the soil, and this young man was a farmer's son, a lout of a very kind heart, and amiable to everyone. Yuan had not spoken to him when he dropped into the seat beside him at a class, but the youth spoke first and then he walked sometimes with Yuan away from the door, and then sometimes lingered in the sunshine and talked a little while with him, and then one day he asked Yuan to walk with him. Yuan had never met with such kindness yet, and he went and it was sweeter to him than he knew, because he lived so solitary.

Soon Yuan found himself telling his own story to this friend he had found. Together they sat down and rested under a tree bent over the roadside, and they talked on and very soon the lad cried out impetuously, "Say, call me Jim! What's your name? Wang. Yuan Wang. Mine's Barnes, Jim Barnes."

Then Yuan explained how in his country the family name came first, for it gave him the strangest reversed feeling to hear his own name called out first as this lad now did. And this amused the lad again, and he tried his own names backwards, and laughed aloud.

In such small talk and frequent laughter their friendship grew, and led to other talk, and Jim told Yuan how he had lived upon a farm his whole life, and when he said, "My father's farm has about two hundred acres," Yuan said, "He must be very rich." And then Jim looked at him surprised and said, "That's only a small farm here. Would it be big in your country?"

To this Yuan did not answer straightly. He suddenly could not bear to say how small a farm was in his country, dreading the other's scorn, and so he only said, "My grandfather had greater lands and he was called a rich man. But our fields are very fertile, and a man needs fewer of them to live upon."

And so through such talk he passed to telling of the great house in the town and of his father Wang the Tiger, whom he now called a general and not a lord of war, and he told of the coastal city and of the lady and Ai-lan his sister and of the modern pleasures Ai-lan had, and day after day Jim listened and pressed his questions and Yuan talked, scarcely knowing that he said so much.

But Yuan found it sweet to talk. He had been very lonely in this foreign country, more lonely than he knew, and the small slights put on him, which, if he had been asked, he would have said proudly were nothing to him, yet were something to him. Again and again his pride had been stabbed, and he was not used to it. Now it eased him to sit and tell this white lad all the glories of his race and of his family and his nation, and it was a balm to all his wounds to see Jim's eyes grow large and full of wonder and to hear him say most humbly, "We must look pretty poor to you—a general's son and all— and all those servants and—I'd like to ask you home with me this summer, but I don't know as I dare, after all you've had!"

Then Yuan thanked him courteously, and with courtesy said, "I am sure your father's house would be very large and pleasant to me," and he drank in with pleasure the other's admiration.

But here was the secret fruit in Yuan of all this talk. He came himself, without his knowing it, to see his country as he said it was. He forgot that he had hated Wang the Tiger's wars and all his lusty soldiery, and he came to think of the Tiger as a great noble general, sitting in his halls. And he forgot the humble little village where Wang Lung lived and starved and struggled up by labor and by guile, and he only remembered from his childhood the many courts of that great house in the town, which his grandfather had made. He forgot even the small old earthen house and all the millions like it, shaped out of earth and thatched with straw, and housing poor folk and sometimes even beasts with them, and he remembered clearly only the coastal town and all its riches and its pleasure houses. So when Jim asked, "Have you automobiles like we have?" or if he asked, "Do you have houses like ours?" Yuan answered simply, "Yes, we have all these things."

Nor did he lie. In a measure he spoke the truth, and in a full measure he believed he spoke the whole truth because as days passed his own distant country grew more perfect in his eyes. He forgot everything not beautiful, miseries such as are to be found anywhere, and it seemed to him that only in his country were the men upon the land all honest and content, and all the serving men loyal and all masters kind and all children filial and all maids virtuous and full of modesty.

So much did Yuan come to believe thus in his own distant country that one day by force of his own belief he was driven to say publicly a thing in her defense. It happened that to this town and to a certain temple in it, which was called a church, there came a white man who had lived in Yuan's country and announced he would show pictures of that far place and tell of its people and their habits. Now Yuan, since he believed in no religion, had never been to this foreign temple, but on this night he went, thinking to hear the man and see what he might show.

In the crowd then Yuan sat. From the first sight of the traveller Yuan did not like him, for he perceived him to be a priest of a sort of whom he had heard but had not seen, and one of those against whom he had been taught in his early school of war, who went abroad with religion as a trade, and enticed humble folk into his sect for some secret purpose, which many guessed at but none knew, except that all know a man does not leave his own land for nothing and with no hope of private gain. Now he stood very tall and grim about the mouth, his eyes sunken in his weathered face, and he began to speak. He told of the poor in Yuan's land and of the famines and of how in places girl babes were killed at birth, and how the people lived in hovels, and he told filthy, gruesome tales. And Yuan heard them all. Then the man began to show his pictures, pictures of the things he said he had seen himself. Now Yuan saw beggars whining at him from the screen, and lepers with their faces eaten off, and starving children, their bellies swollen though empty, and there were narrow crowded streets and men carrying loads too great for beasts. There were such evils shown as Yuan had not seen in all his sheltered life. At the end the man said solemnly, "You see how our gospel is needed in this sad land. We need your prayers; we need your gifts." Then he sat down.

But Yuan could not bear it. All through the hour his anger had been rising, mixed with shame and dismay, so to see revealed before this staring, ignorant foreign crowd his country's faults. And more than faults, for he had not himself seen the things this man had told of, and it seemed to him that this prying priest had searched out every ill that he could find and dragged it forth before the cold eyes of this western world. It was only greater shame to Yuan that at the end the man begged for money for these whom he disclosed thus cruelly.

Yuan's heart broke with anger. He leaped to his feet, he clenched his hands upon the seat in front of him, and he cried loudly, his eyes burning black, his cheeks red, his body trembling, "These are lies this man has told and shown! There are not such things in my country! I myself have never seen these sights—I have not seen those lepers—I have not seen starved children like those —nor houses like those! In my home there are a score of rooms—and there are many houses like mine. This man has shaped lies to tease your money from you. I— I speak for my country! We do not want this man nor do we want your money! We need nothing from you!"

So Yuan shouted, and then he set his lips to keep from weeping and sat down again, and the people sat in great silence and astonishment at what had happened.

As for the man, he listened, smiling thinly, and then he rose and said, and mildly enough, "I see this young man is a modern student. Well, young man, all I can say is that I have lived among the poor, like these I have shown, for more than half my life. When you go back to your own country come into the little city in the inland where I live and I will show you all these things. . . . Shall we close in prayer?"

But Yuan could not stay for such mockery of praying. He rose and went out and stumbled through the streets to his own room. Soon behind him came the footsteps of others who went homeward too, and here was the final stab which Yuan had that night. Two men passed him, not knowing who he was, and he heard one say, "Queer thing, that Chinese fellow getting up like that, wasn't it?—Wonder which of 'em was right?"

And the other said, "Both of them, I reckon. It's safest not to believe all you hear from anybody. But what does it matter what those foreign folks are? It isn't anything to us!" And the man yawned and the other man said carelessly, "That's right—looks like rain tomorrow, doesn't it?" And so they went their way.

Then Yuan, hearing this, was somehow more wounded than if the men had cared. It seemed to him they should have cared, even if the priest had been right, but since he told lies they should have cared to know the truth. He went angry to his bed and lay and tossed and wept a little for very anger's sake, and vowed he would do something yet to make these people know his country great.

After such a thing as this Yuan's new friend assuaged him. He took sound comfort in this simple country youth and poured out his beliefs in his own people to him, and told him of the sages who had shaped the noble minds of his ancestors and framed the systems whereby men lived to this day, so that in that far lovely country there was not such wantonness and willfulness as was to be found here. There men and women walked in decency and ordered goodness, and beauty grew from their goodness. They did not need laws such as were written in these foreign lands, where even children must be protected by a law and women sheltered under law. In his country, Yuan said earnestly, and he believed it, there needed not to be such laws for children were harmed by none, for none there would harm a child, he said, forgetting for the moment the foundlings even his lady mother had told him of, and he said women were always safe and honored in their homes. When the white lad asked, "So it is not true they bind women's feet?" Yuan replied proudly, "It was an old, old custom, like the one of yours when women bound their waists, and now it is long past and no more to be seen anywhere."

So Yuan stood in defense of his own land, and this was now his cause. It made him think of Meng sometimes, and now he could value Meng at his true worth and to himself he thought, "Meng was right. Our country has been defamed and brought so low we ought all to come to her support now. I shall tell Meng he saw more truly, after all, than I did." And he wished he knew where Meng was that he might write and tell him this.

He could write to his father, and so he did. And now Yuan found he could write more kindly and more fully than he ever had. This new love for his country made him love his family more, too, and he wrote saying, "I long often to come home, for no country seems as good to me as my own. Our ways are best, our food the best. As soon as I return I will come gladly home again. I stay here only that I may learn what is to be learned and use it for our country."

And when he had set after this the usual words of courtesy from son to father, he sealed and stamped the letter and went out upon the street to drop it in a box put there for such purpose. It was an evening of a weekly holiday and all the lights were lit in the shops and young men were rollicking and roaring out songs that they knew, and girls laughed and shouted with them. Yuan, seeing all this savage show, drew down his lips in a cold smile, and he let his thoughts follow after his letter into the dignity and stillness where his father lived alone in his own courts. At least his father was surrounded by hundreds of his own men, and at least he, a war lord,

lived honorably according to his code. Yuan seemed to
see the Tiger again as he had often seen him, sitting
stately in his great carved chair, the tiger skin behind
him, before the copper brazier of burning coals, and
all his guard about him, a very king. Then Yuan, in the
midst of all the clattering ribaldry, the loud voices and
the rude unmelodious music streaming out of dancing
places, took greater pride in his own kind than he ever
had before. He withdrew himself and went again alone
into his room and fell upon his books most resolutely,
feeling himself above all such men as were about him
and that he came of old and kingly origin.

This was the third step he took in hatred.

The fourth step came soon, and from a different,
nearer cause, and it was a thing Yuan's new friend did.
The friendship between these two grew less warm than
it was, and Yuan's talk grew cool and distant, always of
work and of the things they heard their teachers say,
and this was because Yuan knew now that often when
Jim came to the house where he lived he came not to
see Yuan but to see that daughter of his landlady.

The thing had begun easily enough. Yuan one evening had brought his new friend to his room, since
the day was wet, and they could not go together to
walk as their growing habit was. When they entered
the house there was the sound of music from a front
room and the door stood ajar. It was the landlady's
daughter who made the music, and be sure she knew the
door was open. But as he passed Jim looked in and saw
the girl, and she saw him and cast him one of her looks
and he caught it and whispered to Yuan, "Why didn't
you tell me you had such a peach here?"

Yuan saw his leering look and could not bear it, and
he answered gravely, "I do not understand you." But
though he did not understand the word he understood
all else and he felt a great discomfort in him. Afterwards
he thought of it more gently and told himself he would
not remember it, nor let so small a thing as that maid

come to mar his friendship, since in this country such things were lightly considered.

But the second time this happened, or that he knew it happened, Yuan was so cut he could have wept. He came late one night, having eaten his night meal away, in order that his work might go on among the books, and when he came in he heard Jim's voice in a room used in common by them all. Now Yuan, being very weary and his very eyes aching with the long reading of the western books, whose lines run to and fro across the page and thus weary very much eyes used to lines from top to bottom, was glad to hear his friend's voice and he longed for an hour's companionship. He pushed open the door, therefore, which was ajar, and cried out gladly and with unwonted freedom in his manner, "I am back, Jim—shall we go upstairs?"

There in that room he saw only these two, Jim, in his hand a box of sweets at whose wrappings he was fumbling, a silly smile upon his face, and opposite him in a deep chair, lying in loose grace, the maid. When she saw Yuan come in, she looked up at him and tossed back her curly, coppery hair and said teasingly, "He came to see *me* this time, Mr. Wang . . ." And then seeing the look between the two young men, how the dark blood came slowly into Yuan's cheeks and how his face, which had been all open and eager, grew closed and smooth and silent, and how on the other's face a bright red shone out and how hostile that one looked as though he did a thing he could do if he liked, she cried petulantly, waving her pretty red-tipped hand, "Of course if he *wants* to go—"

A silence hung between the two men, and the girl laughed and then Yuan said gently and quietly, "Why should he not do what he likes?"

He would not look again at Jim, but he went upstairs and carefully closed his door and sat down for a while upon his bed and wondered at the jealous pain and anger in his heart—and most of all his heart was sick because he could not forget the silly look upon Jim's good face and Yuan was revolted at that look.

Thereafter he turned yet more proud. He told himself these white men and women were the loosest, lustiest race he ever heard of, and their whole inner thoughts were turned to each other wantonly. And when he thought this there rushed into his mind a hundred of the pictures in the theatres where they loved to go, the pictures blazoned on the highways of things to sell and always of some woman half unclothed. He could not, he thought bitterly, come back at night and not see an evil sight in any dark corner—some man who held a woman against him, their arms locked, hands touching in an evil way. Of such sights the town was full. And Yuan sickened at it all, and his very stomach turned proud within him at such coarseness everywhere.

Thereafter, he was never so near to Jim. When he heard Jim's voice in the house somewhere he went silently alone up the stairs to his own room, and fell to his books and he was formal in his speech if Jim came in after a while, and very often he did so because, in some strange way Yuan could not understand, his feeling for the maid was no hindrance to his old friendship for Yuan, so that he was as hearty in his way and seemed not to see Yuan's silence and aloofness. Sometimes, it is true, Yuan forgot the maid and let himself go free again in good talk and even jesting gently. But at least now he waited first for Jim to come to him. The old eager going out to meet him was no longer possible. Yuan said quietly to himself, "I am here if he wants me. I am not changed to him. Let him seek me if he wants me." But he was changed, for all he said he was not. He was alone again.

To assuage himself Yuan began now to notice everything he did not like about this town and school, and every small thing he did not like came to fall like a sword-cut upon his raw heart. He heard the clatter of the foreign tongue among the crowds upon the street and he thought how harsh the voices were and the syllables, and not smooth and like the running waters of his own tongue. He marked the careless looks of students and their stammering speech before their teachers oftentimes, and he grew more jealous of himself and more careful even than he had been, and planned his own speech more perfectly, even though it was foreign to him, and he did his own work more perfectly than they did, and for his country's sake.

Without knowing it he came to despise this race because he wanted to despise them, and yet he could not but envy them their ease and wealth and place and these great buildings and the many inventions they had made and all they had learned of the magic of air and wind and water and lightning. Yet their very wisdom and his very admiration made him like these people less. How had they stolen to such a place of power as this, and how could they be so confident of their own power and not know even how he hated them? One day he sat in the library poring over a certain very wonderful book, which marked out clearly for him how generations of plants could be foretold before even the seed was put into the ground, because the laws of their growth were known so clearly and this thing was so astonishing to Yuan, so far above men's usual knowledge, that he could not but cry out secret admiration in his heart, and yet he thought most bitterly, "We have in our country been sleeping in our beds, the curtains drawn, thinking it still night and all the world asleep with us. But it has long been day, and these foreigners have been awake and working. . . . Shall we ever find what we have lost in all these years?"

Thus Yuan fell into great secret despairs in those six years, and these despairs put into him what the Tiger had begun, and Yuan determined that he would throw himself into his country's cause as he never had, and he came to forget after a while that he was himself. He walked and talked among these foreigners and saw himself no longer as one Wang Yuan, but he saw himself as his people, and one who stood for his whole race in a foreign alien land.

There was only Sheng who could make Yuan feel young and not full of this mission. Sheng would not once in all the six years leave that great city he had chosen to live in. He said, "Why should I leave this place? There is more here than I can learn in a lifetime. I would rather know this place well than many places a little. If I know this city then I know this people, for this city is the mouthpiece of the whole race."

So because Sheng would not come to Yuan and yet he would see Yuan, Yuan could not withstand his letters full of graceful, playful pleading, and so it came about that these two spent their summers in the city together, and Yuan slept in Sheng's small sitting room, and sat and listened to the varied talk that was there often, and sometimes he added to it, but more often he kept silence, because Sheng soon saw how narrow Yuan's life was and that he lived too much alone, and he did not spare Yuan what he thought.

With a new sharpness that Yuan did not know was in him Sheng told Yuan all he ought to know and see, and he said, "We in our country have worshipped books. You see what we are. But these people care less for books than any race on earth does. They care for the goods of life. They do not worship scholars—they laugh at them. Half their jokes are told of their teachers, and they pay them less than their servants are paid. Shall you then think to learn the secrets of this people from these old men alone? And is it well enough to learn of only a farmer's son? You are too narrow-hearted, Yuan. You set yourself on one thing, one person, one place, and miss all else. Less than any people are these people to be found in their books. They gather books from all the world here in their libraries, and use them as they use stores of grain or gold—books are only materials for some plan they have. You may read a thousand books, Yuan, and learn nothing of the secret of their prosperity."

Such things he said over and over to Yuan, and Yuan was very humble before Sheng's ease and wisdom and he asked at last, "Then what ought I to do, Sheng, to learn more?" And Sheng said, "See everything—go everywhere, know all the kinds of people that you can. Let that small plot of land rest for a while and let books be.

I have sat here listening to what you have learned. Now come and let me show you what I have learned."

And Sheng looked so worldly, so sure in the way he sat and spoke and waved the ashes from his cigarette and smoothed down his shining black hair with his graceful ivory-colored hand that Yuan was abashed before him, and felt himself as raw a bumpkin as a man could be. It seemed to him in truth that Sheng knew far more than he did in everything. How much Sheng had changed from the slender dreamy pretty youth he had been! In the few years he had grown quick and vivid; he had bloomed forth into sureness of his beauty and faith in himself. Some heat had forced him. In the electric air of this new country, his indolence was gone. He moved, he spoke, he laughed as these others did, yet with this vividness were still left the grace and ease and inwardness of his own race and kind. And Yuan, seeing all that Sheng now was, thought surely there was never any man like him for beauty and for brilliance. He asked in great humility, "Do you still write the verses and the tales you did?"

And Sheng answered gaily, "I do, and more than I did. I have a group of poems now that I may make into a book. And I have hope of a prize or two for some tales I wrote." This Sheng said not too proudly, but with the confidence of one who knows himself well. Yuan was silent. It seemed to him indeed that he had done very little. He was as cloddish as he had been when he came; he had no friends; all that he could point to for his life these many months was a pile of notebooks, and some seedling plants upon a strip of earth.

Once he asked Sheng, "What will you do when we go home again? Shall you always live there in the city?"

This Yuan asked to feel and see if Sheng were troubled as he was by his own people's lack. But Sheng answered gaily and very surely, "Oh, always! I cannot live elsewhere. The truth is, Yuan, and we may say it here, what we cannot say before strangers, except in such cities there is no other fit place for men like us to live in our country. Where else can one find amusements fit for intelligence to enjoy, and where else cleanliness enough to live in? The little I remember of our village is enough to make me loathe it—the people filthy and the children naked in summer and the dogs savage and everything all black with flies—you know what it is—I cannot, will not, live elsewhere than in the city. After all, these western peoples have something to teach us in the way of comfort and of pleasure. Meng hates them, but I don't forget that left alone for centuries we didn't think of running clean water, or of electricity or motion pictures or any of these things. For me, I mean to have all good that I can and I shall live my life where it is best and easiest, and make my poems."

"That is, to live it selfishly," said Yuan bluntly.

"Have it so," Sheng answered coolly. "But who is not selfish? We are all selfish. Meng is selfish in his very cause. That cause! Look at its leaders, Yuan, and dare to say they are not selfish—one was a robber once—one has shifted back and forth to this winning side and that —how does the third one live except upon the very money he collects for his cause?— No, to me it is more honorable to say straightly, I am selfish. I take this for myself. I take my comfort. So be it that I am selfish. But also I am not greedy. I love beauty. I need a delicacy about me in my house and circumstances. I will not live poorly. I only ask enough to surround myself with peace and beauty and a little pleasure."

"And your countrymen who have no peace or pleasure?" Yuan asked, his heart seething in him.

"Can I help it?" Sheng replied. "Has it not been for centuries that the poor are born and famines come and wars break out, and shall I be so silly as to think that in my one life I can change it all? I would only lose myself in struggle, and in losing myself, my noblest self, this me—why should I struggle against a people's fate? I might as well leap in the sea to make it dry up into productive land—"

Yuan could not answer such smoothness. That night he could only lie awhile after Sheng had gone to sleep and listen to the thunder of that vast changing city beating against the very walls against which he lay.

Thus listening he grew afraid. His mind's eye, seeing through this little narrow wall of security between him and the strange dark roaring world beyond, saw too much and he could not bear his smallness and he clung to the good sense of Sheng's words and to the warmth of the room lighted by the street light, and to the table and the chairs and the common things of life. There was this little spot of safety in the thousand miles of change and death and unknown life. Strange how Sheng's sure choice of safety and of ease could make Yuan feel his dreams so great they were foolish to him! So long as he was near Sheng, Yuan was not himself somehow, not brave or full of hate even, but a child seeking certainty.

But Yuan could not always be thus closely and alone with Sheng. Sheng knew many in this city, and he went dancing many a night with any maid he could, and Yuan was alone even though he went with Sheng. At first he sat on the edge of all the merriment, wondering and half envious of Sheng's beauty and his friendly manner, and his boldness with a woman. Sometimes he wondered if he might follow and then after a while he saw something which made him walk away and swear he would not speak to any woman.

And here was the reason. The women Sheng made friends with in this fashion were women not often of his own race. They were white women or they were mixed in blood, and partly dark and partly white. Now Yuan had never touched one of these women. He could not for some strange reason of the flesh. He had seen them often in the evenings when he had gone with Ai-lan, for in the coastal city people of every hue and shade mingled freely. But he had never taken one to him to dance with her. For one thing, they dressed in such a way as to him seemed shameless, for their backs were bare, and so bare that a man in dancing must place his hand on bare white flesh and this he could not do, because it made a sickness rise in his blood.

Yet now there was another reason why he would not.

For as he watched Sheng and all the women who smiled and nodded when he came near them, it seemed to Yuan that only certain women smiled, and that the best, less shameless ones looked sidewise or away from Sheng when he came near and gave themselves only to the men of their own kind. The more Yuan looked, the more true this seemed, and it even seemed to him that Sheng knew this, too, and that he only took the ones whose smiles were sure and easy. And Yuan grew deeply angry for his cousin's sake, and somehow for his own sake and for his country's sake, although he did not understand fully why the women so behaved, and he was too shy and fearful of hurting Sheng to mention it, and he muttered in his own heart, "I wish Sheng were proud and would not dance with them at all. If he is not held good enough for the best of them, I wish he would scorn them all."

And then Yuan was in an agony of hurt because Sheng was not proud enough and took his pleasure anyhow. Here was a strange thing, that all Meng's angers against foreigners had not moved Yuan to hatred. But seeing these proud women who looked sidewise when Sheng came near, Yuan felt that he could hate them and then that he did, and that because of these few he could hate all their kind. Then Yuan often went away and would not stay to see Sheng scorned and he spent his nights alone, at books, or staring into sky or into city streets and into the questions and confusions of his heart.

Patiently through these summers Yuan followed Sheng hither and thither in his life in that city. Sheng's friends were many. He could not go into the restaurant where commonly he bought his food without some man or maid calling out most heartily, "Hello, Johnnie!" For this was what they called him. The first time Yuan heard it he was shocked at such freedom. He murmured to Sheng, "How do you bear this common name?" But Sheng only laughed and answered, "You should hear what they call each other! I am only glad they call me by so mild a name as this. Besides, they do it in friendship, Yuan. The ones they like best they speak of with the greatest freedom."

And indeed it could be seen that Sheng had many friends. Into his room at night they came, twos and threes of friends, and sometimes twice as many. Piled together on Sheng's bed or on the floor, smoking and talking, these young men strove each with the other to see who could think the wildest quickest thoughts and who could first confound what another had just said. Yuan never had heard such motley talk. Sometimes he thought them rebels against the government and feared for Sheng, until by some new wind the whole several hours' talk might veer away from this and end in the cheerfulest acceptance of what was and in great scorn of any newness, and these young men, reeking of their smoke and of the stuff they brought to drink, would shout their partings, grinning and content and with the mightiest relish for themselves and all the world. Sometimes they talked of women boldly, and Yuan, silent on a theme he knew so little of,—for what did he know except the touch of one maid's hand?—sat listening, sick at what he heard. When they were gone he said to Sheng most gravely, "Can all we hear be true, and are there such evil, forward women as they say? Are all the women of this nation so—no chaste maids, no virtuous wives, no woman unassailable?" Then Sheng laughed teasingly and answered, "They are very young, these men—only students like you and me. And what do you know of women, Yuan?"

And Yuan answered humbly, "It is true, I do know nothing of them—"

Yet thereafter Yuan looked more often at these women whom he saw so freely on the streets. They, too, were part of these people. But he could make nothing of them. They walked quickly, were gay in garb and their faces were painted as gaily. Yet when their sweet bold eyes fell on Yuan's face, the look was empty. They stared at him a second and passed on. To them he was not a man—only a stranger passing by, not worth the effort that a man was worth, their eyes said. And Yuan, not understanding this fully, yet felt the coldness and the emptiness and was shy to his soul. They moved so arrogantly, he thought, so coldly sure of their own worth, that he feared them greatly. Even in passing he took care not to touch one of them heedlessly in any way, lest anger come forth from the casual moment. For there was a shape to their reddened lips, a boldness in the way they held their shining heads, a swing their bodies had, which made him shrink away. He felt no lure of woman in them. Yet they did add their magic of living color to this city. For after days and nights Yuan could see why Sheng said these people were not in their books. One could not, Yuan perceived, his face upturned to the distant golden peak of one great building, put such a thing as that in books.

At first Yuan had seen no beauty in their buildings, his eye being trained to quiet latitudes of low tiled roofs and gentle slopes of houses. But now he saw beauty, —foreign beauty, it was true, yet beauty. And for the first time since he had come to this land, he felt a need to write a verse. One night in his bed, while Sheng slept, he struggled to shape his thought. Rhymes would not do, not usual, quiet rhymes, the rhymes he once had made of fields and clouds. He needed sharp words, rough-edged and cleanly pointed. The words of his own tongue he could not use, they were so round and smooth with long polished use. No, he must search out other words in this newer, foreign tongue. And yet they were like new tools to him, too heavy for his own wielding, and he was not accustomed to their form and sound. And so at last he gave it up. He could not shape the verse and there it lay unshaped in his mind to make him a little restless for a day or two, and longer, because at last he came to feel that if he could but shape it out of him, he could have caught between his hands the meaning of these people. But he could not. They kept their souls away from him and he moved only here and there among their swift bodies.

Now Sheng and Yuan were two very different souls. Sheng's soul was like the rhymes which flowed so easily out from it. He showed these rhymes to Yuan one day, beautifully written on thick paper edged with gold, and said with pretended carelessness, "They are nothing, of course—not my best work. That I shall do some later day. These are only fragments of this country put down as they came to me. But my teachers give me praise for them."

Yuan read them carefully, one by one, in silence and reverence. To him they seemed beautiful, each word well chosen, fitted to its place as neatly as a stone set in a ring of gold embossed with gold. There were some of these verses, Sheng said lightly, which had even been set to music by a certain woman whom he knew. One day after he had spoken a time or two of this woman he took Yuan to her home to hear the music she had made of Sheng's verses, and here Yuan saw another sort of woman still, and still another life of Sheng's.

She was a singer in some hall, not quite a common singer, but still not so great by far as she conceived herself to be. She lived alone in a house where many others lived, each in his own little home in the great house. The room which she had made for herself to live in was dark and still. Although outside the sun shone brightly no sun came here. Candles burned in tall bronze stands. A scent of incense hung heavily upon the thick air. There was no seat hard or uncushioned, and at one end a great divan stretched. Here on this bed the woman lay, a long, fair woman, whose age was inscrutable to Yuan. She cried out when she saw Sheng, waving a holder that she held to smoke by, and she said, "Sheng, darling, I haven't seen you in ages!"

When Sheng sat easily beside her, as though he had sat there many times before, she cried again, and her voice was deep and strange and not like a woman's voice, "That lovely thing of yours—'Temple Bells'—I've finished it! I was just going to call you up—"

When Sheng said, "This is my cousin Yuan," she scarcely looked at Yuan. She was rising as Sheng spoke,

her long legs careless as a child's, and with the holder
in her mouth she flung a twisted word or two, "Oh,
hello, Yuan!" and seeming not to see him, went to the
instrument she had and laying down the thing from out
her mouth, began to slide her fingers slowly from one
handful of notes to another—deep, slow notes such as
Yuan did not know. Soon she began to sing, her voice
deep as the music her hands made, shaking a little, very
passionately.

The thing she sang was short, a little verse of Sheng's
he had once written in his own country, but the music
changed it, somehow. For Sheng had shaped the words
wistfully and slightly, as slightly as bamboos shadowed
in the moonlight on a temple wall. But this foreign
woman singing these pretty little words made them passionate, the shadows black and hard, the moonlight hot.
And Yuan was troubled, feeling the frame of music was
too heavy for the picture the words made. But so the
woman was. Every movement she made was full of
troubled meaning—every word and every look not simple.

Suddenly Yuan did not like her. He did not like the
room she lived in. He did not like her eyes too dark for
the fairness of her hair. He did not like her looks at
Sheng, nor how she called him by the name of "darling"
many times, nor how when she had made the music
she walked about and touched Sheng often as she passed
him, nor how she brought the music to him written
down and leaned over him and once even laid her cheek
against his hair and murmured in her casual negligent
fashion, "Your hair's not painted on, is it, darling? It
shines so smoothly always—"

And Yuan sitting in completest silence felt some gorge
in him rise against this woman, some healthy gorge his
old grandfather had given him, and his father, too, a
simple knowledge that what this woman did and said
and how she looked were not seemly. He looked to
Sheng to repulse her, even gently to repulse her. But
Sheng did not. He did not touch her, it is true, or answer her words with like words, or in any way put out

his hand to meet her hand. But he accepted what she
did and said. When her hand lay upon his for an instant,
he let it lie, and did not draw away from her as Yuan
wished he would. When she sent her gaze into his eyes,
he looked back, half laughing but accepting all her boldness and her flattery until Yuan could scarcely stomach
what he saw. He sat as large and stolid as an image,
seeming to see nothing and hear nothing, until Sheng rose.
Even then this woman clung to his arm with her two
hands, coaxing Sheng to come to some dinner that she
gave, saying, "Darling, I want to show you off, you know
—your verses are something new—you're something new
yourself—I *love* the Orient—the music's rather nice, too,
isn't it? I want the crowd to hear it—not *too* many, you
know—only a few poets and that Russian dancer—darling, here's an idea—she could do a dance to the music
—a sort of Oriental thing—your verses would be divine
to dance to—let's try it—" So she continued coaxing until
Sheng took her two hands in his own and put them down
and promised what she wished, seeming reluctant, yet
as Yuan could see, only seeming.

When they were out away from her at last Yuan
breathed in a time or two and out again and looked about
him gladly at the honest sunshine. They two were silent
for a while, Yuan fearing to speak lest he offend Sheng
in what he thought, and Sheng absorbed in some thinking of his own, a little smile upon his face. At last Yuan
said, half trying Sheng, "I never heard such words upon
a woman's tongue before. I scarcely know such words.
Does she then love you so well?"

But Sheng laughed at this and answered, "Those words
mean nothing. She uses them to any man—it is a way
such women have. The music is not bad, though. She
gets my mood." And Yuan, looking now at Sheng, saw on
his face a look Sheng did not know was there. It was a
look which plainly said that Sheng somehow liked those
sweet and idle words the woman had said, and he liked
her praise of him and liked the flattery of his verses
which her music made. Yuan said no more then. But to
himself he said that Sheng's way was not his, nor Sheng's

life his, and his own way for him was best, though what his way was, he scarcely knew, except it was not this way.

Therefore, though Yuan stayed on awhile in that city and its sights to please his cousin, and saw its subterranean trains and all the streets of show, he knew that in spite of what Sheng said, not all of life was here. His own life was not here. He was lonely. There was nothing here that he knew or understood, or so he thought.

Then one day when it was very hot, and Sheng was indolent with heat and lay asleep, Yuan wandered forth alone, and riding on a public vehicle or two, he came into a region he had not dreamed was here in such a city. For he had been surfeited with its richness. To him the buildings were palaces, and every man took for matter of course that he had all he would of food and drink and garments and his needs were not for these things, for they were his due and only to be expected. Beyond these were the needs of pleasure and of better garments and food made not to live by but to take zest in. Thus were all the citizens of this city or so it seemed to Yuan.

But upon this day he found himself in another city, a city of the poor. He stumbled on it, unknowing, and suddenly it was everywhere about him. These were the poor. He knew them. Though their faces were pale and white, though some were black-skinned as the savages are, he knew them. By their eyes, by the filth upon their bodies, by their dirty scaly hands, by the loud screams of women and the cries of too many children, he knew them. There in his memory were the other poor he knew, very far away in another city, but how like these! He said to himself, recognizing them, "Then this great city, too, is built upon a city of the poor!" Ai-lan and her friends came out at midnight into such men and women as these were.

Yuan thought to himself, and with a sort of triumph, "These people, too, hide their poor! In this rich city, crowded secretly into these few streets, are these poor, as filthy as any to be seen in any country!"

Here then Yuan truly found something not in books.

He walked among these people in a daze, staring into narrow shadowed rooms, choosing his footsteps among the garbage of the streets, where starved children ran half naked in the heat. Lifting up his head to look at misery on misery he thought, "It does not matter that they live in lofty houses—they live in hovels still—the same hovels—"

He went back at last, when darkness fell, and entered into the cool lit darkness of the other streets. When he came into Sheng's room, Sheng was gay again, awake, and ready with a friend or two to sally forth into the street of theatres to make merry there.

When he saw Yuan he cried out, "Where have you been, cousin? I nearly feared you lost."

And Yuan answered slowly, "I have seen some of the life you told me was not in the books. . . . Then all the wealth and strength of these people still cannot keep away the poor." And he told where he had been and a little of what he saw. And one of Sheng's friends said, careful as a judge, "Some day, of course, we will solve the problem of poverty." And the other said, "Of course if these people were capable of more they would have more. They are defective somehow. There is always room at the top."

Then Yuan spoke out quickly "The truth is you hide your poor—you are ashamed of them as a man is ashamed of some secret vile disease—"

But Sheng said gaily, "We'll be late if we let this cousin start us on this talk! The play begins in half an hour!"

In those six years Yuan came near to three others who befriended him among all the strangers among whom he lived. There was a certain old teacher he had, a white-haired man, whose face Yuan early liked to see because it was very kindly marked by gentle thoughts and perfect ways of life. To Yuan this old man showed himself, when time went on, as more than a teacher only. He spent willingly much time in special talk with Yuan, and he read the notes Yuan wrote in planning for a book he hoped to write, and with very mild correction he pointed out a place or two where Yuan was wrong. Whenever Yuan spoke he listened, his blue eyes so smiling and so filled with understanding that Yuan came at length to trust him greatly and at further length to tell him inward things.

He told him, among much else, how he had seen the poor in the city, and how he wondered that in the midst of such vast riches the poor could live so desperately. And this led him on to talk of the foreign priest and how he had besmirched Yuan's people by his vile pictures. The old man listened to it all in his mild silent way and then he said, "I think not everyone can see the whole picture. It has long been said we each see what we look for. You and I, we look at land and think of seed and harvests. A builder looks at the same land and thinks of houses, and a painter of its colors. The priest sees men only as those who need to be saved, and so naturally he sees most clearly those who need to be saved."

And after Yuan had thought of this awhile, unwillingly he knew it to be true, and in all fairness he could not quite hate the foreign priest as wholly as he did, or even as he wished he could, for still he thought him wrong, and still he said, "At least, he saw a very narrow part of my country." To which the old man answered always mildly, "That might be, and must be if he were a narrow man."

Through talk like this in field and schoolroom after others had gone home, Yuan learned to love this old white man. And he loved Yuan and looked on him with increasing tenderness.

One day he said to Yuan, half hesitating, "I wish you would come with me tonight, my son. We are very simple folk—only my wife and my daughter Mary and I —we three—but if you will come and take your supper with us, we'll be glad. I've told them so much about you, they want to know you, too."

This was the first time anyone had spoken thus to Yuan, in these years, and he was very moved by it. It seemed a warm and special thing to him that a teacher would take a pupil to his private home. He said shyly therefore in the courteous way of his own tongue, "I am not worthy."

To which the old man opened his eyes wide and smiled and said, "Wait until you see how plain we are! My wife said when I first told her it would be a pleasure to me if you came, 'I'm afraid he's used to much better than we have.'"

Then Yuan protested again in courtesy and yielded. Thus he found himself walking down the shaded street into a small square court-like yard, and thence to an ancient wooden house, standing back in trees, and set about with porches. There at the door a lady met him who made him think of the lady whom he called his mother. For in these two women, ten thousand miles apart, who spoke two different tongues, whose blood and bones and skin were not alike, there was yet a common look. The white smoothed hair, their full settled look of motherhood, their simple ways and honest eyes, their quiet voices, the wisdom and the patience graven on their lips and brows, these made them like. Yet it was true there was a difference in the two which Yuan could perceive after they were seated in the large main room, for about this lady there was an air of contentment and simple satisfaction of the soul which his lady mother had not. It was as if this one had her heart's desire in her lifetime, but the other had not. By two roads the two had come to a good tranquil age, but the one had come by a happy road and with companionship, while the other had come by a darker way and she walked alone.

But when this lady's daughter came in, she was not like Ai-lan. No, this Mary was a different sort of maid. She was, perhaps, a little more in years than Ai-lan was, much taller and not so pretty, very quiet, seemingly, and governed in her voice and look. Yet when one listened to the words she spoke, there was sense in all she said and her dark, grey-black eyes, somber in hue when she was grave, could flash out merrily to match a witty twist her words might take. She was demure before her parents, yet not afraid, and they deferred to her as to an equal, and Yuan perceived this.

Indeed Yuan saw very soon she was no common maid. For when the old man talked of what Yuan wrote, this Mary knew of it, too, and put a question so quickly and so aptly before Yuan that he was taken aback and asked her, wondering, "How is it that you know the history of my people so well that you can ask me of one so far away in history as Ch'ao Tso?"

To this the maid answered modestly but with a shine of smiling in her eyes. "Oh, I have always had a kinship with your land, I think. I have read books about it. Shall I tell you the very little I know about him? Then you will know I am a sham! I really know nothing. But he wrote about agriculture, didn't he?—in an essay. I remember I memorized a bit I read once in a translation. It was something like this, 'Crime begins in poverty; poverty in insufficiency of food; insufficiency in neglect of tilling of the soil. Without such tilling, man has no tie to bind him to the soil. Without such a tie he readily leaves his birthplace and his home. Then he is like the birds of the air or the beasts of the field. Neither battlemented cities nor deep moats, nor harsh laws, nor cruel punishments, can subdue this roving spirit that is strong within him.' "

These words, which Yuan knew very well, this maid now chanted in a round clear voice, for her voice was very full of meaning. It could be seen she loved the words, because a gravity came upon her face and into her eyes a mystery, as of one who again perceives beauty known before. Her parents listened reverently and in pride while she spoke and the old father turned to Yuan as one who cries out in his heart, only keeping back the words in decent courtesy, "Do you see what my child is for wisdom and intelligence, and have you seen one like her?"

Yuan could not but speak out his pleasure, and hereafter when she spoke he listened, too, and felt a kinship with her, because whatever she said, even if she said a

small thing, was said fitly and well, and as he would
have liked to have said it in her place.

Yet though he felt so used to this house he had entered for the first time this night, so used to these people that he forgot they were not of his kind, yet every
now and again there came a strangeness of some sort, a
foreign thing he did not understand. When they entered into a smaller room and sat about an oval table
spread for the meal, Yuan took up his spoon to eat. But
he saw the others hesitate, and then the old man bowed
his head and so did the others except Yuan, who did
not understand the thing, and while he looked from one
to the other, to see what would happen, the old man
spoke aloud as though to some god not to be seen, a
few words only, but said with feeling, as though he
thanked one for a gift received. After this, without
further rite, they ate, and Yuan asked nothing at that
time, but he gave and received in talk.

But afterwards, being very curious about this rite and
never having seen it heretofore, he asked his teacher of
it as they sat alone in the twilight on the wide veranda,
and he asked so he might know what the courteous thing
was he should do at such a time. Then the old man fell
silent for a while, smoking his pipe and looking peace-
fully away into the shadowed street. At last he held his
pipe in the cup of his hand and said, "Yuan, I have
many times wondered how to speak to you of our religion. What you saw is a religious rite we have, a simple
giving thanks to God for food daily set before us. In itself it is not important and yet it is a symbol of the greatest thing our lives hold—our belief in God. Do you remember you spoke of our prosperity and power? I
believe it is the fruit of our religion. I do not know what
your religion is, Yuan, but I know I should not be true
to my own self or to you if I should let you live here
and daily come and go in my classes and come often, I
hope, to my home, and not tell you of my own faith."

While the old man spoke thus, the two women came
out and seated themselves there, the mother on a chair
in which she rocked gently to and fro as though a wind

were blowing it. There she sat listening to her husband, a mild agreeing smile upon her face, and when he paused a moment, for he went on to talk of gods and mysteries of gods made human flesh, she cried out with a sort of gentle passion, "Oh, Mr. Wang, ever since Dr. Wilson told me how brilliant you are in his classes, how able in all you write, I have counted you for Christ. What a great thing it would be for your country if you could be somehow won for Christ and go back to bear good witness!"

This gave Yuan great astonishment, for he did not know what all these words meant. But being courteous he smiled merely and bowed a little and was even about to speak when Mary's voice broke out sharp and clear as metal, and with a tone Yuan had not heard in it before. She had not sat herself in a chair but on the uppermost step and she had sat there silent while her father had talked, holding her chin in her two hands and listening seemingly. Now out of the dim light her voice came restless, strange, impatient, cutting like a knife across the talk, "Shall we go inside, father? The chairs will be more comfortable—and I like the light—"

To which the old man answered in a vague surprise, "Why yes, Mary, if you wish. But I thought you always liked to sit here of an evening. Every night we sit here awhile—"

But the young woman answered still more restlessly and with a sort of willfulness, "Tonight I want the light, father."

"Very well, my dear," the old man said, and rose slowly and so they went within.

There in the lighted room he spoke no more of mysteries. Instead his daughter led the talk, plying Yuan with a hundred questions of his own country, so quick and deep sometimes that he must in all honesty confess himself confounded by his own ignorance. And while she talked, he could not but feel a pleasure in her. For though he knew she was not beautiful, her face was keen and quickened, and the skin was delicate and very white, her lips narrow and a little red, and her hair was

smooth and very nearly like his own in blackness, but
much finer than his was. Her eyes he saw were beautiful, now near black with earnestness, then changing to
a lovely shining grey when she smiled, and she smiled
often though she did not laugh aloud. Her hands spoke,
too, being very restless, supple, slender hands, not small,
and perhaps too thin and not smooth enough for beauty
but nevertheless with a sort of power in their look and
movement.

But Yuan took no pleasure in these things for themselves. For he saw she was one whose body seemed a
thing not of itself but only a covering for her mind and
soul. And this was new to Yuan, who had known no such
woman. When he thought he saw a sudden beauty in
her as suddenly it was gone and he forgot it in the flash
of light her mind sent out or in a witty word her tongue
spoke. The body was informed here by the mind, and
the mind did not spend itself in thoughts upon the body.
So Yuan saw her scarcely as a woman, but as a being,
changeful, shining, eager, sometimes a little cold, even,
and often suddenly silent. Yet not silent out of emptiness, only silent while her mind took hold of something
that he said and pulled it delicately apart to question
what it was. In such silence she often did forget herself
and forgot that her eyes were still on Yuan's eyes though
he had finished speaking, so that in such silence more
than once he found himself looking deep and deeper into
the soft changing darkening blackness of her eyes.

Not once did she speak of mysteries nor did the elder
two again either, until at last when Yuan rose to take his
leave the old man clinging to his hand a little said, "If
you wish, son, come to church with us next Sunday and
see how you like it."

And Yuan, taking this as further kindness, said he
would, and this he said more willingly because he felt
it would be a very pleasant thing to see these three again,
who made him like a son in the house, who was not even
of their race or kind.

Now after Yuan had gone back to his room, when he
lay in his bed waiting for sleep, he thought about these

three and most of all he thought about the daughter of
the old two. Here was a woman such as he had not seen.
She was of a material different from any he had known,
a stuff more shining than Ai-lan, and this in spite of all
of Ai-lan's mirth and pretty kitten's eyes and little laugh-
ters. This white woman, though grave often, had some
strong inner light, at times too hard, if one compared her
to the vague soft kindness of her mother, but always
clear. She made no misdirected movement, even, of her
body. There were in her none of the constant useless
movements of the body, only, such as the landlady's
daughter made continually to show her thigh or wrist or
foot more clearly forth, blind movements of the flesh.
Nor were her words, nor was her voice like that one's,
who had set Sheng's pretty words to heavy, passionate
music. For this Mary's words were not surcharged with
oversubtle meaning. No, she spoke them out swiftly and
with sharp clearness and each word had its own weight
and meaning and no more, good tools of her mind, but
not messengers of vague suggestion.

When Yuan thought of her he remembered most her
spirit, clothed in color and in substance of her flesh, but
not hidden by it. And he fell to thinking of what she
said and how she said sometimes things he had not
thought upon. Once she said, when they spoke of love
of country, "Idealism and enthusiasm are not the same
thing. Enthusiasm may be only physical—the youth and
strength of body making the spirit gay. But idealism may
live on, though the body be aged or broken, for it is the
essential quality of the soul which has it." And then her
face had changed in its quick, lighting way and looking
at her father very tenderly, she said, "My father has real
idealism, I think."

And the old man answered quietly, "I call it faith, my
child."

To which Yuan now remembered she had answered
nothing.

And so thinking of these three he fell asleep in more
content of soul than he had ever had in this foreign

country, for to him they seemed actual and to be com-
prehended.

When the day came, therefore, for the religious rites
of which the old teacher had spoken Yuan dressed himself with care in his better garments and again he went
to the house. At first he felt some timidity, because the
door opened and there Mary stood. It was plain she
was surprised to see him, for her eyes darkened and she
did not smile. She was moreover clothed in a long blue
coat and a small hat of the same hue, and she seemed
taller than Yuan remembered her and somehow touched
with an austerity. Therefore he stammered forth, "Your
father invited me to go with him to his religious place
today."

She answered gravely, searching out his eyes with
some troubled look within her own, "I know he did.
Will you come in? We are almost ready."

So Yuan went in again to the room where he had remembered such good friendship. But this morning it
did not seem so friendly to him. There was no fire burning on the hearth as there had been that night, and the
hard cold sunshine of the autumn morning fell through
the windows and showed the wornness of the rugs upon
the floor and of the stuffs upon the chairs, so that whereas
by night and firelight and lamplight what had looked
dark and homely and used, by this stern sunshine seemed
too worn and aged and needing newness.

Yet the old man and his lady were very kind when
they came in, clothed decently for their devotions, as
kind as they had been. The old man said, "I am so glad
you came. I did not speak again, because I do not want
to influence you unduly."

But the lady said in her soft, overflowing way, "But I
have *prayed*! I prayed you would be led to come. I pray
about you every night, Mr. Wang. If God will grant my
prayer how proud it will make me, if through us—"

Then sharp as a ray of the piercing sunlight across
the old room the daughter's voice fell, a pleasant voice,
not unkind, but very clear and perfect in its tone, a little

colder yet than Yuan had heard it, "Shall we go now? We have just time to get there."

She led them out and sat herself by the guiding wheel in the car which was to take them to the place they went. The old two sat behind, but Yuan she placed beside her. Yet she did not say any word while she turned the wheel this way and that. And Yuan, being courteous, did not speak, either, nor did he even look at her except as he might turn his head to see a strange sight passed. Yet, without looking straightly at her, he saw her face sidewise against and in front of that which he looked. There was no smile or light in that face now. It was grave even to a sort of sadness, the straight nose not small, the sharply cut, delicately folded lips, the clearly rounded chin lifted out of a dark fur upon her collar, her grey eyes set direct and far upon the road ahead. As she was now, turning the wheel quickly and well, sitting there straight and silent, Yuan was even a little afraid of her. She seemed not that one with whom he had once spoken freely and easily.

Thus they came to a great house into which many men and women and even children were passing. With these they entered and seated themselves, Yuan between the old man and the young woman. Yuan could not but look about him curiously for this was only the second time he had been in such a temple. Temples in his own land he had seen often, but they were for the common and the unlearned, and for women, and he had never worshipped any god in his life. A few times he had entered for curiosity and stared at the vast images, and had listened to the deep warning solitary note the great bell gave forth when it was struck, and he had seen with contempt the grey-robed priests, for his tutor taught him early that such priests were evil and ignorant men who preyed upon the people. So Yuan had never worshipped any god.

Now in this foreign temple he sat and watched. It was a cheerful place, and through long narrow windows the early autumn sunshine streamed in great bars of light, falling upon flowers at an altar, upon the gay garments of women, upon many faces of varied meaning, although not of many young. Soon music flowed out into the air from some unknown source, at first very soft music, then gradually growing in sound and volume until all the air was throbbing with that music. Yuan, turning his head to see what its source was, saw beside him the figure of the old man, his head bowed before him, his eyes closed, upon his face a smile, sweet, ecstatic. And Yuan, looking about, observed others also in this bound speechless silence, and in courtesy he wondered what he should do. But when he looked at Mary, he saw her sitting as she had been at the wheel, straight and proud, her chin lifted, and her eyes opened and fixed in the distance. When he saw her sitting thus, Yuan also therefore did not bow his head in any unknown worship.

Now, remembering what the old man had said, that in the power of their religion these people had found their strength, Yuan watched to know what this power was. But he could not easily discover it. For when the grave music fell soft once more and at last withdrew itself into the place where it hid, a robed priest came out and read certain words to which all seemed to listen decorously, although Yuan, observing, could see that some paid heed to their garments or to others' faces or to some such thing. But the old man and his lady listened carefully, although Mary, her face still set as to a far distance, did not change her look with anything she heard so that Yuan could not know if indeed she listened. Again and again there was music, and there was chanting of words Yuan could not understand, and the robed priest exhorted those in the temple out of the great book from which he had read.

To this Yuan listened, and it seemed a good harmless exhortation by a pleasant, holy man who urged his countrymen to be more kindly to the poor and to deny themselves and to obey their god, and such talk he made as priests do anywhere.

When he had finished, he bade them bow while he cried out a prayer to this god. Again Yuan looked to see what he should do, and again he saw the old pair bow themselves in their devotion. And again the woman by him held her proud head high, and therefore he also did not bow. He held his eyes open and looked to see if any image would be brought forth by the priest, since the people were bowed ready to worship. But the priest brought forth no image and no god was seen anywhere, and after a time when he had finished his speaking, the people waited no more for the god to come, but stirred and rose and went to their homes, and Yuan went back also to his own place, not understanding anything of what he had seen or heard, and out of all of it remembering most the clear line of that proud woman's head, which had not bowed itself.

Yet out of this day grew the next new thing in Yuan's life. For one day when he returned to his room from the field where he was now planting seeds of winter wheat, to see which did best in various rows where he placed them, he found a letter upon his table. Letters were very rare in Yuan's solitary life in this foreign country. Once in three months he knew his father's letter would lie on that table, each time its letters brushed to say the same words nearly, that the Tiger did well, but rested until next spring when he would go out to war again, that Yuan must study hard at what he wished most to know, and that he must come home as soon as his years of study were complete, since he was only son. Or else a letter might lie there from the lady, Ai-lan's mother, a quiet good letter, telling small things that she did, how Ai-lan she thought was to be wed, now three times promised, by her own will, but each time will-fully refusing to be wed to the one promised, so that Yuan smiled a little when he read of Ai-lan's willfulness, and when the mother had spoken of it, she often added as though for her own comfort, "But Mei-ling is my stay. I have taken her into the home with us, and she learns so well and does everything so rightly, and is so filled with every proper sense of fitness, that almost she might be the child I should have had, and sometimes more my daughter than my Ai-lan is."

Such letters Yuan could look for, and once or twice Ai-lan had written, letters mixed in two languages and full of willfulness and teasing and pretty threats if Yuan did not bring her back some western baubles, and vows that she expected perhaps a western sister-in-law. Or Sheng might write, but very seldom and never surely, and Yuan knew, half sadly, that his life was filled with all the many things a young man has who is beautiful in body and skilled in pretty speech, whose foreignness added grace to him in the eyes of those city dwellers who sought restlessly and everywhere for every new thing they could find.

But this letter was none of these. It lay white and square upon the table and his name was there marked clearly in black ink. So Yuan opened it, and it was from Mary Wilson. There her name was, plain and large at the bottom, yet with an energy and keenness in its shape, and very far from the rude letters that the landlady shaped upon her monthly bills. The letter asked Yuan to come for a special purpose on any day he could, since she who wrote it had been troubled since the day they went to church together, and had something unsaid which she wanted said, so she could be free of it toward Yuan.

Then Yuan, wondering very much, dressed himself in his dark better clothes and washed himself free of the stain of earth and that night when he had eaten he went out. And as he went his landlady cried out after him that she had put a letter from a lady on his table that day, and now she reckoned that he went to see her. And all the company laughed aloud, and the young girl laughed loudest of them all. But Yuan said nothing. He was only angry that this rude laughter should come even as near as this to Mary Wilson, who was too high for such as these to touch her name. And Yuan felt his heart grow hot against them and he swore to himself that none should ever hear her name from him, and he wished he had not that laughter and these looks even in his mind when he went to her.

But there the memory was, and it put a constraint

upon him when he stood again before that door, so that
when the door opened and she stood there, he was
cool and shy and did not touch her hand when she put
it warmly forth, but feigned he did not see it, he was
so fastidious against the coarseness of those others. And
she felt his coolness. A light went from her face, and
she put away the little smile she had to greet him, and
asked him gravely to come in and her voice was quiet
and cool.

But when he went in the room was as it had been that
first evening, warm and intimate and lit with the flames
that burned upon the hearth. The old deep chairs invited him and the very stillness and the emptiness received him.

Nevertheless Yuan waited to see where she would
seat herself, so that he might not be more near her than
he ought to be, and she, not looking at him, dropped
with a careless grace upon a low stool before the fire,
and motioned to a great chair near. But Yuan, as he sat
in it, contrived to push it back somewhat, so that while
he was near to her, near enough so that he could see
her face clearly, yet, if he put forth a hand, or if she
did, their hands could not touch each other. So he
wished to have it, and know more surely that the laughter of those common folk was coarse laughter only.

Thus these two sat alone. Of the old pair there was
nothing seen or heard. But without telling of them, the
woman began to speak directly and with abruptness, as
if what she said was hard to say, and yet necessary to
be spoken. "Mr. Wang, you will think it strange of me
that I asked you to come here tonight. We are really
strangers, almost. And yet I have read so much about
your country—you know I work in the library—and I
know a little of your people and admire them a great
deal. I asked you here, not only for your own sake, but
for your sake as a Chinese. And I speak to you as a
modern American to a modern Chinese."

Here she paused, and gazed awhile into the fire, and
at last took up a little twig caught among a heap of logs
upon the hearth, and with this she stirred half idly the

red coals which lay beneath the burning logs. And Yuan
waited, wondering what was to be said, and not wholly
easy with her, since he was not used to being alone with
a woman, until she went on.

"The truth is I have been much embarrassed by my
parents' efforts to interest you in their religion. Of them
I say nothing, except they are the best people I have
ever known. You know my father—you see—anyone can
see—what he is. People talk of saints. He is one. I have
never seen him angry or unkind in all my life. No girl,
no woman, ever had better parents. The only trouble
is that my father, if he did not give me his goodness,
did give me his brain. In my time I have used that brain,
and it has turned against the religion, the energy that
feeds my father's life, really, so that I myself have no
belief in it. I cannot understand how men like my father,
with strong, keen intellect, do not use it upon their
religion. His religion satisfies his emotional needs. His
intellectual life is outside religion, and—there is no passage between the two. . . . My mother, of course, is not
an intellectual. She is simpler—easier to understand. If
father were like her, I should be merely amused when
they try to make a Christian out of you—I should know
they never could."

Now the woman turned her honest eyes straight upon
Yuan, and let her hands grow still, the twig hanging in
her fingers, and looking at him she grew still more earnest. "But—I am afraid—father may influence you. I know
you admire him. You are his pupil. You study the books
he has written, he has been attracted to you as he seldom has been to any pupil. I think he has a sort of vision
of you going back to your country as a great Christian
leader. Has he told you he once wanted to be a missionary? He belongs to the generation when every good
earnest boy or girl was faced with the—the missionary
call, as it was named. But he was engaged to my mother,
and she wasn't strong enough to go. I think both of them
have felt ever since a sense of—of some frustration. . . .
Strange, how generations differ! We feel the same thing
about you, they and I"—there were her deep lovely

eyes, looking straight into his, unashamed, with no co-
quetry—"and yet how we differ! They feel because you
are what you are, how glorious to win you to their
cause! To me, how presumptuous to think you could
be made more than you are—by a religion! You are of
your own race and your own time. How can anyone
dare to impose upon you what is foreign to you?"

These words she said with a sort of ardor streaming
from her, and Yuan was stirred, but not grossly, towards
her. For she seemed to see him not only as himself,
one man, but as one of his whole race. It was as though
through him she spoke to millions. Between them was
a wall of delicacy, of mind, of a withdrawal native to
them both. And he said gratefully, "I understand very
well what you mean. It doesn't, I promise you, weaken
any admiration I feel for your father to know he believes
a thing my mind cannot accept."

Her eyes were turned upon the flames again. The fire
had sunk into coals and ashes, and the glow was steadier
now upon her face and hair, upon her hands, upon the
dark red of her dress. She said thoughtfully, "Who could
not admire him? It was a hard thing for me, I can tell
you, to put aside my childish faith in what he had taught
me. But I was honest with him—I could be—and we
talked again and again. I couldn't talk to mother at all—
she always began to weep, and that made me impatient.
But father met me at every point—and we could talk—he
always respected my disbelief, and I always respected
—more and more—his faith. We would reason very much
alike up to a certain point—when the intellect must stop
and one must begin to believe without understanding.
There we parted. He could take that at a leap—frankly
believing, in faith and hope—I couldn't. My generation
can't."

Suddenly and with energy she rose and taking a log
flung it upon the bed of coals. A mass of sparks flew up
the wide black chimney, and again a blaze burst forth,
and again Yuan saw her shining in the fresh light. She
turned to him, standing above him, leaning against the
mantel, saying seriously, yet with a little half smile at

the corners of her mouth, "I think that's what I wanted to say—that sums it up. Don't forget that I do not believe. When my parents try to influence you, remember their generation—it is not mine—not yours and mine."   .

Yuan rose, too, very grateful, and as he stood beside her, thinking what to say, words came up unexpectedly out of him, which were not what he would have planned to say.

"I wish," he said slowly, looking at her, "that I could speak to you in my own language. For I find your speech never wholly natural to me. You have made me forget we are not one race. Somehow, for the first time since I entered your country I have felt a mind speaking to my mind without a barrier."

This he said honestly and simply, and she looked back at him as straight as a child, their eyes level to each other's, and she answered quietly, but very warmly, "I believe we shall be friends—Yuan?"

And Yuan answered, half timidly and as though he put his foot out to step upon an unknown shore, not knowing where he stepped or what was there, but still he must step forth, "If this is your wish—" and then still looking at her he added, his voice very low with shyness—"Mary."

She smiled then, a quick, brilliant, playful smile, accepting what he said and then stopping him as clearly as though she spoke the words "We have said enough for this day." They spoke then for a while of small things in books or elsewhere until there were steps heard upon the porch and she said at once, "Here they come—my precious two. They went to prayer meeting —they go every Wednesday night."

And she walked swiftly to the door and opened it and welcomed the old two, who came in, their faces fresh and reddened by the chilly autumn air. Soon they were all before the fire, and more than ever they made Yuan one of them, and bade him sit down again, while Mary brought fruit and the hot milk they loved to drink before they slept. And Yuan, though his soul loathed the milk, yet took it and sipped a little of it to feel more one with them, until Mary perceived how it was and laughed and said, "Why didn't I remember?" And she brewed a pot of tea and gave it to him, and they made a little merriment about it.

But the moment which afterwards Yuan thought of most was this. In a pause of talk, the mother sighed and said, "Mary, dear, I wish you had wanted to come tonight. It was a *good* meeting. I think Dr. Jones spoke so well—didn't you, Henry?—about having faith enough to carry us even through the greatest trials." And then she said kindly to Yuan, "You must feel very lonely often, Mr. Wang. I often think how hard it must be to be so far from your dear parents and they, too, how hard it is for them to let you be so far. If you feel you'd like it, we'd love to have you take supper with us Wednesdays and go to church with us."

Then Yuan, perceiving how kindly she was, said only "Thank you," and as he said it his eyes fell on Mary, who sat again upon the stool, so now her eyes were beneath the level of his own, and very near. And there in her eyes and upon her face he saw a lovely tender half-merry meaning, tender towards the mother, but very comprehending too toward Yuan, so that this look bound them together in a sort of mutual understanding, wherein they two were quite alone.

Thereafter Yuan lived with a sense of secret, hidden richness. No longer was this people alien to him wholly nor its ways altogether strange and often he forgot he hated them, and he thought he had not so many slights put on him as before, either. He had now two gateways whereby to enter. The one was the outer gateway, and it was this one house into which he could come and go always with freedom and welcome. The worn brown room became home to him in this foreign place. He had thought his loneliness very sweet and the thing he wanted most, yet now he came to this further knowledge, and it was that loneliness is only sweet to a man if it rids him of presences irksome and unwanted, and it is no longer sweet when the beloved presences are discovered. Here in this room did Yuan discover such beloved presences.

There were the little presences of used books, seeming so small and silent, and yet when sometimes he came alone into this room, and sat alone, the house being empty for the time, he took up a book and he found himself spoken to most mightily. For here books spoke more nearly to him than they did anywhere, because the room enfolded him in learned quiet and in friendliness.

And there was here often the beloved presence of his old teacher. Here more than in any classroom or even in the fields Yuan came to know the full beauty of this man. The old man had lived a very simple childlike life, a farmer's son, a student, then a teacher, many years, and he knew so little of the world that one would say he had not lived in it. Yet did he live in two worlds of mind and spirit, and Yuan, exploring into those two worlds with many questions and long listening silences when he sat and heard the old man speak out his knowledge and beliefs, felt no narrowness here, but the wide ranging simple vastness of a mind unlimited by time or space, to which all things were possible in man and god. It was the vastness of a wise child's mind, to which there are no boundaries between the true and magical. Yet this simplicity was so informed with wisdom that Yuan could not but love it, and ponder, troubled, on his own narrowness of understanding. One day, in such trouble, he said to Mary, when she came in and found him alone and troubled, "Almost your father persuades me to be a Christian!"

And she answered, "Does he not almost so persuade us all? But you will find, as I did, the barrier is the—almost. Our two minds are different, Yuan—less simple, less sure, more exploring."

So she spoke, definitely and calmly, and linked thus with her Yuan felt himself pulled back from some brink towards which he had been drawn against his will, and

yet somehow with his will, too, because he loved the
old man. But she drew him back each time.

If this house was the outer gateway, the woman was
the gateway to its inner heart. For through her he learned
of many things. For him she told the story of her people and how they came to the shores of the land upon
which they lived, gathered out of every nation and tribe
nearly upon the earth, and how by force and by guile
and by every measure of war they wrested the land
from those who possessed it and took it for themselves,
and Yuan listened as he had been used to listen to tales
of the Three Kingdoms in his childhood. Then she told
how her forefathers forced their way always to the far-
thest coasts, boldly and desperately, and while she talked,
sometimes in the room by the fire, sometimes walking
in woods when the leaves fell now before winter, Yuan
seemed to feel in this woman for all her outward gentle-
ness the inner hardness which was in her blood. Her
eyes could grow brilliant and daring and cold, and her
chin set beneath her straight lips, and she would kindle
as she talked, very proud of the past of her race, and
Yuan was half afraid of her.

And here was the strangest thing, that at these times
he felt in her a power that was man, almost, and in himself a lesser, leaning quality which was less than man,
as though they two together might make man and woman,
but interfused, and not clearly he the man and she the
woman. And there was sometimes in her eyes a look so
possessive towards him, as though she felt herself
stronger than he, that his flesh drew back until she
changed her look. So while he often saw her beautiful,
her body arrowy and light with all her energy, and while
he could not but be moved by her darting mind, yet he
never could feel her quite flesh to his flesh, or as a
woman to be touched or loved, for there was that in
her which made him a little afraid of her, and so held
back growing love.

He was glad of this, for he still did not wish to think
of love or woman, and while he could not keep away
from this woman, since there was much in her which

drew him, yet he was glad he did not want to touch her. If any had asked him even now he would have said, "It is not wise nor well for two of different flesh to wed each other. There is the outer difficulty of the two races, neither of which likes such union. But there is also the inner struggle against each other, and this pull away from each other goes as deep as blood does—there is no end to that war between two different bloods."

Yet there were times, too, when he was shaken in his sureness that he was safe against her, for sometimes she seemed not wholly foreign to him even in blood, for she could not only show him her own people, but she showed him his people, too, in such a way as he had never seen them. There was much Yuan did not know of his own kind. He had lived among them in a way, a part of his father's life, a part of the school of war and of young men filled with ardor for a cause, a part of that earthen house, even, and a part too of the great new city, but between these parts there was no unity to make them into one world. When any asked him of his own country or his people, he spoke out of knowledge so separated and disjointed, that even while he spoke he remembered something against what he said, and at last it came about that he did not speak at all of it except to deny such things as the tall priest had shown, for pride's sake.

But through this western woman's eyes, who had never even seen the earth upon which his people had their life, he saw his country as he wished to see it. Now, for his sake, he knew, she read everything she could about his people, all books and sayings of travellers, the stories and the tales which had been put into her language, and the poems, too, and she pored over pictures. From all this she formed within her mind a dream, an inner knowledge, of what Yuan's country was, and to her it seemed a place most perfectly beautiful, where men and women lived in justice and in peace, in a society framed soundly upon the wisdom of its sages.

And Yuan, listening to her, saw it so, too. When she said, "It seems to me, Yuan, that in your country you

have solved all our human problems. The beautiful re-
lationship of father to son, of friend to friend, of man
to man—everything is thought of and expressed simply
and well. And the hatred that your people have for violence and war, how I admire that!" And Yuan, listening,
forgot his own childhood and remembered only that it
was true he did hate violence and war, and since he did,
he felt his people did, and he remembered the villagers,
how they had besought him against any wars, and so her
words seemed true to him and only true.

And sometimes when she gazed at a picture she had
found and saved for him to look at with her, a picture
perhaps of a slender tall pagoda, flung up against the sky
from some craggy mountain top, or perhaps a country
pool fringed about with drooping willows and white
geese floating in the shadows, she caught her breath to
cry softly, "O Yuan—beautiful—*beautiful!* Why is it
when I look at these pictures I seem to feel they are of a
place I have lived in and know very well? There is a
strange longing in me for them. I think yours must be
the most lovely country in the world."

Yuan, staring at the pictures, seeing them through her
eyes, and himself remembering the beauty he had seen
those few days upon the land, where he had seen such
pools, accepted what she said most simply and he answered honestly enough, "It is true, it is a very fair land."

Then she, looking at him troubled, said on, "How
crude we all must seem to you, and how crude our life
—we are so new and crude!" And Yuan suddenly felt
that this, too, was true. He remembered the house in
which he lived, the brawling woman there, often angry
at her daughter, so that in many bickering ways she filled
the house with anger, and he remembered the poor in
the city, but he said only very kindly, "In this house, at
least, I find the peace and courtesy to which I am accustomed."

When she was in a mood like this, Yuan almost loved
her. He thought proudly, "My country has this power
over her, that when she thinks and dreams upon it, she
grows soft and quiet, and her hardness goes away, and

she is all a woman." And he wondered if it might be one day that he would love her in spite of his own wish. Sometimes he thought it so, and then he reasoned thus, "For if she lived in my country, which she has already so much made her own, she would always be like this, gentle and womanish and admiring, and leaning on me for what she needs."

And Yuan at such times thought it might be sweet to have it so, and it would be sweet to teach her how to speak his tongue; sweet, too, to live in the home that she could make, a home like this one he had learned to love very well, its comforts and its homeliness.

But as surely as he let himself be drawn thus, he would come one day to find this Mary changed again, her hardness flashing out, her dominating self the uppermost, so that she could argue and condemn and judge and drive a point home with a keen word or two, even to her father, for she was gentler with Yuan than with anyone, and then he was afraid of her again, and he felt a wildness in her that he could not subdue. So did she draw him to her and so thrust him from her many times.

Thus through the fifth year and the sixth did Yuan continue in this bondage to this woman, and always she was either more than woman to him so that he was afraid of her, or less than woman so that he did not desire her, and yet he never could wholly forget she was a woman. Nevertheless, at last it came about, that with his deep, too narrow nature, she was his only friend.

Thus was it more sure that soon or late he must draw closer to her still, or else grow colder towards her, and he drew away and it came about over a thing not great in itself.

Now Yuan was one who never could take part in all the fooleries of his fellows. There came to the school that last year two brothers who were of his own race, but from the southern parts, where men are light in speech and heart, and variable in mind and laugh too easily. These were two youths so debonair, who so easily lent themselves to the lesser life about them that they were well beloved and often sought for such occasions as demanded what they could do, and they had learned to sing as well as any clown the roaring songs or tricky, halting rhythms which the students loved, so that when they came before a crowd they grinned and danced like clowns and loved the clapping hands of any crowd. Between them and Yuan there was a chasm deeper than between him and the white men, and not only was it that their native language was not his, since south and north have not the same tongue, but because Yuan was secretly ashamed of them. Let these white men, he thought, shake their bodies hither and thither in foolishness but not his countrymen before these foreigners. And when Yuan heard the loud laughter and the roars of praise his own face grew still and cold, because he discerned, or was sure he did, a mockery beneath the merriment.

One day especially he could not bear it. There had been an evening set for amusement in a certain hall and thither Yuan went, inviting with him Mary Wilson, for she now would often go with him to public places, and they sat with all the others. These two Cantonese appeared in their turn that night, tricked out as an old farmer and his wife, the farmer with a long false queue hung down his back, and the wife coarse and loud as any bawdy woman. And Yuan must sit there and see those two play the fool, in pretense quarrelling and cursing over a fowl made of cloth and feathers which they held between them and divided bit by bit, and they spoke so all could understand and yet seemed somehow to be speaking in their own tongue, too. Indeed the sight was very funny, and the two so witty and so clever that none could keep from laughing, and even Yuan smiled a little sometimes, in spite of an uneasy heart, and Mary laughed often and when the two were gone she turned to Yuan, her face still bright with laughter, "It might have been a bit straight out of your country, Yuan! I am so glad to have seen it."

But these words drove the laughter from him. He said

very stiffly, "It was not my country at all. No farmer there wears queues in these days. It was as much a farce as any comedian upon your own stage in New York."

Seeing he was somehow very hurt, she said quickly, "Oh, of course I see that. It was only nonsense, but there was a flavor to it, nevertheless, Yuan?"

But Yuan would not answer. He sat gravely through the evening until it was over, and at the door he bowed and when she asked him to come in he would not, although of late he had looked forward eagerly to coming in and staying awhile in the warm room with her. When now he refused, she looked at him questioningly, not knowing what was wrong, yet knowing something was; suddenly she was a little impatient with him, and felt him foreign and different and difficult, and she let him go, saying only, "Another time, perhaps." Then he went away more hurt because she had not urged him and he thought somberly, "That clownishness made her think less of me, because she saw my race so foolish."

He went home and he was so angry in himself, thinking of her coolness, too, that he went to the house where those two clowns slept and knocked and went into their room and surprised them as they stood half dressed, preparing for sleep. Upon the table were the false queue and the long false whiskers and all the things they used for disguise, and seeing these, Yuan could not but add earnestness to what he said. He said very coldly, "I come only to say I think it wrong that you did what you did tonight. It is not true love of country so to hold one's own up for cause of laughter to a people always too ready for such laughing at us."

At this the two brothers were wholly taken aback, and first they stared at each other and at Yuan, and then one burst into laughter and then the other, and the elder said in the foreign tongue, since they and Yuan spoke differently in any other tongue, "We let you hold up the honor of the country, elder brother! You have dignity enough for a million others!" At this they roared again and Yuan could not bear their wide lips and little merry eyes and their squat bodies. He looked at them while they laughed and then without a word went out and shut the door behind him.

"These men of the south," he muttered, "to us true Chinese they are no kin—petty tribes—"

Lying in his bed that night, the bare branches of the trees patterned in shadows upon the white moonlit wall, he was glad he had no dealings with them, glad he had not even in the old days stayed on in their school of war, and he felt in this foreign country very far away from these very ones whom others counted of his race and nation. He stood alone, he thought, proudly, himself the only one to show forth what his people really were.

Thus Yuan gathered all his pride to strengthen him, for he was delicate in feeling this night, because he could not bear, knowing he valued most Mary's praise of him, to have her see his kind in any foolish light. To him it was as though she saw himself thus, and this he could not endure. He lay, therefore, very proud and solitary, more solitary because from these two even of his countrymen he felt alien, and more solitary because she had not begged him to come into her house. He thought bitterly, "She looked at me differently. She looked at me almost as though I had been myself one of those two fools."

And then he resolved he would not care, and he fostered in himself every memory of her that was not dear, how she could be hard sometimes and her voice incisive as a blade of steel, and how sometimes she was positive as a woman should not be before men, and he remembered her at the wheel of her car, driving it as though it were a beast she owned and forced to great speed and greater, her face set as stone. All these memories he did not love, and at last he ended them by saying in his haughty heart, "I have my work to do, and I will do it well. On the day when I finish what I have to do, I swear there shall not be a name above my name in the lists. Thus is my people honored."

And so he slept at last.

But for all his loneliness, he could not draw again into his solitude, for this Mary would not let him. She wrote him after three days again, and he could not but know his heart stirred strongly in him when he saw the square letter on his table. He felt his loneliness more heavily than he had before, and so now he took up the letter quickly, eager to know what she would say. When he tore it open he was a little cooled, because the words inside were very usual, and not as though she had not seen a friend for three days, whom she had grown used to seeing every day. There were only four lines and they said only that her mother had a certain flower in early bloom which she wished Yuan to see, and would he come the next morning? It would by tomorrow be in full bloom. . . . That was all.

At that moment Yuan was nearer to love for this woman than he ever had been. But her coolness pricked him, too, and he said to himself with a touch of his old childish willfulness, "Well, if she says I am to see her mother, why, then I will see her mother!" and in his little pique he planned that the next day he would devote himself to the mother.

And so he did, and when, as he stood by the flower with the lady, and gazed into its clear whiteness, Mary came by, drawing on her gloves, he only bowed his head a little without speech. But she would not have his coolness. No, although she did not stop except to say some common household thing to her mother, she threw her full look on Yuan, a look so calm and free from any meaning other than her friendship that Yuan forgot his hurt and afterwards, though she was gone, he suddenly found the flower lovely, and he took a new interest in this old mother and in what she had to say, though until this time he thought her usually too full in her speech, too quick to words of praise and of affection which she poured out, or so it seemed to Yuan, too easily on everyone alike. But now he thought in the garden she was only herself, a simple woman, very kind, and always tender to a young thing, so that she could touch a seedling struggling through the soil as tenderly as though it were a little child, and she could almost weep if a young shoot were snapped inadvertently from a rose tree, or if one stepped by accident upon a plant. She loved to feel her two hands in the earth among roots and seeds.

Here today Yuan could share her feelings, and after a while in this dewy garden he helped her pull the weeds and showed her how to move a seedling so it need not wilt but spread its small roots confidently to the new soil. He even promised he would find some seeds from his country, and would see if he could find a sort of cabbage, very green and white and well-flavored, and he was sure she would like it very well. And this slight thing made him feel more again part of this house, and now he wondered how he ever had thought this lady was too free of speech or ever anything other than warm and motherly.

Yet even today he had not much to say to this lady except the little talk of flowers or vegetables she planted. For he soon knew her mind was as simple in its own way as his own country mother's mind, a kindly narrow mind which dwelt on a dish to be cooked or a friend's gossip or the garden and its welfare, or on a bowl of flowers upon the dining table. Her loves were love of God and of her own two, and in these loves she lived most faithfully and so simply that Yuan was confounded sometimes by this simplicity. For he found that this lady, who could read well enough to take up any book and comprehend it, was as filled with strange beliefs as any villager in his own land. By her own talk with him he knew it, for she spoke of a certain festival in spring and she said, "We call it Easter, Yuan, and on this day our dear Lord rose from the dead again and ascended into heaven."

But Yuan had not the heart to smile, for well he knew that there are many tales like this among folk of every nation, and he had read them in his childish days, although he could scarcely think this lady did believe them, except he heard the awe in her kind voice and saw the goodness in her truthful eyes, blue and placid as a child's eyes, under her white hair, and he knew she did believe.

These hours in the garden finished what the quiet full look from Mary's eyes had begun, and when she came back, Yuan had put by all his hurt, and he said nothing of it, but met her as though there had been no three days apart. She said, smiling, when they were alone, "Have you spent all these two hours with mother in her garden? She is merciless if once she gets you there!"

And Yuan felt her smile free him and he smiled back and said, "Does she believe the tales she tells of rising from the dead? We have these stories but they are not believed often, even by women if they are learned."

To this she answered, "She does believe it, Yuan. And will you understand me when I say I would fight to keep you free from such beliefs because for you they would be false, and at the same time I would fight to keep my mother in those same beliefs because for her they are true and necessary? She would be lost without them, for by them she has lived and by them she must die. But you and I—we must have our own beliefs to live and die in!"

As for the lady, she grew that morning to like Yuan very well, so well indeed that often later she forgot his race and kind and would say in mild distress, if he spoke of his home, "Yuan, I declare I forget most of the time now that you are not an American boy. You fit in so well here."

But to this Mary answered quickly, "He will never be quite American, mother." And once she added in a lower voice, "And I am glad of it. I like him as he is."

This Yuan remembered, for when Mary spoke with some secret energy, the mother for once answered nothing, but she looked with trouble in her eyes upon her daughter, and Yuan fancied at that moment she was not quite so warm as she had been towards him. But this passed when he had been with her a time or two more in her garden, for in that early spring a sort of beetle fell upon the rose trees, and Yuan helped her zealously and forgot her little chill towards him. But even in so small a thing as killing beetles Yuan felt a confusion in himself; he furiously hated the cruel tiny things, destroying beauty of bud and leaf with every hour they lived, and he wanted to crush them every one. And yet his fingers loathed the task of plucking them from the trees and his flesh was squeamish afterwards, nor could he wash his hands enough. But the lady had no such feelings. She was only glad for every one she plucked away, and killed them gladly for the plague they were.

So did Yuan come to friendliness with the lady, and he drew near, too, to his old teacher, as near as he could. But the truth was that none drew very near to this old man, who was so strange a compound of depth and simplicity, of faith and intelligence. Yuan could and did talk often with him of his books and of the thoughts there, but often even in the midst of learned talk of some scientific law, the old man's thoughts would steal away into a farther nebulous world, where Yuan could not follow him and he would muse aloud, "Perhaps, Yuan, such laws as this are only keys to unlock a door to a closed garden, and we must throw the key recklessly away and go forth into that garden boldly by imagination —or call it faith, Yuan—and the garden is the garden of God—God infinite, unchangeable, in whose very being are wisdom, justice, goodness, and truth—all those ideals to which our poor human laws try to lead us."

So he mused, until Yuan, listening and comprehending nothing, one day said, "Sir, leave me at the gate. I cannot throw away the key."

To which the old man smiled a little sadly and answered, "You are just like Mary. You young people— you are like young birds—afraid to try your wings and fly out of the little world you know. Ah, until you cease to cling to reason only and begin to trust to dreams and imaginations there will come forth no great scientists from among you. No great poets—no great scientists— the same age produces both."

But Yuan out of all these words remembered most the one saying, "You are just like Mary."

It was true he was like Mary. Between these two, born ten thousand miles apart, and of two bloods never mingled, there was a likeness, and it was twofold, the likeness of youth to any youth in any age, alike in their rebellions, and the other likeness, which is that between a man and maid in spite of time or blood.

For now as the full spring drew near and the trees grew green again and in the woods near the house little flowers sprang out from under the dead winter leaves, Yuan felt in himself a new freedom of the blood. Here surely in this home there was nothing to make his flesh shrink back. Here he forgot he was an alien. He could look at these three and forget their difference, so that the blue eyes of the old pair were natural to him and Mary's eyes were lovely for their changefulness and no longer strange.

And she grew more lovely to him. Some mildness came upon her always now. She was never sharp, her voice even not incisive as it used to be. Her face grew a little fuller, her cheeks less pale, and her lips were softer and not so tightly pressed together and she moved more languidly and with some ease she had not before.

Sometimes on Yuan's coming she seemed very busy, and she came and went so that he seldom saw her. But as spring came full in this she changed, and, not knowing that they did it, each began to plan to meet every morning in the garden. There she came to him, fresh as the day was, her dark hair smooth about her ears. To Yuan she was most lovely when she was dressed in blue, so one day he said, smiling at her, "It is the blue the country people wear in my land. It suits you." And she smiled back and answered, "I am glad."

One day Yuan remembered, for he came early to take his morning meal with them, and while he waited in the garden for her he bent over a bed of small pansy seedlings to take the weeds carefully from their roots. Then she came and stood there watching him, her face strangely warm and lighted, and as he looked, she put forth her hand and took from his hair a leaf or bit of weed lodged there, and he felt her quick hand touch

his cheek as it dropped. He knew she did not touch
him purposely, for she was always careful against such
touching, so that she seemed to draw away even from an
aid given her at some roughness in the road. She did
not, as many maids will do, put forth a hand to touch a
man for any small cause. It was in truth the first time he
had ever felt her hand, except in the cool casual touch
of greeting.

But now she did not excuse herself. By her frank eyes
and by the sudden faint red in her cheeks he knew she
felt the touch and that she knew he did. They looked
at each other quickly, and turned away again and she
said tranquilly, "Shall we go in for breakfast?"

And he answered as tranquilly, "I must just wash my
hands."

So the moment passed.

Afterwards he thought a little of it and his mind flew
to bring him the memory of that other touch so long
ago, given by the maid now dead. Strangely, beside
that ardent open touch, this new light touch seemed
less than nothing and still the other burned more real.
He muttered to himself, "Doubtless she did not know
she did it. I am a fool." And he resolved to forget it all,
and to control his mind more sternly against such
thoughts, for he truly did not welcome them.

So through the months of that last spring Yuan lived
in a strange double way. Within himself he held a certain place of his own, secure against this woman. The
softness of the new season, the mildness of a moonlight
night when he and she might walk together down the
street under the budding new-leaved trees into lonely
roads leading to the country, or the stillness of a room
where sometimes they sat alone while the musical steady
rains of spring beat upon the window panes, even such
hours alone with her could not break through into that
place. And Yuan wondered at himself, not knowing how
he could be so stirred as he sometimes knew he was
and yet not want to yield.

For in some ways this white woman could stir him

and yet hold him off, and by the same things he loved
and did not love. Because he loved beauty and never
could escape it, he often saw her beautiful, her brow
and neck so white against her dark hair. And yet he
did not love such whiteness. He often saw her lighted
eyes, clear and grey underneath her dark brows, and he
could admire the mind which made them shine and
flash, and yet he did not love grey eyes. So, too, with
her hands, quick, vivid, speaking, moving hands, beautiful and angular in strength. But he did not love such
hands somehow.

Yet was he drawn to her again and yet again by some
power in her, so that over and over in that busy spring
he would pause in the midst of his work in fields or in
his room or in the hall of books, to find her suddenly
in his mind. He came to ask himself at such times, "Shall
I miss her when I go away? Am I bound somehow to
this country through this woman?" He dallied with the
thought that he might stay on and study more, and yet
he could ask himself plainly, "Why do I really stay? If
in truth for this woman, to what end, seeing I do not
want to wed one of her race?" Yet he felt a pang when
he thought further, "No, I will go home." Then he
thought further that perhaps he would never see her
again, once he was gone, for how could he return again?
When he thought he might never see her again, then it
seemed he must indeed put off his going.

So might the questioning have dragged itself into an
answer and he stayed on, except there came across the
sea news which was like his country's voice demanding
him.

Now these years while Yuan had been away he had
scarcely known how his country did. He knew that there
were little wars, but to these he paid no heed, for there
had always been little wars.

In these six years Wang the Tiger wrote him of one
or two such petty wars he undertook; one against a little new bandit chieftain, and a second time against a
lord of war who passed unbidden through his regions.

But Yuan passed quickly over such news, partly because he never loved wars, and partly because such things seemed not real at all to him, living in this peaceful foreign country, so that when some fellow pupil called out blithely, "Say, Wang, what's this new war you're getting up in China? I see it in the papers. Some Chang or Tang or Wang—" And Yuan, ashamed, would answer quickly, "It is nothing—no more than any robbery anywhere."

Sometimes his lady mother, who wrote him faithfully once a season, said in her letters, "The revolution grows apace, but I do not know how. Now that Meng is gone we have no revolutionists in our family. I only hear that at last from the south the new revolution breaks. But Meng cannot yet come home. He is there among them, for he has written so, but he does not yet come home, even if he would, for the rulers here are afraid and still very bitter in their hunting of those like him."

But Yuan did not lay aside wholly the thought of his own country and as he could he followed all the news he could find of that revolution, and he seized eagerly on every little printed line which told of some change, such as, "The old calendar of the moon is changed to the new western calendar," or he read, "It is forbidden any more to bind the feet of women," or he read, "The new laws will not let a man have more wives than one," and many such things he read in those days. Every change Yuan read with joy and believed, and through all he could see his whole country changing, so that he thought to himself and wrote to Sheng so also, "When we go back next summer we will not know our land. It seems not possible that so soon, in six short years, so great a change has been brought about."

To which Sheng wrote back after many days. "Do you go home this summer? But I am not ready. I have a year or two yet I want to live here, if my father will send the money for it."

At these words Yuan could not but remember with great discomfort that woman who put Sheng's little poems to such languid heavy music, and then he would not think of her. But he wished Sheng would hasten and go home. It was true he had not yet won his degree, although he had spent more time at it than he should, and then troubled, Yuan thought how Sheng never spoke of the new things in their own country. But he excused Sheng quickly, because indeed it was not easy in this rich peaceful land to think of revolutions and of battles for a cause, and Yuan did too forget these things often in his own days of peace.

And yet, as he knew afterwards, the revolution was even then coming to its height. Surely in its old way, up from the south, while Yuan spent his days upon his books, while he questioned himself what he felt for this white woman whom he loved and did not love, the grey army of the revolution, in which Meng was, crossed through the heart of his country to the great river. There it battled, but Yuan, ten thousand miles away, lived in peace.

In such great peace he might thus have lived forever. For suddenly one day the warmth between him and the woman deepened. So long they had stood where they were, a little more than friends, a little less than lovers, that Yuan had come to take it as a thing accepted that every evening for a while they walked and talked together after the old pair slept. Before these two they showed nothing. And Mary would have said very honestly to any question, "But there is nothing to tell. What is there between us except friendship?" And it was true there had never been a speech between them which others could not hear and wonder nothing at it.

Yet every night these two felt the day not ended unless they had been alone a little while together, even though each talked idly only of the day's happenings. But in this little hour they grew more to know each other's minds and hearts than by days of other hours.

One night in that spring, they walked thus together up and down between the rose trees planted by a certain winding path. At the end of this path there was a clump of trees, six elm trees once planted in a circle and now grown large and old and full of shadows.

Within these shadows the old man had placed a wooden seat, because he loved to come and sit there for meditation. On this night the shadows were very black, because it was a night of clear moon and all the garden was full of light except where the six elms grew. Once did the two pause within the circle of shadow and the woman said half carelessly, "See how dark these shadows are— we seem lost once we step within them."

In silence they stood and Yuan saw with a strange, uneasy pleasure how clear the moonlight was and he said, "The moonlight is so bright one can almost see the color of the new leaves."

"Or almost feel the shadow cold and the moonlight warm," said Mary, stepping out again into the light.

Yet again they paused when they had walked to and fro, and this time Yuan paused first and he said, "Are you cold, Mary?" For now he spoke her name easily.

She answered, "No—" half stammering, and then, without knowing how it came about, they stood uncertain in the shadow and then quickly she moved to him, touched his hands, and Yuan felt this woman in his arms, and his arms about her, too, his cheek against her hair. And he felt her trembling and knew he was trembling and then as one they sank upon the bench, and she lifted up her head and looked at him and put up her two hands and held his head, her hands upon his cheeks, and she whispered, "Kiss me!"

Then Yuan, who had seen such things pictured in amusement houses but never had he done it, felt his head drawn down and her lips hot against his lips, and she was pressed and centered on his lips.

In that instant he drew back. Why he must draw back he could not tell, for there was that in him, too, which wanted to press on and on, deeper and long. But stronger than that desire was a distaste he could not understand, except it was the distaste of flesh for flesh that was not its own kind. He drew back, and stood up quickly, hot and cold and shamed and confused together. But the woman sat on, amazed. Even in the shadow he could see her white face upturned to him, amazed, questioning him why he drew back. But for his very life he could say nothing, nothing! He only knew he must draw back. At last he said half above his breath, and not in his usual voice, "It is cold—you must go in to the house— I must go back."

Still she did not move, and then after a little time she said, "You go if you must. I want to stay here awhile—"

And he, feeling himself somehow lacking in what he should have been, yet knowing he had done only what he must do, said in attempted courtesy, "You must come in. You will be chilled."

She answered deliberately without moving at all, "I am chilled already. What does it matter?"

And Yuan, hearing how cold and dead her voice, turned quickly and left her there and went away.

But hour after hour he could not sleep. He thought of her only, and wondered if she still sat there in those shadows alone and he was troubled for her and yet he knew he had done only what he must. Like any child he muttered to excuse himself, "I did not like it. I truly did not like it."

How it might have been between them after that Yuan did not know. For as though she knew his plight his country now called him home.

The next morning he awoke, knowing he must go to see Mary, and yet he delayed, half fearful, for now in the morning still there were these truths clear to him, that he had somehow failed her, though he knew he could have done no other thing than what he did.

But when at last he went to the house he found the three of them in great gravity and consternation over what they saw in a paper. The old man asked anxiously as Yuan came in with him, "Yuan, can this be true?"

Yuan looked with them at the paper and there in great letters were the words that the new revolutionists had fallen upon the white men and women in a certain city in his land and had driven them from their homes and even killed some among them, a priest or two, an old teacher and a physician, and some others. Yuan's heart stopped, and he cried out, "There is a mistake here—"

And the old lady murmured, for she had sat waiting for his word, "Oh, Yuan, I *knew* it must be wrong!"

But Mary said nothing. Though Yuan did not look at her when he came in, and not now, either, yet he saw her sitting there, silent, her chin resting on her crossed hands, looking at him. But he would not look at her fully. He read quickly down the page, crying over and over, "It is not true—it cannot be true—such a thing would never happen in my country! Or if it did there is some dreadful cause—"

His eye searched for that cause. Then Mary spoke. She said, and now he knew her well enough to perceive her heart from the very way she spoke, her words clipped and clear and seemingly careless, her voice a little hard and casual, "I looked for the cause, too, Yuan. But there is none—it seems they were all quite innocent and friendly people, surprised in their homes and with their children—"

At this Yuan looked at her, and she looked at him, her eyes as clear and grey and cold as ice. And they accused him and he cried out to her silently, "I only did what I could not help!" But they steadily accused him.

Then Yuan, trying to be his usual self, sat down and talking more than was his wont, said eagerly, "I shall call up my cousin Sheng—he will know, being in that large city, what the truth is. I know my people—they could not do a thing like this—we are a civilized race—not savage—we love peace—we hate bloodshed. There is a mistake here, I know."

And the old lady repeated fervently, "I know there is a mistake, Yuan. I know God could not let such a thing happen to our good missionaries."

But suddenly Yuan felt his breath stopped by this simple speech, and he was about to cry out, "If they were those priests—" and then his eyes fell on Mary again, and he was silent. For now she was looking at him still and it was with a great speechless sadness, and he could not say a word. His heart longed for forgiveness from her. Yet his very heart drew back, lest in seeking forgiveness it yield to that to which his flesh did not wish to yield.

He said no more, and none spoke except the old man, who, when he was finished, said to Yuan as he rose, "Will you tell me, Yuan, what news you learn?" Then Yuan rose, too, suddenly not wanting to be left alone with Mary, lest the lady leave them so, and he went away very heavy of heart, afraid because he did not want the news to be true. He could not bear to be put to such shame, and this the more because he felt the woman judged him secretly for his withdrawal and counted it for weakness in him. Therefore the more must he show his people blameless of this thing.

Never again were these two near to each other. For as day passed into day, Yuan was swept into this passion to show his country clear, and he came to feel that if he could do it, he would be justified himself. In all the busy ending weeks of that year of school he so busied himself. Step by step he must prove it not his country's fault. It was true, Sheng said, his voice coming calm and like itself across the wires that first day, it was true the thing was done. And Yuan cried back impatiently, "But why—but why?" And Sheng's voice came back so careless Yuan could almost see him shrug himself, "Who knows? A mob—communists—some fanatic cause—who can know the truth?"

But Yuan was in an agony. "I will not believe it—there was a cause—some aggression—*something!*"

And Sheng said quietly, "We can never know the truth—" and changing he asked, "When shall we meet again, Yuan? I have not seen you in too long—when do you go home?"

But Yuan was able only to say "Soon!" He knew that he must go home; if he could not clear his country, then he must go home as quickly as he could finish what remained to be done.

Thereafter he went no more into the garden, nor were there hours alone with Mary any more. They were

A HOUSE DIVIDED

friendly outwardly, but there was nothing to be said between them, and Yuan planned so he need not meet her. For more and more as he could not prove his country blameless, he turned somehow against these very friends of his.

The old pair perceived this and though they were still gentle with him always, yet they drew themselves a little apart, too, not blaming him at all, and sensitive to his distress, though not understanding it.

But Yuan felt they blamed him. Upon his shoulders he carried the weight of all his country did. Now as he daily read the papers and read of things that any army does in victory and marching through a vanquished country, he felt himself in agony. Sometimes he wondered about his father, for the army moved steadily towards the northern plains, everywhere victorious.

But his father seemed very far away. Near, too near, were these gentle silent aliens, to whose home he must sometimes still go, for they would have it so, who never spoke one word of what the papers said, sparing him all mention of what they knew must torture him with shame. And yet in spite of all their silence, they accused. Their very silence accused. The woman's gravity and coolness, the prayers of the old two, for sometimes before a meal to which they pressed him the old man would say low and troubled words and he would add to his thanks such words as these, "Save them, O God, who are Thy servants in a distant land, who live in such peril of their lives." And the lady would add to it most earnestly her soft "Amen."

Yuan could not bear this prayer, nor this amen, and he could bear it less because even Mary, who had warned him against the faith of the old pair, now bowed her head in new respect of them, not, he knew, that she believed more than she did, but only because she felt the dangers against which they prayed. So was she leagued with them against him, or so he thought.

Again Yuan was alone, and alone he worked to the year's finish and to the hour when with the others he stood for his degree. Alone among them all, the single one of his own people, he received the symbol of his scholarship. Alone he heard his name mentioned for high honors. There were a few who came to give him congratulations, but Yuan told himself he did not care if they came or not.

Alone he packed his books and clothes. At the last it came into his mind that the old pair were even glad to see him go, although their kindness did not change, and then Yuan in his pride thought to himself, "I wonder if they have been uneasy lest I wed their daughter, and so are glad to see me go!"

He smiled bitterly and believed this so. And then thinking of her he thought to himself again, "But I have this to thank her for—she saved me from turning a Christian. Yes, once she saved me—but once, too, I saved myself!"

III

EVEN as Yuan had loved and hated his father in his childhood, so now he left that foreign country loving and hating it. He could not but love it, however unwillingly, as anyone must love a thing beautiful and young and strong. He loved beauty and so he must love the beauty of trees upon mountains, and of meadows free from graves of the dead and beasts upon the land fed and healthy and content and cities clean of human refuse. Then he did not love these very things because if they were beautiful he was not sure if there could be beauty in the bare hills of his own country and he felt it wrong that the dead should lie in the good land of the living so that their graves were in the midst of fields, and he remembered such things there. When he looked upon the rich countryside passing him in the train, he thought, "If this were mine I would love it very well. But it is not mine." He could not, somehow, love wholly a beauty or a good that was not his. He could not like very greatly the people even who possessed this good which was not his.

When once more he went upon the ship and turned to his own country again, he spent much time in questioning himself what gain he had from these six years away. He had gained, doubtless, in learning. His brain was stuffed with useful learning, and he had a small trunk full of notebooks and books of other sorts, and there was a long dissertation he had made himself upon a theme of the inheritance of certain strains of wheat. He had, moreover, little bags of seed wheat, which he had chosen carefully from other seeds he had planted himself in experiment, and he planned to put this seed into his own ground, and raise more and then more until there was enough to give to others, and so might all harvests be improved. Such things he knew he had.

He had more than this. He had some certainties. He knew that when he wed, the woman must be of his own flesh and kind. He was not like Sheng. For him there was now no magic in white flesh and pale eyes and tangled hair. Wherever his mate was she was like him, her eyes black as his, her hair smooth and straight and black, her skin the hue of his. He must have his own.

For, ever after that night beneath the elms, the white woman whom in some ways he knew very well had become to him completely strange. She was not changed, she maintained herself day after day as she had always been, steady, courteous always, quick to understand what he said or felt, but a stranger. Their two minds might know each other, but their minds were housed in two different habitations. Only for one moment had she striven to draw near to him again. She went with him, and the old pair also, to see him at his train and when he put forth his hand to say farewell, she held it for an instant strongly, and her grey eyes warmed and darkened and she cried in a low voice, "Shall we not even write to each other?"

Then Yuan, never able to give pain for any cause, and confused by the pain in her darkening eyes, said, stammering, "Yes—of course—why should we not?"

But she, searching his face, dropped his hand and her look changed, and she said no more, not even when the old mother broke in quietly, "But of course Yuan will write to us."

Then again Yuan promised that he would write and tell them everything. But he knew, and as the train drew away and he must look at Mary's face, he saw that she knew also that he would never write and tell them anything. He was going home, and they were aliens, and he could tell them nothing. As though he cast aside a garment no longer to be used, he cast aside these whole six years of his life except the knowledge in his brain and his box of books. . . . Yet now upon the ship when he thought of the years, there was the unwilling love in his heart, because this foreign country had so much he would have, and because he could not hate these three, since they were truly good; but the love was unwilling because now he was turned homeward he began to remember certain things he had forgotten. He remembered his father, and he remembered small crowded streets, not clean or beautiful, and he remembered the three days he had spent once in prison.

But against these things he argued thus, that in these six years the revolution had come about and doubtless all was changed. Was not all changed? For when he left Meng had been a fugitive, and now Sheng told him Meng was a captain in the army of the revolution and free to go anywhere and everywhere. There was more changed, too, for on this ship Yuan was not the only one of his kind. There were a score or so of young men and women who returned to their own land as he did, and they all talked much together and ate together at the same tables, and they talked of all that was come about, and Yuan heard how old narrow streets were torn away and great streets, as wide as any in the world, were driven through the old cities, and how there were motor vehicles far in the country along country roads, and farmers rode in them who used always to plod afoot, or at best sit across an ass's back, and he heard how many cannon and how many bombing planes and how many weaponed soldiers the new revolution had, and they told how men and women were equal in these days, and how it was against the new law to sell or to smoke opium, and how all such old evils were now gone.

They told so many things Yuan had not heard that he began to wonder why he ever had those old memories, and he grew more than ever eager to be in his new country. He was glad of his youth, in these days, and among these of his own kind he said one day as they sat at a table together and his heart leaped within him when he spoke, "How great a thing it is that we are born now when we may be free and do as we will with our own lives!"

And they all looked at each other, these young eager men and women, and they smiled in exultation, and one girl thrust out her pretty foot and said, "Look at me! If

I had been born in my mother's time, do you think I could have walked on two good sound feet like these?" and they all laughed as children do over some little joke of their own. But the girls' laughter had a deeper meaning in it than only merriment, and one said, "It is the first time in our people's history that we are all free— the first time since Confucius!"

And then a merry youth cried out, "Down with Confucius!" And they all cried, "Yes, down with Confucius!" and they said, "Let's put him down and keep him down with all those old things which we hate—him and his filial piety!"

Then at other times they talked more gravely and at these times they grew anxious to think and plan what they could do for country's sake, for there was not one of these companions of Yuan's who was not filled with yearning so to serve his country. In every sentence they made, the words "country" and "love of country" could be heard, and they seriously weighed their faults and their abilities and compared them to those of other men. They said, "Those men of the west excel us in inventiveness, and in the energy in their bodies, and in their dauntlessness to go ahead in what they do." And another said, "How do we excel?" and they looked at each other and took thought, and they said, "We excel in patience and in understanding and in long endurance."

At this the girl who had thrust out her pretty foot cried impatiently, "It is our weakness that we do endure so long! For myself, I am determined to endure nothing—nothing at all I do not like, and I shall try to teach all my countrywomen not to endure anything. I never saw any woman in the foreign country endure anything she did not like and that is how they have come as far as they have!"

And one who was a wag cried out, "Yes, it is the men who endure there, and now it seems we must learn it, brothers!" and then they all laughed together, as the young will laugh easily, but the wag looked secretly with admiration at the bold pretty impatient girl, who must have her own way.

So did all these young men and women and Yuan among them pass the days upon the ship in the highest good humor and most eager expectation of their homecoming. They paid no heed to any except themselves, for they all were filled with the strength of their sureness of their own youth and sufficient to themselves in their knowledge and zest to be going home again, confident each one that he was significant and marked for some special value and service to his times. Yet for all their pleasure in themselves, Yuan could not but see how the very words they used were foreign words, and how even when they spoke their own tongues they must add words of a foreign sort to supply some idea they had for which there was no suited word in their own tongue, and the girls were half foreign in their dress, and the men all foreign, so that if one saw another in the back, it could not be said what his race was. And every night they danced, man and maid together, in the way foreigners did, and even sometimes as shamelessly, cheek pressed to cheek, and hand put into hand. Only Yuan did not dance. In such small ways he held himself apart even from these his own people when they did that which was foreign to him. He said to himself, forgetting he used to do it, "It is a foreign thing, this dancing." But partly he drew back because now he did not want to take one of these new women in his arms. He was afraid of them because they put out their hands so easily to touch a man, and Yuan was always one who feared a clinging touch.

So those days passed, and Yuan wondered more and more what his country would seem to him after all these years. On the day when he was to reach it, he went alone to the front of the ship and there watched the coming of the land. The land put forth its shadow into the ocean long before it could be seen. Into the clear cold green of ocean water Yuan looked down and saw the yellow line of clay which was the earth the river tore away in its passing through thousands of miles of land, and carried turbulently down to throw into the sea. There the line was as clearly as though a hand had drawn it, so that every wave was pushed back and held away. Yuan one moment saw himself upon the ocean, and the next moment, as though the ship had leaped a barrier he looked down into swirling yellow waves and knew himself at home.

When later he went to bathe himself, for the day was in the midst of summer and of great heat, the water rushed out yellow, and Yuan thought first, "Shall I bathe myself in it?" For at first it seemed to him not clean. Then he said, "Why should I not bathe myself in it? It is dark with the good earth of my fathers," and he did bathe himself and felt himself cooled and cleansed.

Then the ship crept into the river's mouth, and there the land was on either side, stolid and yellow and low and not beautiful, and on it were the small low houses of the same color, and there was no making it beautiful, as though that land did not care if men found it beautiful or not. There it was as it always was, low yellow banks the rivers had laid to push the sea back and claim more for their own.

Even Yuan must see it was not beautiful. He stood upon the decks along the many others of every race and kind upon the ship, and they all stood staring at this new country, and Yuan heard some cry, "It's not beautiful, is it?" "It is not as pretty as the mountains of other countries." But he would not answer anything. He was proud and thought to himself, "My country hides her beauty. She is like a virtuous woman who puts on sober clothes before strangers at the gates, and only within the walls of her own home does she wear colors and put rings on her hands and jewels in her ears."

For the first time in many years this thought shaped itself into a small poem, and he felt the impulse to write four lines down, and he drew out a little book he kept in his pocket, and instantly the verse was there, and this flying moment added its point of brightness to the exultation of this day.

Then suddenly out of the flat grave country towers arose, and these towers Yuan had not seen when he went away, awaking as he had within a ship's cabin at night with Sheng. Now he gazed on them as strangely as all these other travellers did, and they rose glittering in the hot sunshine, tall out of the flatness, and Yuan heard a white man say, "I did not dream it was such a big modern city," and he marked with secret pride the respect in the man's voice, though he said nothing and he did not let his face move, but only leaned as he was upon the rail and looked steadfastly at his country.

But even as this pride rose in him, the ship was docked and instantly a horde of common men leaped on the ship, fellows from the wharf and docks who pressed about to find a little work to do, a bag or box to hoist upon their backs, or some such lowly task. And in the harbor small dingy boats crept out into the hot summer sunshine, and in these boats beggars whined and held up baskets on long poles, and of these beggars many were diseased. Among these common fellows, too, many were half naked for the heat, and in their eagerness for work they pressed rudely among the delicately gowned white women, their bodies grimed and sweating.

Then Yuan saw those white women draw back, some afraid of the men and all afraid of dirt and sweat and commonness, and Yuan felt a shame in his heart, for these beggars and these common fellows were his own people. And here was the strangest thing, that while he hated these white shrinking women very much, suddenly he hated the beggars and the naked common fellows, too, and he cried passionately within himself, "The rulers ought not to allow these people to come out and show themselves like this before everyone. It is not right that all the world should see them first, and some never see any but these—"

He resolved he must set himself to right this wrong somehow, for he could not bear it; small as it might seem to some, it was not small to him.

Then suddenly he was soothed. For now he stepped from the ship, and he saw his mother there to greet him, and with her Ai-lan. There among many they stood, but in one look of his eyes, Yuan saw with a great flush of pleasure that there was none among all the many who

could compare to Ai-lan. Even as he gave greeting to his
mother, and felt the joy of her steadfast hand against his,
and the great welcome in her eyes and smile, he could
not but see how the eyes of all from that ship turned
to Ai-lan, and he was glad they had her to see, who was
his own race and blood. She could wipe out the sight
of all the poor and common men.

For Ai-lan was beautiful. When Yuan had seen her last
he was still a boy and he had not valued all her prettiness. Now as they lingered on the docks he saw Ai-lan
truly could have stood among the beauties of the world
and lost nothing.

It suited her well that she had lost the kitten-like
coquettishness of her young girlhood. Now, although
her eyes were bright and quick, her voice as light and
flexible as ever, she had learned somehow a softer, finished dignity, from out of which only sometimes her
laughter sparkled forth. About her warm lovely face her
short hair was black and smoothly shaped. She did not
curl it as some do, but kept it straight and smooth as
ebony and cut across her forehead. On this day she wore
a long straight silver gown of newest fashion, high-
collared, but the sleeves short to her pretty elbows, and it
was shaped to her body, so that without a breaking line,
there flowed the smooth perfection of shoulder, waist,
thigh, ankle.

So Yuan saw her proudly, comforted for much by her
perfection. There were such women as this in his own
land!

A little behind his lady mother there stood a tall girl,
no more a child, but still not wholly maiden. She was
not beautiful as Ai-lan was but she had a clear and noble
gaze, and if Ai-lan had not been by, she would have
seemed fair enough, for though she was tall, she moved
gracefully and well, and her face was pale and oval, and
the black eyes wide and set truly beneath full straight
brows. Now no one thought in all the talk and welcom-
ing laughter to say anything to Yuan of who she was.
But even as he was about to ask the question, it came to
him that she was the child Mei-ling who had cried out

at the prison gate that day because she had seen him first. He bowed to her in silence, and she to him in the same way, though Yuan took time to know her face was not one easily forgotten.

There was one other who was the story teller whom Yuan remembered even still, the one surnamed Wu, against whom the lady had asked Yuan to guard his sister. Now he stood confidently among these others, very debonair in western garb, a small moustache beneath his nostrils, his hair as waxed and black as though it had been polished so, and in his whole look a sort of sureness that he was where he had a right to be. This Yuan soon understood, for after the first cries of greeting and the bows were over, the lady took this young man's hand delicately and took Yuan's, and she said, "Yuan, here is the man who is to wed our Ai-lan. We have put off the wedding day until you came, for Ai-lan chose it so."

Now Yuan, remembering very well how the lady felt against this man, wondered that she never wrote of this, and yet now he could say nothing here except kind things, and so he took the other's smooth hand and shook it in the new fashion and he smiled and said, "I am glad I can be at my sister's wedding—I am very fortunate."

And the other laughed easily and a little indolently, and he let his eyelids droop in a way he had and he looked at Yuan and drawled out in English of a modish certain sort, "It is I who am fortunate, I am sure!" and across his hair he passed his other hand, whose strange loveliness Yuan remembered, now he saw it again.

Yuan, not used to this speech, dropped the hand he held, and turned away uncertainly, and then he remembered this man had been already wed to some other woman and he wondered yet more and resolved to ask his mother secretly how all this came about, since now nothing could be said. Yet when a few minutes later they all walked out to the street to where the cars awaited them, Yuan could not but see how very fairly mated these two were, and each like their race, and yet somehow they were not, too. It was almost as though some old sturdy rooted tree had put forth exquisite blossoms from its gnarled and knotted trunk.

Then the lady took Yuan's hand again and said, "We must go home because the sun is so hot here shining up from the water," and he let himself be led into the streets, and there were motors waiting for them. His lady mother had her own to which she led Yuan, still clinging to his hand, and Mei-ling walked on her other side.

But Ai-lan stepped into a small scarlet motor shaped for two, and with her was her lover. In that glowing vehicle these two might have been god and goddess for their beauty, for the top of it was thrown back, and the sun fell full upon their black and shining hair, upon the faultless smoothness of their golden skins, and the brightness of the scarlet did not daunt their beauty but only showed more clearly the flawless perfect shape and grace in which their bodies grew.

And Yuan could not but admire again such beauty and feel the pride of race rush to his heart. Why, never once in that foreign land had he seen clear beauty like to this! He needed not to be afraid to come home.

Then even as he gazed a beggar writhed himself out of the gaping multitude who stood to see these rich folk pass, and he rushed to the lordly, scarlet car and laid his hands upon the edge of the door and clung there whining the old cry of his kind, "A little silver, sir, a little silver!"

At this the young lord within shouted very harshly, "Remove your filthy hands!" But the beggar continued to whine yet more earnestly and at last when he would cling so, the young man reached down and slipped from his foot his shoe, his western shoe, hard and leathern, and with its heel he struck down upon the beggar's clutching fingers and he struck with all his force so that the beggar murmured, "Oh, my mother!" and fell back into the crowd and put his wounded hands to his mouth.

Then waving his beautiful pale hand to Yuan the young man drove off his car in a roar of noise, and the scarlet thing leaped through the sunshine.

In the first days in his own country Yuan let his own heart stay in abeyance until he could see in proportion what was about him. At first he thought with a relief, "It is not so different here—after all, my country is like all other countries of this day, and why was I afraid?"

And indeed so it seemed to him, and Yuan, who had secretly feared to find that houses and streets and people might seem poor and mean to him, was pleased he did not find them so. This was the more true because in these years while he had been away the lady removed herself from the small house where she used to live into a large good house built in a foreign fashion. On the first day when Yuan came with her into it, she said, "I did it for Ai-lan. She felt the other house too small and poor to have her friends come to it. And I have done, moreover, what I said I would. I have taken Mei-ling to live with me. . . . Yuan, she might be my own child. Did I tell you she will be a physician as my father was? I have taught her all he taught me, and now she goes to a foreign school of medicine. She has two more years to learn, and then she must work in their hospital for more years. I say to her do not forget that for internal humors it is we who know best our own frames. Nevertheless, it cannot be denied that for cutting and sewing up again the foreign physicians are best. Mei-ling will know both. And she helps me besides with my girl babes whom I still find unwanted in the streets—and many of them these days, Yuan, after the revolution, when men and maids have learned to be so free!"

Yuan said, wondering, "But I thought Mei-ling only a child—I remember her only a child—"

"She is twenty years old," the lady answered quietly, "and very far past childhood. In mind she is much older than that, and older than Ai-lan, who is three years more than twenty——a very brave quiet maid Mei-ling is. I went one day and saw her help the doctor who cut a great thing from a woman's neck, and her hands were as steady as a man's to do it, and the doctor praised her because she did not tremble and was not frightened by the gush of blood. Nothing frightens her—a very brave quiet maid.

Yet she and Ai-lan like each other, though she will not
follow Ai-lan to her pleasures, and Ai-lan would not see
the things that Mei-ling does."

By now they sat in the lady's sitting room alone, for
Mei-ling had gone away at once, and no one was near
except the servant who brought tea and comfits in and
out, and Yuan asked curiously, "I thought this Wu was
bound to another wife, my mother—"

At this the lady sighed and answered, "I knew you
would wonder. I have been through such a trouble with
Ai-lan! Yuan, she would have him and he would have
her, and there was nothing to be said,—no way to persuade her to anything. That was the reason why I took
this greater house, because I thought if they must meet
it might be here—since meet they would, and all that I
could do was to fend off more until he could divorce his
old wife and be free. . . . And it was true she was an old-
fashioned woman, Yuan, one his parents had chosen for
him and wed to him when he was sixteen. Ai, I do not
know whom to pity most, the man or that poor soul!
I seem to feel in me the sorrows of them both. I was
wed like that, too, and not loved, and so I felt myself
her. And yet I promised myself I would let my daughter wed where she would because I know what it is to
be not loved, and so it is that I feel the troubles of them
both. But it is arranged now, Yuan, in the way such
things are arranged—too easily, I fear, nowadays. He is
free, and she, poor woman, returns to the inland city
of her birth. I went to see her at the last, for she lived
here with him—though not really, she said, with him.
There she was with her two maids putting her garments in the red leathern boxes she had brought as part
of her marriage portion. And all she said to me was, 'I
knew this end must come—I knew this end must come,'
—a woman not beautiful and older by five years than he,
speaking no foreign tongue, as all must speak these days,
and even with her feet once bound, though she strove
to hide this in big foreign shoes. For her indeed it is
the end—what is left to her now? I did not ask. I must
think most of Ai-lan now. We can do nothing in these

days, we old ones, except let the new sweep us on as
it will. . . . Who can do anything? The country is upset,
and anyhow, and there is nothing left to guide us—no
rule, no punishment."

Yuan only smiled a little when she ended thus. She
sat, old and quiet and always a little sad, her hair white,
and she said the things the old always say.

For in himself he felt only courage and hopefulness.
In the day he had been back, in the few hours even,
this city somehow gave him courage. It was so busy and
so rich. Everywhere even in his quick passing he saw
great new shops were raised up, shops to sell machines,
and shops to sell goods of every kind from all parts of
the world. No longer were there many humble streets
lined with the low-roofed simple shops of homely
merchandise. The city was a center of the world, and
new buildings heaped on buildings, higher and higher.
In the six years he had been gone a score of mighty
buildings had flung themselves up against the sky.

That first night before he slept he stood at the window of his room and looked out across the city, and he
thought, "It looks almost like the city where Sheng is
abroad." There about him were blazing lights and noise
of motors and the deep hum of a million humans and
all the rush and throb of restless growing pushing life.
This was his country. The letters hung in flame against
the moonless clouds were letters of his own tongue,
proclaiming goods his own countrymen were making.
The city was his own, and great as any in the world. He
thought for a moment of that woman pushed aside to
make way for Ai-lan, but he hardened himself as he
thought, and in his heart he said, "So must all be pushed
aside who cannot stand in this new day. It is right. Ai-
lan and the man are right. The new cannot be denied."

And in a sort of hard clear joy he laid himself to sleep.

Now Yuan went everywhere these few first days in
this lift of joy through this great city. It seemed to him
his fortune was good beyond his dreams, for he left
this country from a prison, and now he was truly home

again, and it seemed to him that all the prison gates
were opened, not only his own prison, but all the bond-
ages. It was an evil dream forgotten that his father had
ever said he must wed against his will, and it was an
evil dream that youths and maidens had once been
seized and shot for seeking freedom. This freedom for
which they died, why, now it was achieved for all! Upon
the streets of the city he saw the young come and go,
their looks free and bold and ready to do what they
would, men and women, too, and there was no bondage
anywhere. And in a day or two a letter came from
Meng which said, "I would have come to meet you, but
I am tied here at the new capital. We make the old city
new, my cousin, and we tear down the old houses and
we have put up a great new road which sweeps through
the city like a cleansing wind, and we shall build more
streets everywhere, and we have planned to tear down
old unwanted temples and put schools in them, for the
people have no need of temples any more in these new
days. We teach them science instead. . . . As for me, I
am a captain in the army, and near to my general, who
knew you once, Yuan, in that school of war. He says,
'Tell Yuan there is a place here for him to do his work.'
And so there is, my cousin, for he has spoken to a man
above him very high, and that one has spoken in a place
of influence, and in the college here there is a place
where you may teach what you like, and you can live
here and help us to build this city."

Then Yuan, reading these bold swelling words, thought
to himself with exultation, "This is from Meng, who was
in hiding—and see what he is come to!" It was a warmth
in Yuan that already his country had a place for him. He
turned it over in his mind a time or two. . . . Did he
indeed wish to teach young men and women? It might
be the quickest way to serve his people. He put the
thought into his mind to wait a day or two or more, until his duty was fulfilled.

For first he must go and see his uncle and his household, and then there was Ai-lan's wedding three days
off, and then he must go to see his father. Yuan found

two letters from his father waiting at the coast for him, and when he saw the square trembling letters, scrawled upon a page or two, big and uncertain as old men write, he was touched with an old tenderness, and he forgot he had ever feared or hated his father, for now in this new day the Tiger seemed as futile as an old actor on a forgotten stage. Yes, he must go and see his father.

Now if the six years had made Ai-lan more beautiful and had led the child Mei-ling into womanhood, they had laid old age heavily upon Wang the Landlord and his lady. For where Yuan's lady mother seemed to hold herself at much the same place all these years, her hair only a little whiter, her wise face a little more wise and more patient and a little less round, these other two Yuan found were truly old. They lived now no more in their own house, but with their elder son, and thither Yuan went and found them, the house a western house the son had built and set into a pleasant garden.

In this garden the old man sat beneath a banana palm tree, and Yuan found him there as placid and as happy as any aged saint. For now he had given up all his seeking lustful ways, and the worst he did was to buy a picture now and then whereon was painted a pretty maid, so that he had some hundreds of these pictures, and when he felt inclined he called to a servant that they be brought to him, and he turned the pictures over one by one and gazed at them. So he sat when Yuan came, and the maidservant who stood beside him to fan off the flies turned the pictures for him as she might have turned pages for a child to see.

Yuan scarcely knew him for his uncle. For this old man had by his very lustiness fended off his age until the last moment, so that whether it was because he now sometimes smoked a little opium as the old will often do, or what it was, when his age was come at last upon him it came as suddenly as a withering blast, shriveling him and driving off his fat, so that now he sat as loosely in his skin as though it were a garment cut too largely for him. Where his fat had stood out firm and full, folds of yellow skin hung down. His very robes he had not changed, and they also hung too loose upon him, very rich in textured satins, but still his old robes cut to suit his old fullness, and now gathered round his heels and the sleeves falling over his hands and the collar hanging to show his lean wrinkled throat.

When Yuan stood before him the old man gave him vague greeting and said, "I sit here alone to look at these pictures, because my lady will have it that they are evil." And he laughed a little in his old leering way, but it was ghastly laughter somehow on his ravaged face, and when he laughed he looked at the maidservant and she laughed with false heartiness to cheer him, while she stared at Yuan. But to Yuan the old man's very voice and laughter seemed thinner than they used to be.

And after a while the old man asked again, while he still looked at his pictures, "How long is it since you went away?" and when Yuan told him he asked, "And how does my second son?" and when Yuan told him, he muttered as though it were a thing he always thought when Sheng was in his mind, "He uses too much money in that foreign country—my eldest son says Sheng uses too much money—" And he fell into a gravity until Yuan said to cheer him, "He returns next summer, he tells me," and the old man murmured, staring at another picture of a maid beneath a young bamboo, "Oh, aye, he says he does." Then he bethought himself of something and he said suddenly with great pride, "You know my son Meng is a captain?" And when Yuan smiled and said he did the old man said proudly, 'Yes, he is a very great captain now, and he has a fine large wage, and it is a good thing to have a warrior in the family somewhere in time of trouble—my son Meng, he is very high these days. He came to see me and he wore a soldier's garb such as they wear abroad, they tell me, and he had a pistol in his belt and spurs to his heels—I saw them."

Yuan held his peace, but he could not keep the smile from his face to think how in these few years Meng had turned from a fugitive against whom his father cried aloud into this captain of whom his father boasted.

All the time the two had talked the old man seemed

not at ease with Yuan and he kept beginning little courtesies such as one does to a guest and not to a nephew,
and he fumbled at his teapot on a little table there beside him, making as though to pour tea for Yuan until
Yuan stopped him, and he fumbled in his bosom for his
pipe for Yuan to smoke until at last Yuan perceived that
indeed this uncle felt him like a guest, staring at him
with troubled old eyes, and at last the old man said,
"You look like a foreigner somehow—your clothes and
how you walk and move make you look foreign to me."

Now though Yuan laughed he was not overpleased at
this, and a constraint came on him since after all he could
not answer it. And very soon, even though he had been
six years away, he knew he had nothing to say to this
old man, nor this old man to him, and so he took his
leave. . . . Once he looked back, but his uncle had forgotten him. He had settled himself in sleep, his jaws
moving a little and then dropping open and his eyes
closing. Even as Yuan looked at him he was asleep, for
a fly settled on his cheek bone while the maid stared at
Yuan's foreignness and forgot to wave her fan, and it
wandered down to his old hanging lips and the old man
did not move.

When Yuan had left him thus he went in search of his
aunt, to whom also he must pay his respects, and while
he waited he sat in the guest hall and looked about him.
Since he had returned he found himself measuring everything he saw in new ways, and always, although he
did not know it, the standard by which he measured was
what he had seen in the foreign country. He was very
well content with this room, which it seemed to him
was finer than anything he had seen anywhere. Upon the
floor was a large carpet covered with beasts and flowers
in a very rich confusion, red and yellow and blue together, and on the walls were foreign pictures of sunny
mountains and blue waters, all set in bright gold frames,
and at the windows were heavy curtains of red velvet,
and the chairs were all alike, red, very deep and soft to
sit upon, and there were little tables of fine black carven
wood set about here and there, and the very spittoons

were not a common sort, but were covered with bright
blue painted birds and gold flowers. At the farther end
of the room between the windows there were hung four
scrolls painted for the four seasons, red plum blossoms
for spring, white lilies for summer, golden chrysanthe-
mums for autumn, and the scarlet berries of heavenly
bamboo lying under snow for the winter.

To Yuan this seemed the gayest richest room he had
ever seen, full enough of things to amuse a guest for
hours, for on every table were set little carven images
and toys of ivory and silver. It was far more to see than
that distant worn brown room he had thought warm
and friendly for a while. He walked about, waiting for
the maidservant to return and tell him he might go in,
and while he waited a roar of a vehicle stopped at the
doors, and his cousin and his wife came.

Both these two looked prosperous beyond anything
Yuan had remembered. The man was in his middle years,
and gaining all his father's flesh, and he looked even
fatter than he was, since he wore the foreign dress, which
hid nothing of his shape, and above its severity, which
shaped clear his large belly, his round smooth face was
like a ripe yellow melon, for against the heat he had
shaved away even his hair. Now he came in mopping
the sweat from himself, and when he turned to give his
straw hat to a servant, Yuan saw his neck in three great
rolls of flesh beneath his shaven crown.

But his wife was exquisite. She was no longer young,
and she had had five children, but none would know it,
since after every childbirth, as the custom was with such
ladies of fashion in the city, she gave her child to some
poor woman to be nursed and she bound her breasts
and body back again into slenderness. Now Yuan saw her
slender as a virgin, and though she was forty years of
age, her face was pink and ivory, her hair smooth and
black, her whole look untouched by any care or age.
Nor did the heat touch her. She came slowly forward,
greeting Yuan prettily and gravely, and only in the quick
look of distaste which she cast at her huge sweating
husband could Yuan see the petulance she used to have.

But she was courteous to Yuan for she looked on him no longer as a raw youth from the small old home city, and only a child in the family. He was a man now who had been abroad, and he had won a foreign degree and he saw it mattered to her what he thought of her.

Then to while the time away when they were seated after courtesies, and his cousin had shouted for tea to be brought, Yuan asked, "What do you now, elder cousin? For I see your fortunes have risen."

At this the man laughed and was well pleased and he fumbled at a thick gold chain hung across his great belly, and he answered, "I am a vice president of a newly opened bank now, Yuan. There is good business these days in banks in this foreign place where wars cannot touch us, and they have opened everywhere. People used to put their silver into land. I remember our old grandfather never rested until all he had was made over into land and yet more land. But land is not so sure as it once was. There are even places where the tenants have arisen and taken land from landlords."

"Are they not stopped?" Yuan asked, astonished.

And the lady thrust in sharply, "They ought to be killed!"

But the cousin shrugged himself a little in the tightness of his foreign coat and flung up his pudgy hands and he said, "Who shall stop them? Who knows how to stop anything these days?" And when Yuan murmured, "Government?" he repeated, "Government! This new confusion of war lord and student and that we call government! What can they stop? No, each man for himself these days, and so the money pours into our banks and we are safe enough guarded by foreign soldiery and under foreign law. . . . Yes, it is a good prosperous place I hold, and I have it through the grace of friends."

"*My* friends," his lady put in quickly. "If it had not been for me and that I grew friends with a great banker's wife and through her came to know her husband and begged for you—"

"Yes, yes," the man said hastily. "I know that—" and he fell into silence and discomfort of a sort, as though there were something there he would not discuss too clearly, and as though he had paid some secret price for what he had. Then the lady asked Yuan very prettily, for there was a sort of cool polished prettiness in all she said and did now, as though she had said and done everything before a mirror first, "So, Yuan, you are home again and a man and you know everything!"

When Yuan smiled mutely to deny his knowledge, she laughed a little set laugh and put her silken kerchief to her lips and said again, "Oh, I am sure you know much you will not tell of, for you have not come out of such years knowing as little as you did when you began them!"

What Yuan would have said to this he did not know and he felt uneasy, as though his cousin's wife was false and strange, and as though she were encased about with falseness so he could not know how she really was, but at this moment a servant came in leading her old mistress, and Yuan rose to greet his aunt.

Into this rich foreign room the old lady came, leaning on her servant. She was a thin upright figure, her hair still black, but her face wrinkled into many crossing lines, though her eyes were as they were, very sharp and critical of all they saw. To her son and son's wife she paid no heed, but she let Yuan bow to her and took his greeting and sat down and called to the servant, saying, "Fetch me the spittoon!"

When the servant had so done, she coughed and spat very decently, and then she said to Yuan, "I am as sound as ever I was, thanks to the gods, except that I have this cough and the phlegm comes up in me especially in the mornings."

At this her daughter-in-law looked at her with great distaste, but her son said soothingly, "It is always so with the aged, my mother."

The lady paid no heed to him. She looked Yuan up and down and asked, "How does my second son in that outer country?" And when she heard Yuan say Sheng was well she said positively, "I shall wed him when he comes home."

Now her daughter-in-law laughed out and said uncautiously, "I do not see Sheng being wed against his will, my mother—not as the young are nowadays."

The old lady cast a look at her daughter-in-law, a look which showed she had spoken her feelings against her many times and now it was no use, so she said on to Yuan, "My third son is an official. Doubtless you have heard. Yes, Meng is now a captain over many men in the new army."

This Yuan heard again, and again he smiled secretly remembering how this lady had once cried against Meng. His cousin saw the smile and put down the bowl of tea he had been sipping loudly and he said, "It is so. My brother came in with the triumphant armies from the south, and now he holds a very good high place in the new capital and has his own soldiers under him, and we hear very brave and ruthless tales of him. He could come any day now to see us, for he is safe enough since the old rulers are swept so clean and flown to every foreign land for safety, only he is busy and cannot be spared."

But the old lady would not suffer any talk but her own. She coughed and spat again loudly and then she asked, "What position shall you take, Yuan, now that you have been abroad? You ought to win a very good high pay!"

To this Yuan answered mildly, "First, as you know, Ai-lan is to be wed three days hence and then I go to my father, and then I shall see how the way opens up before me."

"That Ai-lan!" said the old lady, suddenly, fastening on the name. "*I* would not let my daughter wed a man like that! I would put her in a nunnery first!"

"Ai-lan in a nunnery!" cried her son's wife, hearing this, and she laughed her little false and bitter laugh.

"If she were my daughter, so I would!" the old lady said firmly, staring at her daughter-in-law, and she would have said more except that she choked suddenly, and she coughed until the servant must rub her shoulders and strike her back to let her breathe again.

At last Yuan took his leave, and when he went homeward through the sunny streets, choosing to walk this fair day, he thought how good as dead this old pair were. Yes, all the old were good as dead, he thought joyously. But he was young and the times were young, and on this brilliant summer's morning it seemed to him he met none but young in this whole city—young laughing girls in light-colored robes, their pretty arms bare in the new foreign fashion, and young men with them free and laughing. In this city all today were rich and young, and Yuan felt himself one of these rich and young, and his life was good to him.

But soon none had time to think of anything these days except Ai-lan's wedding. For Ai-lan and the man were well known everywhere among the young rich of the city not only of their own race, but among those of other peoples too, and there were bidden to the marriage more than a thousand guests, and to the feast afterwards very nearly as many. Yuan had no time for any speech with Ai-lan alone, except for a little hour on the first day when he came back. Yet even then he felt he did not truly talk with her. For her old teasing laughing self was gone, and he could not penetrate into the lovely finish and assuredness that wrapped her about now. She asked him with what seemed her old frank look, "You are glad to be home, Yuan?" But when he answered he saw that her eyes, for all they looked at him, did not see him at all, but were turned inward in some thought of her own, and they were only lovely shapes of dark liquid light. So through all the hour, until Yuan was bewildered by the distance all about her and he asked uneasily, blurting out the words, "You are different—you do not seem happy—do you want to marry?"

But there the distance still was. She opened her pretty eyes very widely and made her voice very cool and silvery and laughed a small clear laugh and said, "Am I not so pretty, Yuan? I have grown old and pale and ugly!" And Yuan said hastily, "No—no—you are prettier, but—" and she said, mocking him a little as she used to

do, "What—shall I be so bold as to say I want to be
wed and must be wed to this man? Did I ever do anything I did not want to do, brother? Have I not always
been naughty and willful? At least I hear my aunt say
so, and mother is too good to say it, but I know she
thinks it—"

But Yuan, although she made her eyes mischievous
and arch in shape and twisted her pretty brows above
them, still saw her eyes were empty and he said no
more. Thereafter he spoke no more alone with her, for
each night of those three days she went forth in a new
dress and wrapped about with silks of every hue, and
even if Yuan was bidden with her as a guest, he saw her
only in the distance, a lovely, brilliant figure, strange to
him these days, engrossed in her own self and seeing
everyone as in a dream. She was silent as she had never
been before—her laughter only smiles now, her eyes
soft instead of bright, and all her body round and soft
and gentle, moving slowly and with cool grace, instead
of with her old light leaping merriment. She had cast
aside the charm of her gay youth, and had learned this
new charm of silence and of grace.

By day she slept exhausted. Yuan and the mother and
Mei-ling met and ate alone, and moved gently about
the house and all noise was shut out until nightfall when
again Ai-lan came forth to meet her love and go forth
with him to some house where they were bidden as
guests. If she rose earlier it was only that she might
have fitted to her form, by the many tailors who came
for this, the gowns of silk and satin that she wanted,
and among them was the pale peach-hued satin wedding
gown with its trailing silvery foreign veil.

Now Yuan noted how silent and how grave the mother
was through the few days before the marriage. She spoke
very little to anyone except to Mei-ling, and on her she
seemed to lean for many things. She said, "Did you
take the broth in to Ai-lan?" Or she said, "Ai-lan must
have soup to drink or that dried foreign milk she likes
when she comes in tonight. I thought her pale." Or she

said, "Ai-lan wants two pearls to hold the veil, you know. Bid a jeweller send what he has for her to see."

Her mind was full of all these many small things for Ai-lan, and Yuan knew it natural for a mother to be so and he was glad she had this young girl to help her. Once when the mother was not there and they two happened to be alone in the room and waiting for the meal to come, Yuan said to Mei-ling, not knowing what to say and feeling something must be said, "You are very helpful to my mother."

The girl turned her honest look on him and said, "She saved me in my babyhood." Yuan answered, "Yes, I know," and he was surprised because there was no shame at all in the girl's eyes, such shame as she might have had to say she was a foundling, of what parents she did not know. And then Yuan, feeling her like one of his house, because of her feeling to his mother, said, "I wish she seemed happier to see my sister wed. Most mothers are glad, I thought, if their daughters wed."

But to this Mei-ling answered nothing. She turned her head away and at that moment the servant came in with bowls of meats, and she went forward herself to set them on the table. Yuan watched her do it, and she did it very simply and not at all as though she shared a servant's task. He watched her, forgetting that he did so, and he saw how slight yet strong her lithe body was, how firm and quick were her hands, not making one useless movement, and he remembered how not once when his mother asked if a thing were done or not, had it been undone.

Thus the days drew on quickly to Ai-lan's marriage day. It was to be a very great wedding, and to the largest and most fashionable hotel in the whole city the guests were bidden to come at an hour before noon. Since Ai-lan's father was not there, and since the old uncle could not stand so long, her elder cousin took his place, and beside her was her mother, who never left her at all.

This marriage was according to a new fashion, and

very different from the simple way in which her grandfather Wang Lung had taken his wives, and very different too from the old formal weddings of his sons in ways set and appointed by the forefathers. In these days the city people wed their sons and daughters in many ways, in some more old and in some more new, but be sure Ai-lan and her lover must have the very newest. Therefore there was much music from foreign instruments hired for the day and there were flowers set everywhere, and these alone cost many hundreds of silver pieces. The guests came in all the various garb of their races, for Ai-lan and her lover counted such people among their friends. These all gathered in a vast hall of the hotel. Outside, the streets were choked with their vehicles and with the idle and the poor who pressed to see what they could, and to try what they could do to gain something from the day, to beg or to slip their hands unseen into pockets of the throng and take what they found there, although guards had been hired to hold them back.

Through this great throng Yuan and the mother and Ai-lan rode, the driver incessantly sounding his horn lest some be crushed, and when the guards saw their vehicle and the bride within, they darted forward shouting out, "Make way—make way!"

Through all this din Ai-lan rode proudly, silent now, her head bent a little beneath the long veil held to her head by the two pearls and by a circle of small fragrant orange flowers. She held between her hands a great cluster of white lilies and small white roses, very fragrant.

Never had there been so beautiful a creature. Even Yuan was awed by her beauty. A little cool set smile hung on her lips, though she would not let it out, and her eyes glittered black and white beneath her lowered lids, for well she knew her own beauty, and there was not one whit of it she did not know and had not fostered to its utmost height. The very crowd fell silent before her, and when she stepped out, its thousand eyes fastened on her hungrily and drank in all her beauty, at first silently and then with restless murmurings,—"Ah, see her!" "Ah, how fair, how fair!" "Ah, never such a bride was seen!" And be sure Ai-lan heard it all, but she made as if she did not.

So, too, when she came into the great hall, when the music set the moment, did all the crowded guests turn their heads and that same wondering silence came upon them. Yuan, who had gone first and stood with the man who was to wed her, saw her coming slowly between the guests, two little white-clad children before her scattering roses for her to tread upon, and maidens with her, too, clad in silks of many hues, and he could not but share the wonder at her beauty. Yet, even so, even at that moment, although he did not know it until afterwards, he saw Mei-ling very clearly, for she was with Ai-lan as attendant.

Yes, after all the wedding was over, and the contract read between the two, and when they had bowed to those who stood for the two families, and bowed to the guests and all to whom such courtesy was due, when all was over, the mighty feast and the merry-making and the wedded pair were gone to have a holiday together, then thinking of it all upon his return to his home, Yuan remembered, and he was surprised he did, the girl Mei-ling. She had walked alone before Ai-lan, and even Ai-lan's radiance had not made Mei-ling seem unnoticeable. Now Yuan remembered very well she wore a soft long robe of apple green, the sleeves cut very short, and the collar high, so that above the color her face looked clear and somewhat pale and resolute. The very difference to Ai-lan made her hold her own against such beauty. For Mei-ling's face owed nothing to its color or to its changefulness or sparkling eyes or smile, as Ai-lan's did. Its good high look was from the perfect line of bone beneath the firm clear flesh, a line which, Yuan thought, would keep its strength and nobleness long past its youth. She looked older now than her age was. But some day in her age her straight low nose, her clean oval cheeks and chin, her sharp-cut lips, the straightness of her short black hair shaped smoothly against her head, would give her youth again. Life could

not greatly change her. Even as now a certain gravity
was hers, so in her maturity she would still be young.

Yuan remembered this gravity. Of all that wedding
party only two were grave, the mother and Mei-ling.
Yes, even at the feast, when wines of every foreign sort
were poured out, and all the tables full of guests were
crying out such wit as they did not know they had before, when glass was lifted high to glass, and the bride
and groom joined in the laughter as they made their way
between the guests, even then Yuan saw at his table that
the mother's face was grave, and so was Mei-ling's. These
two talked together in low tones often and directed the
servants here and there, and took counsel with the master of the hotel, and Yuan thought they were grave because of all these cares, and he let it pass and looked
about the brilliant hall.

But that night when they were alone after all was
over, and the house was silent save for servants passing
here and there to set covers right again and bring order
everywhere, the lady sat in her chair so silent and downcast that Yuan felt he must say something to make her
lift her heart up somehow, and so he said kindly, "Ai-
lan was beautiful—the loveliest I ever saw—the loveliest
woman."

The lady answered listlessly, "Yes, she was beautiful.
She has these three years been counted the most beautiful among the young rich ladies of this city—famous
for her beauty." She sat awhile and then she said with
strange bitterness, "Yes, and I wish it had not been so.
It has been the curse of my own life and of my poor
child's that she has been so beautiful. She has needed
to do nothing. She has not needed to use her mind or
hands or anything—only to let people look at her, and
praise flowed in upon her and desire and all that others
work to gain. Such beauty only a very great spirit can
withstand, and Ai-lan is not great enough to bear it!"

At this Mei-ling looked up from a piece of sewing
she had in her hands and cried softly and beseechingly,
"Mother!"

But the lady would say on, as if for once her bitter-

ness was more than she could bear, "I say only what is
true, my child. Against this beauty have I fought my
whole life, but I have lost. . . . Yuan, you are my son. I
can tell you. You wonder that I let her wed this man.
So may you wonder, for I do not like or trust him. But
it had to be—Ai-lan is with child by him."

So simply did the lady say these dreadful words. Yuan,
hearing them, felt the beating of his heart stop. He was
yet young enough to feel the horror of this thing, that
his own sister . . . He glanced in great shame at Mei-
ling. Her head was bent over the bit of cloth she held,
and she said nothing. Her face was not changed, only
more grave and quiet.

But the lady caught Yuan's glance and understood it.
She said, "You need not mind, for Mei-ling knows everything. I could not have borne my life if I had not
had her. She it was who helped me to plan and know
what I must do. I had no one, Yuan. And she stayed a
sister to my poor pretty foolish child, and that one leaned
upon her, too. She even would not let me send for you,
Yuan. Once I thought I must have a son to help me, for
I am not used in all these new ways of divorce, and I
could not tell your eldest cousin even, not anything, for
I was ashamed. But Mei-ling would not let me spoil
your years abroad."

Still Yuan could not say a word. His blood flushed up
to his cheeks and he sat confused and shamed, and angry too. And the lady, understanding very well this confusion, smiled sadly and said once more, "I dared not tell
your father, Yuan, whose only simple remedy is killing.
And even if he had not been so, I could not tell him. It is
a sorry end to all my care for Ai-lan, to train and school
my daughter in such freedom as this! Is this the new
day, then? In the old days the two would have suffered
death for such a sin! But now they will suffer nothing.
They will come back and live merrily and Ai-lan's child
will come too soon, but none will whisper more loudly
than behind their hands, because today many children
come too soon. It is the new day."

The lady smiled a mirthless smile but there were tears

in her eyes. Then Mei-ling folded up the bit of silk she sewed and thrust her needle in it and came and said soothingly, "You are so tired you do not know what you say. You have done everything for Ai-lan and well she knows it and so do we all. Come and sleep and I will fetch a broth for you to drink."

Then the lady rose obedient to the young girl as though it were a thing she had often done, and went out leaning on her shoulder gratefully, and Yuan watched the two go, still having nothing he could say, so confounded was he by what he had heard.

So Ai-lan, his own sister, had done so wild a thing! Thus had she used her freedom. Into his own life through her had come again this hot wild thing which he had twice escaped. He went slowly to his own room, very troubled, and troubled in his old divided way, as though nothing could ever come clearly and simply to him, neither love nor pain. For now half he was ashamed of Ai-lan's recklessness, because such things ought not to happen to his own sister, in whom he wanted to have nothing but whole pride, and yet half he was troubled because there was a hidden sweetness in this wild thing and he wanted it for himself. It was the first doubtfulness to fall upon him in his own country.

When this marriage day was over Yuan knew he must not in decency delay his going to his father, and he was eager to be gone, and the more eager because he found it sad in this home now. The mother was more quiet even than she ever had been and Mei-ling devoted her time steadfastly to her school. In the two days while Yuan made ready to go away, he scarcely saw the girl. Once he thought she avoided him, and then he said to himself, "It is because of what my mother said of Ai-lan. It is natural for a maid so modest to remember that," and he liked this modesty. Yet when the time came when he must set forth and take the train north, he found he wanted to bid Mei-ling good-bye, and not leave to be away the month or two and not to see her again. He even waited, therefore, and chose a later train by night, so that he could see her come home from her school, could dine alone with the lady and with her and talk a little quietly with them before he went.

And as they talked he found he listened for the girl's speech, very clear and soft and pleasant, always, and not shy and giggling as the laughter of maids is sometimes. She seemed always busy at some bit of sewing, and once or twice when a servant came in to ask a question of the next day's meats or some such thing, Yuan heard her ask Mei-ling instead of the lady, and Mei-ling gave directions as though she had done it many times. Nor was she shy in speech. This night, since the lady was more quiet than usual, and Yuan silent, too, Mei-ling talked on and told of what she did in school, and how she had long hoped to be a doctor.

"My foster mother made me think of it at first," she said and threw her quiet beaming look upon the lady. "And now I like it very well. Only it has meant a long time to study, and a great cost, and this my foster mother has done for me, and I shall always care for her in return; where I am she shall be, too. I want a hospital of my own one day in some city, a place for children and for women, and I want a garden in the center, and round it buildings full of beds and places for the sick,— not too large, not more than I could do, but all very clean and pretty."

So this young woman planned out her wish and in her earnestness she let her sewing lie, and her eyes began to beam and her lips to smile, and Yuan watching her, his cigarette between his fingers, thought in surprise, "Why, this maid is fair enough," and he forgot to listen to her while he looked at her. Suddenly he felt he was not pleased and when he looked into himself to see why it was, he found he did not like to hear this maid plan out a life alone for herself and so sufficient that she needed no one else in it. It seemed then to him that women ought not to think it well to have no thought of marriage in their minds. But even as he was so thinking, he saw the lady's face. For the first time since the marriage day her eyes were lit with interest and she heard all the young' girl said. And now she said warmly, "If I were not too old I would myself do something in that hospital. It is a better day than mine was. It is a very good day when women are not forced to wed!"

This Yuan heard her say, and while he believed it, or would have said he did, still it made him feel a little strangely, too. Somehow he took it as a thing not to be gainsaid or questioned that all women ought to wed, although it was not what a man could talk about with two women. Yet their eagerness for freedom left a little coolness in him, so that when he said farewell he felt less warmly than he thought he would and bewildered in himself because he was hurt somewhere within him, but he did not know just where or how the hurt was.

Long after he had lain himself down in the narrow berth of the train he thought of this, and of the new women of his country, and of how they were, Ai-lan so free she made her mother sad, and yet this same mother rejoiced in all Mei-ling's great free plans for her life. Then Yuan thought with a little bitterness, "I doubt she can be so very free. She will find it hard to do all she plans. And she will want a husband and children some day as all women do, doubtless."

And he remembered the women he had known, how in any land they turned at least secretly to a man. Yet, when his memory searched Mei-ling's face and speech, he could not truly say he had ever seen one sign of that searching in her look or voice. And he wondered if there were some youth she dreamed about, and he remembered that in the school she went to there were young men, too. Suddenly as a wind blows out of a still summer's night he was jealous of those youths he did not know, so jealous he could not even smile at himself or ask himself why he should care what Mei-ling dreamed. He planned soberly how he must hint to the lady that she ought to warn Mei-ling, and how she ought to guard the young woman better, and he took a heed for her he never had taken for any living soul, and never once did he think to ask why he did.

So planning, as the train swayed and creaked beneath him, he fell into a troubled sleep at last.

There came much now to drive all these thoughts from Yuan's mind for a while. Since his return from the foreign country he had lived only in the great coastal city. Not once had he seen any other thing than its wide streets, filled by day and night with vehicles of every sort, with motors and with public tramways and with people warm and brightly dressed and busy each in his own way. If there were poor ones, the sweating ricksha pullers, the lesser vendors, yet these in summer seemed not so piteous and there were not the winter beggars, who had fled from flood or famine to try a life in city streets. Rather the city seemed very gay to Yuan, a place measuring well beside any he had seen anywhere, and in it there was the comfort and the wealth of his cousin's new house and the display of the marriage and all the shining wedding gifts. And as he left the lady had pressed into his hand a thick folded heap of paper which he knew was money, and he took it easily, thinking that his father sent it to her for him. He had almost forgotten now that there were poor even in the world, his own house seemed so rich and easily fed.

But when he woke in the train the next day and looked out of the window, it was not to see such a country as he thought was his. The train had stopped beside a certain mighty river, and there all must descend and cross in boats and take up their journey again on the other side. So Yuan did also, crowding with the others on an open, wide-bottomed ferry boat, which still seemed not wide enough for all the people on it, so that Yuan, coming last, must stand upon the outside near the water.

He remembered very well that he had crossed this river when he went south before, but then he did not see what he now saw. For now his eyes, long shaped to other sights, saw these things newly. He saw upon the river a very city of small boats, tightly packed together, from whence a stench rose that sickened him.

This was the eighth month of the year, and though it was scarcely more than dawn the day was thick with heat. There was no great light from the sun, the sky was dark and low with clouds, pressing down so that it seemed to cover the water and the land, and there was no least wind anywhere. In the dull sluggish light the people pushed their boats aside to make way for the ferry, and men scrambled out of little hatches, nearly naked, their faces sunk and sodden with the sleepless night of heat, and women screamed at crying children and scratched their tangled hair, and naked children wailed, hungry and unwashed. These crowded tiny boats held each its fill of men and women and many children, and from the very water where they lived and which they drank the stench arose of filth they had poured into it.

Upon this, then, Yuan suddenly opened his eyes that morning. The picture lasted scarcely a moment and was gone, for the ferry boat swung clear of the little boats against the shore, into the cleanness of the middle of the river, and as suddenly Yuan was looking no more into sodden faces but into the swift yellow water of the river. Then almost before he could grasp the change, the ferry half turned against the current, and crept past a vast white-painted ship, rising as clean as a snowy peak against the grey sky, and Yuan and all the crowd looked up to see above them the prow of a foreign ship, and the hanging blue and red of a foreign flag. But when the ferry had crept through to the other side, there were also the black points of cannon and these were foreign cannon.

Then Yuan forgot the stench of the poor and their little crowded boats. He looked up and down the river as he went on and upon its yellow breast he counted seven of these great foreign ships of war, here in the heart of his country. He forgot all else for this moment as he counted them. An anger rose in him against these ships. Even as he stepped on shore he could not but look back on them with hate and question why they were there. Yet they were there, white, immaculate, invincible. Out of those black cannon, aimed steadily at

shore and shore, had more than once leaped fire and
death upon the land. Yuan remembered very well that it
was so. Staring at the ships, he forgot everything except
that out of those cannon fire could come upon his people and he muttered bitterly, "They have no right to
be here—we ought to drive them out of all our waters!",
and remembering and in bitterness he mounted into
another train and took up his way again to his father.

Now here was a strange thing that Yuan found in himself; so long as he could maintain his anger against these
white ships and remember how they had fired on his
people, and so long as he could remember every evil
thing whereby his people had been oppressed by other
outer peoples, and these were many, for he had learned
in school of evil treaties forced upon the emperors of
old by armies sent to ravage and to plunder, and even in
his lifetime had there been such things, and even in
the great city while he had been away young lads had
been shot down by white guards for crying out their
country's cause—so long as he could remember all these
wrongs that day, he was happy enough and filled with a
sort of fire, and he thought in all he did, while he ate,
and while he sat and looked out over the passing fields
and villages, "I must do something for my country.
Meng is right and better than I am. He is more true than
I am because he is so single. I am too weak. I think
them all good because of one good old teacher or—or a
woman clever with her tongue. I ought to be like Meng
and hate them heartily, and so help my people by my
strong hating. For only hate is strong enough to help
us, now—" So he thought to himself, remembering the
alien ships.

But even as Yuan would have clung to this wish of
his, he could not but feel himself grow cooler, and this
coolness grew in little subtle ways. A great fat man sat
in the seat across from him, so near that Yuan could
not always keep his eyes away from his mighty bulk.
As the day wore on to greater heat, the sun burning
through the windless clouds upon the metal roof of the
train, the air within grew burning, too, and this man

took off all his garments, save his little inner trousers, and there he sat in all his naked flesh, his breasts, his belly rolls of thick yellow oily flesh, and his very jowls hanging to his shoulders. And as if this were not enough, he coughed, in spite of summer, and he made much of his cough and rumbled at it all he could and spat his phlegm out so often, that stay where he would Yuan could not avoid it always. So into his right anger for his country's sake crept his petulance against this man who was his own countryman. At last a gloom came into Yuan. It was almost too hot for life in this shaking train, and he began to see what he did not want to see. For in the heat and weariness, the travellers were past caring for anything except how to live to the journey's end. Children wailed and dragged at their mothers' breasts and at every station flies flew into open windows and settled on the sweating flesh and on the spittle upon the floors and on the food and on the children's faces. And Yuan, who never noticed a fly in his youth because flies were everywhere and why should they matter, now that he had been elsewhere and learned the death they carried, was in an agony of daintiness against them, and he could not bear to have one settle on his glass of tea or on a bit of bread he bought from a vendor or on the dish of rice and eggs he bought at noon from the servant in the train. Yet he could not but ask himself what use was all this hatred against the flies when he saw the blackness of the servant's hands, and the sticky grime upon the cloth with which the man wiped the dish before he poured the rice in. Then in his bitterness Yuan shouted at him, "Leave the dish unwiped rather than touch it with such a rag as that!"

At this the man stared and grinned most amiably and then at this moment feeling how very great the heat was, he took the cloth and wiped his sweating face and hung it on his neck again where he carried it. Now Yuan indeed could scarcely bear to touch his food. He put down his spoon and cried out against the man and he cried out against the flies and all the filth upon the floor. Then the man was outraged at such injustice and he cried out for heaven to witness and he said, "Here am I, one man, and I have only one man's work to do, and floors are not my work and flies are not my work! And who can spend his life in summer to kill flies? I swear if all the people in this nation spent all their lives to kill the flies they could not prevail against them, for flies are natural!" Then rid of his anger thus the man burst out laughing very heartily, for he was of a good temper even under anger, and he went his way laughing.

But all the travellers, being so weary and ready to look at anything or listen anywhere, had listened to everything said, and they all took part against Yuan and with the servant and some cried out, "It is true there is no end of flies. They come from none knows where but they have their life to live too, doubtless!" And one aged lady said, "Aye, and they have a right to it. As for me, I would not dare to take life even from a fly!" And another said scornfully, "He is one of those students come back from abroad to try his little foreign notions on us!"

At this the large fat man near Yuan, who had eaten mightily of rice and meats and was now drinking tea very gravely, belching loudly as he drank, said suddenly, "So that is what he is! Here I have sat my whole day through staring at him to see what he was and making nothing of him!" And he gazed on at Yuan in pleased wonder, now that he knew what he was, drinking as he stared and belching up his wind until Yuan could not bear to see him, and looked steadfastly away into the flat green country.

He was too proud to answer. Nor could he eat. He sat on looking out of the window hour after hour. Under the hot cloudy sky the country grew more poor, more flat, more flat with wastes of water as the train sped north. At every station the people looked to Yuan more wretched, more plagued with boils and sore eyes and even though there was water everywhere they were not washed, and many of the women had their feet bound still in the old evil way he thought was gone. He looked at them and he could not bear them. "These are my

people!" he said bitterly within himself at last, and he
forgot the white foreign ships of war.

Yet there was one more bitterness that he must bear.
At the far end of the car sat a white man whom Yuan
had not seen. Now he came past to descend from the
train, at a certain little mud-walled country town where
he lived. And as he passed Yuan he noted him and his
young sad face, and he remembered how Yuan had cried
out against the flies, and he said in his own tongue,
meaning to be kind and seeing what Yuan was, "Don't
be discouraged, friend! I fight against the flies, too, and
shall keep on fighting!"

Yuan looked up suddenly at the foreign voice and
words. There he saw a small thin white man, a little
common-looking fellow in a grey cotton suit of clothes
and a white sun helmet, and with a common face, not
newly shaven, though the pale blue eyes were kind
enough, and Yuan saw he was a foreign priest. He could
not answer. This was the bitterest thing to bear, that here
was a white man to see what he had seen, and know what
he had known this day. He turned away and would not
answer. But from his seat he saw the man get off the
train and trudge through the crowd and turn towards
the mud-walled city. Then Yuan remembered that other
white man who had said, "If you would live as I have
lived—"

And Yuan asked himself accusingly, "Why did I
never see all this before? I have seen nothing until
now!"

Yet it was only the beginning of what Yuan must see.
For when at last he stood before his father, Wang the
Tiger, he saw him as he never knew he was. There the
Tiger stood, clinging to the door post of his hall waiting
for his son, and all his old strength was gone, even his
old petulance, and there was only an old grey man, whose
long white whiskers dropped down sparsely on his chin,
and whose eyes were red and filmed with age and with
too much wine-drinking, so that until Yuan came near
he could not see him, but must listen for his voice.

Now Yuan had seen with wonder how weedy were the courts that he came through and how few the soldiers were who stood about, a few ragged idle fellows, and how the very guard at the gate had no gun and let him come in as he would and asked no questions and gave no courteous greeting as he should to his general's son. But Yuan was not ready to see his father look so gaunt and thin. The old Tiger stood there in an old robe of grey stuff, and it was even patched upon the elbows where his bones had worn through upon the arm of his chair, and on his feet were slippers of cloth and the heels turned under, and his sword was not in his hand now.

Then Yuan cried out, "My father!" and the old man answered, trembling, "Is it really you, my son?" And they held each other's hands, and Yuan felt tears rush to his eyes to see his father's old face, the nose and mouth and dimmed eyes all somehow bigger than they used to be and too big in the shrunken face. It seemed to Yuan, staring at the face, that this could not be his father, not the Tiger whom he used to fear, whose frowns and black brows were once so terrible, whose sword was never far from his hand, even when he slept. Yet it was the Tiger, for when he knew it was Yuan he called out, "Bring the wine!"

There was a slow stirring and the hare-lipped trusty man, himself aged now, but still his general's man, came forward, and he gave his greeting to his general's son, his crooked face beaming, and he poured out wine, while the father took the son's hand and led him in.

Now did another show himself, and yet another whom Yuan had not seen before, or thought he had not, two grave little prosperous men, one old, one young. The elder was a small, shriveled man, dressed very neatly in an old fashion of long robe of dark grey small-patterned silk, and on his upper body was a sleeved jacket of dull black silk, and on his head a little round silk cap and on it a white cord button denoting mourning for some near relative. About his ankles, too, higher than the black velvet shoes he wore, his trousers were tied with bands of white cotton cloth. Above this somber garb his small old face peered out, smooth as though he still could not grow a beard, but very wrinkled, his eyes as shining sharp as a weasel's eyes are.

The young man was like him except his robe was dull blue, and he wore the mourning that a son wears for his dead mother, and his eyes were not sharp, but wistful as an ape's little hollow eyes are when it looks at human men to whom it is akin and yet not near enough to understand them or be understood. This was the other's son.

Now as Yuan looked at them uncertainly, the elder said in his dried high voice, "I am your second uncle, nephew. I have not seen you since you were a lad, I think. This is my eldest son, your cousin."

At this Yuan gave surprised greeting to the two, not too gladly, because they were very strange to him in their staid old-fashioned looks and ways, but still he was courteous, and more courteous than the Tiger, who paid no heed to them at all, but only sat now and stared joyfully at Yuan.

And indeed Yuan was much moved by this childlike pleasure his father had in his return. The old Tiger could not take his eyes from Yuan, and when he had stared awhile he burst into silent laughter, and rose from his seat and went to Yuan and felt his arms and his strong shoulders and laughed again and muttered, "Strong as I was at his age—aye, I remember I had such arms I could throw an eight-foot spear of iron and wield a great stone weight. In the south under that old general I used to do it of an evening to amuse my fellows. Stand up and let me see your thighs!"

Yuan stood up obediently, amused and patient, and the Tiger turned to his brother and laughed aloud and cried in some of his old vigor, "You see this son of mine? I'll swear you have not one to match him out of all your four!"

Wang the Merchant answered nothing to this, except he smiled his little forbearing meager smile. But the younger man said patiently and carefully, "I think my two younger brothers are as large, and my next brother is larger than I, since I am smallest of them all, although the eldest." And he blinked his mournful eyes at them as he made his report.

Now Yuan, listening, asked curiously, "How are these other cousins of mine and what do they do?"

The son of Wang the Merchant here looked at his father, but since that elder sat silent, and wore the same small smile, he took courage and answered Yuan. "It is I who work to aid my father with his rents and grain shop. Once we all did it, but the times are very evil now in these parts. The tenants have grown so lordly that they will not pay the rents they should. And the grain, too, is harvested in lesser quantities. My elder brother is your father's, for my father gave him to my uncle. And my next brother, he would go out to see the world and he went and is in a shop in the south, an accountant, because he fingers the abacus very well, and he is prosperous, since much silver passes through his hands. My third brother is at home, and his family, and the youngest; he goes to school, for we have a school now in our town of a new sort, and we expect him to be wed as soon as it is decent, for my mother died a few months back."

Then Yuan remembering, remembered a great blowsy lively country woman he had seen in his uncle's house the once his father took him there, and how she made merry always, and he wondered to think she must lie still and dead while this little creeping man, his uncle, lived on and on so little changed. He asked, "How did it happen?"

Then the son looked at his father and they were both silent until the Tiger hearing what was asked answered, as if here were a thing which had to do with him, "How did it happen? Why, we have an enemy, our family has, and now he is a little wandering robber chieftain in the hills about our old village. Once I took a city from him in the fairest way, by open guile and siege, but he has not forgiven me for it. I swear he settled near our lands on purpose and he watched for my kin, I know. And this brother of mine is cautious and found out this robber hated us and he would not go himself to take his share of crops and taxes from the tenants, but he sent his wife, she being only a woman and the robbers caught her on her homeward way, and robbed her and cut her head off and rolled it down beside the road. I tell my brother, 'Wait a few months now until I gather up my men again. I swear I'll search that robber out—I swear I'll— I swear I'll . . .'" The Tiger's voice dragged in weakening wrath and he put out his hand blindly, searching, and the old trusty man standing near put a wine bowl in it and said drowsily, as if from long habit, "Quiet yourself, my general. Do not be angry, lest you grow ill." And he shifted on his tired old feet and yawned a little and stared happily at Yuan, admiring him.

Now though Wang the Merchant had said nothing during all this tale, when Yuan looked at him to speak some courteous comfort, he was surprised to see his uncle's little old shining eyes were wet with tears, and still silent, the old man took the edge of first one sleeve and then the other and carefully wiped each eye, and then in his spare stealthy fashion he drew his dry old hand across his nose and Yuan was so astonished he could not speak, to see this cold old man shed tears.

The son saw it, too, and with his small wistful eyes upon his father he said mournfully to Yuan, "The servant who was with her said if she had been silent and more obedient to them they would not have been so quick to kill. But she had a very swift loud tongue and all her life long she had used it as she liked, and she had a temper always quick to boil, and she shouted at the very first, 'Shall I give you my good silver, you sons of cursed mothers?' Yes, the servant ran as fast as his feet could take him when she cried so loudly, but when he looked back her head was off already, and we lost the whole of those rents with her for they took everything."

Thus the son spoke in the evenest little garrulous voice, the words running out one like another in flatness, as though he had his mother's loose tongue inside his father's body. But he was a good son, too, who had loved his mother, and now his voice broke and he went out to the court and coughed to ease himself and wipe his eyes and mourn a little.

As for Yuan, not knowing what else to do, he rose and poured a bowl of tea for his uncle and felt himself in a dream here in this room, a stranger with these folk who were his own blood. Yes, he had a life to live they could not conceive, and their life was small as death to him. Suddenly, though why he did not know, he remembered Mary, of whom for a long time he had not thought. . . . Why now should she come to his mind as clearly as though a door were opened to show her there, as he had been used to see her on a windy day in spring across the sea, her fine dark hair blown about her face, her skin white and red, her eyes their steady grey? She had no place here. This place she could not know. The pictures of his country she had been used to speak of, the pictures she had made for her own mind, were only pictures. It was well, Yuan thought passionately, staring at his father and at these others, sunk back in themselves, now that the first keen edge of meeting was over,—oh, it was very well he had not loved her! He looked about the old hall. There was dust everywhere, the dust long left by a few old careless servants. Between the tiles upon the floor, the green mold grew, and there were stains upon the tiles of spilt wine and of old spittle and of ashes and of dripped greasy food. The broken lattices of shell had been mended with paper, hanging now in sheets, and even in this daylight rats ran to and fro upon the beams above. The old Tiger sat nodding, his warm wine drunk, and his jaw dropped and all his great old body slack and helpless. Above him on a nail his sword hung in its scabbard. Now for the first time Yuan saw it, although he had missed its shining nearness the first moment when he saw his father. It was still beautiful, though sheathed. The scabbard was beautiful in spite of dust in all the carven patterns on it and although the red silken tassels hung down faded and gnawed by rats.

. . . Ah, he was very glad he had not loved that

foreign woman. Let her keep her dreams of what his country was! Let her never know the truth!

A great sob rose in Yuan's throat. . . . Had the old passed forever from him? He thought of the old Tiger, and of the little shriveled mean-faced man, his uncle, and his son. These, these were still his own and he was tied to them by the blood in his own veins, which he could not spill out if he would. However he might long to be free of all their kind, their blood must run in him so long as he lived.

It was very well that Yuan should know his youth was over and that he must be a man now, and look only to himself, for on that night while he lay alone in the old room where he had slept as a child and as a lad, his guards about him, and where he had sat alone and wept himself to sleep when he ran home from the school of war, the old trusty man came creeping in. Yuan had but just lain himself down to sleep, for his father had made a little feast for him that night and he had bidden his two captains in and they had eaten and drunk together for welcome to Yuan. Afterwards Yuan had let his father lean on him and taken him to his own door before he came to bed himself.

For a while, lying in his bed before he slept, he listened to what he never used to hear, the night sounds of the little town where his father had lived so long encamped. He thought to himself, "If I had been asked I would have said there were no sounds in this little town at night." And yet there were the barking of the dogs up the street, the crying of a child, a murmur of voices not yet stilled in sleep, a solitary tolling note now and again of some temple bell, and clear and wailing above it all, although not near, the crying agony of some woman's voice seeking for the wandering soul of her child now dying. No sound was loud, for there were silent courts between him and the gate, and yet Yuan, somehow newly keen to everything because he felt himself a stranger here where once he was not strange, heard each separate sound.

Then suddenly there was the squeak of his door upon its wooden hinges and the flare of a candle, and he saw the door open and there was the old trusty man, who bent and set his candle carefully on the floor, and panting a little because his back was stiff he stood again and closed the door and thrust the bar through. Yuan waited, wondering in surprise what he had to say.

He came on his slow old feet up to Yuan's bed, and seeing Yuan had not drawn the curtains he said, "You are not sleeping, young sir? I have something I must say."

Then Yuan, seeing how this man's old body bent at the knees, said kindly, "Sit, then, while you speak." But the man knew his place and was unwilling for a while, until at last he yielded to Yuan's kindness, and sat down on the footstool beside the bed and he began to hiss and whisper through his split lip and though his eyes were kind and honest, he was so hideous that Yuan could not bear to see him, however good he was.

Yet soon he forgot how the old man looked, in his dismay at what he heard. For out of a long, winding, broken story Yuan's mind began to discern something more and more clearly, and at last the old man put his two hands upon his dried old knees and whispered loudly, "So every year, little general, your father has borrowed more heavily of your uncle. First he borrowed a great sum to set you free out of that prison, little general, and then every year to keep you safe abroad he borrowed more. Well, and he let his soldiers go and let them go until now I swear he has not a hundred left to fight with. He could not go to war; his men have left him for other lords of war. They were but hirelings and when the wage is stopped, shall hirelings stay? And the handful he has left are not soldiers. They are ragged thieves and wastrels of his army who live here because he gives them food, and the townspeople hate them because they go from door to door demanding money, and having guns they must be feared. Yet they are only armed beggars. Once I told the general what they did, because he has always been so honorable, he has never let his men take more than their due for booty, and never did he let them take from people in times of peace. Well, and then he went out and roared and drew his brows down and pulled his whiskers at them, but what of that, little sir? They saw him old and shaking even while he roared, and though they pretended to be afraid, when he was gone I saw them laugh and they went straight out again to their begging and still they do as they like. And what use to tell my general more? It is better for him to have peace. And so he borrows money every month, I know, because your uncle comes here often now, and he would not if it were not something for money. And your father gets money somehow, because he has it and I know people do not give him much tax these days, and his soldiers who force what is given keep most of it, and he could not have enough if your uncle did not give it."

But Yuan could not believe it all at once and he said in dismay, "Yet if my father has dispersed his army as much as you say he has, and he gives only food to his men now, he cannot need so much money as he did. And his father left him land, I think."

Then the old man bent close and he whispered piercingly, "That land is all your uncle's now, I swear—or else as good as his, for how will your father pay him what is owed? And, little general, do you think it has cost nothing for you to go to foreign countries? Yes, he has let your mother do with little enough, and your own two sisters have been wed to tradesmen in this little town, but every month your father has sent this money to that other lady for you."

In this moment Yuan perceived how childish he had been all these years. Year after year he had taken it as a thing not to be doubted that his father should pay for all he had wanted. He had not been wasteful and he had not gamed or wanted many fine garments or done those things that young men sometimes do to waste their parents' goods. But year after year his least needs had cost his father hundreds of pieces of silver. And now he thought of Ai-lan's silken gowns and of her wedding, yes, and of the lady's house and of her foundlings. And while Yuan knew the lady had some silver left her from her own father, whose only child she had been, so that he left her no mean sum of money, yet Yuan doubted if it could pay for all.

Then Yuan felt his heart rush out to his old father that all these years he had made no complaint, but by borrowing and contriving he had not let his son suffer for a want of silver. And Yuan said in the gravity of his new manhood, "I thank you that you have told me. Tomorrow I will see my uncle and my cousin and know what has taken place and what their hold is on my father—" and then as though this suddenly came to him as a new thought he added, "and on me!"

Through the night Yuan could not forget this thought. Again and again he woke and though he might comfort himself and remember that after all they were of one blood, and therefore debt is not really debt, yet Yuan felt a weight upon him when he thought of these two. Yes, they were his flesh and blood though he felt himself as alien from them as though his were another race. Once, pondering on this in the black loneliness of night, it came to him that here in his own childhood bed, within his father's house, he felt as foreign as he had across the sea. It struck with a sudden bleakness, "How is it I have no home anywhere?" And all the days upon the train and all he had seen rose up to sicken him again and make him shrink away and he said suddenly aloud in a low whispering cry, "I am homeless!"

Then he hastened his heart from that cry, for it was dreadful to him and he could not bear to understand it.

So on the next day he reminded himself many times that these were his own blood after all, and that he was no true stranger, and this his own blood could not harm him. Nor would he blame his old father. He told himself he knew easily how his father had been compelled by age and by his very love for his son to go into debt, and who better to borrow of than his own brother? So

in the morning Yuan comforted himself. But he was glad
it was a fair day, very fair and cool with little winds of
coming autumn, for he felt it easier to find comfort when
the sun shone into the courts, and the heat was blown
out of the rooms by the stirring winds.

Now after they had eaten, on the next morning the
Tiger went out to see his men, and this day he made a
show before Yuan that he was very busy for his men,
and he took down his sword and shouted to the trusty
man to come and wipe it clean and he stood quarrelling
because it was so dusty, so that Yuan could not but smile
and comprehend a little sadly, too, what was the truth.

But when he saw his father gone it came to Yuan that
here was a good time to talk privately with his uncle
and his cousin and so he said frankly, after courtesies,
"Uncle, I know my father owes you certain moneys.
Since he is older than he was, I want to know what
burdens are on him, and do my share."

Now Yuan was prepared for much, but he was not
prepared for such obligations as he now found. For those
two men of business looked at each other and the
younger went and fetched an account book, such a book
as is used to tally moneys in a shop, a large soft paper-
covered book, and this he gave with both hands to his
father, and his father took it and opened it and began to
read forth in his dry voice the year, the month, the day,
when the Tiger had begun to borrow sums from him.
And Yuan listening, heard the years begin with that one
when he had gone south to school, and it continued even
until now, the sums mounting every time and with such
interest that at the end Wang the Merchant read forth
this sum, "Eleven thousand and five hundred and seventeen pieces of silver in all."

These words Yuan heard and he sat as though he had
been struck down by a stone. The merchant closed up
the book again and gave it to his son and his son placed
it on the table and the two men waited. And Yuan said
in a voice smaller than his was usually, though he tried
to make it his own, "What security did my father give?"

Then Wang the Merchant answered carefully and

drily, scarcely moving his lips at all, as his way was when he spoke, "I did naturally remember that he is my brother, and I required no such security as I might from a stranger. Moreover, for a while your father's rank and army were a safeguard for me, but now no longer. For since my son's mother died as she did, I feel my safety is all gone when I go out into the countryside. I feel no one fears me any more, and all know your father's power is not what it once was. But truly, no war lord's power is what it once was, with the new revolution in the south and threatening to press its way even here to the north. The times are very evil. There is rebellion everywhere and tenants are bold upon the land as they have never been. Yet I remember that your father is my brother, and I have not even taken his land for security, though indeed it is not enough for all the silver I have given your father for you."

At these last two words, "for you," Yuan looked at his uncle but he said nothing. He waited for the uncle to go on. And the old man said, "I have preferred to put my moneys out for you, and let you be security in what ways you could be. There are many things you can do for me, Yuan, and for my sons, who are your kin."

So this old man spoke, not unkindly, either, but very reasonably and as any elder in a great family may to his junior. But when Yuan heard these few words and heard the dry small voice and saw his uncle's little weazened face, he was dismayed, and he asked, "And what can I do, uncle, who have not even any work yet fixed for myself?"

"You must find that work," the uncle replied. "It is well known these days that any young man who has been to foreign countries can ask a very high wage, as much wage as in the old days a governor could hope for. I have taken pains, before I lent so much for you, to know this from my second son who is accountant in the south, and he tells me it is so, that this foreign learning is as good a business nowadays as can be found. And it is best of all if you can find a place where money passes by, because my son says there are higher taxes taken now for all the new things to be done than ever have been taken from the people, and the new rulers have the highest plans of great highways and mighty tombs for their heroes and foreign houses and every sort of thing. If you could find a good high place where silver must go in and out, it would be easy for you and a help to us all."

This the old man said, and Yuan could answer nothing. He saw before him in this clear instant the life his uncle planned for him. But he said nothing, only stared at his uncle, yet not seeing him, either, only seeing the narrow mean old mind shaping these plans. He knew that according to the old laws his uncle might so plan and might so claim his years, and when he remembered this, Yuan's heart rose as it never had against the miserable rights of those old times, which had been like logs chained to the feet of the young, so that they might never run swiftly. Yet he did not cry this forth. For when he thought of this, he thought of his old father, too, and how not in any willfulness the old Tiger had bound his son like this, but only because there was no other way whereby he could find money to give Yuan his desire. So in uncertainty Yuan could only sit and loathe his uncle secretly.

But the old man did not catch the young man's loathing. He went on again in the same flat little voice, "There are also other things that you may do. I have my two younger sons who have no livelihood. The times are so ill now that my business is not what it was, and ever since I heard how well my elder brother's son does in a bank, I have wondered why my sons should not, too. So when you have found a good place for yourself, if you will take my two younger sons with you and find places for them under you, it will be part payment of the debt, and so I shall consider it, depending on the size of the sum they have each month."

Now Yuan cried out bitterly, and he could no longer hold back his bitterness, "So I am sold as security—my years are yours!"

But the old man opened his eyes at this and answered

very peaceably, "I do not know how you mean those
words. Is it not a duty to help one's own family as one
can? Surely I have spent myself for my two brothers,
and one of them your father. I have been their agent
on the land these many years, and I have kept the great
house which our father left us, and paid all taxes, and
done everything for the land which our father left to us.
But it has been my duty and I have not refused to do
it, and after me this eldest son must do it. Yet the land
is not what it was. Our father left us enough in lands
and rents so that we were accounted rich. But our children are not rich. The times are hard. Taxes are high
and tenants pay little and they fear no one. Therefore my
two younger sons must seek places for themselves even
as my second has, and this is your duty in your turn
to help your brother-cousins. From ancient times the
most able in a family has helped the others."

So was the old bondage laid upon Yuan. He could
make no answer. Well he knew that some young men
in his place would have refused the bondage, and they
would have run away and lived where they pleased and
cast aside all thought of family, for these were the new
times. And Yuan wished most passionately that he could
be free like that; he longed, even as he sat there in that
dark old dusty room, looking at these two who were
his kin, to rise and shout out, "The debt is not mine!
I owe no debt except to myself!"

But he knew he could not shout it. Meng could have
said it for his cause's sake, and Sheng could have laughed
and seemed to accept the bondage, and then he would
forget it, and live as he liked in spite of it. But Yuan was
differently shaped. He could not refuse this bondage
which in ignorant love his father had set upon him.
Nor could he blame his father still, nor when he pondered yet more upon it, think of any other way his
father could have done.

He stared down on a square of sunlight falling through
the open door, and in the silence he heard a twittering
quarrel among the little wild birds in the bamboos in
the court. At last he said somberly, "I am really your

investment, then, my uncle. You have used me as a means to make your sons and your old age safe."

The old man heard this and considered it and poured out a little tea into a bowl and sipped it slowly and then he wiped his dried old hand about his mouth and said again, "It is what every generation does and must do. So will you when your own sons come."

"No, I will not," said Yuan quickly. Never had he seen in his mind a son of his until this moment. But now these words of the old man seemed to call the future into life. Yes, one day he would have sons. There would be a woman for him and they would have sons. But those sons—they should be free—free of any shaping from him who was their father! They should not be made for soldiers, nor shaped for any destiny, nor bound to any family cause.

And suddenly he hated all his kind, his uncles and his cousins,—yes, and even his own father, for at this moment the Tiger came in, weary from his rounds among his men and eager to sit down before his bowl and look at Yuan awhile and hear him talk of anything. But Yuan could not bear it. . . . He rose quickly and without a word he went away to be alone.

Now in his own old room upon his bed Yuan lay weeping and shivering and weeping as he used to do when he was a lad, but not long, because the old Tiger stayed behind him only long enough to discover from the other two what had gone amiss, and he came after Yuan and pushed the door open and came as fast as his two old feet would carry him to Yuan's bed. But Yuan would not turn to his father. He lay with his face buried in his arms and the old Tiger sat beside him and smoothed his shoulder with his hand and patted it and poured forth eager promises and broken pleadings, and he said, "See, my son, you are not to do anything but what you like. I am no old man yet. I have been too idle. I will gather up my men once more and sally forth again to a battle and make the region mine again and have the taxes that robber lord has taken from me. I downed him once and I can again, and you shall have everything. You shall stay here with me and have everything. Yes, and wed whom you like. I was wrong before. I am not so old-fashioned now, Yuan—I know how young men do now. . . ."

Now the old Tiger had truly said the thing most needed to strengthen Yuan out of his weeping and his pity for himself. He turned over and he cried violently, "I will not let you battle any more, father, and I—"

And Yuan was about to cry out, "I will not wed." He had so long said it to his father that the words ran off his tongue of their own accord. But in the midst of all his misery he stopped. A sudden question came to him. Did he indeed not wish to wed? But not an hour ago he had cried out that his sons should be free. Of course one day he would wed. He delayed his words upon his tongue and then more slowly he told his father, "Yes, some day I will wed the one I want to wed."

But the old Tiger was so pleased to see Yuan turn his face about and cease his weeping that he answered merrily, "You shall—you shall—only tell me who she is, my son, and let me send the go-between and do it, and I will tell your mother—after all, what cursed country maid is worthy of my son?"

Then Yuan, staring at his father while he spoke, began to see a thing in his own mind he had not known was there. "I do not need a go-between," he said slowly, but his mind was not on these words. He began to see a face shape in his mind—a woman's young face. "I can speak for myself. We speak for ourselves, these days, we young men—"

Now it was the Tiger's turn to stare, and he said severely, "Son, what woman is there decent who can be so spoken to? You have not forgotten my old warnings against such women, son? Have you chosen a good woman, son?"

But Yuan smiled. He forgot debts and wars and all the troubles of these days. Suddenly his divided mind joined upon one clear way he had not seen at all. There was one to whom he could tell everything, and know

what he must do! These old ones never could understand him nor his needs, they could not see that he belonged no more among them. No, they could not see
any more than aliens could. But he knew a woman of
his own times, not rooted in the old as he was and forever divided because he had no power to pull the roots
up and plant them in the new and necessary times
wherein his life must be—he saw her face clearer than
any face in his whole life, its clearness making every face
grow dim, dimming even his father's face that was before his very eyes. She could only set him free from
himself—only Mei-ling could set him free and tell him
what he ought to do. She, who ordered everything she
touched, could tell him what to do! His heart began to
lift within him out of its own lightness. He must go
back to her. He sat up quickly and put his feet to the
floor. Then he remembered his father had put a question to him and he answered out of his dazing new joy,
"A good woman? Yes, I have chosen a good woman, my
father!"

And he felt such an impatience as he had not known
before in all his life. Here were no doubts and no with-
drawals. He would go at once to her.

And yet for all his sudden new impatience Yuan found
he must stay his month out with his father. For when
Yuan thought how he might find excuse to go away, the
Tiger grew so hurt and downcast that Yuan could not
but be moved and draw back the hints he had put forth
of some business calling him to the coastal city. And he
knew it was not fitting that he should not stay to see his
mother, who during these days had been in the country
where her old home once was. For this woman, ever
since she had gone to the earthen house for Yuan, had
returned to her childhood love of country life, and now
that her two daughters were wed she went often to the
village where once she had been a maid, and she found
a home there with her eldest brother who suffered her
willingly enough because she paid out silver and made
a little lavish show as wife of a lord of war, and her

brother's wife liked the show because it set her up above the other village women. Though the trusty man sent a messenger to tell the mother Yuan was come, yet she had delayed a day or two.

And Yuan was the more willing and even anxious to see his mother and make plain to her that he would choose his own wife, and that he had chosen her already, and it only remained that he tell her so. Therefore he could and did live on the month, and this more easily because his uncle and the son went back soon to the old great house and Yuan was alone with his father.

But this joyful knowledge of Mei-ling made it easier for Yuan even to be courteous to his uncle, and he thought secretly with deep relief, "She will help me to find a way to settle off this debt. I will say nothing angry now—not until I have told her." And so thinking he could say to his uncle steadily at parting, "Be sure I shall not forget the debt. But lend us no more moneys, uncle, for now my first care when this month is past, will be to find a good place for myself. As for your sons, I will do what I can for them."

And the Tiger hearing it said stoutly, "Be sure, brother, that all will come back to you, for what I cannot do by war my son will do by government, for doubtless he will find a good official place, with all his knowledge."

"Yes, doubtless, if he tries," returned the merchant. But as he went he said to his son, "Put in Yuan's hand the paper you have written." And the son pulled a folded paper from his sleeve and handed it to Yuan and said in his little wordy way, "It is only the full counting out, my cousin, of those sums. We thought, my father and I, that you would want to know it all clearly."

Even then Yuan could not be angry with these two little men. He took the paper gravely, smiling inwardly, and with every outward courtesy he sent them on their way.

Yes, nothing was so confused now as it had been for Yuan. He could be courteous to these two, and when they were gone he could be very patient with his father in the evenings when the old man told long garrulous

tales of his wars and victories. For his son the Tiger lived
his life over, and made much of all his battles and while
he talked he drew down his old brows and pulled at his
ragged whiskers and his eyes grew bright, and after all
to him it seemed as he talked to his son that he had
lived a very glorious life. But Yuan, sitting in calmness,
half smiling when he heard the old Tiger's shouts and
saw his drawn brows and the thrust he made to show
how he had stabbed the Leopard, only wondered how
he ever could have feared his father.

Yet in the end the days passed not too slowly. For
the thought of Mei-ling had come so suddenly to Yuan
that he needed to live with only the thought for a while,
and sometimes he was glad for the delay, even, and for
the hours when he could sit and seem to listen to his
father's talk. Secretly he wondered to himself that he
had been so dull to his own heart that he had not known
before, even on the day of Ai-lan's wedding, when,
while he watched the marriage procession and had seen
Ai-lan's beauty, he had seen Mei-ling and thought her
still more beautiful. That moment he should have known.
And he should have known a score of times thereafter,
when he had seen her here and there about the house,
her hands ordering all, her voice directing and helping
servants. But he had not known, not until he lay weeping and in loneliness.

Across such dreaming broke again and again the Tiger's
happy old voice, and Yuan could bear to sit and listen
as he never could have done, had he not this new
growing love inside himself. He listened in a dream to
all his father said, not discerning at all between wars past
or wars his father planned for the future, and his father
prattled on, "I still do have a little revenue from that
son my elder brother gave me. But he is no lord of
war, no real lord. I dare not trust him much, he is so idle
in his love of laughter—a born clown and he will die a
clown, I swear. He says he is my lieutenant, but he
sends me very little, and I have not been there now
these six years. I must go in the spring—aye, I must
make my rounds of battle in the spring. That nephew

of mine, well I know he will turn straight over to any coming enemy, even against me he will turn—"

And Yuan, half listening, cared nothing for this cousin of his whom he scarcely could remember except his elder aunt liked to say, "My son who is a general in the north."

Yes, it was pleasant to sit and answer his father a little now and then, and think of the maid he knew he loved. And many comforts came to him in these thoughts. He told himself he would not be ashamed to have her see these courts, for she would understand his shames. They both were of a kind, this was their country, whatever its shames were. He could even say to her, "My father is an old foolish war lord, so full of tales he does not know which is false and which is true. He sees himself a mighty man he never was." Yes, he could say such things as those to her, and know she would comprehend. And when he thought of this simplicity she had he felt the false shames fall away from him. Oh, let him go to her, and be himself again, no more divided, but as he was those few days on the land, in that earthen home of his grandfather's, when he had been alone and free! With her he could be alone and free and once more simple.

At last he could think of nothing else than pouring out his need before her. So steadily did he know that she would help him, that when his mother came at last, he could greet her as he should and look upon her without suffering to think she was his mother and yet one to whom he had nothing to say. For she was now, for all her withered rosy healthy looks, a very plain old country woman. She looked up at him, leaning on a peeled staff she used these days to walk with, and her old eyes asked, wondering, "What is this I have for a son?"

And Yuan, tall and different in the foreign clothes he wore, looked down upon the woman in her old-fashioned coat and skirt of black cotton stuff and asked himself, "Was I indeed shaped in this old woman's body? I feel no kinship in our flesh."

But he did not suffer or now feel ashamed. To that

white woman, had he loved her, he would have said with great shame, "This is my mother." But he could say to Mei-ling, "This is my mother," and she, knowing that a thousand men like him had sprung from such mothers, would not think it strange, for nothing was strange to her. To her it would be enough that it was so. . . . Even to Ai-lan he might feel shame, but not to Mei-ling. He could uncover all his heart to her and never be ashamed. This knowledge made him tranquil therefore, even in his impatience, and later on a certain day he told his mother plainly, "I am betrothed, or good as betrothed. I have chosen the maid."

And the old woman answered mildly, "Your father told me so. Well, I had talked of a maid or two I knew, but your father has always let you do what you wished. His son you have ever been, and scarcely mine, and he with the hottest temper ever was so I cannot go against him. Aye, that learned one, she could escape it and go out, but I have stayed and let him use me for his anger. But I hope she is a decent maid and can cut a coat and turn a fish as it should be turned, and I hope I may see her sometimes, though I know very well these new times are anyhow, and the young do what they will, and daughters-in-law do not even come to see their husband's mothers as they ought to do."

But Yuan thought she seemed glad she need not bestir herself beyond this and she sat and stared at nothing in a way she had and moved her eyes and jaws a little and forgot him, and slept gently, or seemed to do so. They were not of the same world, these two, and that he was her son was meaningless to him. In truth, everything was meaningless to him now, except that he come again into the presence of that one.

When his farewells had been said to his parents, and he forced himself to say them courteously and as though he grieved to leave them, he went again on the train south, and now it was strange how little he saw the travellers on that train. Whether they behaved fittingly or not was all one to him. For he could think of nothing but Mei-ling. He thought of all he knew of her. He remembered that she had a narrow hand, very strong, but narrow across the palm, the fingers very delicate, and then he wondered to think that hand could be swift and stern to cut away an evil growth in human flesh. Her whole body had this slender strength, the strength of good bones well knitted under the fine pale skin. He remembered again and again how able she was in everything and how the servants looked to her, and how Ai-lan had cried out that Mei-ling must say if a coat hung well about the edge, and only Mei-ling could do for the lady what she liked to have done. And Yuan said, comforting himself, "At twenty she is as able as many a woman ten years older."

For the maid had this double charm for Yuan when he remembered her. She had sedateness and gravity as the older women had, whom he looked to, his lady mother, his aunt, and all those reared in the old ways for rearing maids. And yet she had this new thing, too, that she was not shy and silent before men. She could speak openly and plainly anywhere, and be as easy, in her different way, as Ai-lan was. Thus in the turmoil of the train and while the fields and towns went past, Yuan saw nothing. He only sat and shaped his dreams of Mei-ling, and in his mind he gathered every least word and look of hers and made the precious picture whole. When he remembered all he could, he let his mind leap to the moment when he would see her and how he would speak and what he would tell her of his love. Perfectly as though the hour were there he could see her grave good look, watching him while he spoke. And afterwards —oh, he must remember still how young she was, and that she was no bold, ready maid, but gentle and very reticent. But still he might take that narrow hand of hers, that cool kind narrow hand. . . .

Yet who can shape an hour to his wish, or what lover knows how the hour will find even himself? For Yuan's tongue, which shaped the words so easily upon the train, could shape nothing when the hour was come.

The house was quiet when he came into its hallway, and only a servant stood there. The stillness struck him like a chill.

"Where is she?" he cried to the servant, and then remembering, he said more quietly, "Where is the lady, my mother?"

The servant replied, "They are gone to the foundling home to see to a babe newly left there who is ill. They may be late, they said."

So then Yuan could only cool his heart and wait. He waited and tried to turn his thoughts here or there, but his mind was not his own—it would turn back of its own will to the one great hope it had. Night came and still the two did not come, and when the servant called the evening meal, Yuan must go to the dining room and eat there alone, and the food was dry and tasteless on his tongue. Almost he hated the little child who so delayed the hour he had longed for all these weeks.

Then even as he was about to rise because he could not eat, the door opened and the lady came in, very weary and spent and downcast in her look, and Mei-ling with her, silent and sad as Yuan had never seen her. She looked at Yuan as though she did not see him and she cried out to him in a low voice, as though Yuan had not been away at all, "The little baby died. We did all we could, but she died!"

The lady sighed and sat down and said, grieving too, "You are back, my son? . . . I never saw a lovelier little newborn child, Yuan—left three days since on the threshold—not poor, either, for its little coat was silk. At first we thought it sound, but this morning there were convulsions, and it was that old ancient woe that curses newborn babes, and takes them before the tenth day is gone. I have seen the fairest, soundest children seized by it, as by an evil wind, and nothing can prevail against it."

To this the maid sat listening, and she could not eat. Her narrow hands were clenched upon the table and she cried angrily, "I know what it is. It need not be!"

But Yuan, looking at her angry face, more moved than

he had ever seen it, perceived her eyes were full of tears. That anger and those tears were ice upon his hot heart. For he saw they closed the maid's mind against him. Yes, he thought of her and her only, but at this moment she did not dream of him; although he had been weeks away, she did not think of him. He sat and listened, therefore, and answered quietly questions that the lady mother put to him of his father's house. But he could not but see that Mei-ling did not even hear the questions or how he answered them. She sat there strangely idle, her hands quiet in her lap, and though she looked from face to face, she said nothing at all. Only more than once her eyes were full of tears. And because he saw her mind was very far from him, on that night Yuan could not speak.

Yet how could he rest until he had spoken? All night he dreamed brokenly, strange dreams of love, but never love come clear.

In the morning he woke exhausted by his dreams. It was a grey day, too, a day when summer passes certainly into autumn. When Yuan rose and looked out of the window he saw nothing but greyness everywhere, a still smooth grey sky curved above the flat grey city and upon the grey streets the people moving sluggishly, small and grey upon the earth. His ardor seeped from him under this lifelessness, and Yuan wondered at himself that ever he could have dreamed of Mei-ling.

In such a mood he sat himself down to eat his breakfast, and while he ate listlessly, for the very food on this day seemed to him saltless and without flavor, the lady came in, too. She had not eaten or exchanged much more than morning greetings with Yuan before she saw something was wrong with him. So she began to press him gently with her questions. And he, feeling it not possible to speak of his new love, told her instead of how his father had borrowed so much silver of his uncle, and she was very taken back by this and cried out, "Why did he not tell me he was so hard pressed for money? I could have used less. I am glad I have used my own silver for Mei-ling. Yes, I had a sort of pride to do that, and my father left me enough, since he had no son, before he died, and he put his moneys in a good sound foreign bank where they have lain safely all these years. He loved me very well, and sold many of his inherited lands even, and turned them into silver for me. If I had known, I might have——"

But Yuan said dully, "And why should you have done it? No, I will seek out a place where what I have learned will serve me, and I will save my wage, as much as I can, and return it to my uncle."

Then it came to him that if he did this, how could he have enough to wed on and set up his house and do all those things for which a young man hopes? In the old days the sons lived with the father, and son's wife and son's children ate from the common pot. But Yuan in his day could not bear to do this. When he thought of the courts where the Tiger lived and of that old mother who must be Mei-ling's mother-in-law, he swore he would not live there with Mei-ling. They would have their own home somewhere, a home such as Yuan had learned to love, pictures on the walls and chairs easy to sit upon and cleanliness everywhere—and only they two in it to make it what they liked. And thinking of all this he fell into such longing before the lady's very eyes that she said very kindly, "You still have not told me everything."

Then suddenly Yuan's heart burst from him and he cried, his face all red and his eyes so hot he could feel them burning underneath their lids, "I have more to tell —I do have more to tell! I have somehow learned to love her and if I do not have her I shall die."

"Her?" asked the lady, wondering. "What her?" And she cast about in her mind. But Yuan cried, "And who but Mei-ling?"

Then the lady was full of astonishment, for she had not dreamed of such a thing, since Mei-ling was to her only a child yet, the child she had lifted up from the street one cold day and taken into her own home. Now she looked at Yuan and was silent for a while and she

said thoughtfully, "She is yet young and full of her plans."
And then she said again, "Her parents are unknown. I do
not know how it will be with your father if he knows she
was a foundling."

But Yuan cried in impatience now, "My father can say
nothing on this thing. In this day I will not be bound
by their old ways. I will choose for myself."

The lady bore this mildly, being by now very well
used to all such talk, since Ai-lan had cried it often, and
she knew from talk with other parents that all young
men and women said the same thing and their elders
must bear it as they could. So she only asked, "And
have you spoken to her?"

Then Yuan forgot his boldness straightway and he said,
shy as any old-fashioned lover, "No, and I do not know
how to begin." And after a little thought he said, "It always seems as though her thoughts are set on some
busy matter of her own. Other maids begin somehow
with eyes or even touch of hands, or so I have heard,
but she never does."

"No," the lady answered proudly, "Mei-ling never
does."

Now even as Yuan sat in his dejection this came to
him. He would ask the lady to speak for him. And after
all, his mind said swiftly to itself, it was really better so.
Mei-ling would listen to the lady whom she so loved
and honored and it would be something for him.

So it seemed better to him suddenly not to say the
words himself in spite of the new times. This would be
a sort of new and yet an old way, and the maid, being so
young yet, might like it more, too. All this Yuan thought,
and he said to the lady very eagerly, "Will you speak
for me, my mother? It is true she is very young. It may
be if I speak it would frighten her—"

At this the lady smiled a little and she gazed with
some tenderness at Yuan and answered, "If she wants
to marry you, my son, let it be so, if your father will let
it be. But I will not compel her. That one thing I will
never do—compel a maid to any man. It is the only

great new good these times have brought to women—
that they need not be compelled to marriage."

"No, no—" cried Yuan.

But he did not dream the maid would need com-
pelling, because it is natural for all maids to wed.

Now while they talked and finished the meal as they
did, Mei-ling came in, very fresh and clean to see in her
robe of a dark blue silk she wore to school, and her short
straight black hair brushed behind her ears and no
jewels in her ears or on her hands, such as Ai-lan must
always wear or feel herself unclothed. Her look was
quiet, the eyes cool and steady, and her mouth curved
and not very red in hue, as Ai-lan's always was, and her
cheeks pale and smooth. Yet though Mei-ling was never
ruddy, she had always a clear gold skin which was full
of health, it was so fine and smooth. Now she gave greeting courteously, and Yuan saw the night's sleep had taken
the yesterday's distress away from her, so that she was
tranquil again and ready for this day.

Even as he watched her seat herself and take up her
bowl to eat, the lady began to speak out, a small half
smile upon her lips and in her eyes. Suddenly if Yuan
could have stopped her or chosen another hour, he would
have done so. He wished anyhow to put the moment
off, and a shyness rushed upon him and he dropped his
eyes and sat all hot with misery. But the lady said, and
the secret smile was shining in her eyes now for she
saw how Yuan was, "Child, here is a question I have to
put to you. This young man, this Yuan, for all he is a
mighty modern and will choose his wife, turns weak at
the last moment and goes back to old ways and asks a go-
between after all. And I am the go-between, and you
are the maid, and will you have him?"

As baldly as this the lady put it, in a very dry bald
voice, and Yuan almost hated her because it seemed to
him it could not have been worse done, and enough
to frighten any maid.

And Mei-ling was frightened. She set her bowl down
carefully and put her chopsticks down and stared at the

lady in a panic. Then in a very small low voice she whispered, *"Must* I do it?"

"No, child," the lady answered and now she was grave. "You need not if you do not wish it."

"Then I will not," the maid answered joyfully, her face all lit with her relief. And then she said again, "There have been others of my schoolmates who have to wed, mother, and they weep and weep because they must leave school to wed. And so I was frightened. Ah, I thank you, mother," and this young woman Mei-ling, who was always so quiet and contained, rose quickly from her seat and went and fell before the lady in the old obeisance of gratitude and bowed herself down. But the lady lifted her up and held her by an arm about her.

Then the lady's eyes fell on Yuan, and there he sat, his hot blood all flying from his face and leaving him pale, his very lips pale that he bit between his teeth to hold them still, for he would not weep. And the lady pitied him, and she said kindly, looking at the girl, "Still, you like our Yuan, Mei-ling?"

And the girl answered quickly, "Oh, yes, he is my brother. I like him, but not to wed. I do not want to wed, mother. I want to finish school and be a doctor. I want to learn and learn. Every woman weds. I do not want only to wed and take care of a house and children. I have set my heart to be a doctor!"

Now when Mei-ling said these words, the lady looked at Yuan in a sort of triumph. And Yuan looking back at the two women, felt them leagued against him, women leagued against a man, and he could not bear it. There was something good about the old ways, after all, for it was the natural right thing that women should be wed and bear children and Mei-ling ought to want to marry, and there was some perversion in her that she would not. He thought to himself, angry in his manhood against these women, "It is a strange thing if women are like this nowadays! Whoever heard of a girl not marrying when the time comes? A very strange thing if young women are not to wed—a sorry thing for the nation and the next generation!" He thought, after all, how foolish

even wisest women are, and he looked and met Mei-
ling's calm eyes and for once he thought them hard and
cold to be so calm and sure, and he looked at her angrily.
But the lady answered for her very certainly, "She shall
not marry until she wishes. She shall use her own life
as seems best to her, and you must bear it, Yuan."

And the two women looked at him, even hostile in
their new freedom, the younger held within the circle of
the elder's arm. . . . Yes, he must bear it!

Later in that gloomy day Yuan left his room where he
had thrown himself upon the bed, and he went wandering through the streets, his mind all confusion once
again. He had even wept and wept in his distress, and
his heart sat in his side aching with an actual pain, as
though it had been too hot and now was too cold and
could not beat as it should.

What should he do now? Yuan asked himself in dreariness. Here and there about the streets he wandered,
pushed and pushing, and seeing no one. . . . Well, and
if joy was gone, his duty still remained. There was the
debt he owed. At least alone he could fulfill his debt.
He had his old father left to think of and he cast about
to think what he could do, and where find a place to
work and live, and save his wage to pay his debt. He
would do his duty, he said to himself, and felt himself
most hardly used.

So the day wore on and he wandered everywhere
throughout that whole city, and it grew hateful to him.
He hated all its foreignness, the foreign faces on the
streets, the foreign garments even his own kind wore,
the very garb upon his own body. It seemed to him at
this one hour at least that old ways were better. He
cried furiously to his cold, stopped heart, "It is these
foreign ways that set our women to all this stubbornness
and talk of freedom, so that they set nature aside and
live like nuns or courtesans!" And he remembered with
especial hatred that landlady's daughter and her lewdness and Mary, whose lips had been too ready, and he
blamed even them. At last he looked at every foreign

female that he passed with such hatred that he could not bear them and he uttered, "I will get out of this city somehow. I will go away where I shall see nothing foreign and nothing new and live and find my life there in my own country. I wish I had not gone abroad! I wish I had never left the earthen house!"

And suddenly he bethought himself of that old farmer whom he once knew, who had taught him how to wield a hoe. He would go there and see that man and feel his own kind again, not tainted with these foreigners and all their ways.

At once he struck aside and took a public vehicle to hasten on his way, and when the vehicle was gone as far as it would, he walked on. Very far he walked that day searching for the land he once had planted and for the farmer and his home. But he could not find it until nearly evening, for the streets were changed and built up and full of people. When he reached at last the place he knew and recognized, there was no land to plant. There on the earth which only a few years ago had borne so fertilely, where the farmer had been proud to say his family had lived for a hundred years, now stood a factory for weaving silk. It was a great new thing, large as a village used to be, and the bricks new and red and many windows shone upon its roofs, and from its chimneys the black smoke gushed. Even as Yuan stood and looked at it, a shrieking whistle blew, the iron gates sprang open, and out of their vastness came a slow thick stream of men and women and little children, spent with their day's labor and with the knowledge of tomorrow's day to come and many days and many days which they must live like this one. Their clothes were drenched with sweat, and about them hung the vile stench of the dead worms in the cocoons from which the silk was wound.

Yuan stood looking at these faces, thinking half frantically that one of them must be the farmer's face, that he must be swallowed, even as his land had been, by this new monster. But no, he was not there. These were pale city folk, who crept out of their hovels in the morning and returned to them at night. The farmer had gone elsewhere. He and his old wife and their old buffalo had gone to other lands. Of course they had, Yuan told himself. Somewhere they lived their own life, stoutly as they ever had. And thinking of them he smiled a little, and for the moment forgetting his own pain, he went thoughtfully to his home. So would he also somehow find his own life.

IV

Two things came on the next day to shape Yuan's life. The lady said to him very early in the morning, "My son, it is not fitting somehow that you live in this house for the time. Think yourself how hard it is for Mei-ling now to see you day after day knowing what is in your heart towards her."

To this Yuan answered with anger left from his angers of the day before, "I do know very well, for so I feel also. I feel I want to be where I must not see her every day, too, and where I need not remember every time I see her or hear her voice that she will not have me."

These words Yuan started bravely enough and in anger, but before he came to the end his voice trembled and however he tried to hold his anger and say he wanted to be where he could not see Mei-ling, yet when he thought of it he knew miserably that the truth was he had rather be where he could see her and hear her voice and this in spite of anything. But this morning the lady was her old mild self and now that she needed not to defend Mei-ling or the cause of women against men she could be gentle and comprehending, and she heard very well the tremble in Yuan's voice and marked how he broke off speaking and fell very quickly to his bowl of food, for it was at table they met now, only Mei-ling did not come. So she said to comfort him, "This is your first love, son, and it comes hardly. I know what your nature is, and it is very much like your father's and they all tell me he was like his mother who was a grave quiet soul, always holding too hard to those she loved. Yes, and Ai-lan is like your grandfather, and your uncle tells me she has his merry eye. . . . Well, son, you are too young to hold so hard on anything. Go away and find a place you like and a work of some sort, and set

276

yourself to your debt to your second uncle, and know young men and women and after a year or two—" She paused here and looked at Yuan, and Yuan waited, looking back. "After a year or two perhaps Mei-ling will be changed. Who can tell?"

But Yuan would not be hopeful. He said doggedly, "No, she is not a changing sort, mother, and I can see she cannot bear me. It came to me all in a moment that she was the one I wanted. I do not want the foreign sort of maid—I do not like them. But she is right for me. She is the kind I like— Somehow she is new and old, too—"

At this Yuan stopped again suddenly and filled his mouth with his food, and then could not swallow it because his throat was stiff with tears he was ashamed to shed, because it seemed a childish thing to weep for love, and he longed to think he did not care.

The lady knew this perfectly and she let him be awhile and at last she said peaceably, "Well, let it be now, and we will wait. You are young enough to wait, and it is true you have your debt. It is a necessity that you remember you have a son's duty to do, and duty is duty in spite of all."

The lady said this with a purpose to stir Yuan out of his dejection and it did, for he swallowed hard a time or two and burst out, although it was only what he had said yesterday himself, but today he could not bear it, "Yes, that is what they always say, but I swear I am tired of it. I did my duty always to my father and how did he reward me? He would have tied me to an unlettered country wife and let me be tied forever and never know what he did to me. Now he has tied me again to my uncle, and I'll do what I did before—I'll go and join Meng and throw my life in against what old people call duty—I'll do it again—it is no excuse that he did it innocently. It is wicked to be so innocent and injure me as he has—"

Now Yuan knew he spoke unreasonably and that if the Tiger had tried to force him, still he had freed him from the prison with all the money he could find to do it. He kept his anger high therefore and ready to meet the lady's reminder of this. But instead of her expected words she said tranquilly, "It would be a very good thing, I think, for you to go and live with Meng in the new capital." And in his surprise at this lack of argument from her Yuan had no words and so the matter lay and they spoke no more.

On the same day by chance a letter came again from Meng to Yuan, and when Yuan opened it he found first a rebuke from his cousin that no answering word had come and Meng said impatiently, "With difficulty I have held this position waiting for you, for in these days to every such chance a hundred men are to be found. Come quickly and this very day, for on the third day from now the great school opens and there is no time for writing back and forth like this." And then Meng ended ardently, "It is not every man who has this opportunity to work in the new capital. There are thousands here waiting and hoping for work these days. The whole city is being made new—everything is being made which any great city has. The old winding streets are torn away and everything is to be made new. Come and do your share!"

Yuan, reading these bold words, felt his heart leap and he threw the letter down upon his table and cried aloud, "I will, then!" At that instant he began to put together his books and clothing and all his notes and writings and so he made ready for this next part of his life.

At noon he told the lady of Meng's letter and he said, "It is the best way for me to go, since all is as it must be." And the lady agreed mildly that it was so, and again they talked no more, only the lady was her usual self, kindly and a little remote from what was before her.

But that night when Yuan came to take his evening meal with her as usual she talked of many common things, of how Ai-lan would be home that day fortnight, for she was gone with her husband to play a month away in the old northern capital, and half the month was gone, and she told of a cough that had come into her foundling home and spread from child to child until today eight had it. Then she said calmly, "Mei-ling has been there all day, trying a sort of medicine the foreigners use against this cough by thrusting a liquid drug through a needle into the blood. But I told her you might go away very soon, and I told her to come home tonight that we might all be together this one more evening."

Now underneath all his other thoughts and plans through this whole day Yuan had wondered many times if he would see Mei-ling again, and sometimes he hoped he would not, and yet when he felt so he thought again with a great rush of longing that he would like once more to see her when she did not know it, perhaps, and let his eyes cling to how she looked and moved, even though he did not hear her voice. But he could not ask to see her. If it happened, let it be so, but if she stayed so it could not happen, he must bear it.

For his thwarted love worked a sort of ferment in him. In his room, he halted a score of times during that day and he threw himself sometimes on his bed and fell to melancholy thinking of how Mei-ling would not have him and he even wept, since he was alone, or sometimes he wandered to the window and leaned against it, staring out across the city, as careless of him as a merry woman and glittering in a shimmer of hot sunshine, and then he was angry in his heart that he loved and was not loved. He felt himself most bitterly used, until at one such time there came to him a thing he had forgotten, which was that twice a woman had loved him and he had given no love in return. When he thought of this he had a great fear and he cried in his heart, "Is it that she can never love me as I never did love them? Does she hate my flesh as I hated theirs, so that she cannot help it?" But he found this fear too great to be borne and he bethought himself very quickly, "It is not the same—they never loved me truly—not as I love her. No one has ever loved as I do." And again he thought proudly, "I love her most purely and highly. I have not thought of touching even her hand—well, I have not thought of it but a very little, and then only if she should love me—" And it seemed to him as if she must—she must—comprehend how great and pure was the love he gave her and so he ought to see her once more and let her see how steadfast he was even though she would not have him.

Yet now when he heard the lady say these words he felt his blood fly to his face, and for an instant he hoped in a fever that she would not come and now he did not want to see her at all before he went away.

But before he could devise an escape, Mei-ling came in quietly and usually. He could not look at her fully at first. He rose until she sat down and he saw the dark green silk of her robe and then he saw her lovely narrow hands take up the ivory chopsticks, which were the same hue as her flesh. He could say nothing, and the lady saw it, and so she said very usually to Mei-ling, "Did you finish all the work?"

And Mei-ling answered in the same way, "Yes, the last child. But I think with some I am too late. They are already coughing, but at least it will help it." Then she laughed a little, very softly, and said, "You know the six-year-old they call Little Goose? She cried out when she saw me come with the needle and wept loudly and said, 'Oh, little mother, let me cough—I'd so much rather cough—hear me, I cough already!' And then she coughed a loud false cough."

They laughed then, and Yuan a little, too, at the child, and in the laughter he found himself looking at Mei-ling without knowing it. And to his shame he could not leave off looking at her once he saw her. No, his eyes clung to hers, though he was speechless, and he drew his breath in hard, imploring her with his eyes. Then though he saw her pale clear cheeks grow red, yet she met his gaze very fully and clearly and she said breathlessly and quickly and as he had never heard her speak before, and as though he had asked a question of her, though he did not know himself what question it was, "But at least I will write to you, Yuan, and you may write to me." And then as though not able to bear his look any more she turned very shy and looked at the lady, her face still burning, but her head held high and brave and she asked, "Are you willing, my mother?"

To which the lady answered, making her voice quiet and as though she spoke of any common thing, "And why not, child? It is only letters between brother and sister, and even if it were not, what of it in these days?"

"Yes," said the maid happily, and she turned a shining look on Yuan. And Yuan smiled at her look for look, and his heart, which had been so confined all day in sorrow, found a sudden door of escape thrown open to it. He thought, "I can tell her everything!" And it was ecstasy, since not in his whole life had there been one to whom he could tell everything, and he loved her still more than he had before.

That night on the train he thought to himself, "I can do without love all my life, I think, if I can have her for a friend to whom to tell everything." He lay in the narrow berth and felt himself full of high pure thoughts and shriven by his love and filled with stoutest courage, as swept aloft by these few words of hers as he had been cast down before.

In the early morning the train ran swiftly through a cluster of low hills green in the new sunlight and then pounded for a mile or two at the foot of a vast old echoing city wall, and stopped suddenly beside a great new building shaped of grey cement and made in a foreign fashion. Yuan at a window saw very clearly against this greyness a man whom he knew instantly to be Meng. There he stood, the sun shining full upon his sword, upon a pistol thrust in his belt, upon his brass buttons, upon his white gloves, upon his lean high-cheeked face. Behind was a guard of soldiers drawn up exactly, and each man's hand was on the holster of his pistol.

Now until this moment Yuan had been no more than a common passenger, but when he came down out of the train and when it was seen he was greeted by so bold an officer, at once the crowd gave way for him and common ragged fellows who had been begging other passengers to let them hoist their bags and baskets on their shoulders now forsook them and ran to Yuan and besought him instead. But Meng, seeing them clamoring, shouted out in a great voice, "Begone, you dogs!" and turning to his own men he commanded them as sharply, "See to my cousin's goods!" And then without a word more to them he took Yuan's hand and led him through the crowd saying in his old impatient way, "I thought you would never come. Why did you not answer my letter? Never mind, you are here! I have been very busy or I should have come to meet you at your ship— Yuan, you come back at a fortunate time, a time of great need of men like you. Everywhere the country is in need of us. The people are as ignorant as sheep—"

At this instant he paused before a petty official and cried out, "When my soldiers bring my cousin's bags, you are to let them pass!"

At this the official, who was a humble anxious man and new in his place, said, "Sir, we are commanded to open all bags for opium or for arms or for anti-revolutionary books."

Then Meng grew furious and he shouted very terribly and made his eyes wide and drew down his black brows, "Do you know who I am? My general is the highest in the party, and I am his first captain and this is my cousin! Am I to be insulted by these petty rules made for common passengers?" And as he spoke he laid his white gloved hand upon his pistol, so that the little official said quickly, "Sir, forgive me! I did not indeed perceive who you were," and at that moment when the soldiers came, he marked his mark upon Yuan's box and bag, and let them go free, and all the crowd parted patiently to let them pass, staring open-mouthed. The very beggars were silent and shrank away from Meng and waited to beg until he was passed.

Thus striding through the crowd Meng led Yuan to a motor car, and a soldier leaped to open it, and Meng bade Yuan mount and then he followed and instantly the door was shut and the soldiers leaped upon the sides and the car rushed at great speed away.

Now since it was early morning, there was a great crowd in the street. Many farmers had come in with their produce of vegetables in baskets upon their poles slung across their shoulders, and there were caravans of asses carrying great bags of rice crossed upon their swaying backs, and there were wheelbarrows loaded full of water from the river near by to take into the city and sell to folk, and there were men and women going out to work, and men going to teahouses for their early meal and every sort of person on his business. But the soldier who drove the car was very able to do it, and fearless, and he sounded his horn unceasingly with a great noise, and blew his way by force among the crowd, so that people ran to either side of the street as though a mighty wind divided them, and they jerked their asses hither and thither that they might save the beasts, and women clutched their children aside, so that Yuan was afraid, and he looked at Meng to see if he would not speak to go more slowly among the frightened common people.

But Meng was used to this swiftness. He sat erect and stared ahead and pointed out to Yuan with a sort of fierce exultation all there was to see.

"You see this road, Yuan? A bare year ago it was scarcely four feet wide and a car could not pass through it. Rickshas, sedan chairs, and that was all! Even in the best wide streets the only other mode was a small carriage pulled by a single horse. Now see this road!"

Yuan answered, "I do see it," and he stared out between the soldiers' bodies and he saw the wide and hard street, and on either side were ruins of the houses and the shops which were torn down to make way for it. Yet along the edge of these ruins were already being built new shops and new houses from the ruins, frail buildings raised too quickly, but brave in their foreign shapes, and in bright paint and big glass windows.

But across this wide new street there fell suddenly a shadow, and Yuan saw it was the high old city wall, and here was the gate, and looking he saw at the foot of the wall, and especially in a sheltered curve it made, a cluster of small huts made of mats. In them lived the very poor, and now in this morning they bestirred themselves, and the women lit small fires underneath cauldrons set on four bricks, and picked over bits of cabbage they had found on refuse heaps and made ready a meal. Children ran out naked and unwashed and men came forth, still weary, to pull at rickshas or to drag great loads.

When Meng saw where Yuan's eyes were he said with irritation, "Next year they are not to be allowed, these huts. It is a shame to us all to have folk like that about. It is necessary that the great of foreign parts should come to our new capital—even princes come here—and such sights are shameful."

Now Yuan very well saw this, and he felt with Meng that these huts ought not to be there, and it was true these men and women were very low to see, and something should be done to put them out of sight. He pondered on this for a while and at last he said, "I suppose they could be put to work," and Meng said gustily, "Of course they can be put to work, and sent home to their fields, and so they shall be—"

And then Meng's look changed as though at some old remembered grievance and he cried very passionately, "Oh, it is these people who hold back our country! I wish we could sweep the country clean and build it only of the young! I want to tear this whole city down —this old foolish wall which is no use now when we make war with cannon instead of arrows! What wall can guard against an airplane dropping bombs? Away with it, and let us use the bricks to make factories and schools and places for the young to work and learn! But these people, they understand nothing—they will not let the wall be torn away—they threaten—"

Now Yuan, hearing Meng so speak, asked, "But I thought you used to grieve for the poor, Meng? It seems to me I remember you used to be angry when the poor were oppressed and you were always angry when a man was struck by a foreigner or by an official of the police."

"So I am still," said Meng quickly, turning to look at Yuan, so that Yuan saw how black and burning was his gaze. "If I saw a foreigner lay his hand even on the poorest beggar here I would be as angry as I ever was and more, because I fear no foreigner and I would draw my weapon on him. But I know more than I used to know. I know that the chief hindrance against all we do is these very poor for whom we do it. There are too many — Who can teach them anything? There is no hope for them. So I say, let famine take them and flood and war. Let us keep only their children and shape them in the ways of revolution."

So Meng spoke in his loud, lordly way, and to Yuan, listening and considering in his slower fashion, there was truth in what he said. He remembered suddenly that foreign priest who stood before the curious crowd and showed them those vile sights. Yes, even here in this new great city, upon this wide street, among the brave new shops and houses, Yuan saw some of the things the priest showed—a beggar with his eyes sightless and eaten by disease, these hovels, running filthy cesspools at their doors so that there was a stench already upon the freshness of the morning air. Then his angry shame against that foreign priest rose up in Yuan again, an anger stabbed through with pain, too, and he cried in his heart passionately as Meng had cried aloud, "It is true we must somehow sweep all this filth away!" and Yuan thought to himself resolutely that Meng was right. In this new day what use were all these hopeless, ignorant poor? He had been too soft always. Let him learn now to be hard as Meng was hard, and not waste himself on feeling for the useless poor.

So they came at last to Meng's quarters. Yuan, not being of the soldiers' company, could not live there, but Meng had hired a room in an inn near by, and he made apology somewhat when Yuan seemed doubtful because it was small and dark and not clean, and he said, "The city is so crowded in these days I cannot find a room easily at any price. Houses are not built quickly enough —the city grows beyond all power of keeping up with it." This Meng said in pride, and then he said proudly, "It is for the good cause, cousin,—we can bear anything for this time of building the new capital!" And Yuan took heart and said he could willingly, and that the room did very well.

The same night alone he sat before the small writing table beneath the one window in the room where he was now to live, and there he began his first letter to Mei-ling. He pondered long what to say at the beginning, and wondered if he should begin with all the old courteous words of greeting. But there was something reckless in him at the end of this day. The old houses lying in ruins, the little bold new shops, the wide unfinished street tearing its ruthless way through the old city, and all Meng's ardent, fearless, angry talk made him reckless, too. He thought a moment more and then began in the sharp foreign fashion, "Dear Mei-ling—" And when the words were set down black and bold, he sat and pondered on them before he wrote more and stared at them and filled them full of tenderness. "Dear"—what was that but beloved?—and Mei-ling—that was herself —she was there. . . . Then he took up his pen again and in quick sentences he told of what he had seen that day —a new city rising out of ruins, the city of the young.

This new city now caught Yuan up into its life. He had never been so busy or so happy, or so he thought. There was everywhere work to be done, and here was the pleasure in the work, that every hour of it was full of meaning for the future of many people. Among all those to whom Meng led him, Yuan felt this great same urgency of work and life. Everywhere in this city, which was the newly beating heart of the country, there were men, none much older than Yuan himself, who were writing plans and shaping ways of life not for themselves but for the people. There were those who planned the city, and the chief of these was a small fiery southerner, impatient in speech and quick in every step he took and in the movement of his small, beautiful, childlike hands. He, too, was a friend of Meng's, and when Meng said to him of Yuan, "This is my cousin," it was enough and he poured out to Yuan his plans of the city, and how he would tear down the old foolish city wall and use the ancient bricks, which after hundreds of years were still beautiful and whole as blocks of stone, and better than those which could be made nowadays. These bricks, he said, his little eyes kindling to points of light, should be made into new great halls for the new seat of government, worthy halls built in a new fashion. And one day he took Yuan to his offices, which were in an old sagging house and full of dust and flying cobwebs. He said, "It is not worth while to do anything to these old rooms. We let them go until the new ones are ready, and then these will be torn down and the land used for other new houses."

The dusty rooms were full of tables and at these tables were many young men drawing plans and measuring lines upon paper and some were coloring very brightly the roofs and cornices they drew, and even though the rooms were so old and ruined, they were full of life from these young men and their plans.

Then their chief called aloud and one came running, and he said in a lordly way, "Bring the plans for the new seat of government!" When these were brought he unrolled them before Yuan, and there were pictured very high noble buildings indeed, built of the old bricks, and set in large new lines, and from every roof flew the new flag of the revolution. There were the streets pictured forth, too, the trees green on either side, the people, very richly dressed, men and women together, walking by the sides of the streets, and in the streets there were no caravans of asses or wheelbarrows or rickshas, or any such humble vehicles as were to be seen now, but only great motor cars colored brightly in red and blue and green and filled with rich folk. Nor was there any beggar pictured.

Yuan, looking at the plans, could not but find them very beautiful. He said, entranced, "When can it be finished?"

The young chief answered certainly, "Within five years! Everything is moving quickly now."

Five years! It was nothing. Yuan—in his dingy room again, musing, looked about upon the streets where as yet there was no such building as he had seen planned. No, and there were no trees and no rich people, and the poor still were brawling and struggling. But he thought to himself that five years were nothing. It was as good as done. That night he wrote to Mei-ling what was planned, and when he set it down and told in all detail what the picture of the new city was to be, more than ever it seemed as good as done, since all the plans were clearly made, so that the very colors of the roofs were planned in tiles of bright blue, and the trees planned and painted full of leaf, and he remembered there was even a fountain running before a statue of a certain hero in the revolution. Without knowing it he wrote thus to Mei-ling, as if all were finished. "There is a noble hall—there is a great gate—there are trees beside a wide street—"

It was the same in many other things also. Young men who were physicians learned in the foreign ways of cutting diseases out of people's bodies and who scorned the old doctoring of their fathers, planned great hospitals, and others planned great schools where all the children of the country folk even might be taught, so that in the whole land there would be no one who could not read and write, and some sat and planned new laws to govern other people, and these laws were written down in every detail, and prisons were planned for those who disobeyed them. And there were yet others who planned new books to be written in a free new way of writing, and full of the new free sort of love between men and women everywhere.

Among all the planning there was a new sort of lord of war who planned new armies and new ships of war and new ways of warfare and some day he planned a great new war to show the world his nation was now mighty as any, and this one was Yuan's old tutor, who was afterwards his captain, and now general over Meng, to whose army Meng had escaped secretly when Yuan was betrayed in prison.

Now Yuan was uneasy when he knew Meng's general was this man, and he wished it could have been another,

for he did not know how much the general would remember against him. Yet he did not dare to refuse him
either when he commanded Meng to bring his cousin
to him.

So on a certain day Yuan went with Meng, and though
he kept his face straight and calm, his heart was doubtful.

Yet when he had walked through a gate at which
guards stood, very cleanly and bravely dressed, their
guns shining and ready in their hands and through courts
cleaned and ordered, and when he went into a room and
saw the general there, sitting at a table, he need not
have been afraid. In a moment Yuan saw this old tutor
of his would not call to speech any old grievance against
him. He was older than when Yuan saw him last, and
now a known and famous leader of the armies, and although his face was not smiling or easy or lenient, yet
it was not an angry face. When Yuan came in he did
not rise but nodded his head towards a seat, and when
Yuan sat edgewise on it, for he had once been this
man's pupil, he saw the two sharp eyes he remembered
gazing from behind the foreign spectacles, and the harsh
voice he remembered, which was not unkind nevertheless, asked him abruptly, "So now you have joined us,
after all?"

Yuan nodded and as simply as he used to speak when
he was a child he said, "My father pushed me to it,"
and he told his story.

Then the general asked again, looking at him very
keenly, "But still you do not love the army? With all I
taught you, you are not a soldier?"

Yuan in a little of his old confusion hesitated and then
decided willfully he would be bold and not fear this
man and he said, "I hate war still, but I can do my share
in other ways."

"What?" the general asked, and Yuan replied, "I shall
teach in the new great school here for the present, for
I have need to earn, and then I shall see how the road
opens."

But now the general grew restless, and he looked at a

foreign clock that was on his desk, as though his interest
was no more in Yuan if he were not a soldier, and so
Yuan rose, and waited while the general said to Meng,
"Have you the plans made for the new encampment?
The new military law calls for an increase of men levied
from each province, and the new contingents come in
a month from today."

At this Meng struck his heels together, for he had not
sat in his general's presence, and he saluted sharply and
he said in a very clear proud voice, "The plans are made,
my general, and await your seal, and then they will be
carried out."

So was the brief meeting over and Yuan, for all his
old distaste which rose up in him strongly as he passed
between many soldiers who now filed in from grounds
where they had been practicing their ways of war, yet
could not but see these men were different from his
father's lounging, laughing followers. These were all
young, so young that half at least were less than twenty.
And they did not laugh. The Tiger's men were always
full of brawling and of laughter, and when they straggled
home to rest after practice they pushed each other in
rude trickery and shouted and made jokes, so that the
courts were full of rough merriment. Daily in his youth
Yuan knew the hours for meals because he heard guf-
faws and curses and loud laughter outside his inner court
where he lived with his father. But these young men
came back silently, and their footsteps were in such
solemn unison the sound was like a great single foot-
step. There was no laughter. Yuan walked past them,
soldier after soldier, and he saw their faces, all young, all
simple and all grave. These were the new armies.

That night he wrote to Mei-ling, "They looked too
young to be soldiers and their faces were the faces of
country boys." Then he thought awhile, remembering
their faces, and he wrote again, "Yet they had a certain
soldier's look. You do not know it, for you have not
lived as I have. I mean their faces were simple, so simple that I knew, looking at them, they can kill as simply
as they eat their food,—a simplicity fearful as death."

In this new city Yuan now found his own life and share. He opened at last his box of books and placed them in some shelves he bought. There were also the foreign seeds he had grown to fruition in the foreign country. He looked at them doubtfully, each kind still sealed in its packet, questioning himself how they would grow if he planted them in this darker heavier earth. Then he tore one packet open and shook the seeds into his palm. They lay in his hand, large, golden, waiting grains of wheat. He must find a bit of land in which to try them.

Now he was caught in a wheel of days and weeks and months, each following swiftly after the last. His days were spent in the school. In the morning he went to the buildings, some new, some old. The new buildings were gaunt grey halls, foreign-shaped, built too quickly of cement and slender iron rods, and already flaking into pieces, but Yuan had his classrooms in an old building, and since the building was old the leaders of that school would not so much as mend a broken window. The autumn drew out long and warm and golden, and at first Yuan said nothing when a door hung cracked with age and would not close. But autumn became sharp with winter and the eleventh month howled in on the wings of a mighty wind from the northwest deserts, and fine yellow sands sifted through every break. Yuan, wrapped in his greatcoat, stood before his shivering pupils and corrected their ill-written essays and with the sandy wind blowing through his hair he set upon the blackboard rules for them on writing poetry. But it was nearly useless, for all their minds were bent on huddling in their clothes, which were for many too scanty in spite of their huddling.

First Yuan made report of it by letter to his head, an official who spent five weeks out of seven in the great coastal city, but to such letters the man paid no heed, for he had many offices and his chief work was to collect all his salaries. Then Yuan grew angry and he went himself to the high head of the school and he told the plight of his students, how the glass was broken in the windows, and how there were boards so cracked in the wooden floors the fierce wind came up between their feet, and how doors would not close.

But the high head, who had many duties, said impatiently, "Bear it awhile—bear it awhile! Such money as we have must go to making new—not patching up the useless old!" These were the same words to be heard everywhere in that city.

Now Yuan thought the words rightly enough said, and he could dream of a new hall and fine warm rooms sealed against the cold, yet here were these days, and every day colder than the last as the winter deepened. If Yuan could have done it he would have taken his own wage and hired a carpenter and made the one room closed against the winter. For after a while he came to like this work he did and he felt a sort of love for these young boys he taught. They were not often rich, for the rich sent their sons to private colleges where they had foreign teachers everywhere and fires in the school houses to keep them warm and good food every day. But to this school, which was public and opened by the new state, there were no fees, and here sons of little merchants came, and sons of ill-paid teachers of the old classics and a few bright village boys who hoped to be more than their fathers were upon the land. They were all young and poorly clad and not well fed, and Yuan loved them for they were eager and strained to understand what he taught them, though very often they did not, for although some knew more and some less, still all knew too little. Yes, looking at their pale faces and eager watching eyes, Yuan wished he had the money to mend their schoolroom.

But he had not. Even his wage was not paid to him regularly, for those above him were given their pay first, and if the moneys were not enough that month, or if some had been stopped for another cause, for army or for a new house for some official, or if some stuck in a private pocket, then Yuan and the newer teachers must wait in what patience they could. And Yuan was not patient, for he longed to be free of his debt to his uncle.

At least he could be free of one debt. He wrote and told Wang the Merchant, "As for your sons, I can do nothing for them. I have no power here. It is all I can do to hold my own place. But I will send you half of what I earn until all is paid my father borrowed. Only I will not be responsible for your sons." So he cast off in these new times at least so much of the bondage of blood kin.

Therefore he dared not use his money for his pupils. To Mei-ling he wrote of it, and how he wished he could mend the room, and how cold the winter drew down, but he did not know what to do. She answered quickly that one time, "Why do you not take them out of that old useless house into some warm court? If it does not rain or snow, take them out into the sun."

Yuan, holding her letter in his hand, wondered he had not thought of this, for the winters were dry and there were many sunny days, and after that for many days he taught his pupils in a sunny place he found, where two walls met into a corner between two buildings. If some laughed in passing he let them laugh, for the sun was warm. He could not but love Mei-ling the more because so swiftly she had thought of a small simple thing to do before the new building was made. Then this swiftness taught him something. She always answered him more quickly when he put a question to her of a thing he did not know what to do about, and he grew cunning and poured out all his perplexities. She would not answer if he spoke of love, but she answered eagerly if he spoke of trouble, and soon letters flew back and forth between these two as thick as leaves blown by the autumn winds.

There was another way Yuan found to make blood warm these cold days of coming winter, and it was by labor on the land and by planting the foreign seeds in the land. He must in this school teach many things, for the teachers were not enough for all those young who wanted to learn. Everywhere great new schools were opened to teach every new foreign thing which had not been taught before, and the young crowded into the schools to learn, and there were not to be found teachers enough to teach them all they craved to know in these new days. Since Yuan, therefore, had been to foreign parts, he was given some honor and urged to teach everything he knew, and among those things he taught was the new way of planting and tending of seeds. A piece of land was given him outside the city wall, and near a little hamlet, and thither he led his pupils, forming them like a small army into fours, and he marched through the city streets at their head, but instead of guns he bought hoes for them, and these they carried over their shoulders. The people who passed stared to see them, and many paused in their business to stare and call out in wonder, "What sort of a new thing is this?" And Yuan heard one man shout, a very honest dull fellow who pulled a ricksha, "Well, I see a new thing every day in this city now, but this is the newest thing I ever did see, to go to war with hoes!"

Then Yuan grinned to hear this and he answered, "It is the newest army of the revolution!"

The conceit pleased him, too, as he swung along in the winter sunshine. This was truly a sort of army, the only sort of army he would ever lead, an army of young men who went out to sow seed on the land. As he walked he set his feet down in the old rhythm he learned in his childhood from his father's armies, although he did not know he did it, and his footsteps rang so loudly and clearly that the ragged marching of his followers began to shape evenly and to his pace. Soon the rhythm of their marching set a rhythm moving in his blood, and when they had passed through the dark old city gate, where the mossy bricks gave echo to their steps, and were come into the country, this rhythm began in Yuan's mind to shape into short sharp words. For very long this had not happened to him. It was as though he had gone through a confusion and now work made him tranquil again and made his soul come clear and distil itself into a verse. Breathless he waited for the words and as they came he caught them in the old remembered delight of the few days in the earthen house. And they came clear, three living lines, but he lacked the fourth. In sudden uneasy haste, for the road was nearly ended and the land in sight, he tried to force it and then it would not come at all.

Then he had to let it all drop from his mind, for now murmurings and complainings began to break from his followers, and they caught their breath and cried out that he led them too quickly and they could not walk so fast and the hoes were heavy, and they were not used to such labor.

So Yuan must forget his verse and he called heartily to console them, "We are here; there is the land! Rest a little before we begin to hoe."

And the young men threw themselves down upon a bank by the edge of the field, and it was true the sweat poured down their pale faces and their bodies heaved with their panting. Only the two or three country lads among them were not in such a plight.

Then while they rested Yuan opened up his good foreign seed, and each youth held his two hands cupped and into their hands Yuan poured the full golden grains. This seed seemed very precious to him now. He remembered how he had grown it ten thousand miles away on foreign soil, and he remembered the old white-haired man. He could not but remember also the foreign woman who had put her lips to his. Pouring the grain out steadfastly, that moment came again into his mind. He wished she had not! Yet that moment after all had saved him and sent him on alone until he found Mei-ling. He took up his hoe swiftly and began to swing it up and down into the earth. "See," he cried to the watching pupils, "so the hoe must be swung! At first it is possible to waste much strength because one does not wield the hoe like this—"

Up and down his hoe swung in the way that old farmer had taught him, its point flashing in the sunlight. One by one the young men rose and tried to swing as he did. But the last and slowest to rise were the two country lads, and they, although they very well knew how to swing their hoes, moved slowly and reluctantly. Then Yuan saw it and he called out sharply, "How is it you will not work?"

At first the lads would not answer, but then one muttered sullenly, "I did not come to school to learn what I have done all my life at home. I came to learn a better way to earn my living."

Now Yuan grew angry when he heard this, and he answered swiftly, "Yes, and if you know how to do it better you would not need to leave home to find a way to earn more. Better seed and better ways to plant it and greater harvests would have made your life better, too."

Now there had gathered about Yuan and these pupils of his a handful of farmers from the village, and they stood staring in great wonder to see these young students come out with hoes and seed. At first they were afraid and silent, but soon they began to laugh to see how the young men could not strike their hoes into the soil. When Yuan said these words, they felt at ease and one shouted out, "You are wrong, teacher! However man works himself and whatever seed he sows, the harvests rest with heaven!"

But Yuan somehow could not bear to be contradicted so before his pupils, and so he would not answer this ignorant man. Without seeming to have heard the foolish speech, he showed his pupils how to scatter the seed into the rows, and then how deep to press the soil above the seed, and how to put a sign at the end of each row to show the name of the kind of seed, and when it was planted and by whom.

All these things the farmers watched agape, making merry over such great care, and they laughed freely and cried out, "Did you count each seed, brother?" And they cried, "Have you given each little seed its name, brother, and marked the color of its skin?" And another cried, "My mother! And if we took such care of every little seed, we would not have time to reap more than one harvest in ten years!"

But the young men who followed Yuan were disdainful of these coarse jests, and the two country lads were angriest of all and cried out, "These are foreign seeds and not such common stuff as you plant in your fields!" And the jokes of the farmers made them work with more zeal than their teacher could.

But after a while the merriment died out of the watching men, and their looks grew sullen and they fell silent. One by one they spat as if by chance, and turned and went back to their hamlet.

But Yuan was very happy. It was good to sow seed again and to feel the earth in his hands. It was thick and rich and fertile, black against the yellow foreign grain. . . . So the day's work was done. Yuan felt his body fresh with good weariness, and when he looked he saw the young men, even the palest one, had a new healthy look, and all were warmed, although a sharp wind blew against them from the west.

"It is a good way to be warmed," Yuan said, smiling at them. "Better than any other fire." The young men laughed to please Yuan, for they liked him. But the village lads stayed sullen in spite of their reddened cheeks.

That night in his room alone Yuan wrote it all down to Mei-ling, for it had come to be a thing as necessary as food and drink to him to end his day by telling her what it held. When he was finished he rose and went to the window and looked out over the city. The dark tiled roofs of the old houses huddled here and there, black in the moonlight. But thrusting up everywhere among them sharply were the tall new houses, red roofed—angular and foreign, their many windows shining with inner light. Across the city the few great new streets flung out wide pathways of light and glitter and dimmed the moon.

Looking at this changing city, seeing it and yet not seeing it much either, because he saw most clearly Mei-ling's face, very clear and young before his mind, the city only a background for her face, suddenly the fourth line of his verse came to his mind as finished as though he saw it printed down. He ran to the table and seized the letter he had just sealed, and tearing it open he added to it these words, "These four lines came to me today, the first three on the land, but I could not find the last perfecting line until I came back to the city and I thought of you. Then it came as simply as though you had spoken it to me."

So Yuan lived in this city, his days full of his work, and his nights full of his letters to Mei-ling. She did not write so often to him. Her letters were sedately put, the words few and exact. But they were not dull, because her words, since they were so few, were full of her meaning. She told him Ai-lan had come back after her months away, for those two had stayed their month of play over several times and were only now come home, and Mei-ling said, "Ai-lan is more beautiful than ever, but some warmth has gone out of her. Perhaps her child will bring this back. It will be born in less than a month. She comes home often because she says she sleeps better in her old bed." And she told him, "Today I did my first real operation. It was to cut off the foot of a woman which had been bound in childhood until it was gangrened. I was not frightened." And she said, "I ever love to go and play with the foundling babes, of whom I am one. They are my sisters." And she told often of some merry childish thing they said.

Once she wrote, "Your uncle and his eldest son have sent a command for Sheng to come home. He spends too much silver, they say, since they can collect no rents these days from the old lands, and the eldest son's wife is not willing for her husband's wage to be sent abroad and there is no great sum to be found otherwise. Therefore Sheng must come, because he is to have no more money."

This Yuan read thoughtfully, remembering Sheng as he had last seen him, excellently clothed in new garments, swinging a small shining cane as he walked along a sunny street in that great foreign city. It was true he spent much money since he was careful of his beauty. Doubtless he must come home—doubtless it was the only way to make him come home. Then Yuan thought,

remembering the fawning woman, "It is better for him
to come home. I am glad he must leave her at last."

Always Mei-ling answered very carefully every question Yuan wrote to her. As the winter deepened she
cautioned him to wear a thicker coat and to eat well, and
he must sleep long and not work too hard. Many times
she bade him take care against the winds in the old
schoolroom. But there was one thing she never answered
in his letters. He said in every letter, "I am not changed.
I love you—and I wait." This she did not answer.

Nevertheless Yuan thought her letters very perfect
ones. Four times a month, as certain as the day came,
he knew he could expect to find upon his table when
he went to his room at night the long shape of her
letter and her writing on it, clear and somewhat small
in shape. These four days in each month came to be
his feast days, and for sheer pleasure in his certainty he
bought a little calendar and marked ahead the days he
would have her letters. He marked them in red, and
there were twelve in all until the New Year, when there
was holiday and then he might go home to her and see
her face. Beyond that he would not mark because he
had his secret hope.

Thus Yuan lived from seventh day to seventh day,
scarcely caring to go elsewhere than to his work, and
needing no friends because his heart was fed.

Yet Meng would come sometimes and force him forth
and then Yuan sat in a teahouse somewhere for an evening and listened to Meng and his friends cry out their
impatience. For Meng was not so triumphant as he
seemed at first. Yuan listened and he heard Meng angry
still, and still he cried out against the times, even these
new times. On one such night in a teahouse newly
opened in the new street Yuan sat at dinner with him
and four young fellow captains, and these were all dis-
satisfied with everything. The lights above the table
were first too bright and then not bright enough, and
the food was not brought fast enough to please them,
and they wanted a certain white foreign wine that was

not to be had. Between Meng and the other four the serving man was in a sweat, and he mopped his shaven head and panted and ran to and fro, afraid not to please these young captains who carried shining weapons at their belts. Even when the singing girls came in and after the new foreign fashion danced and threw their limbs about, the young men would not be satisfied, but spoke loudly of how this one's eyes were small as any pig's eyes, and that one had a nose like a leek, and one was too fat and one too old, until the girls' eyes were full of tears and anger. And Yuan, though he did not think them beautiful, could not but pity them and so he said at last, "Let be. They have their rice to earn some-how."

At this one young captain said loudly, "Better they starve, I say," and laughing their loud bitter young laugh-ter they rose at last with a great clatter of their swords and parted.

But that night Meng went on foot with Yuan to his room and as they walked along the streets together, he spoke his discontent and he said, "The truth is we are all angry because our leaders are not just to us. In the revolution it is a principle that we shall all be equal and all have equal opportunity. Yet even now our leaders are oppressing us. That general of mine—you know him, Yuan! You saw him. Well, and there he sits like any old war lord, drawing a great pay each month as head of the armies of this region, and we younger ones are kept al-ways in one place. I rose quickly to be a captain, and so quickly I was full of hope and ready to do anything in our good cause, expecting to rise yet higher. Yet though I work and spend myself I stick here, a captain. We all can rise no higher than being captains. Do you know why? It is because that general fears us. He is afraid we will be greater than he is some day. We are younger and more able, and so he keeps us down. Is this the spirit of the revolution?" And Meng stopped beneath a light and poured out his hot questions at Yuan, and Yuan saw Meng's face as angry as it used to be in his sullen boyhood. By now the few passers-by were staring sidewise curiously and Meng saw them and he dropped his voice and went on again and at last said very sullenly, "Yuan, this is not the true revolution. There must be another. These are not our true leaders—they are as selfish as the old lords of war. Yuan, we young ones, we must start again—the common people are as oppressed as they ever were—we must strike again for their sakes —these leaders we have now have forgotten wholly that the common people—"

Now even as Meng said this he paused and stared, for just ahead at a certain gateway to a very famous pleasure house there was a brawl arising. The lights from that pleasure house shone down as red and bright as blood, and in the light they saw a very hateful sight. A foreign sailor from some foreign ship, such as Yuan had seen upon the great river which flowed past the city, in half drunkenness was beating with his coarse clenched fists the man who had pulled him to that pleasure house in his vehicle. He was shouting in his drunkenness and anger and staggering stupidly upon his clumsy feet. Now Meng when he saw how the white man struck the other, started forward and he began to run swiftly and Yuan ran after him. As they came near they heard the white man cursing foully the ricksha puller because he dared to ask for more coin than the white man wished to give and under his blows the man cowered, shielding himself with his upraised arms, for the white man was large and rude in body, and his drunken blows were cruel when they fell.

Now Meng had reached them and he shouted at the foreigner, "You dare—you dare—!" and he leaped at the man and caught his arms and pinioned them behind his back. But the sailor would not submit so easily, and he did not care that Meng was a captain or what he was. To him all men not of his kind were the same and all to be despised and he turned his curses on to Meng, and the two would have jumped upon each other then and there in mutual hatred, except that Yuan and the ricksha puller sprang between them and fended off the blows, and Yuan besought Meng, saying in an agony,

"He is drunk—this fellow—a common fellow—you forget yourself," and while he cried he made haste to push the drunken sailor through the gate to the pleasure house, where he forgot the quarrel and went on his way.

Then Yuan put his hand to his pocket and brought forth some scattered copper coin and gave them to the ricksha man, and so settled the quarrel, and the man, who was a small old weazened fellow, never fed well enough in a day, was pleased to have the thing end thus, and in his gratitude he cackled out a little laughter, and he said, "You understand the doctrines, sir! It is true enough one ought not to blame a child, nor a woman, nor a man drunk!"

Now Meng had stood there panting and very hot with anger all this time, and since he had not freed his anger fully on the sailor it was more than half in him still, and he was beside himself. When he saw how easily the beaten man was assuaged with a few copper coins and when he heard the poor laughter and the old adage he put into words again, Meng could not bear it. No, in some strange way his clean right anger against the foreigner's insult to his own kind soured and without a word his eyes blazed out anew now upon the ricksha puller, and he leaned and gave the man's face a blow across the mouth. Yuan saw Meng do this thing, and he cried out, "Meng, what is it you do!" And he made haste to find a coin again to give the man for such a cruel blow.

But the man did not take the money. He stood in a daze. The blow came so swiftly and without any expectation, that he stood with his jaw hanging, and a little blood began to stream out from the corner of his mouth. Suddenly he bent and picked up the shafts of the ricksha, and he said to Yuan simply, "It was a harder blow than any the foreigner gave me." And so he went away.

But Meng had not stayed a moment after he gave the blow. He strode off and Yuan ran after him. When he came up to Meng he was about to ask him why he gave the blow, but first he looked at Meng's face, and then he kept silent for to his astonishment he saw in the bright light of the streets that tears were running down Meng's cheeks. Through these tears Meng stared ahead, until at last he muttered furiously, "What is the use of fighting in any cause for people like these, who will not even hate the ones who oppress them,—a little money sets everything right for such as these—" And he left Yuan at that instant and turned without another word into a dark side street.

Then Yuan stood irresolute a moment, questioning if perhaps he should not follow Meng to see he did not do some further angry deed. But he was eager to reach his room, for it was the night of a seventh day, and he could see before him the shape of the letter waiting for him, and so once more he let Meng go his angry way alone.

At last the days drew near to the end of the year, and it came within a handful of days to the holidays when Yuan could see Mei-ling again. In those days whatever he did seemed only a means of waiting until the one day when he would be freed. His work he did as well as he was able, but even his pupils ceased for him to have any life or meaning and he could not greatly care if they did well or ill, or what they did. He went to bed early to hasten the night, and he rose early to begin the day and pass it over, and yet in spite of all he did, the time went as slowly as though a clock were stopped.

Once he went to see Meng and made a plan to take the same train homewards, for this time Meng was free for holiday, too, and though he always said he was a revolutionist and he cared nothing if he never saw home again, yet he was very restless in these days, and eager for some change or other he could not make, and he was willing to go home, having nothing better then to do. He never spoke to Yuan again of that night he had struck the common fellow. It seemed he had forgotten the thing, for now he was full of a new anger, and here it was, that the common people were so willful they would not make the great feast day for the New Year on the day the new government had said it must be. The truth was the people were used to a year timed by the moon, and now these new young men would have it timed by the sun as it was in foreign countries, and the people were doubtful, and on the streets where there were placards put commanding all to make merry at the foreign new year, the people gathered to look or to listen, if they could not read, to some scholar in their midst, who read out the commands. Thus the people muttered everywhere, "How can the year be put anyhow like this? If we send up the kitchen god a month too soon, what will heaven think? Heaven does not count by any foreign sun, we swear!" And so they stayed willful and women would not make their cakes and meats and men would not buy the mottoes of red paper to paste upon their doors for good fortune.

Then the new young rulers grew very angry at such willfulness, and they made mottoes of their own, not of old foolish sayings of the gods, but of the sayings of the revolution and they sent their own hirelings and pasted these mottoes on the doors by force.

Of this Meng was full on the day when Yuan went to see him, and he ended all the story triumphantly, "So whether they will or not the people must be taught and forced out of old superstitious ways!"

But Yuan answered nothing, not knowing indeed what to say, since he could see the two sides of the thing.

In those next two days left, Yuan looked and it was true he saw everywhere the new mottoes being pasted upon doors. There was no word said against it. Everywhere men and women watched the new red papers put upon their doors and they stayed silent. A man here and there might laugh a little, or he spat into the dust, and went his way as though he were full of something he would not tell, but men and women worked as usual everywhere and as though there was no feast day for them in that whole year anywhere. Though all the doors were gay and newly red, the common people seemed not to see anything at all, but went with ostentatious usualness to their usual work. And Yuan could not but smile a little secretly, although he knew Meng's anger had a cause, and although if he had been asked he would have acknowledged the people ought to obey.

But then Yuan smiled more easily these days about any small thing because somehow he felt Mei-ling must be changed and warmer. Though she had not answered any word of love he wrote, at least she read the words and he could not believe she forgot them all. For him at least it was the happiest gayest year he ever had begun in his life, because he hoped much from it.

In such expectation Yuan began his holidays that Meng's angers even could not throw a cloud upon him, although Meng came as near to a quarrel with Yuan upon that day's journey as Yuan would let him. The truth was that Meng was in some such fierce secret inner discontent that nothing pleased him and in the train he was inflamed immediately against a rich man who spread his fur robes to take twice the space he should upon a seat, so that a lesser-seeming man must stand, and then he was inflamed as much against the lesser man because he bore it. At last Yuan could not forbear smiling and he made a little thrust at Meng half merrily and said, "Nothing will please you, Meng, not rich because they are rich, nor poor because they are poor!"

But Meng was too sore secretly to hear any merriment at all about himself. He turned furiously on Yuan then and said in a fierce low tone, "Yes, and you are the same —you bear anything—you are the lukewarmest soul I ever knew—never fit to be a true revolutionist!"

At Meng's fierceness Yuan could not but grow grave. He answered nothing, for all the people stared at Meng, and though he made his voice too low to let them hear what he said, still his face was so angry and his eyes so blazing under his black brows drawn down that they were afraid of such a one, who had a pistol thrust into his belt besides. . . . Therefore Yuan sat silent. But in his silence he could not but acknowledge Meng spoke the truth and he was wounded a little, although he knew Meng was angry at some hidden thing and not at him. So Yuan sat in soberness for a while as the train wound its way through the valleys, hills and fields, and he fell to thinking and to asking himself what he was and what he wanted most. It was true he was no great revolutionist, and never would be, because he could not hold his hates long, as Meng could. No, he could be angry for a while and hate for a moment, but not for long. The thing he truly wanted was a peace in which to do his work. And the work he loved best was what he did now. The best hours he had spent were those he used to teach his pupils—except his hours of writing to his love. . . .

Across his dreaming Meng's voice broke scornfully, saying, "What are you thinking of, Yuan? You sit there smiling as silly as a boy who has had barley sugar thrust unawares into his mouth!"

Then Yuan could not but laugh shamefacedly, and curse the heat he felt rush into his face, for Meng was not one to whom he could tell such thoughts as now were his.

Yet what meeting can ever be so sweet as it is dreamed? When Yuan reached his home on the evening of that day he leaped up the steps and into the house. But again there was only silence, and after a moment a serving woman came and gave him greeting and said, "My mistress says you are to go at once to your eldest cousin's house, where there is a family feast made for the homecoming of the young lord who has been in foreign countries. She awaits you there."

Now above his interest in this news of Sheng's coming home was Yuan's eagerness to know if Mei-ling was gone with the lady or not. Yet however he longed to know he would not ask a servant of her, for there is no mind so quick as a servant's mind to put a man and a maid together. Therefore he must make his heart wait until he could get to his uncle's house and see for himself if Mei-ling were there.

All during these many days Yuan had dreamed of how he would first see Mei-ling, and always he dreamed it that he saw her alone. They met, magically alone, inside the door as he stepped into the house. Somehow she would be there. But she was not there, and even if she were at his cousin's house, he could not hope to see her alone, and he dare not seem other to her than cool and courteous before the eyes of his family.

And so it was. He went to his cousin's house and into the large room which was full of rich foreign ornaments and chairs and there were they all gathered. Meng was before Yuan, and they had only finished making welcome for him when Yuan came in and fresh welcome must begin for him. He must go and bow before his old uncle, now wakeful and very merry with all his sons about him except the one he gave the Tiger and the one who was hunchback and a priest, but these neither he nor his lady counted any more as sons. There the old pair sat in their best holiday robes, and the lady was full of her place and dignity and she smoked very gravely a water pipe a maid stood and filled for her every puff or two, and in her hand she held a rosary, whose brown beads she passed constantly between her fingers, and still she took it on herself to say a balancing moral word to every jest the old man made. When he had given reply to Yuan he shouted, his old loose face in a thousand wrinkles, "Well, Yuan, here is this son of mine home again as pretty as a girl, and all our fears of a foreign wife were needless—he is still unwed!"

At this the aged lady said very sedately, "My lord, Sheng was ever much too wise to think of such wickedness. I pray you do not speak foolishly in your age!"

But for once the old man would not be afraid of the lady's tongue. He felt himself the head of this house, and head of all these goodly young men and women in this rich house and he grew waggish and he was made bold by the presence of others and he cried, "It is nothing untoward to speak of marriage for a son, I suppose? I suppose Sheng will be wed?" To which the lady answered with majesty, "I know what is the proper way in these new days, and my son need not complain that his mother forced him against his will."

Then Yuan, who had listened half smiling to this bickering between the old pair, saw a strange thing. He saw Sheng smile a little cold sad smile and he said, "No,

mother, I am not so new after all. Wed me as you like
—I do not care—women are the same to me anywhere,
I think."

At this Ai-lan laughed and said, "It is only because you
are too young, Sheng—" And in her laughter the others
joined and the moment passed, except Yuan did not forget Sheng's look, the look in his eyes while he steadily
smiled and while the others laughed. It was the look of
one who greatly cares for nothing, not even for what
woman he is to wed.

Yet how could Yuan think deeply on this night of
Sheng? Before even he had bowed to the old pair, his
eyes sought and found Mei-ling. He saw her first of all,
standing very still and quiet beside the lady, her foster
mother, and for one flying second their eyes met, although they did not smile. But there she was, and Yuan
could not be wholly disappointed even though it was
not as he dreamed. It was now enough that she was
here in this room, even though he did not say a word
to her. Then he thought he would not say a word to
her—not now, not in this crowded room. Let their true
meeting be afterwards and in some other place. Yet
though Yuan looked at her very often, he never caught
her eyes after that one first time. But the lady his mother
gave him very warm greeting, and when he went to her
she caught his hand and patted it a little before she
dropped it, and Yuan stayed by her a moment, although
when he did Mei-ling made excuse to slip away to fetch
some small thing she wanted. Nevertheless, although he
gave himself to all these others, there was the warmth
of knowing her presence, and when he could do it he
let his eyes find her again and again as she moved to
pour tea into some bowl or to give a sweetmeat to a
child.

All the talk and greetings were mostly for Sheng this
night, and Meng and Yuan were soon only part of the
others. Sheng was more beautiful than ever and so beautiful and seeming so to know everything and be at ease
in all he said and did, that Yuan was shy before him as
he always used to be and he felt himself a youth again

before this finished man. But Sheng would not have it
so. He took Yuan's hand in his old friendly way and
held it, and Yuan felt the touch of Sheng's smooth
graceful fingers, shaped so like a woman's hands, and the
touch was pleasant and yet somehow distasteful, and so
was the look Sheng had now in his eyes. For all its
sweet seeming frankness there was in these days something near to evil in Sheng's face and way, as there is in
a flower too fully blown and whose scent is heavy with
something more than fragrance, but why this was Yuan
did not know. Sometimes he felt he imagined it, and
yet again he knew he did not. For Sheng, although he
laughed and talked and his laughter was always nicely,
rightly made, and his voice even as a bell, not high nor
low, but very softly toned, and although he seemed to
enter into all the family gossip with readiness and pleasure, yet Yuan felt Sheng himself was not there at all but
somewhere very far away. He could not but wonder if
Sheng were sorry to be home again, and once he seized
a chance when he was near to ask him quietly, "Sheng,
were you sorry to leave that foreign city?"

He watched Sheng's face for answer, but the face was
smooth and golden and untroubled, and his eyes as
smooth as dark jade, and telling nothing more, and Sheng
smiled his lovely ready smile and answered, "Oh, no, I
was ready to come home. It makes no difference to me
where I am."

Again Yuan asked, "Have you written more verse?"
And Sheng answered carelessly, "Yes, I have a little book
printed now of my verses, a few of them you saw, but
nearly all new since you left— If you like, I will give
you a copy before you go tonight." And he only smiled
when Yuan said simply he would like to have them.
Once more Yuan asked a question and he asked, "Shall
you stay here to live or come to the new capital?"

Then only did Sheng answer quickly and as though
here were one thing which mattered to him, and he said,
"Oh, I stay here, of course. I have been so long away I
am used to modern life. I could not, of course, live in
so raw a city as that is. Meng has told me something,

and though he is so proud of the new streets and houses, still he had to tell me when I asked him, that there is no modern way to bathe one's self, no amusement houses worth the name, no good theatres—nothing in fact for a cultivated man to enjoy. I said, 'My dear Meng, what is there, pray, in this city of which you are so proud!' And then he went into one of his glowering silences! How little Meng has changed!" And all this Sheng said in the foreign tongue he now spoke so easily and well that it came more quickly to his tongue than his own native one.

But his elder brother's wife found Sheng very perfect, and so did Ai-lan and her husband. These three could not look at him enough, and Ai-lan, though she was then big with child, laughed more in her old merry way than she did usually, nowadays, and made free with Sheng and took great delight in him. And Sheng answered all her wit and paid her praise, and Ai-lan took it willingly, and it was true she was still as pretty as she ever was in spite of her burden. Yes, when other women grow thick and dark in the face and sluggish in their blood, Ai-lan was only like a lovely flower at its height, a rose wide in the sun. To Yuan she cried a lively greeting as her brother, but to Sheng she gave her smiles and wit, and her handsome husband watched her carelessly and lazily and without jealousy, for however beautiful Sheng might be, he still thought himself more beautiful and more to be preferred by any woman and most of all by the one whom he had chosen. He loved himself too well for jealousy.

So in the talk and laugher the feast began and they all sat together, not as in ancient times divided into old and young. No, in these days there was not such division. It is true the old lord and his lady sat in the highest seats, but their voices were not heard in the laughing back and forth of Ai-lan and Sheng and of the others who took part sometimes. It was a very merry hour, and Yuan could not but be proud of all these his blood kin, these rich well-clad folk, every women in the finest gayest hue of satin robe cut to the hour's fashion, and

the men, except the old uncle, in their foreign garb, and
Meng haughty in his captain's uniform, and even the
children gay in silks and foreign ribbons, and the table
covered with dishes of every foreign sort and foreign
sweets and foreign wines.

Then Yuan thought of something and here it was.
These were not all his family. No, many miles in from
the sea, the Tiger, his own father, lived as he ever did,
and so did Wang the Merchant and all his sons and
daughters. They spoke no foreign tongue. They ate no
foreign thing, and they lived as their own forefathers
did. If they were brought into this room, Yuan thought,
half troubled, they would be very ill at ease. The old
Tiger would soon be pettish because he could not spit
as freely as he was used, for on this floor was spread a
flowered silken carpet, and though he was not a poor
man, he was used at best to brick or tile. And the merchant would be in a misery at all this money spent on
pictures and on satin-covered seats and little foreign toys,
and all those foreign rings and trinkets which the women
wore. Nor could this half of Wang Lung's house have
borne the life the Tiger lived, nor even the life in the
home where Wang the Merchant lived, which Wang
Lung had left for his sons in that old town. These grand-
children and great-grandchildren would hold it too mean
to live in, cold in winter except where the southern sun
struck in, and unceiled and not modern anywhere, and
not a fit house for them. As for the earthen house, it
was no more than a hovel, and they had forgot it was,
even.

But Yuan did not forget. In the strangeness of memory, sitting at this feast and looking all about the table,
white-clothed in the new foreign fashion, he suddenly
remembered that earthen house and when he remembered it, he liked it, somehow, still. . . . He was not
wholly one of them, he thought slowly—not with Ai-lan,
not with Sheng. . . . Their foreign looks and ways made
him wish to be less foreign even than he was. Yet he
could not live in that earthen house, either,—no, though
he liked something about it very deeply, he knew now

he could not live there as his grandfather once had lived in content, and feel it home. He was between, some-how, and it was a lonely place—between, as he was, this foreign house and the house of earth. He had no real home, and his was a very lonely heart which could not be wholly here nor there.

His eyes rested on Sheng a moment. Except for his gold skin, and for his dark, pointed eyes, Sheng might be completely foreign. The very movements of his body now were foreign, and he spoke as a man from the west does. Yes, and Ai-lan liked it, and so did the cousin's wife, and even the eldest cousin felt Sheng very new and full of something modish, and he was silent and abashed and somewhat envious and for solace he ate heavily in silence.

Then quickly and secretly Yuan looked at Mei-ling, jealous because he had thought of a thing when he saw the praise of Sheng in Ai-lan's eyes. Did Mei-ling also watch Sheng as the other younger women did and laugh at all he said to make them laugh, and admire him with her eyes, too? He saw her look at Sheng calmly, and turn her gaze away again tranquilly. His heart eased itself. Why, she was like himself! She was between, too, not wholly new, and yet different from the old. He looked at her once more, hot and longing, and he let the waves of talk and laughter break over him and for a moment took his fill of her through his eyes. There she sat beside the lady, and now she leaned and with her chopsticks picked a bit of white meat daintily from a central dish and put it on the lady's dish, and smiled at her. She was, Yuan said most passionately within him-self, as far from Ai-lan and her kind as a lily growing wild beneath bamboos is different from a forced ca-mellia. Yes, she was between, too,—well, then he was not lonely!

Suddenly, Yuan's heart was so warm and ready that he could not believe Mei-ling would not be ready, too. In this one love of his his heart flowed out and all his many feelings fused most ardently into this one swift course.

That night he went to bed and lay sleepless, planning how he would talk with Mei-ling alone the next day and feel how her heart was to him now, for surely, or so he thought, the many letters he had written must mean some change in her to warmth. He planned how they would sit and talk, or perhaps he might persuade her to a walk with him, even, since many maids walked alone these days with young men whom they knew and trusted. And he bethought himself how he might say he was a sort of brother to her if she hesitated, and then quickly he rejected this excuse and he said stoutly in himself, "No, I am not her brother, whatever else I may not be." Only at last could he fall asleep and then to dream awry and without completion of any dream.

But who could foretell that this was the night when Ai-lan would give birth to her child? Yet so it was. When Yuan woke in the morning it was to hear confusion through all the house, and the noise of servants running here and there, and when he rose and washed and clothed himself and went to the dining room, there was the table only half set for the meal, and a sleepy maidservant moved to and fro languidly, and the only other in the room was Ai-lan's husband, who sat there dressed as he had been the night before. When Yuan came in he said gaily, "Never be a father, Yuan, if one's wife is the new sort of woman! I have had as hard a time as though I bore the child—sleepless, and Ai-lan crying out and making such a wailing I thought her near her end, except the doctor and Mei-ling promised me she did very well. These women nowadays bear their children very hardly. Lucky it is a boy, I say, because Ai-lan has already called me to her bed this morning to swear me there will never be another child from her!" He laughed again, and passed his beautiful smooth hand across his laughing, half-rueful face, and then he sat down to eat with great appetite the food the serving maid set there for he had been father several times before this, and so it was no great thing to him now.

Thus was Ai-lan's child born in this house, and all

the household was absorbed and busied in it, and Yuan caught no glance at Mei-ling scarcely beyond a passing moment here and there. Three times a day the physician came, and nothing would please Ai-lan except a foreign one, and so he came, a tall red-haired Englishman, and he saw her and talked with Mei-ling and the lady and told them what Ai-lan must eat and how many days she must rest. There was the child, too, to be cared for, and Ai-lan would have it that Mei-ling must do this herself, and so Mei-ling did, and the child wept much, because the milk of the nurse they hired at first was not suited to its needs, and so this one and that must be found and tried.

For Ai-lan, like many of her kind these days, would not feed her son from her own breasts, lest they grow too large and full and spoil her slender looks. This was the only great quarrel Mei-ling ever made with her. She cried accusingly to Ai-lan, "You are not fit to have this good sweet son! Here he is born strong and lusty and starving, and your two breasts running full, and you will not feed him! Shame, shame, Ai-lan!"

Then Ai-lan wept with anger, and she pitied herself, too, and she cried back at Mei-ling, "You know nothing of it—how can you know who are a virgin? You don't know how hard it has been to have a child in me for months and months and my clothes hideous on me, and now after all my pain am I to go hideous another year or two? No, let such coarse work be done by serving women! I will not—I will not!"

Yet though Ai-lan wept, her pretty face all flushed and distraught, Mei-ling would not give in so lightly, and this was how Yuan heard of the quarrel, for Mei-ling carried it to Ai-lan's husband and Yuan was in the room. While she besought the father Yuan listened in enchantment, for it seemed to him he never had seen how true and lovely Mei-ling was. She came in swiftly, full of her anger and without seeing Yuan she began to speak earnestly to the father, "Will you let this be? Will you let Ai-lan hold back her own milk from the child? The child is hungry, and she will not feed it!"

But the man only laughed and shrugged himself and said, "Has anyone ever made Ai-lan do what she would not? At least I have never tried, and could not dare it, now, most certainly. Ai-lan is a modern woman, you know!"

He laughed and glanced at Yuan. But Yuan was watching Mei-ling. Her grave eyes grew large as she held them to the man's smiling face, and her clear pale face went paler and she said quickly beneath her breath, "Oh, wicked—wicked—wicked!" and turned and went away again.

When she had gone the husband said affably to Yuan, as men may speak when no women are by, "After all, I cannot blame Ai-lan,—it is a very binding thing to nurse a brat, and force one's self to be home every hour or two, and I could not ask her to give up her pleasure, and the truth is, I like to have her keep her beauty, too. Besides, the child will do as well on some servant's milk as hers."

But when he heard this, Yuan felt a passionate defense of Mei-ling. She was right in all she said and did! He rose abruptly to leave this man whom somehow now he did not like. "As for me," he said coldly, "I think a woman may be too modern, sometimes. I think Ai-lan is wrong here." And he went slowly to his room, hoping on the way to meet Mei-ling, but he did not.

Thus one by one the few days of his holidays crept past, and not on any one day did he see Mei-ling above ten minutes or so, and never then alone, for she and the lady were always bent together over the newborn babe, the lady in a sort of ecstasy, because here was the son at last she had so longed for once. Though she was so used to new ways, yet now she took a sweet half-shamed pleasure in a few old ways, too, and she dyed some eggs red and bought some silver trinkets and made ready for his month-old birthday feast although the time was still far off. And in every plan she made she must talk with Mei-ling, and almost she seemed to forget Ai-lan was the child's mother, she depended so on the foster daughter.

But long before this birthday was come Yuan must go back to the new city to do his work. Now as the days passed, they passed very empty for him, and after a while he grew sullen and then he told himself that Mei-ling need not be so busy and that she could make time for him if she would, and when he had so thought for a day or two, while the last day drew very near, he grew sure he felt rightly and that Mei-ling did what she did on purpose not to see him any time alone. And in her new pleasure in the child even the lady seemed to forget him and that he loved Mei-ling.

So it was even until the day he must go back. On that day Sheng came in very gaily and he said to Yuan and to Ai-lan's husband, "I am bid to a great merry-making tonight at a certain house, and they lack a youth or two in number, and will you two forget your age for once and pretend you are young again and be partners to some pretty ladies?"

Ai-lan's husband answered with ready laughter that he would very willingly, and that he had been so tied to Ai-lan these fourteen days he had forgot what pleasure was. But Yuan drew back somewhat, for he had gone to no such merry-making for years now, and not since he used to go with Ai-lan, and he felt the old shyness on him when he thought of strange women. But Sheng would have him and the two pressed him, and though at first Yuan would not go, then he thought recklessly, "Why should I not? It is a stupid thing to sit in this house and wait for the hour that never comes. What does Mei-ling care how I make merry?" So forced by this thought he said aloud, "Well, then, I will go."

Now all these days Mei-ling had not seemed to see Yuan, so busy had she been, but that one night when he came out of his room dressed in his black foreign clothes which he had been used to wear at evening, she happened to pass him, holding in her arms the new little boy who was asleep. She asked wonderingly, "Where are you going, Yuan?" He answered, "To an evening's merry-making with Sheng and Ai-lan's husband."

He fancied at that moment he saw a look change in Mei-ling's face. But he was not sure, and then he thought he must be wrong, for she only held the sleeping child more closely to her and said quietly, "I hope you have a merry time, then," and so she went on.

As for Yuan, he went his way hardened against her, and to himself he thought, "Well, then, I *will* be merry. This is my last evening and I will see how to make it very merry."

And so he did. That night Yuan did what he had never done before. He drank wine freely and whenever anyone called out to him to drink, and he drank until he did not see clearly the face of any maid he danced with, but he only knew he had some maid or other in his arms. He drank so much of foreign wines to which he was not used, that all the great flower-decked pleasure hall grew before his eyes into a sort of swimming glittering moving maze of brightness. Yet for all this he held his drunkenness inside him very well, so that none knew except himself how drunken he truly was. Even Sheng cried out in praise of him, and said, "Yuan, you are a lucky fellow! You are one of those who grow paler as he drinks instead of red as we lesser fellows do! I swear it is only your eyes that betray you, but they burn as hot as coals!"

Now in this night's drinking he met one whom he had seen somewhere before. She was a woman whom Sheng brought to him, saying, "Here is a new friend of mine, Yuan! I'll lend her to you for a dance, and then you must tell me if you have found one who does so well!" So Yuan found himself with her in his arms, a strange little slender creature in a long foreign dress of white glittering stuff, and when he looked down at her face he thought he knew it, for it was not a face easily forgotten, very round and dark, and the lips thick and passionate, a face not beautiful, but strange and to be looked at more than once. Then she said herself, half wondering, "Why, I know you—we were on the same boat, do you remember?" Then Yuan forced his hot brain and he did remember and he said, smiling, "You are the girl who cried you would be free always."

At this her great black eyes grew grave and her full lips, which were painted thick and very red, pouted and she answered, "It is not easy being free here. Oh, I suppose I am free enough—but horribly lonely—" And suddenly she stopped dancing and pulled Yuan's sleeve and cried, "Come and sit down somewhere and talk with me. Have you been as miserable as I? . . . Look, I am the youngest child of my mother who is dead, and my father is next to the chief governor of the city. . . . He has four concubines—all nothing but singsong girls—you can imagine the life I lead! I know your sister. She is pretty, but she is like all the others. Do you know what their life is? It is gamble all day, gossip, dance all night! I *can't* like it—I want to *do* something—What are *you* doing?"

These earnest words came so strangely from her painted lips that Yuan could not but heed them. She listened restlessly after a while when Yuan told her of the new city and his work there, and how he had found a little place of his own, and, he thought, a small work to do. When Sheng came and took her hand to bring her back into the dance, she thrust him pettishly away, and pouted her too full lips at him, and she cried earnestly, "Leave me alone! I want to talk seriously with him—"

At this Sheng laughed, and said teasingly, "Yuan, you would make me jealous if I thought she could be serious about anything!"

But the girl had turned already again to Yuan and she began to pour out her passionate heart to him, and all her body spoke, too, the little round bare shoulders shrugging, and her pretty plump hands moving in her earnestness, "Oh, I hate it all so—don't you? I can't go abroad again—my father won't give me the money—he says he can't waste any more on me—and all those wives gambling from morning to night! I hate it here! The concubines all say nasty things about me because I go places with men!"

Now Yuan did not like this girl at all, for he was repelled by her naked bosom and by her foreign garb and by her too red lips, but still he could feel her earnestness and be sorry for her plight and so he said, "Why do you not find something to do?"

"What can I do?" she asked. "Do you know what I specialized in in college? Interior decoration for western homes! I've done my own room over. I've done a little in a friend's house, but not for pay. Who here wants what I have? I want to belong here, it's my country, but I've been away too long. I have no place anywhere—no country—"

By now Yuan had forgotten this was an evening meant for pleasure, he was so moved by the poor creature's plight. There she sat before his pitying gaze, gay in her silly shining clothes, and her painted eyes full of tears.

But before he could think of a thing to say for her comfort Sheng was back again. And now he would not have refusal. He did not see her tears. He put his arm about her waist and laughing at her he swept her off with him into the whirling music, and Yuan was left alone.

Somehow he had no heart to dance more, and all the gaiety was gone from the noisy hall. Once the girl came by in Sheng's arms, and now her face was turned up to his, and it was bright and empty again and as though she had never spoken the words she had to Yuan. . . . He sat thoughtfully awhile, and let a servant fill his glass again and again, while he sat on alone.

At the end of that night of pleasure, when they went home again, Yuan was steady still, though it was true the wine burned inside him like a fever. Yet he could be strong enough to let Ai-lan's husband lean on him, for that one could not walk alone any more, he was so drunken, and his whole face was crimson and he babbled like a foolish child.

Now when Yuan struck at the door to be let in that night it opened suddenly and there by the manservant who had opened it was Mei-ling herself, and when the drunken man saw her he seemed to think of something he remembered between Yuan and Mei-ling, and he cried, "You—you—should have gone—there was a—a pretty rival—she wouldn't—leave Yuan—dangerous, eh?" And he fell to laughing foolishly.

Mei-ling answered nothing. When she saw the two she said to the servant coldly, "Take my sister's lord to his bed, since he is so drunken!"

But when he was gone she held Yuan there with a sudden blazing gaze. Thus were these two alone at last, and when Yuan felt Mei-ling's great angry eyes on him, it was like a sobering blast of cold north wind upon him. He felt the heat within him die down quickly, and for an instant he almost feared her, she was so tall and straight and angry, and he was speechless.

But she was not. No, all these days she had scarcely spoken to him, but now she did, and her words leaped from her, and she said, "You are like all the others, Yuan, —like all the other foolish idle Wangs! I have made myself a fool. I thought, 'Yuan is different—he is not a half-foreign fop, drinking and dancing all his good years away!' But you are—you are! Look at you! Look at your silly foreign clothes—you reek of wine—you are drunk, too!"

But Yuan grew angry at this and sulky as a boy and he muttered, "You would not give me anything—you know how I have waited for you—and you have made excuses and excuses—"

"I did not!" she cried, and then beside herself this maid stamped her foot and she leaned forward and gave Yuan's face a swift sharp slap, as though he were indeed a naughty child. "You know how busy I have been—who was that woman he told of?—and this was your last evening—and I had planned— Oh, I hate you!"

And she burst into weeping and ran quickly away, and Yuan stood in an agony, not comprehending anything except she said she hated him. So ended his poor holiday.

The next day Yuan returned to his work, and alone, for Meng had shorter holiday and was already gone. The rains of late winter were begun, and the train drove through the dark day, and the water dropped down the window pane, so that he could scarcely see the sodden fields. At every town the streets ran with liquid filth and the stations were empty except for the shivering few men who must be there for some duty, and Yuan, remembering how he had not seen Mei-ling again, for he left in the early morning and she was not there to bid him good-bye, said to himself this was the dreariest hour of his life. . . .

At last weary of watching the rain and in restless dreariness he took from his bag the book of verses Sheng had given him the first night, and which he had not read yet, and he began to turn the thick ivory paper, not caring much if he read or not. On each page were printed clear and black a few lines or words, a little group of strung phrases, seeming exquisite, Yuan thought, until he grew curious and half forgot his trouble, and read the book again more carefully, and then he saw these little poems Sheng had made were only empty shapes. They were only small lovely empty shapes, all exquisite and empty although they were so fluent in their line and sound that almost Yuan forgot their emptiness until, the shape seized, he found there was nothing there within them.

He closed the pretty silver-bound book, and put it in its cover again and laid it down. . . . Outside the villages slipped past, dark and huddled in the rain. At doorways men looked sullenly into the rains that beat through the thatched roofs above their heads. In sunshine these folk could live outdoors as beasts do, and thrive merrily somehow, but the days of rains drove them into their hovels and too many days of rain drove them half-mad with quarrelling and cold misery, and now they looked out with hate against heaven who sent such long rains down.

. . . The verses were of lovely delicacies, the light of the moon upon a dead woman's golden hair, an ice-bound fountain in a park, a faëry island in a smooth green sea, narrow between pale sands. . . .

Yuan saw the sullen beast-like faces, and he thought,

very troubled, "As for me, I can write nothing. If I wrote these things Sheng does, which I can well enough see are exquisite, why, then I remember these dark faces and these hovels and all this deep under-life of which he knows nothing and will not know. And yet I cannot write of such life either. I wonder why I am so speechless and troubled?"

And so he fell to brooding and to thinking perhaps that no man can create anything who lives not wholly anywhere. He remembered how on that feast day he had thought himself between the old and the new. And then he smiled sadly, thinking how foolish he had been to think himself not alone. He was alone.

. . . So it rained on to his journey's end, and he came down from the train in rain and dusk, and in the rain the old city wall stood grim and black and high. He called a ricksha and climbed in, and sat chill and lonely while the man dragged the vehicle along the slippery running streets. Once the man stumbled and fell, and while he righted himself and waited for a moment to pant and wipe the rain from his dripping face, Yuan looked out and saw the hovels still clinging against the wall. The rains had flooded them and the wretched helpless folk within sat in the flood and waited silently for heaven to change.

Thus began for Yuan the new year, which he had thought would be his best and happiest year. Instead it began in every sort of evil. For the rains held that spring beyond all bearing, and though priests in temples made many prayers, nothing came of all their prayers and sacrifices except new evil, for such superstitions stirred up ardent angers in the young rulers who believed in no gods at all except their own heroes, and they commanded the temples in those parts to be closed, and ruthlessly they sent soldiers to live in those temples and drive the priests into the smallest worst rooms. Then this in turn made angry the farmer folk, who could be wroth enough against those selfsame priests for one cause or another when they came begging; but who feared now that the gods might be angry anew, and they cried that doubtless all these evil rains were because of these new rulers, and so for once they joined the priests against the young rulers.

For a month the rains held, and still they held, and the great river began to swell and rise and flow into the lesser rivers and canals and everywhere men began to see the coming of the same ancient floods, and if flood, then famine. Now the people had believed that the new times would bring them somehow a new heaven and a new earth, and when they found this was not true, and heaven behaved as carelessly as ever it did, and the earth gave forth no more for harvest in flood or drought than ever it did, they cried out the new rulers were false and no better than the old ones, and old discontents, stilled for a while by new promises of new times, began to rise again.

And Yuan found himself divided again, too, for Meng was pent in his narrow quarters all these many days and not able to spend the vigor of his young body in his usual training of his men, and he came often to Yuan's room and quarrelled with everything Yuan said and he cursed the rains and he cursed his general and he cursed the new leaders whom every day he said grew more selfish and careless of the people's good. He was so unjust sometimes that Yuan could not forbear saying one day, very mildly, "Yet we can hardly blame them that it rains so much, and even if there is a flood, we cannot blame them for that."

But Meng shouted savagely, "I will blame them, nevertheless, for they are no true revolutionists!" And then he let his voice drop and he said restlessly, "Yuan, I'll tell you something no one else knows. But I tell you because though you are so spineless and join in no cause clearly, still you are good enough in your way and faithful and always the same. Hear me—when one day I am gone, you are not to be surprised! Tell my parents not to be afraid. The truth is within this revolution there grows now another, a better, truer one, Yuan—a new revolution! And I and four of my fellows are determined to go and join it—we shall take our loyal men, and go into the west where the thing is shaping. Already thousands of young good eager men have joined secretly. I'll have my chance yet to fight against this old general who keeps me down so low!" And Meng stood glowering for a moment until suddenly his dark face grew bright, or bright as it ever did, for it was a sullen face at best, and then he said thoughtfully and more quietly, "That true revolution, Yuan, is for the people's good. We shall seize the country and hold it for the common people's good, and there shall be no more rich and no more poor—"

And so Meng talked on and Yuan let him talk in half-sad silence. He had, he thought heavily, heard these words all his life somewhere, and still there were these poor, and still there were these words. He remembered how he had seen the poor even in that rich foreign country. Yes, there were always the poor. He let Meng talk, and when at last he was gone, Yuan went and stood by the window for a while and watched the few people trudging through the rain. He saw Meng come out and stride along the street, his head high even in the rain. But he was the only proud one. For the most part the only figures were the rain-soaked ricksha pullers, struggling over the slippery stones. . . . He remembered again what he never could wholly forget, that Mei-ling had not written to him once. Nor had he written to her, for, or so he said simply to himself, "There is no use in writing if she hates me so." And this set the seal of sadness to the day.

There remained therefore only his work, and into this he would have poured his strength, but even here the year did him evil. For the discontent of the times spread among the schools, and the students quarrelled with the laws laid down for them, and they felt too much the rights their youth gave them, and they quarrelled with their rulers and their teachers and refused to work and stayed out of school, so that often when Yuan went to his windy classroom, it was empty and there was no one for him to teach and he must go home again and sit and read his old books he knew before, for he dared not spend money for new ones, since steadfastly he sent half of all he earned to his uncle for his debt. In these long dark nights the end of his debt seemed as hopeless to him as the dream he once had had of Mei-ling.

One day in despair at his own idleness, for seven days on end he had gone only to find his schoolroom empty, he walked through mud and drifting rain out to the land where he had planted the foreign wheat that day. But even here there was to be no harvest, for whether the foreign wheat was not used to such long rains, or whether the black and heavy clay held the water beyond what the roots could bear, or what the wrong was, the foreign wheat lay rotting on the mucky earth. It had sprung up quick and tall and every seed had been alive and swift and eager to put forth. But the earth and skies were not native to it, and it took no deep natural root, and so it lay spoiled and rotted.

Even while Yuan stood and looked sorrowfully at this hope gone, too, a farmer saw him, and ran out in all the rain to cry out with malice and pleasure, "You see the foreign wheat is not good, after all! It sprang up very tall and fair, but it has no staying strength! I said at the time, it is not in nature to have such large pale seeds— look at my wheat—too wet, to be sure, but it will not die!"

In silence Yuan looked. It was true enough; in the next field the small strong wheat stood sturdily even in all the mud, scanty and short, but not dead. . . . He could not answer. He could not bear the man's common face and pleased stupid laughter. For one swift moment he saw why Meng struck the ricksha puller. But Yuan could never strike. He only turned in silence and went his own way again.

Now what would have been the end of Yuan's despair in this dull spring he did not know. That night he lay and sobbed on his bed he was so melancholy, although he wept for no one single cause. It seemed to him as he sobbed that he grieved because the times were so hopeless, the poor still poor, the new city unfinished and drab and dreary in the rains, the wheat rotted, the revolution weakened and new wars threatening, his work delayed by the strife of the students. There was nothing not awry to Yuan that night, but deepest awry of all was this, that for forty days there was no letter from Mei-ling and her last words still were as clear in his mind as the moment she spoke them, and he had not seen her again after she had cried, "Oh, I hate you!"

Once the lady wrote him, it is true, and Yuan seized the letter eagerly to see if perhaps Mei-ling's name was there, but it was not. The lady spoke only now of Ai-lan's little son, and how rejoiced she was because though Ai-lan was gone home again to her husband, she left the child with her mother to be cared for, since she felt the child too much trouble for her, and the lady said gratefully, "I am weak enough almost to be glad Ai-lan so loves her freedom and her pleasures, for it leaves this child to me. I know it is wrong in her. . . . But I sit and hold him all day long."

Now thinking of this letter as he lay in his dark and lonely room it added one more small sadness to him. The new little son seemed to have taken all the lady's heart so even she needed Yuan no more. In a great rush of pity for himself he thought, "I am not needed anywhere, it seems!" And so he wept himself at last to sleep.

Soon the discontents of these times were everywhere very widespread, and much more widely spread than Yuan could know, bound as he was by his solitary life in the new city. It was true he wrote dutifully once in every month to his father, and every other month the Tiger answered his son's letter. But Yuan had not been home again to visit him, partly because he wished to be steadfast to his work, the more because there were not many steadfast in these changing times, and partly because in the little holiday he had he longed most to see Mei-ling.

Nor could he have perceived clearly how the times were from the Tiger's letters, for the old man wrote only the same thing again and again without knowing he did, and always he wrote bravely of how in the spring he planned a great attack against the robber chieftain in those parts, for that robber was growing too bold by half, but he, the Tiger, vowed he would put him down yet with his loyal men, and for the sake of all good people.

Such words Yuan read scarcely heeding them any more. It did not make him angry now to hear his old father boast, and if he answered anything it was only to smile somewhat sadly because such boasting had once a power to frighten him, and now he knew it was only poor empty words. Sometimes he thought to himself, "My father grows old indeed. I must go to him in the summer and see how he does." And once he thought moodily, "I might as well have gone this holiday for all the good it did me." And he sighed and fell to reckoning how much of his debt could be paid by the summer, at the rate he could pay it, and hoping his wage would not be delayed or held back as it now was often in these troubled times which were not wholly old or wholly new and full of many uncertainties.

So there was nothing in the Tiger's letters to prepare his son for what befell him.

One day when Yuan had only just risen from his bed and stood half washed beside his little stove, where every morning he laid his own fire and lighted it for warmth against the cold wet air, there was at his door a knock, timorous and yet persistent. He cried out, "Enter!" and there entered the last man he would have said could stand there, and it was his country cousin, the eldest son of his uncle, Wang the Merchant.

Yuan could see at once that some evil had befallen this little careworn man, for there were black bruises on his skinny yellow throat, and deep bloody scratches on his small withered face, and he had a finger gone from his right hand, and a foul rag dark with blood was tied about the stub.

All these violent marks Yuan saw, and he stood speechless, not knowing what to say or think, he was so surprised. This little man, when he saw Yuan, began to sob but he held his sobs noiseless under his breath and Yuan saw he had some terrible tale to tell. He drew his garments quickly about him, therefore, and he made his cousin sit down, and he fetched some tea leaves in a pot, and poured water from the boiling kettle in the little stove and then he said, "Speak when you can and tell me what has happened. I can see it is some very fearful thing." And he waited.

Then the man caught his breath and he began, but in a low small voice, looking often at the closed door to see it did not move, and he said, "Nine days ago and one night the robber bands came against our town. It was your father's fault. He came to spend awhile at my father's house and wait for the old moon year to pass and he would not be still as an old man ought to be. Time and again we besought him to be silent, but he would boast everywhere how he planned to go out to war against this robber chieftain as soon as spring was come and how he would down him as he had before. And we have enemies enough upon the land, for tenants hate their landlords always, and be sure those somehow told the robbers to incite them. At last the chieftain grew angry and he sent men out to cry everywhere in scorn that he feared no old toothless Tiger, and he would not wait for spring, but he would begin war now against the Tiger and all his house. . . . Even so, my cousin, we might have stayed him, for hearing this, my father and I, we made haste to send him a great sum of money and twenty head of oxen and fifty head of sheep for his men to kill and eat, and we made amends for your father's insult, and besought the chieftain not to heed an old man's talk. So I say it might have passed except for a trouble in our own town."

Here the man paused and fell into a fit of trembling and Yuan steadied him and said, "Do not hurry yourself. Drink the hot tea. You need not be afraid. I will do all I can. Tell on when you are able."

So at last the man could go on, subduing his shivering

somewhat, and he said, his voice still strained low and half whispering, "Well, and the troubles in these new times I do not understand. But there is a new revolutionary school in our town nowadays, and all the young men go there and they sing songs and bow their heads before some new god whose picture they have hanging on the wall and they hate the old gods. Well, and even that would not matter much, except they enticed one who was once our cousin before he took vows—a hunchback—you never saw him, doubtless." Here the man paused to make his question, and Yuan answered gravely, "I have seen him once, long ago," and he remembered now that hunchbacked lad, and he remembered his father had told him be believed the boy had a soldier's heart in him because once when the Tiger passed by the earthen house the hunchback would have his foreign gun and he took the weapon and looked at its every part as fondly as though it were his own, and the Tiger always said, musing, "If it were not for that hump of his, I would ask my brother for him."—Yes, Yuan remembered him, and he nodded and said, "Go on—go on!"

The little man went on then, and he cried, "This priest cousin of ours was seized by this madness, too, and we heard it said he was restless and not like himself for these last two years, ever since his foster mother, who was a nun nearby, died of a cough she had for long. When she lived she used to sew his robes and bring him some sweetmeats sometimes she made which had no beast's fat in them, and then he lived quiet. But once she died he grew rebellious in the temple and at last he ran away one day and joined a band of a new sort I do not understand, except they entice the farming folk to seize the land for their own. Well, and this band joined with the old robbers and filled our whole town and countryside with confusion beyond any we have ever had, and their talk is so vile I cannot tell you what they say except they hate their parents and their brothers, and when they kill they kill first their own households. And then such rains as never were have fallen on the lands this year, and the people knowing flood sure and famine after, and made more fearless by the weak new times, have thrown aside their decency—"

Now the man grew so long at his tale and began trembling so again that Yuan could not bear it and he grew impatient and forced him on, saying, "Yes, yes, I know —we have had the same rains—but what has happened?"

At this the little man said solemnly, "This—they all joined together, robbers old and new and farming folk, and they fell on our town and sacked it clean, and my father and my brothers and our wives and children escaped with nothing but the little we could hide about us—and we fled to my eldest brother's house, who is a sort of governor in a city for your father—but your father would not flee—no, he still boasted like an old fool, and the most he would do was to go to the earthen house on the land which was our grandfather's—"

Here the man paused and then shivering more violently he said breathlessly, "But they were soon there— the chieftain and his men—and they seized your father and tied him by his thumbs to a beam in the middle room where he sat, and they robbed him clean and they took especially his sword which he loved, and left not one of his soldiers except his old hare-lipped servant who saved himself by hiding in a well—and when I heard and went secretly to his aid, they came back before I knew it and they caught me, and cut my finger off, and I did not tell them who I was or they would have killed me, and they thought me a serving man and they said, 'Go and tell his son he hangs here!' So I am come."

And the man began to sob very bitterly and he made haste and unwrapped from his finger the bloody rag, and showed Yuan the splintered bone and ragged flesh, and the stump began to bleed again before his eyes.

Now Yuan was beside himself indeed and he sat down and held his head, trying to think most swiftly what he must do. First he must go to his father. But if his father were already dead—well, he must have hope somehow since the trusty man was there. "Are the robbers gone?" he asked, lifting up his head suddenly.

"Yes, they went away when they had everything," the man replied, and then he wept again and said, "But the great house—the great house—it is burned and empty! The tenants did it—they helped the robbers, the tenants, who ought to have joined to save us—they have taken it all from us—the good house our grandfather—they say they will take back the land, too, and divide it—I heard it said—but who dares go to see what the truth is?"

When Yuan heard this it smote him almost more than what his father suffered. Now would they be robbed indeed, he and his house, if they had no land left. He rose heavily, dazed by what was come about.

"I will go at once to my father," he said—and then after further thought he said, "As for you, you are to go to the coastal city and to this house whose directions I will write for you, and there find my father's lady and tell her I am gone ahead, and let her come if she will to her lord."

So Yuan decided and when the man had eaten and was on his way Yuan started the same day for his father.

All the two days and nights upon the train it seemed this must be only an evil story out of some old ancient book. It was not possible, Yuan told himself, in these new times, that such an ancient evil thing had happened. He thought of the great ordered peaceful coastal city where Sheng lived out his idle pleasant days, where Ai-lan lived secure and careless and full of her pretty laughter and ignorant—yes, as ignorant of such tales as these as that white woman was who lived ten thousand miles away. . . . He sighed heavily and stared out of the window.

Before he left the new city he had gone and found Meng and took him aside into a teahouse corner, and told him what had happened, and this he did in some faint hope that Meng would be angry for his family's sake and cry he would come too, and help his cousin. But Meng did not. He listened and he lifted his black brows and he argued thus, "I suppose the truth is my uncles have oppressed the people. Well, let them suffer, then. I will not share their suffering who have not shared their sin." And he said further, "You are foolish, to my thought. Why should you go and risk your life for an old man who may be dead already? What has your father ever done for you? I care nothing for any of them." Then he looked at Yuan awhile, who sat silent and wistful and helpless in this new trouble, and Meng, who was not wholly hard in heart, leaned and put his hand on Yuan's as it lay on the table and he made his voice low and said, "Come with me, Yuan! Once before you came, but not with your heart—join now and truly in our new good cause— This time it is the real revolution!"

But Yuan, though he let his hand lie, shook his head. And at this Meng took his hand off abruptly and he rose and said, "Then this is farewell. When you come back, I shall be gone. It may be we meet no more. . . ." Sitting in the train, Yuan remembered how Meng looked, how tall and brave and impetuous he looked in his soldier's uniform, and how quickly when he said these words, he was gone.

The train swayed on its way through the afternoon. Yuan sighed and looked about him. There were the travellers who seem always the same on any train, fat merchants wrapped in silk and fur, the soldiers, the students, mothers with their crying children. But across the aisle from his seat were two young men, brothers, who were, it could be seen, newly come home from foreign parts. Their clothes were new and cut in the newest foreign way, loose short trousers and long bright-colored stockings and leather shoes of a yellow color, and on their upper bodies they wore thick garments of knitted yarn, and on their breasts were sewed foreign letters, and their leather bags were shining and new. They laughed easily and spoke freely in the foreign tongue and one had a foreign lute he strummed, and sometimes they sang a foreign song together and all the people listened astonished at the noise. What they said Yuan understood very well, but he made no sign of understanding for he was too weary and downhearted

for any talk. Once when the train stopped he heard one
say to the other, "The sooner we get the factories started
the better it will be, for then we can get these wretched
creatures at work." And once he heard the other rail
against the serving man for the blackness of the rag he
hung across his shoulder with which he wiped the tea
bowls, and they both threw fiery looks at the merchant
who sat next to Yuan when he coughed and spat upon
the floor.

These things Yuan saw and understood, for so had he
spoken and felt once, too. But now he watched the fat
man cough and cough and spit at last upon the floor
and he let it be. Now he could see it and feel no shame
nor outrage, but only let it be. Yes, though he could
not so do himself, he could let others do as they would
these days. He could see the serving man's black rag
and not cry out against it, and he could bear at least in
silence the filth of vendors at the stations. He was
numbed and yet he did not know why he was, except
it seemed without hope to change so many people. Yet
he knew he could not be like Sheng and live for his
pleasures only, nor like Meng and forget his old duty to
his father. Better for him, if he could, doubtless, be
wholly new and careless as they were each in his own
way and see nothing they did not like to see, and feel
no tie which was irksome. But he was as he was, and
his father was his father still. He could not so lay aside
his duty to that old which was his own past, too, and
still somehow part of him. And so he went patiently to
the long journey's end.

The train stopped at last at the town near the earthen
house, and Yuan descended and he walked through the
town quickly, and though he stayed to see nothing, he
could not fail to see it was a town which robbers had
possessed not long since. The people were silent and
frightened, and here and there were burned houses,
and only now did the owners who were left dare to
come and survey ruefully the ruins. But Yuan went

straight through the chief street, not stopping at all to see the great house, and he passed out of the other gate and turned across the fields towards the hamlet he remembered and so he came again to the earthen house.

Once again he stooped to enter the middle room upon whose walls he saw his young verses still as he brushed them. But he could not stay to see how they seemed to him now; he called, and two came to his call, and one was the old tenant, now withered and toothless and very near his end and alone, for his old wife was dead already, and the other was the aged trusty man. These two cried out to see Yuan, and the old trusty man seized Yuan's hand without a word, not even bowing to him as to his young lord, he was in such haste, and he led him into the inner room where Yuan had slept before, and there on the bed the Tiger lay.

He lay long and stiff and still, but not dead, for his eyes were fixed, and he kept muttering something to himself continually. When he saw Yuan he showed no surprise at all. Instead, like a piteous child, he held up his two hands and said simply, "See my two hands!" And Yuan looked at the two old mangled hands and cried out, agonized, "Oh, my poor father!" Then the old man seemed for the first time to feel the pain and the cloudy tears gathered in his eyes and he whimpered a little and said, "They hurt me—" And Yuan soothed him and touched the old man's swollen thumbs delicately and said over and over, "I know they do—I am sure they do—"

And he began to weep silently, and so did the old man, and so the two wept together, father and son.

Yet what could Yuan do beyong weeping? He saw the Tiger was very near his death. A dreadful yellow pallor was on his flesh, and even while he wept his breath came so short that Yuan was frightened and besought him to be tranquil, and forced himself not to weep. But the Tiger had another trouble to tell and he cried again to Yuan, "They took my good sword—" Then his lips trembled afresh, and he would have put his hand to them in the old habit he had, but the hand pained him if he moved it, and so he let it lie, and looked up at Yuan as he was.

Never in all his life had Yuan felt so tender as he now did to his father. He forgot all the years passed and he seemed to see his father always as he was now with this simple childish heart, and he soothed him over and over, saying, "I will fetch it back somehow, my father—I will send a sum of silver and buy it back."

This Yuan knew he could not do, but he doubted if tomorrow the old man could live to think of his sword and so he promised anything to soothe him.

Yet what could be done after soothing? The old man slept at last, comforted a little, and Yuan sat beside him and the trusty man brought him a little food, stealing quietly in and out, and speechless lest he wake his master's light sick sleeping. Silently Yuan sat there, and so he sat while his old father slept, and at last he laid his head down upon the table by him and slept a little too.

But as night drew near, Yuan awoke and he ached in every bone so that he must rise, and he did, and he went noiselessly away into the other room and there the old trusty man was, who, weeping, told him again the tale he already knew. Then the old man added this, "We must somehow leave this earthen house, because the farmers hereabouts are full of hatred, and they know how helpless my old master is and they would have fallen on us, I am sure, little general, if you had not come. Seeing you come, young and strong, they will hold off awhile perhaps—"

Then the old tenant put in his word, and he said doubtfully, looking at Yuan, "But I wish you had a garment not foreign, young lord, for the country folk hate these young new men so much these days because in spite of all their promises of better times rains are come and there will be certain floods, and if they see your foreign clothes such as the others wear—" He paused and went away and came back with his own best robe of blue cotton cloth, not patched more than once or twice, and he said coaxingly, "Wear this to save us, sir, and I have some shoes, too, and then if you are seen——"

So Yuan put on the robe, willing if it made more safety, for he knew the wounded Tiger could not be taken anywhere now, but must die where he had fallen, though he did not say so, knowing the old trusty man could never bear to hear the word death.

Two days Yuan stayed beside his father waiting, and still the old Tiger did not die, and while he waited Yuan wondered if the lady would come or not. Perhaps she would not, since she had the child to care for whom she loved so well.

But she did come. At the end of the afternoon of the second day Yuan sat beside his father, who lay now as though he slept continually unless he were forced to eat or move. The pallor had grown darker, and from his poisoned dying flesh a faint stench passed off into the air of the room. Outside, the early spring drew on, but Yuan had not once gone out to see sky or earth. He was mindful of what the old men said, that he was hated, and he would not stir that hatred now, for the Tiger's sake, that at least he might die in peace in this old house.

So he sat beside the bed and thought of many things, and most of all how strange his life was and how confused and how there was not one known hope to which to hold. These elders, in their times, they were clear and simple—money, war, pleasure—these were good and worth giving all one's life for. And some few gave all for gods, as his old aunt did, or as that old foreign pair across the sea did. Everywhere the old were the same, simple as children, understanding nothing. But the young, his own kind, how confused they were—how little satisfied by the old gods and gains! For a moment he remembered the woman Mary and wondered what her life was,—perhaps like his; perhaps marked for no clear great goal. . . . Out of all he knew there was only Mei-ling who put her hand surely to a certain thing she

knew she wanted to do. If he could have married Mei-
ling. . . .

Then across this useless thinking he heard a voice and
it was the lady's. She was come! He rose quickly and
went out, greatly cheered to hear her. More than he
knew he had hoped for her coming. And there she was
—and by her, with her, there was Mei-ling!

Now Yuan had never once thought or hoped for this
and he was so astonished, he could only look at Mei-
ling and stammer forth, "I thought— Who is with the
child?"

And Mei-ling answered in her tranquil, sure way, "I
told Ai-lan for once she must come and see to him, and
the fates helped, because she has had a great quarrel
with her husband over some woman she says he looked
at too often, and so it suited her to come home for a
few days. Where is your father?"

"Let us go to him at once," said the lady. "Yuan, I
brought Mei-ling, thinking she would know by her skill
how he did." Then Yuan made no delay, but he took
them in and there they three stood beside the Tiger's
bedside.

Now whether it was the noise of talking or whether
it was the sound of women's voices to which he was
not used, or what it was, the old Tiger came for a passing moment out of his stupor, and seeing his heavy eyes
open on her the lady said gently, "My lord, do you remember me?" And the old Tiger answered, "Aye, I
do—" and drowsed again, so they could not be sure
whether he spoke the truth or not. But soon he opened
his eyes once more and now he stared at Mei-ling, and
he said, dreamily, "My daughter—"

At this Yuan would have spoken who she was, but
Mei-ling stopped him, saying pityingly, "Let him call me
daughter. He is very near the last breath now. Do not
disturb him—"

So Yuan stayed silent after his father's glance wavered
again to him because even though he knew the Tiger
did not know clearly what he said, it was sweet to hear

him call Mei-ling by that name. There they three stood, united somehow, waiting, but the old Tiger sank deeper into his sleep.

That night Yuan took counsel with the lady and with Mei-ling and together they planned what must be done. Mei-ling said gravely, "He will not live through this night, if I see rightly. It is a wonder he has lived these three days—he has a stout old heart, but it is not stout enough for all he has had to bear, to know himself defeated. Besides, the poison from his wounded hands has gone into his blood and made it fevered. I marked it when I washed and dressed his hands."

For while the Tiger slept his half-dead sleep Mei-ling in the skilfulest fashion had cleansed and eased the old man's torn flesh, and Yuan stood by humbly watching her, and all the while he watched he could not but ask himself if this gentle tender creature was that same angry woman who had cried she hated him. About the rude old house she moved as naturally as though she lived always in it, and from its poverty she found somehow the things she needed for her ministrations, such things as Yuan would not have dreamed could be so used,—straw she tied into a mat and slipped under the dying man so he could lie more easily upon the boards, and a brick she took up from the edge of the small dried pool and heated in the hot ashes of the earthen oven and put to his chilling feet, and she made a millet gruel delicately and fed it to him and though he never spoke he did not moan so much as he had. Then Yuan, while he blamed himself because he had not done these things himself, knew humbly that he could not do them. Her strong narrow hands could stir about so gently that they seemed not to move the great old fleshless frame, and yet they eased it.

Now when she spoke he listened, trusting all she said, and they planned, and the lady listened when the old trusty man said they must go away as soon as the death was over, because ill-will gathered blacker every day about them. And the old tenant put his voice to a whisper and he said, "It is true, for today I went about and heard and everywhere there was muttering because they said the young lord was come back to claim the land. It is better for you to go away again, and wait until these evil times are over. I and this old harelip will stay here and we will pretend we are with them, and secretly we will be for you, young lord. For it is evil to break the law of the land. The gods will not forgive us if we use such lawless means—the gods in the earth, they know the rightful owners—"

So all was planned, and the old tenant went into the town and found a plain coffin and had it carried back by night while folk slept. When the old trusty man saw this coffin, which was such as any common man had at his death, he wept a little because his master must lie there and he laid hold of Yuan and begged him, saying, "Promise me you will come back one day and dig up his bones and bury him as he should be buried in a great double coffin—the bravest man I ever knew and always kind!"

And Yuan promised, doubting, too, it ever could be done. For who could say what days lay ahead? There was no more surety in these days—not even surety of the earth in which the Tiger must soon lie beside his father.

At this moment they heard a voice cry out, and it was the Tiger's voice, and Yuan ran in and Mei-ling after him, and the old Tiger looked at them wildly and awake, and he said clearly, "Where is my sword?"

But he did not wait for answer. Before Yuan could say his promise over, the Tiger dropped his two eyes shut and slept again and spoke no more.

In the night Yuan rose from his chair where he watched and he felt very restless. He went first and laid his hand upon his father's throat as he did every little while. Still the faint breath came and went weakly. It was a stout old heart, indeed. The souls were gone, but still the heart beat on, and it might beat so for hours more.

And then Yuan felt so restless he must go out for a little while, shut as he had been these three days within the earthen house. He would, he thought, steal out upon the threshing floor and breathe in the good cool air for a few minutes.

So he did, and in spite of every trouble pressing on him the air was good. He looked about upon the fields. These nearest fields were his by law, this house his when his father died, for so it had been apportioned in the old times after his grandfather died. Then he thought of what the old tenant had told him, how fierce the men upon the land were grown, and he remembered how even in those earlier days they had been hostile to him and held him foreign though he did not feel it then so sharp. There was nothing sure these days. He was afraid. In these new times who could say what was his own? He had nothing surely of his own except his own two hands, his brain, his heart to love—and that one whom he loved he could not call his own.

Even while he so thought, he heard his name called softly and he looked and there stood Mei-ling in the doorway. He went near her quickly and she said, "I thought he might be worse?"

"The pulse in his throat is weaker every time I feel it. I dread the dawn," Yuan answered.

"I will not sleep now," she said. "We will wait together."

When she said this Yuan's heart beat very hard once or twice, for it seemed to him he had never heard that word "together" so sweetly used. But he found nothing he could say. Instead he leaned against the earthen wall, while Mei-ling stood in the door, and they looked gravely across the moonlit fields. It was near the middle of the month, and the moon was very clear and round. Between them while they watched the silence gathered and grew too full to bear. At last Yuan felt his heart so hot and thick and drawn to this woman that he must say something usual and hear his voice speak and hers answer, lest he be foolish and put forth his hand to touch her who hated him. So he said, half stammering, "I am glad you came—you have so eased my old father." To which she answered calmly, "I am glad to help. I wanted to come," and she was as quiet as before. Then Yuan must speak again and now he said, keeping his voice low to suit the night, "Do you—would you be afraid to live in a lonely place like this? I used to think I would like it—when I was a boy, I mean— Now I don't know—"

She looked about upon the shining fields and on the silvery thatch of the little hamlet and she said, thoughtfully, "I can live anywhere, I think, but it is better for such people as we are to live in the new city. I keep thinking about that new city. I want to see it. I want to work there—perhaps I'll make a hospital there one day—add my life to its new life. We belong there—we new ones—we—"

She stopped, tangled in her speech, and then suddenly she laughed a little and Yuan heard the laughter and looked at her. In that one look they two forgot where they were and they forgot the old dying man and that the land was no more sure and they forgot everything except the look they shared. Then Yuan whispered, his eyes still caught to hers, "You said you hated me!"

And she said breathlessly, "I did hate you, Yuan—only for that moment—"

Her lips parted while she looked at him and still their eyes sank deeper into each other's. Indeed, Yuan could not move his eyes until he saw her little tongue slip out delicately and touch her parted lips, and then his eyes did move to those lips. Suddenly he felt his own lips burn. Once a woman's lips had touched his and made his heart sick. . . . But he wanted to touch this woman's lips! Suddenly and clearly as he had never wanted anything, he wanted this one thing. He could think of nothing else except he must do this one thing. He bent forward quickly and put his lips on hers.

She stood straight and still and let him try her lips. This flesh was his—his own kind. . . . He drew away at last and looked at her. She looked back at him, smiling, but even in the moonlight he could see her cheeks flushed and her eyes shining.

Then she said, striving to be usual, "You are different in that long cotton robe. I am not used to see you so."

For a moment he could not answer. He wondered that she could speak so like herself after the touch upon her, could stand so composed, her hands still clasped behind her as she stood. He said unsteadily, "You do not like it? I look a farmer—"

"I like it," she said simply, and then considering him thoughtfully she said, "It becomes you—it looks more natural on you than the foreign clothes."

"If you like," he said fervently, "I will wear robes always."

She shook her head, smiling again, and answered, "Not always—sometimes one, sometimes the other, as the occasion is—one cannot always be the same—"

Again somehow they fell to looking at each other, speechless. They had forgotten death wholly; for them there was no more death. But now he must speak, else how could he longer bear this full united look?

"That—that which I just did—it is a foreign custom—if you disliked—" he said, still looking at her, and he would have gone on to beg her forgiveness if she disliked it, and then he wondered if she knew he meant the kiss. But he could not say the word, and there he stopped, still looking at her.

Then quietly she said, "Not all foreign things are bad!" and suddenly she would not look at him. She hung her head down and looked at the ground, and now she was as shy as any old-fashioned maid could ever be. He saw her eyelids flutter once or twice upon her cheeks and for a moment she seemed wavering and about to turn away and leave him alone again.

Then she would not. She held herself bravely and she straightened her shoulders square and sure, and she lifted up her head and looked back to him steadfastly, smiling, waiting, and Yuan saw her so.

His heart began to mount and mount until his body was full of all his beating heart. He laughed into the night. What was it he had feared a little while ago?

"We two," he said—"we two—we need not be afraid of anything."